Third Life

The Ten Plagues of Oluceps

Book One of the Creation Saga

A.D. Honecker

Credits

Jeff Brown: Book cover creator

"The Dictionary of Obscure Sorrows," by John Koenig: Usage of the word "Sonder".

Acknowledgments

Mom and dad for guiding and congratulating me every step of the way to publishing my first book. My military family for being my beta readers. I know I made some of you read my work repeatedly (As many as five times...), and I appreciate all of the encouragement and constructive criticism you gave. ROCKHOUNDS!

Chapter 1

A Flower of Protection

Quiet as the void preceding creation, Atha crept through the bright first-grade hallway toward the classroom door decorated with images of white heather flowers. He was short for his age, teetering atop the tips of his toes to grasp the door's handle and struggling ever so slightly to pull it down.

His teacher Miss Morry's voice warmly announced, "Good morning, Atha," to him from her place in front of the whiteboard. "First one in, as per the usual." She continued writing out math problems on the board. Like the door, the room was decorated in an array of pleasant colors that took on the shapes of scholarly topics. The trees painted across the walls were blocked only slightly by shelves of books. Cursive letters lined the tops of the walls.

"Good morning, ma'am," Atha replied in his eternally whispering voice, scurrying toward his seat.

Miss Morry was just barely into her thirties and always wore multiple articles of clothing adorned with flowers. She was skinny and blond, both of which were typically noticed before her abnormally perceptive nature. She watched as Atha pulled a single book out of his backpack.

"Did you forget your math book, young man?" she asked.

"Don't need it," Atha whispered back, propping the book open atop his desk, the top of his short brown hair barely visible over it. She turned to look him in the eye but instead only saw the title of the book: *Great Expectations.*

"*Great Expectations*. A fan of Charles Dickens, eh? Quite a good read, but not exactly appropriate for a six-year-old. Does your dad know you have that?" Miss Morry asked as Atha peeked an eye over the binding.

"Yes, ma'am," he replied.

"Then it's not my place to take it away, but we do have the library visit today. Would you mind hearing a few of my literature suggestions?" Miss Morry asked with a warm smile.

"Elementary library limited," Atha replied, ducking back behind the binding.

"Limited to your age group, yes," Miss Morry said. "If I can get permission, could I interest you in a trip to the high school library?" Atha peeked a twinkling orb back up over his book. "If we can go, I'll let you check out a book that *I* approve of, but I do recognize that more nutrition is needed to spur your growth."

"Yes please, ma'am," Atha whispered back with a touch of pep in his voice.

"Dazzling! I have a slew of titles in mind I'm sure you'll enjoy, kiddo. Now, go over to Mr. Lendon's room and get a loaner math book." She smiled as she turned back and began to write another problem. Atha pulled a sparkling geode from his pocket and let it dance in his fingers as he studied the board and the extra credit advanced problems.

"27. -16. 104. 52," Atha began as Miss Morry turned back to him yet again.

"-8. 15. 22. -4," Atha finished. He sat the sparkling rock down on his desk.

She was stunned for long seconds, the ticking clock on the wall the only sound filling the void. Her great expectations had been torn asunder, and she soon gave up trying to find the right words to convey her amazement.

"Y-yes that's... absolutely correct," she said, noticing the rock in his hand.

Atha had failed first grader last year, falling short in each subject. This year he'd been placed in Miss Morry's class. During recess a few weeks ago, she'd discovered him scribbling out the day's lesson in the dirt. A nondescript rock from the playground bounced in his fingers, seemingly calming the raging seas of his mind. She purchased the geode to take the rock's place and secured permission for him to bring it to class. Now he was an honor-roll student and completely bored with the grade's subject level.

The rest of the class eventually filled the room. Atha's best and only friend, Chris, sat in the seat behind him.

"What's up, midget?" Chris asked.

"Nothing. You?" Atha replied.

"Same as yesterday! Kicking butt online in Dragon Stargate Supreme! I'm telling you, man, you gotta get a Funsystem so we can play together," Chris replied.

"Can't have one," Atha whispered back as he nudged Chris's head away.

Atha read his book through the rest of the day, his heart sinking at the sound of the final bell that spelled the end of school.

***

The class filed out of the room in a line, Chris wrapping his arms over Atha's shoulders to say goodbye. "Hit me up over the weekend, okay? And let me know if you need anything," he told Atha with soberness in his voice.

"Okay. Thank you," Atha replied quietly as Chris gave him a shake before running toward the car pick-up line. Atha waved goodbye as Miss Morry walked toward him.

 "I spoke with your father," she said. "He gave permission for me to take you to the library. Come on, my car's parked in the back of the lot." Miss Morry extended her hand down to him and he graciously grasped it. They weren't near it yet, but Atha already knew which car was hers, coming to a stop at a van covered in painted-on flowers.

"What's with that look?" she asked, helping Atha into the front seat.

"Flowers," he replied, poking at a sunflower ornament that hung from the rearview mirror before sitting down in his seat.

She chuckled at this accurate statement as she got into the driver's seat.

"I fill my life with only the things I love and enjoy," she said, twisting the key to spur the vehicle to life.

They drove for a few lights in silence. Clearing her throat in a recognizable start-of-class fashion, Atha instinctively became attentive.

"There's something I wanted to talk to you about. A few things, actually. I'm planning on discussing bumping you up to the fourth grade at our next conference. I know that might sound intimidating, but you're being stunted in the first grade," she said as thoughts of Chris crossed his mind.

"No thank you, ma'am."

"May I ask why?"

"My friend."

"You'll find new friends, kiddo. Just keep it in mind for now. We still have a few weeks before then. I just wanted to get an idea of how you felt about it," she replied as Atha nodded into his backpack.

She thumped her finger on the steering wheel before speaking up again. "There's something else I wanted to talk to you about, Atha, but first I want you to know you're completely safe with me, okay?" she said, absent the usual pep in her voice. Atha pulled his eyes from his bag to look at her.

"How's your situation at *home*? Regarding the relationship between you and your father," she asked, turning into the library parking lot.

"What about it?" Atha asked back, his attention now completely with her as she continued to thump a finger against the wheel.

"Does he ever get extremely mad? Maybe over small things? Spank you or your sister with a closed hand?" she continued, balling a hand into a fist to give Atha an illustrated description. A brilliant smile filled Atha's normally dismal face as his voice picked up.

"He could never do that, ma'am. He loves me and Melinda more than anything. Dad may seem a bit stressed from work, but he never takes anything out on us."

She'd never heard a full sentence from him and never seen more than a partial smile.

"I-I see," she replied, flustered and stunned.

"Library now?" Atha asked, pointing a finger to the building before them as she sat silently.

"Yes, let's go," she replied as Atha unbuckled, catching his arm before he could get out.

"Are you being honest with me? Anything you tell me can *never* be used to hurt you," she continued as Atha's face returned to normal.

"Yes, ma'am," he replied as she sighed and nodded.

Atha's eye widened in disbelief as they walked through the door, the sight of thousands of books stretching toward the ceiling filling his eyes. He stood paralyzed for a moment, regaining sense as Miss Morry spoke.

"Take my advice and move up a few grades, and this will be a visit among many. Go on, then. I have some business to take care of, so don't wander too far or leave the building."

Atha took off at a slow run. He hurried down the walls of books that stretched toward the ceiling lights like trees fighting for the sun. His interest in science and the world around him was vast, but one topic fanned his curiosity to no end: outer space, the only place his still-blooming mind imagined could possibly hold more wonders than the library. He quickly located a book titled *Life Beyond Earth: A Theory of Undeniability.* He ripped it from the shelf and located another titled *Wormholes Are the Cars of the Future* and pulled it down next. He dashed back down the aisle, hoping to glance through a few more sections before his time was up, eyeing over the cover of *Wormholes* with awe. His clumsy feet caught each other and he tumbled down, losing his grip on *Life Beyond Earth,* which hurtled down past the end of the row. He quickly regained his footing, snapping his head up in surprise.

A woman seemingly appeared from nowhere and reached down to clasp the book at her feet. Her clothes were foreign, resembling what a knight's armor might look like if it were made from pure white cloth. She looked about Miss Morry's age and stood about two feet taller than him with piercing blue eyes. But even they didn't compare to her light blue hair which flowed all the way to the backs of her knees like a waterfall. Not a single imperfection or trace of dirt marred her flawless appearance.

"*Undeniable* indeed. An aptly titled book, yet strange to find such advanced research in the hands of child so young in age." Her even voice rung through Atha's head like church bells.

He was shaken, but stepped slowly forward, raising an open hand to the woman.

"My book please, ma'am," Atha whispered, but she continued to eye it over and noticed the other space book he held.

"I see. Unfortunately, the answers you seek won't be so easy to find in a pair of books. Still, I'm intrigued by such a polite and equally intelligent young man," she replied, completely ignoring his waiting hand.

Atha remained silent, his eyes fixed on the space of carpet between their feet.

"I also see you are not much of a conversationalist. Understandable. Allow me to return your property. My aim is not to taunt you." She placed the book in his hand.

"Thank you," Atha replied. He froze as her hand clasped his.

Her touch had a strange warmth, faint yet overpowering, that flowed through Atha.

"Take care to protect what you hold close to heart with firmer grip than that which held the book. Should you fail, it will be lost and never returned to pleading hands." She stepped back and headed around the row of books and out of sight.

"There you are!" Miss Morry exclaimed from the opposite end of the aisle. "You're a hard man to find when you wander past where you were *supposed* to be." She walked to Atha. "Still that curious fixation on the stars above, eh? Now, what did I say? Only one today."

"Please?" Atha begged.

"You can get another next time. Put them back where—" She stopped at the sight of Atha's tiny arms tightening around the books. "*Fine*. Next time just one, though." A slight smile quivered onto Atha's face.

"Thank you," he replied and stepped closer to hug her leg.

"You're welcome," she replied, rubbing her hand across Atha's head.

Chapter 2

A Man Possessed

They left the library and headed for Atha's home, one that stunned Miss Morry with its colossal size when they arrived. Hidden down a long asphalt road—which snaked through the woods, secluded from the world—was a log cabin that must have taken its toll from half a forest.

Atha's heart sank as he noticed his father's flashy sports car in the circular driveway. He'd come home early today. Dread filled Atha, and he hid the three books inside his backpack, hoping they would weather the coming storm.

Miss Morry parked in front of the house and led Atha up the walkway toward the wooden door. He reached for the handle, but it swung open and away, causing him to topple forward. A long, skinny arm caught him.

"Careful, boy," Dr. Schneider warned Atha before letting him regain his balance. The doctor wore a white lab coat that covered his narrow, tall frame. Black hair covered his head, slicked back toward his neck.

"Daddy!" Atha beamed, giving the lowered arm a hug.

"And Miss Morry, a pleasure as always." The doctor extended his free hand to shake hers.

"Good to see you again, doctor," she replied, a bit taken aback by his abrupt appearance.

"Can we throw the football today? You promised we would," Atha asked.

"Don't be rude, son. Miss Morry took you to the library and what do we say when someone does us a favor?" he replied as Atha turned back to her.

"Thank you, ma'am," he announced.

"You're very welcome. I never realized you were such a fan, Atha, but I know better than to keep boys from their sports, so I'll see you at school on Monday, okay?" she replied, patting Atha's head and stepping backwards to her car. She hesitated before getting into the van, but continued when Atha and his father began waving to her energetically. She pulled away, waving goodbye as she did so.

Atha's heart was pounding with fear as she vanished. The doctor's voice was tight as it commanded, "Get inside." Atha's face turned to the floor as he hurried in behind the doctor as the commanding voice spoke again. "Close the door."

Atha complied without raising his eyes.

"Get your books out." Again, Atha complied, pulling his two library and one school book out before dropping his empty bag. "Now rip every single page from every last one."

Atha's lips quivered at this, but he held *Great Expectations* open and tore out page after page, watching sadly as they wafted to the ground like petals from a plucked flower.

Dr. Schneider's hand ripped across his face, sending the boy crashing to the floor.

"Did I say do it right here, boy?! Trying to make a mess to piss me off instead of just putting them in the trash can, huh?!" he screamed, as Atha whimpered but regained his footing.

"N-no, sir, I—" Another hard slap sent him back to the floor as his eyes involuntarily began to water.

"Did I tell you to talk?! All the goddamn things I do for you and you spit in my face every chance you get!"

Atha's face began to shine red with marks. It was always like this. Nothing was ever right and nothing ever made things better. Most parents received a God-given extra sense to the original five that compelled them to protect their children. Father had received something else in its place from the beast below, diseasing his mind and corrupting him. Tears fell from Atha's face from the stinging pain, but this only sent his father further into his fit.

"I don't believe this! If anybody here should be crying it should be me, you wretch!" His father fell to his knees in front of Atha to show him his open hands. "See these hands?! They've done so much for you pair of rats! Get up! Get up!" he screamed into Atha's ear, watching Atha hobble back to his feet again.

The doctor's fist tightened and smashed into Atha's face, nearly rendering him unconscious as he fell a third time. "Again?! You're a mess, boy. Get up!" he screamed, and kicked him in the side with enough force to slam Atha against the door and knock the air from his lungs.

Melinda, Atha's older sister, came running down the stairs, screaming, "Leave him alone!" Melinda was seven years older than Atha, and a full head and shoulders taller.

"Stay out of this," Dr. Schneider ordered. "He's going to grow up to be just as worthless as you unless I teach him."

"I-I'm, okay—okay—" Atha gasped as he stood again. He knew where this was headed, and filled the void of his words with the sound of pages ripping from his book and stuffing them into his backpack. The doctor turned back to Atha.

"At least you can learn despite being slow to do it." He chuckled as Melinda dashed across the room.

"It's okay." Atha spoke up. "Dad's just stressed."

"Look at you, on a roll," said the doctor. "The question now is *why* exactly am I stressed, boy?"

"Unexpected school call," Atha replied, continuing to bastardize the book he held.

"And we all know how I feel about those. To add insult to injury, you bring that bitch to my house. I don't like the look she had in her eye. Did she say anything to you that would explain it?" He grabbed Atha's jaw and turned his face toward his own. Atha nodded. "What?"

"Asked about you," he replied. The slender fingers dug into his cheeks.

"Be more specific! All that time you spend reading, how can you possibly be this inarticulate?!"

"Closed hand spanking," said Atha, feeling relief as his face was released.

"And what did you say?" Dr. Schneider spat as he stood back up and straightened his lab coat.

"What you told me to.".

"Show me. Exactly as you said it."

A brilliant smile filled Atha's face, corrupted by the welts covering it.

"He could never do that, ma'am. He loves Melinda and me more than anything! Dad may seem a little stressed out from work, but he never takes anything out on us!" Atha replied as the doctor nodded with approval.

"Good. I'm transferring you out of that nosy bitch's class. Get in your room and don't disturb me again."

With that Melinda grabbed Atha, all but carrying him up the stairs.

I was right. Keep attention on me and he'll ignore her, he thought as they stepped into her lavish room. Despite how they were treated, the doctor was a master at keeping up appearances. Her room was packed full of toys, clothing, and trinkets from a multitude of shopping trips.

There was one factor that hid the truth with supernatural ease. Beatings were commonplace, yet the bruises, cuts, even the occasional broken bone never lasted longer than the night, vanishing along with all evidence of foul play.

Melinda sat Atha down on her bed. She pulled out a white bag from the drawer in her bedside table, giving it a few shakes to turn it to ice. She pressed it against his face that had already begun to turn purple.

"Why do you always do things you know he won't like?" she asked with a cracking voice.

"Hits me. Leaves you alone," Atha replied. Tears began to roll down her face as she huffed with grief. "What's wrong?"

"Stop doing this, please, Atha. I'm so scared all the time. I'm so scared that—that he won't *stop* every time it starts," she sobbed, grasping a hand mirror to hold in front of him. "God, just look at your face."

He nudged the mirror away, placing his small hands on her cheeks to whisper.

"I'm fine," he said, patting a hand gently against her cheek. "You're what matters."

"No, I'm older. I should be looking out for you." Reaching a hand up to place atop his. "I'm just so *scared*. So, so *scared*."

"Age irrelevant. Brotherly duty takes precedence," he replied with a gentle pat to drive the point home.

She caught the hand and continued holding it against her cheek. "What would I do without you, Atha?"

"Never know. Always be here," he responded, noticing the tears beginning to slow. He planted a kiss on her forehead and waited patiently for the tears to stop.

The night wore on and, as usual, Atha fell asleep in her room, feeling a sense of security with her at arm's reach. A loud crash sounded and he flung up, reaching his hand for Melinda only to notice her absence. Panic took hold. The door was open. He jumped out of bed, the sound of voices coming from downstairs.

"What the fuck are you putting in my food? Is this... This is manchineel!" The doctor's slurred voice rose as Atha reached the bottom floor. He headed through the darkness toward the kitchen and the sound of Melinda sobbing.

Panic turned to terror as he entered the dimly lit kitchen. His father held Melinda by the throat with one hand. With his other, he yanked a plant from her grasp. A plastic food container was overturned on the floor, its contents spewed across the tiles. On the counter sat a bottle of hospital grade morphine and needles, the doctor's drug of choice, which explained why he was befogged.

"You little bitch! Trying to poison me?!" his father yelled while pulling her back and forth, continuing to crush her neck.

"N-no! No!" she wailed as Atha remained unnoticed, frozen with panic. He snapped out of it, making his presence known by knocking a pile of china plates off the counter beside him. The doctor jumped at the sound of them, his eyes flashing to Atha. A grotesque smile crossed the doctor's face.

"I know what you're doing, boy. Don't think you're smarter than me," he sneered, remaining in place as he used his free hand to slap Melinda across the face, keeping eyes locked on Atha.

Atha stared in disbelief as his father struck again, glancing back to the floor to reaffirm the plates' destruction.

"Wondering why your game isn't working right now? No, I get it, you just act up to keep the spotlight off her, don't you?" He laughed, slapping a hand across her face again as he exploded with anger.

"DON'T YOU?! Answer me when I ask you a question, boy!" More hard slaps tore across Melinda's face as Atha finally found his voice.

"Stop it." Atha clenched his teeth as he tried to remain calm. The doctor did stop, if only momentarily.

"See now, *there's* the look I've been waiting for. Been wondering why you don't ever so much as flinch, but now it all makes sense." He laughed, tightening his grip, smiling with disgusting pleasure as a gurgle from Melinda escaped her mouth.

"Why?" Atha asked as tears fell from his eyes.

"Because you make me sick," the doctor replied with hatred burning in his eyes.

Atha ran to the next counter, grasping the morphine bottle.

"Stop!" he yelled at the doctor, louder than his timid voice had ever raised in his entire life.

"Put that down!" the doctor screamed frantically.

Atha ran back to the far side of the kitchen, but his foot caught a shard of broken plate and his leg went limp beneath him. The vial shattered across the floor as Atha fell, pure horror settling into him as he realized what he'd just done. The doctor stood in disbelief as well, unintendedly lessening his grip on Melinda's neck.

"Run, Atha! Get out!" she croaked, her words halted by fingers tightening again, pulling her off her feet and into the air. The doctor slammed her up against the refrigerator with force enough to cause it to teeter.

"Yeah, that's right. You fucked up, boy." The doctor's dizzy eyes struggled to focus on Atha. "Now you're gonna watch her die."

Atha turned back helplessly to see watched Melinda's legs flailing beneath her, her hands slapping at his arm and just nearly breaking free until the doctor's attention returned to her. He placed his free hand on her throat. A dull crunch sounded from her neck, and the struggle slowed, her arms and legs barely twitching.

I'm so weak, Atha thought. There was only one thing he could imagine that would possibly be able to fix this: the memory of a TV show he'd seen that demonstrated the power of a gun. Those metal shards propelled by fiery explosion could solve this. *I need a gun*, he thought. He drew the image of one in his mind, his photographic memory perfectly recalling and tracing every detail of the double-action revolver in his mind, from the intricate etchings upon the side all the way down to the six .357 Magnum cartridges loaded into the chambers. The revolver clattered to the tile by his face. Atha stared in disbelief as he reached a hand slowly toward it. He half expected it to vanish, but the cold metal met his fingertips.

This is real. Logic be damned, he had the only tool that could alleviate his problem. He found his courage. He rose to the occasion, rose to his feet, and raised the barrel up like he'd seen in the show. The doctor hadn't noticed yet as Atha's fingers strained to pull the trigger. A flash lit the room, followed immediately by a *BLAM* as the powerful load practically ripped the pistol from his hands. The recoil knocked Atha back, and his ears rang. His shot had missed wide, the window to the doctor's right shattered to pieces. The doctor glanced over at the window before dropping Melinda in disbelief.

"Did you just...shoot at me?" His vision slowly traced the pistol in Atha's hand. "That's a fucking six-shooter! Where did you get that, you little psycho?!" he roared, bursting toward Atha on wobbly legs.

Atha's target grew larger as it neared and he slowly raised the pistol again. His hands were practically numb from the first shot, but it made no difference with a large target slowly hobbling toward him. Another *BLAM* and another flash lit the room, crimson spraying across the floor from the doctor's leg, sending him crashing down.

Atha's ears screamed in pain, but Atha could still hear screams coming from the downed man.

"You idiot! Do-do you r-realize what you—what you just did? I'm—I'm a hero!"

Atha raised the pistol one last time.

"You're a monster." *BLAM.* This time the explosion was matched with an explosion of brains across the floor. Atha dropped the gun, bursting to his feet, and scrambled to the pale Melinda. He watched in disbelief as a black circle expanded beneath her, stopping as it reached just past her head and feet. In an instant, she vanished down into it, all traces of her disappearing as the black circle closed.

"No!" Atha screamed, slipping backwards on slick blood that covered the tile floor and landing hard on his head. Everything went black as he laid motionless—it was the closest thing to peace he would know for a long time.

Chapter 3

Short Life Expectancy

Atha awoke, unsure of what had just happened and confused about his surroundings. The first thing he realized was that he wasn't in Melinda's room anymore. White curtains surrounded the bed he was in, and he was barely able to peer through the slight opening in them that revealed what appeared to be a hospital room.

"Melinda?" Atha called as he sat up, groaning at the stinging pain on the back of his head. He was halted by an unknown restraint as he tried to move his right arm. A handcuff chained him to the metal bed frame, and he yanked on it in confusion as the curtains were snatched open.

"Finally up, eh?" a police officer asked, staring at Atha for a moment before taking a seat beside another cop. Both were large men. The one who'd spoken to Atha was smiling while the other looked on silently with anger.

"Melinda," Atha said again, rubbing the back of his sore head. "Where's Melinda?"

"Ha-ha, what a coincidence! We were gonna ask you that! Kid's a riot, ain't he, Smith?" the smiling officer replied, elbowing his partner in the side.

"Hilarious." The unamused cop got to his feet. "Gonna give the captain a call. We're clear to relocate him since the CAT scan came back negative," he said before leaving the curtained area. Atha could hear a door open and close as he listened in confusion.

"You don't have the slightest clue how much trouble you're in right now, do you?" the smiling cop asked, forming a pistol with his index finger and thumb to place against his temple. "Shot dear old dad and did God knows what with your sister. Made the front page of the paper. They're calling you America's youngest serial killer. Hell, I heard they're gonna try you as an adult."

He stood and leaned down to Atha. "Know what that means? You could end up in prison with the *big boys* who got a couple hundred pounds on you." He thumped a finger against Atha's forehead. "'Bout damn time they started cracking down on your lot. But it don't need to go down like that. Let me make you a deal." He smiled, leaning in closer to Atha, breath reeking of cigarettes and coffee. "Tell me where the girl's body's at and I'll put in a good word, say you were conflicted afterwards about what you'd done. You'll probably end up in a psych ward, but that's a big step up from where the road's leading now." The officer paused, visibly amused as Atha struggled with the handcuff restraining him.

He flashed a silver handcuff key to Atha. "Ain't going nowhere without this." Atha studied it before it vanished back into a pouch. "Your face is on every TV right now, and mine will be too if I can blow this thing open. So how about it?"

Atha glanced back down at his sheets.

"Gone," he replied, hardly able to speak as fear continued to paralyze him.

"No deal, then? Whatever, bigwigs would probably take all the credit anyways." He shrugged before returning to his seat and pulling out his phone.

Need to leave. Need to find Melinda, Atha thought as electronic noises from the phone filled the room. *Need that key.* Atha drew the image of the silvery key into his mind and he felt something land in his open hand. He glanced down to see a key now occupying the space within his partially curled fingers.

He threw it? Atha wondered, looking back to the officer who payed Atha no mind as he continued playing a game on his phone. Atha turned back and stared at the key, a sense of confusion settling over him.

Like the gun. From nowhere. He reached his left hand over to take it from his right, slowly placing it in the handcuff's slot. Turning it over, a dull click signaled the cuff had lost its hold. He eyed the open door to plan his avenue of escape. There were no windows in his room, but one sat open across the small lobby outside. He burst from the bed, covers flying off of him as he sprinted out the door.

The smiling cop's expression fled along with Atha, as he watched in disbelief as Atha's feet clapped against the white tiled floor. "What the fuck?!" he yelled. "Smith! Runner!" He stumbled to his feet to give chase.

To Atha's dismay, the other cop came into view beside the window, so he quickly hooked a left down the nearest hallway. He hit a quick right into another empty hall and pressed against the wall as the sound of thudding boots got closer.

"You let him go?!" Smith yelled.

"No, he fucking Houdinied out of the handcuffs! Damn it, where the hell did he go?"

Atha slid behind a door and into a darkened room, leaving the door partially open to allow a stream of light to illuminate his surroundings and give no audible clue to his location. They stopped just short as they passed his door.

"He musta hid or he's the fastest kid alive." Smith groaned as Atha grabbed an IV bag, the closest thing to him. He hurled it blindly across the hallway into the opposite dark room, hoping they didn't see him do it. It landed with a dull splat.

"There!" The officers stormed into the opposite room. Atha ran out into the hallway, back the way he'd came. He stopped at the window but quickly realized he was on the top floor. A red sign illustrating stairs pointed him in another direction, and he quickly located the door. He reached for the handle and gave it a yank. Locked. He continued down the hallway, finding a bank of elevators around the next bend. He ran as fast as he could, coming upon them as they pinged and opened. Six more officers stood within, looking equally dumbfounded as the smiling officer had when Atha escaped from the cuffs.

"Wasn't the kid supposed to be cuffed to a bed, Captain?" one asked the oldest one in the middle. The captain sighed as he stepped out.

"Those idiots. They assured me we wouldn't need a full set of seven guards, and look where we are," he replied.

Atha's whispering voice begged, "No, no, no." The captain raised a hand to the others.

"Don't make this any worse than it is. Lay on your belly with both hands on your back," he instructed and Atha's eyes grew hot. He complied, and a new set of cuffs clicked over his wrists before being pulled back to his feet.

"Burgess, radio in a successful pick up with no errors. Gomez, call those two idiots and inform them of this fact as well. Reporters don't need any more ammunition. This could bury his case. Stay tight around the kid when we get to the first floor. We have a hurricane of reports and rubberneckers out there. On that note"—he knelt beside Atha—"don't give them anything to work with okay, Atha? These people are going to want a rise out of you and will say some nasty things to get it. Keep your head down, mouth shut, and we'll get you to transport without incident. Do you understand what I'm telling you?"

Atha nodded.

The elevator doors opened a minute later and they walked into the main lobby. Five officers surrounded Atha as people waiting to see a doctor lifted cell phones to snap pictures. Some tried to get closer to them, but the officers pushed them back as they escorted him toward the door. From between their legs, he got a brief glimpse of the scene outside. Hundreds of cameras flashed like an apocalyptic lightning storm as reporters waited outside the glass walls. A dull roar sounded as the thousands who had gathered outside noticed their approach. It became deafening as the automatic doors parted.

Atha did as he was instructed and kept his head fixated on the asphalt beneath his feet. The yells and flashes roared to new heights as every person took notice of Atha. They were held back by lines of cops and yellow police tape.

"Where's the girl's body?!"

"Dr. Schneider was a hero!"

"Burn in hell, murderer!"

Atha caught full sentences every now and then amidst the crowd's roar. He whimpered, awaiting the second he'd wake from the nightmare. At the same time, he knew he would not.

They'd only gone a few steps when rotten vegetables began pelting the officers surrounding him. Bits and pieces dashed Atha. A tomato ricocheted off an officer's arm and splattered across his cheek. A convoy composed of a van with its windows blacked out and flashing police cruisers sat nearby. The back of the van popped open as they neared, allowing the captain to enter. A second officer helped Atha get in, and the captain pulled the door closed as the van sped away.

"That was worse than I thought it'd be. It was like the Middle Ages out there." The captain sighed as he pulled out a towel to clean Atha's face off.

"Where now?" Atha asked.

"Not even shook after that? You're brave, I'll give you that. We're headed for the station where the FBI will begin their investigation. I only picked you up because they thought it was important that the public recognize their hometown police force was reluctantly handing the case over. In truth, every bigwig in the state is here to try to make a name for themselves, but they want to appear humble about the worldwide attention given to you." His head lowered. "Political dogs."

"Search for Melinda?"

"After gunshots were reported at your residence, we found you unconscious and Dr. Schneider dead. Forensics is still reviewing the scene, but that haven't found anything that could point us in her direction. With no weapon located and gunshot residue on your hands, the only conclusion at this point is pointing to you. To be blunt, it's not looking good. Don't lose hope just yet, though. Your school teacher, Lisa Morry, was reported to be the last person to have contact with you, making her the closest thing we have to a witness. She's been going to bat for you, Atha." Atha's heart picked up, feeling a spark of hope.

"Now, I've answered all of your questions honestly. Could you answer a pair of mine?" he asked. Atha nodded. "Where's the pistol you used? We can tell by the residue on your hands that you fired three shots, but we can't locate the weapon."

"Don't know," Atha replied.

"Were you or your sister abused in any way, physically or mentally?" he asked. He stared in disbelief as a brimming smile overtook Atha's face.

"He could never do that, sir," said Atha. "He loves Melinda and me more than anything! Dad may seem a bit stressed from work, but he never takes anything out on us."

The captain's mouth fell open, no good response coming to him for such an erratic display.

The next few weeks were long. Endless questions filled Atha's ears both in and out of the courtroom. Miss Morry and Chris went to the stand on his behalf, but with Atha's inability to say what happened, the case was looking grim. Miss Morry almost seemed to have the judge on her side when posing as a character witness, but the prosecution, led by a district attorney running for re-election, ripped apart her testimony like a lion rending meat from bone. Eventually the discussion of innocence turned to talk of sentencing severity, and even that was grim with the world screaming for justice.

Atha sat in the courtroom in a tiny suit; his always cheerful lawyer was a middle-aged man who spat the words "rockstar case" a minimum of six times a day. At least he was honest about being the only one benefitting from the nonexistent defense he supplied. The judge sat before them in the massive courtroom brimming with faces, including Miss Morry and Chris with his family.

"Atha Schneider, please rise," the Honorable Judge Hammonds ordered, his emotionless face staring down at Atha, who complied. "Your case has been nothing short of revolutionary. It will stand as a timeless monument to the last day the courts yielded to child psychopaths of which the numbers have quadrupled over just the past decade." He paused as the crowd's whispers began to rise, banging his gavel to silence them. "The jury has spoken and your fate is sealed, yet I find my own thoughts conflicted. Further questioning at this stage is pointless, but regardless my own consciousness begs me to ask just once more. Atha Schneider, did Paul Schneider in *any* conceivable way, compel you to murder him in order to protect yourself?" Atha attempted to fight his scripted response, but with force it pulled itself off his tongue.

"No, sir, he could never—"Atha began. The judge shook his head in disbelief until Atha finished.

"Then with a clear conscious I give the final sentencing. Atha Schneider, you are hereby sentenced to prison until your eighteenth birthday..." he began. but an awestruck crowd roared with disapproval over the lax sentencing. Officers held the rumbling onlookers back aa the judge slammed his gavel a few times and screamed, "Order!" Eventually, silence returned to the courtroom. Atha had become numb to it all, ignoring even the fact that he would be behind bars for eleven years as he looked emptily up at the judge.

"And on the day of your eighteenth birthday, by unanimous vote, you shall be put to death. May God have mercy on your soul."

The entire room became silent at this, and even Atha's numbness dissipated as terror sunk into his body. The silence lasted for a moment that felt like an ironic lifetime. Then a thunderous cheer broke out. Atha's legs gave out as he fell back into his chair. The jury received a standing ovation as if they were war heroes returning from battle. A group of guards flanked Atha, trapping him in darkness despite the brightly lit room as they cuffed him.

He waited for someone to call out that this was all a mistake. Instead, the officers lifted him by the arms to carried him toward the exit.

Atha was taken to a transport van outside. A massive crowd that had been awaiting the final verdict encircled the entire area. Restrained only by a few officers and yellow tape, Atha glanced them over, awaiting a pelting of vegetables, but instead caught a glimpse of Miss Morry. She wore a dark suit, something completely different from her normal wardrobe, but it paired well with the tears streaming through her fingers as she cried into her hands. Her salty tears mixed with sweet cola as a drink was poured over her blond head by a taunting man behind her. Atha couldn't locate Chris but didn't need to. His friend ducked beneath the tape and burst forward, quickly being caught by an officer who pulled him back toward his parents.

"I'm sorry, Atha! The adults wouldn't listen to anything I said!" he screamed. Atha was unable to give a reply as he was pushed into the vehicle.

They were on the road for hours until finally coming to a stop, the doors flinging open to blindingly bright light and roaring heat. Atha's eyes adjusted to see an endless dry wasteland surrounding him in all directions, blocked out only slightly by rows of wired fences. He was pulled around to see a massive building six stories tall and stretching far in either direction before him. He was headed to a set of front doors as a tall bald man leading corrections officers came toward him.

"Atha Schneider, welcome to your new home! I'm Warden Delmato. Not exactly white picket fences, eh?" the man announced with resounding cheer as Atha was handed over to the new set of officers. With yellow teeth, he smiled down at Atha before glancing over to a mass of distant reporters beyond the fence. "We're very grateful to have you here. You're easily the youngest to receive the death penalty in the modern era in a first-world country, and that's exactly the kind of thing that awakens primitive curiosity in people. And curiosity leads to attention, and attention leads to *money* and that's all the incentive I need to keep you alive until you die. Sounds so *funny* saying that out loud, doesn't it?" He smirked, but Atha's silence held firm, and the man knelt in front of him. "Enjoy your new life."

Chapter 4

Godfather, and Now a Godfather

Atha walked through the front door and into a room where he changed into an orange T-shirt and pants. He didn't get a regular jumpsuit due to the fact they didn't have one in his size. He was led to death row, which was housed in a cold, damp building comprised entirely of stone and metal that sat separated from general population. Atha, encircled by an entourage of corrections officers, walked down a center walkway, rows of barred cells stretching up six stories high on either side of them. Hundreds of death row inmates watched and whispered from their cells, surveying the newest addition to the epidemic that would eventually claim them all.

"Light him up, boys!" one of the corrections officers yelled up to them, but they remained quiet. Every set of eyes turned up to a single figure on the sixth floor.

From above, a deep voice laced with a thick Italian accent quietly commanded, "Lock it up." Despite its placid tone, the voice sliced through the whispers, which stopped at the command. The silence was now only broken by the disheartened CO's thudding footsteps. The figure, so well shadowed that he could have been mistaken for a silhouette scarecrow, shifted away from the balcony back into his cell.

 "Fucking Honorati. Can't have no fun around this shithole," one of the guards mumbled so quietly that even Atha almost missed it. They led him up to the third level before stopping in front of a cell. A long, monotonous buzzer droned as a guard pulled open the door to the cell and pushed Atha inside. Bare and made entirely of cement and metal save two cots in parallel placement along either wall, the cell was grim. A man occupied one of the beds, and he groaned from beneath stained white sheets as he looked at Atha with partially open eyes. Suddenly, he burst to his feet.

"Hijo de puto! You the kid! Mierda, what are the chances you'd bunk with me!?" He laughed before starting forward with excitement. "I see on the TV what you did! Capped that old rich puto right in the dome! Ain't been a damn thing else for over a month now! Big fucking cojones!"

He continued, calming down as Atha ignored him and stared into oblivion. "Hey, I don't mean no offense, hombre. Name's Rodrigo. Atha, right?"

"Yes, sir."

Rodrigo shook his head at this. "I ain't no 'sir.'"

"Elderly respect."

"No such thing in here. Orange makes everyone equal. You a man now, same as me," he replied as Atha recalled the memory of the shadowy prisoner from the sixth floor.

"Leader?" he questioned, pointing a finger at the ceiling.

"You catch on quick. The only exception to what I call the orange rule. Man up top is Lenny Honorati, big-time Godfather in the Italian mafia way back in the day. He got hit with that RICO. Make no mistake, he ain't no prisoner like you or me; he runs the big house more than that puto warden. Ain't so bad really, 'cause he keeps the rest of the *monstruo* in line. See, he don't like no noise, especially the alarm that goes off during a lockdown. Last time a stabbing happened they went off, some small-timer got pushed too far and snapped. Now man's either dead or rotting in SHU 'cause ain't no one seen him since." Rodrigo embellished his words, telling it like a campfire story, but Atha blankly met his gaze.

"Damn, bro, ain't nothing able to shake you? Never seen a first timer take this shit so well," he said, pausing as the door buzzer sounded again. A pair of COs came into view, followed by a pair of prisoners. A CO gestured for Rodrigo.

"Hernandez, let's go for a walk," he announced, and without a word, the man shot up, practically running out of the cell as the door pulled open.

"Take as much time as you need, Mr. Honorati," the CO said, naming one of the figures before leading Rodrigo away.

Oh no, Atha thought as his heart rate quickened. *Here to hurt me. Should I run? Fight?* He glanced nervously at the two prisoners, who were whispering indistinctly to one another outside the door. *Can't think. Need my geode.* Drawing the image of the sparking rock into his mind, it landed with a thump on the bunk. Atha quickly snatched it up. Turning it in his fingers, he realized it was his exact geode. A plan began to form in his now-clear mind. *They won't suspect me to put up a fight, so I'll use that negligence to take them by surprise. First, I need a weapon, but I don't want to use another gun.*

He snuck one of his socks off, dropping the rock down into the sock's toe and gripping the sock by the ankle portion to form a makeshift blackjack. *I can stun the first with this and the other should freeze up in surprise, just like how the officers did when I was escaping the hospital*

33

room. I need enough time to run out and get help. The warden sees value in my life, so he likely has the guards that escorted my roommate away keeping an eye on me. Atha pushed the rock end of the sock into his pocket in preparation. The mobsters finished chatting and Atha's heart sunk as only one of them entered the cell. His plan would be difficult to execute while the extra man remained outside the cell door.

"Keep an eye out, Giuseppe," the man said. It was none other than the godfather, and despite the label, he was not a particularly intimidating man. Short, with a fair amount of chub on his middle-aged body, he had grey hair that was well kept in a fade. He looked more like a grandfather than a godfather.

"The infamous Atha Schneider. Any guesses as to the reason of my sudden visit?" he asked in his thick Italian accent, smiling with the confidence of an amateur Texas Hold'em player who knew he had a superior hand. Little did he know, Atha wasn't playing poker; he was playing blackjack and held his hand for the best chance to strike. Atha remained silent. The mobster sighed, sinking down onto a knee before him.

"Listen kid, I know…" he started, glancing at the floor. Atha saw his chance. He snapped to his feet and swung the rock bound in cotton toward the man's head. Honorati's hand shot up as if he'd been expecting this all along, snatching the sock from Atha's hand and pushing him gently back onto the bunk with the other. Atha yelped with surprise and attempted to stand again, but a firm hand rested on his shoulder to hold him in place.

"No! No!" Atha whispered in a panic, but the mobster spoke again in a soothing voice.

"I was asking for that after leaving you to guess why exactly I showed up, but old habits die hard. Used to get a kick out of watching wannabe wise guys sweat. Name's Lenny Honorati—"

"Don't hurt me," Atha cut in fearfully.

"Calm down, I'm not here to hurt you," he continued as he pulled his hand back. "Never was good with kids, so let me just cut to the chase, okay? My reason for coming to you is to invite you to join the Honorati family's prison branch. You are young and in need of protection, protection I can provide you with and then some. I ask nothing from you in return. What are your thoughts on this proposition?"

"Don't know you. Don't trust you," Atha whispered back.

"Fair points. You're a smart kid," he replied, noticing Atha glancing to the sock. He lifted it up, shaking the rock out as a look of surprise crossed his face.

"Not what I was expecting to see. Where did you get this from?" he asked, but Atha remained silent. "The Spaniard who was with you—did he give it to you?"

Atha shook his head.

"It is imperative that you be truthful with me. I alone control the flow of contraband that comes in here, and while rocks have been on the manifest before, never one that *sparkled*." He chuckled but Atha remained silent as Lenny's face hardened again. "It is problematic because it being here signifies someone went around me. You are not in trouble here, Atha, but let me ask once more. Where did you get this from?"

He held the rock up in front of Atha who, again, remained silent.

"Giuseppe, tell them to bring the Spaniard to see me once we have concluded business here," he called back to the other man, Atha twitching fretfully.

"Last chance, where'd you get it from?" he asked as Atha tapped his own head.

"Think of it. It appears," he replied.

"I don't catch the meaning of your words," said Lenny. Atha fell silent again. "Look, kid, if you think you need to cover for your cellmate, don't. If he comes to me and speaks the truth, then this one time I will turn the other cheek. If he is worthy of this protection from you, let him prove it. If he is not, then only he will be responsible for what happens after that."

Lenny finished, but Atha had already cleared his mind and had begun drawing the image of a bag of beef jerky into it. It plopped into his lap as the man's eyes widened. He lifted it up in utter disbelief. "*Holy fucking shit.*" He turned to Giuseppe. "Nobody comes within fifty fucking feet of this cell until I say otherwise! Can you do that again?"

Atha nodded as a second bag fell into his lap. Lenny's eyes opened further, practically popping from his head. "This is real. This is really happening," he whispered under his breath as he felt the bag. "How did you do this? Are you an alien? God? The fucking anti-Christ?"

"Don't know."

"When did this start?" he asked. Atha paused, before using his index finger and thumb to form a pistol and placed it to his head.

"Pictured a gun." A shiver ran down Lenny's back that Atha guessed came as the Godfather recalled images of the doctor's exploded brains that had been shown on every TV screen in America during the trial.

"All right, let's review this as logically as possible." Lenny rubbed a hand over his face. "How many others know of this besides you and me?"

"None."

"That's good. Explains why they sent you to prison and not an off-the-books test facility. The things they'd make you do."

"What about you?" Atha asked as Lenny eyed the beef jerky over.

"If only you knew how lucky you are that I was the one who learned of this first. Giuseppe, dispose of these. Let no one see." He extended the bags and geode.

"My rock," Atha cried, pointing to it.

Lenny glanced to the glistening stone. "Yeah, what of it?"

"Gift from Miss Morry."

"This is proof of what you can do. It could put you in more trouble than I could ever deal with. This is for the best," Lenny explained. He paused as a touch of sadness graced Atha's face.

"I'll join you. Please, my geode."

Giuseppe reached for it, but Lenny sighed and handed it to Atha.

"Not a smart decision, Len," Giuseppe cut in, and Lenny nodded.

"No, it's not. Add fifty sparkling rocks to the next order to cover this up. Till that order comes through, keep the rock out of sight. And for absolutely no reason use this—this power. Do you understand me, Atha?"

"Yes, sir," Atha replied before pocketing the geode.

"The order alone will bring us unnecessary attention," Giuseppe contended, and Lenny nodded as he stood.

"We'll need to formulate reasoning for it, but it's not the craziest thing we've ever done, G."

"But it is the most foolish," Giuseppe replied, and Lenny huffed with laughter.

"True. And kid—call me Len. Speaking of etiquette, sorry for all the swearing. Nasty habit. Be sure it remains one held only by me. G, take him up to an empty room on the sixth floor, I will inform the guards of the housing change." Len stepped out and headed for the stairs.

Atha hadn't gotten a very good look at the other man before, but now he had ample time. He was a middle-aged man, probably only a few years off from Len. Tall, skinny, and not a single trace of hair, including his eyebrows. But one distinct feature of his stood out above the rest— his eyes. Wide open and erratic, they jolted from place to place at dizzying speed, halting only occasionally on Atha's face as he spoke to him.

"Len won't state it plainly, but he was very expectant of your arrival here. I am more straight-forward than he is," Giuseppe stated in a toneless voice as he waved for Atha to walk with him. They headed for the stairs leading upward as Atha watched inmates behind bars shift their eyes away from them.

"Not fond of using your words? Or perhaps the true weight of your situation is sinking in?" Giuseppe asked as Atha hurried to keep up with him.

"Had worse."

"I assume you refer to your abusive father. Cue the scripted response," said Giuseppe, as Atha began to smile.

"He could never do that, sir, he loves—"

"Yes, I've heard. Fortunately, this redundant speech of yours has clear reasoning to me for I, too, have my own puppeteer. It is not by choice that we regurgitate words chosen for us by a ventriloquist. The difference between us is, I've had decades to learn how to restrain it, and Len hopes that I might instill that knowledge on you. From this day forth, I am your teacher and will be referred to as Mr. G. Understood?"

"Yes, Mr. G. Like me?" Atha asked as they reached the sixth floor and headed to the left.

"In a sense. I too carry a certain darkness that I am unable to stop," he replied as they entered cell seven. "We will have time to discuss that in more depth later. How far along were you in the first grade?"

Atha noticed a bookshelf filled with familiar books from school. "Complete, Mr. G," he said, causing the man's eyes to go ballistic.

"You underestimate our resources. I am aware you failed first grade once already." Giuseppe's eyes paused on Atha as he nodded.

"Miss Morry helped. Her idea."

G's eyes went back into motion but he paused and held his chin in thought for a few moments.

"Lisa Morry appeared to be quite intelligent when she took to the stand on your behalf. If that is truly her recommendation, it may be wise to follow it." G pulled the chair out from under a desk and motioned for Atha to sit. He produced paper and a pen, setting them down in front of him. "To keep you informed, I was arrested for multiple accounts of homicide, just like you. Take that as you will. More importantly, I was a college professor and am familiar with every lower level of education. You claim to be prepared for the fourth grade and should you prove that you are, we'll start there."

Atha pulled his geode from his pocket, dancing it around in his fingers before nodding to Giuseppe. He read off a series of questions and Atha scribbled out answers. They continued like this until Len knocked on the open door.

"All set. Now let's have a conversation about your future," he started but Giuseppe shot by, gesturing for Len to follow him.

Atha put down his pen and began contemplating his new life. Atha had never voluntarily cried before in his entire life. Before he'd even learned to read, he'd learned that tears angered the doctor in a way few things could, and had voided his body of outward signs of emotion in the form of both speech and bodily indications. Until now, he'd been able to assure himself that things could still get worse. That sentiment no longer applied.

He glanced around the cold cell of metal and stone, at first unsure of what the warm wet presence was that was trickling down his face. He sniffled, huffed, and burst into tears, burying his face into his incredibly thin pillow. He kicked and thrashed until he fell off the metal bed frame, both literally and figuratively reaching rock bottom as he continued to sob on the floor.

"Oh, Melinda, where'd you go?" Atha whimpered. Len snapped his fingers to a distant guard who was sitting in a protected metal room with massive, bulletproof windows on the bottom floor, pointing to Atha's door as its buzzer rang. Atha quickly recomposed himself, wiping the tears from his face as Len came to sit on the edge of his bed.

"Any breakdown is a breakthrough. Marshall McLuhan said that," Len said, pulling a handkerchief from his pocket to dab at Atha's tears. "Giuseppe informed me that you are well past first grade. Did you enjoy conventional school?"

"No," he replied. Len cocked an eyebrow in surprise.

"Then why did you study so far in advance?" he asked, watching Atha feel over his rock.

"School safe. Felt safe studying."

"Well, I think I can do you one better. Here, you *are* safe. Here, you can *choose* what you want to learn about. What interests you?"

"Nothing."

"Nothing in this world fascinates you?" Len asked, receiving a silent nod. "Let me tell you something, kid." Len stood from the bed, kneeling to stare Atha in the eye. "You're in prison now. That means your body is restricted, caged. What you are doing is that exact same thing except"—he,reached a finger out to poke Atha in the forehead— "caging your mind. Don't be so ready to hand over the only freedom you have left. You don't need to leap straight back into education because, well, we have plenty of time for that. But keep my words in mind for now, okay?"

Atha mumbled back just a single word. "Space."

Len paused, wondering if the quiet child had spoken at all.

"What was that?" he asked.

"I want to learn about space."

Chapter 5

A Debt Not Yet Incurred

Ten years, nine months, and sixteen days later.

Atha, now seventeen years old, had not grown into a large man. He was still shorter than most at five feet, seven inches, and there was only the slightest hint of muscle on his skinny frame. Brown hair kept short at Len's behest, stating it gave an enemy less to grab hold of. Atha's deadline was nearing, and Len broke the silence on Atha's abilities to the mafia family on the outside. Sending a series of coded messages, he explained Atha's gift ability and gained their undivided attention. They agreed to break Atha out, setting the date just sixteen days shy of his execution. Today.

Atha awoke at four a.m. for breakfast. His door buzzed open, but despite other prisoners filing by, he remained in place. The Honorati family occupied the entirety of the sixth floor and members chatted as they walked by.

"Could y'all shut the hell up?" Atha screamed and they fell silent, filing by quietly as he buried his head beneath his pillow. A tiny creak sounded from the door and Atha burst from his sheets as a figure shot toward him. His eyes were still blurry but his reflexes weren't. He threw a fist straight toward the intruder's face, but it was swept away with ease. The intruder caught his arm, pulling him forward and sweeping his leg to send him crashing down. Simultaneously, he wrapped another arm around Atha's neck. Atha pulled at it, straining for air, giving up and tapping the arm a few times to signal defeat. It tightened for a few moments as he choked, finally releasing him to catch his breath as his eyes cleared to see Giuseppe.

"What a poor defense. Have I not taught you to be aware of your surroundings at all times?" he asked with blitzing eyes.

"I was *tapping,* G! I'm not in the mood for this shit today!" Atha replied as he huffed and stood. His teacher had gotten older, but it hardly showed, only a few extra lines creased his face. "Jesus, what's the score now? Trained assassin 3,942 to skinny teen's zero?" Atha asked watching as G's eyes sped up.

"Sarcasm will do nothing to improve your flaws. Your movements were unmotivated and sluggish. Either will get you killed," Giuseppe replied. Atha rolled his eyes.

"Not this again. We go through the same scenario every day, I think I got it down." He turned on the metal sink and dashed water across his face.

"Your arbitrary reaction contradicts that statement. Repetition is key, and you must treat every awareness test as if your life depends on it. Someday it will," Giuseppe replied as Atha toweled his face off.

"Yeah, yeah. I got it. Too bad nothing's as easy as it should be and everything sucks. Thank God almighty I don't have to spend another day in this—" Giuseppe burst toward him, pulling a hand up over his mouth as his eyes momentarily focused on Atha's.

"Not another word. Today is just another day. Think it, act it, believe it, live it," he whispered as his eyes returned to dancing crazily in their sockets. Atha sighed and pushed away, pulling out a black rock and dancing it around in his fingers. "And kick that habit." G pointed down to the rock as Atha felt a slight smile cross his face.

"Tomorrow, G. I'm serious this time."

This advice from Giuseppe had turned more to an inside joke between the two of them, as the same advice was given every time Giuseppe noticed a rock bouncing around Atha's fingers, which was at least once a day. Or, at least, it was a joke for Atha; he couldn't tell if Giuseppe found it as humorous as he did. He still had his sparkling geode, but the black meteorite that currently danced in his fingers had been given to him for his eighth birthday by Len, and he regularly carried both on his person.

"Len's expecting a morning briefing in the chow hall," G said, and Atha nodded, heading toward the door where three more Honorati family members awaited him.

Ever since an attempted rape on Atha when he was thirteen, Len never let him go anywhere without an entourage. He didn't particularly like having them constantly around, but he knew better than to argue with the old mobster about certain things. Atha snatched a folder from his desk and stepped out, the bodyguards following behind as he went down the stairs. They were the last to arrive, but they skipped the long line for chow, instead striding straight by to the front and picking up hot trays of mystery meat. The Honorati family sat at the far back section of tables with Len at the center. Atha and Giuseppe's empty seats were to his right. Atha sat in the first chair next to Lenny, with Giuseppe next in line, a symbol of hierarchy.

"Thirteen minutes late. Don't keep me waiting again, Atha," Len growled with fabricated malice in his voice. If being a mobster had fallen through for Len, he could have easily been an actor, displaying a flawless façade despite the planned breakout happening later that day.

"G's fault. Figured it was time for another awareness test this morning." Atha smirked, digging an elbow into the erratic Giuseppe's side.

"'He that is good for making excuses is seldom good for anything else.' Benj—"

"Yeah, yeah, Benjamin Franklin. Heard it," Atha cut in, Len's chubby face panging with scarlet from genuine annoyance.

"Then you should know better. Now why am I not hearing the morning report?" Len spat as Atha grumbled and pulled the papers out.

"The decrease in sales we've been experiencing has dipped an additional five percent as compared to last month's sales," Atha started, hardly glancing at the paper as he spoke. He'd already memorized the material but preferred having it on hand. "Considering that prisoner allowances are increasing, this flux concerns me. The most likely reasons are: A. a guard has gone rogue; B. multiple guards have gone rogue; C. multiple inmates have started a covert contraband business; or lastly D. inmates have lost interest in contraband. Ordered from most to least likely." Atha took a swig of the overly sweet milk followed by a slight nibble of mystery meat.

"Greedy guards is your diagnosis, eh? We need to reassert dominance," Len said dryly. "Get to the bottom of this shit. Get me a name. I expect a resolution in six days." Len glanced toward the clock to realize they only had a few hours left. "You do good work, kid. Letting a wound fester like this is unlike you." He sighed, looping an arm over Atha.

"Smooth sailing never made for skilled sailors," Atha slurred back through a mouthful of food.

"Well, skipper, you plan on sailing out of the fucking storm any time soon?"

"Like hell! Full speed ahead, boys! Gotta hurry or we'll miss the cyclone!"

"If nothing else, at least you're honest! Got a talent for finding every rough patch!"

"Honest and handsome to boot," Atha replied, flicking his hair across his face.

"Calm down, Adonis, ain't no one in here to impress but the lady-men." Atha's face fell. "I didn't mean to..."

"I'm fucking over it. Can we get out of here? I'm done eating," Atha replied, changing the subject.

"Just remember that this grief you feel now is the effect of having felt such love and be thankful for that."

"We need to leave. This isn't the place to be showing weakness," Atha said, knowing that Len would drop the subject with this observation in mind.

"True. Let's retire to my cell," Len replied to Atha's dismay.

"Gonna make me flat out say it, Len? Fine. I don't want to talk about Emilia." Atha stood to his feet. Emilia, Atha's literally short-lived love interest. Murdered in cold-blood just a month ago.

"Yes, you have made that clear, you little shit. We'll leave it alone, but just answer me a single question." Len strode beside a glaring Atha. "Why do you have evil thoughts?"

"Because the world is evil. By putting myself in its head, it allows me to outthink its next move," Atha growled back as Len nodded.

Len smiled like a proud father as they headed for the stairs.

Atha, Giuseppe, and Len entered Len's lavish cell. Not a trace of the regular concrete showed from beneath an Arabian carpet, which in turn was hardly visible beneath the large pinewood desk and several bookshelves atop it. The desk was dual-purposed, its wood lending the room a lingering festive smell to cover the typical moldy musk.

The three Honorati family members sat around the desk. Atha's bodyguards, who were unaware of the impending breakout, posted guard outside of the barred door.

"Let's go over the plan again. If this goes to shit, we'll be forced to use the brute force strategy. Putting Atha's ability on display is an *absolute last resort*." Len glanced between the two men. "At six a.m. sharp, Atha and myself will be accompanied out by COs Hays, Skinner, and Sierra, all of whom are on our payroll. They'll be leading us to the conjugal section whereupon they will hand over a card key that can open every door from there to the exit. After rendering them unconscious, Atha will continue alone while taking care to avoid the six hallway cameras and the thirteen monitoring the main CO lounge area.

"At that point, you'll reach an area where the cameras simply can't be avoided, but I will be patched into the hard-line by then, replaying last week's recording with an altered time-stamp. This will give you *exactly* thirteen minutes before camera errors are noticed by the computer, time you'll use to get into the parking lot where a series of identical vehicles await. Locate the black coupe that has its hazard lights on, get into the trunk, and slip under the false bottom. You will be taken straight to the airport where a private jet awaits to take you on a nonstop flight to Mozambique. Any questions?"

"Clear as mud," said Atha.

"Punk ass. Giuseppe, your part is to start a riot during the initial phase. It's imperative you maintain a mid- to low-level or the alarm will be raised, lockdown initiated, and we're back to brute force," Len finished as the others nodded. Atha's head sagged; the thought of leaving prison was bittersweet. "What's with that look, kid? Show some gratitude. Paying the guards off on something like this is costly, and I called in every favor I have to make this happen."

"Can't you and G come with me?" Atha asked, a slight crack to his voice. "Any member of the Honorati could take G's job and with this"— Atha flashed his open palms—"I could get us out of here, no problem."

"No, we stick to the plan. Brute force is last-ditch only, to avoid the *worst* possible outcome. Using your power will expand your infamy to *unfathomable* heights. Either way, I ain't coming with you. My place is here. To this day I'm astonished you grew up so well, but I ain't about to put another bullet in the gun and play roulette again."

Atha's eyes shifted to Giuseppe.

"I go where Len goes," Giuseppe replied.

"Can't blame me for trying, right?" Atha chuckled, flicking his head back up. "Thank you both for all you've done for me. And I know why you can't leave each other. My two prison dads, both refusing to leave the... *other's behind*." Len's hand flew up to shove his face away.

"You little fucking rat!" Len reached up to give Atha another shove, but he was nimble and easily avoided the second.

"Too slow, old man. Did you get the joke?! I said other's behind! *Other's behind*!" Atha roared, laughing so hard he fell to the floor clutching his chest.

"Your joke is becoming redundant," said Giuseppe.

"Fucking brat! Every fucking time!" Len spat as he turned to Giuseppe. "I speak momentary praise, and this is what greets me?"

"I am but a product of your labors, old man!" Atha replied, calming as the voice of an Honorati member called out from beyond the cell wall.

"Hey, Len, got some COs up here waiting here to take Atha to conjugal."

Atha hopped back to his feet.

"Tell them to wait a minute," Len called before returning his attention to Atha, who had leapt to his feet. "I love you, son. I'm proud of the man you've become."

"Stay aware of your surroundings," Giuseppe added. Keep the skills and knowledge I have taught you in mind and you'll survive."

"Come on, you guys know I don't do the sappy shit. Let's go," Atha replied.

The three stepped out, striding past the Honorati family members. Three COs awaited as Len and Atha headed in their direction. Giuseppe headed the opposite way to begin his portion of the plan. Atha didn't recognize two of the guards, but knew Hays well. Six years older than Atha, he was the youngest guard in the prison. Len would call him an ally, but Atha would call him a friend—though never out loud.

"What's up, boys?" Atha asked as he glanced across the guards. Hays only gave him a cold smile, gesturing for them to follow. "Who pissed in your Wheaties?" Atha laughed, following beside him and receiving another glance from Hays. "All business today eh? Bipolar weirdo." Atha scoffed as a smile broke across Hays's face.

"Naw man, I'm jus' kiddin ya," Hays replied in a thick country accent.

"Everything all right?" Atha asked, this time paying close attention to Hays's face, watching for a tell. *Are you holding something up your sleeve, Hays?*

"Everything's gravy," Hays replied with a single twitch in his lip. That single twitch telegraphed a deeper meaning to Atha. A tell that warned Atha of a liar. To be fair, even a master of facial readings could be wrong. It was not a perfect science. *The question now is do you feel like you're playing me for the fool, or the prison?*

"Swell. Let's hit it then," Atha replied. Atha scratched his ear, a hand signal meaning *something's wrong* to Len who followed behind. They were led down the stairs and into a hallway, cameras and guards everywhere until they reached the last bend before the conjugal door finally came into view.

Maybe I read that wrong. I could just be on edge. They entered the next hallway, which was lined with heavy metal doors on either side. All was silent as they walked, the final and longest hallway stretching before them.

Hays broke the silence. "I've waited a long time for this, Atha." Atha instantly noticed Hays' trademark country accent had vanished. "Think you could just *take* what you want without any concern for where it came from?"

"I haven't taken shit from nobody, as you'll see if you keep on talking to me like that," Atha replied but paused as the convoy came to a halt. Atha's heart sank as Hays drew his baton. The other guards followed suit. "The hell's this about? I thought we were cool." Atha eased back closer to Lenny.

"You haven't done it *yet*, but you will. Oh, you will," Hays replied.

"Done what? You're not making any sense—" Atha started but was cut short as the doors around them burst open. Dozens of baton-wielding guards swarmed down on them. Atha and Len simultaneously came to the same response and burst toward the lone guard who had entered through a heavy metal door. He swung at Atha, but with a swift jab to the jaw, he reeled back as the prisoners slid into the room, slamming the door shut behind them.

"You're a dead man, Hays! You hear me?" Atha screamed at the metal door, giving it a heavy kick before turning to Len. "So, what now?! Plan B, huh?" Atha asked, attempting to hide the excitement in his voice.

"Do it," Len replied and Atha smiled, drawing the image of a loaded Tommy gun in his mind. It fell into his hands, cold and heavy with a hundred-round drum magazine weighing it down. He handed it off to Len.

"A thing of beauty," Len chuckled.

Loaded automatic shotgun Atha pictured, and the firearm fell into his hungry hands.

"You can have your old-timey relic, I'll take modern technology." Atha smirked, a small-door charge falling into his free hand.

"Stick to the plan. We free as many prisoners as possible to use as a smokescreen. Give Giuseppe the signal."

A machine fell into Atha's hands next. He sat it down and pulled up a receiver as the prison's PA system crackled on.

"The cuckoo is grounded!" he yelled as a lower, distorted version of his voice repeated the words over the PA.

Atha sat the machine back down, retrieved the explosive, and moved toward the door. A cacophony of screams came from the far side, and Atha glanced back to Len, who shrugged and motioned for him to continue. Reaching the charge up toward the center of the door, he reeled back in surprise as an explosion rocked the opposite side of the door, caving the thick metal inches away from Atha's face.

"What the—? Len, what was *that*?" he yelled to the other man, but stopped as a black circle began to form on the wall behind Len. "Holy shit! Look! It's just like the one that took Melinda!" He hurried forward as Len glanced back.

"Hold it together, kid, all hell's breaking loose out there!" he yelled as Atha reached his shotgun up to tap the wall.

"You don't see this?! It's like, I don't know, a portal or something!" Atha stared in disbelief, leaning his hands up to touch it and nearly falling straight into it. Atha's arms vanished into the wall up to his elbows.

"What the hell?! I'm stuck. I can't pull my arms back out!" Atha struggled fruitlessly, only succeeding in slipping in further as Len felt over the darkness surrounding Atha's arm.

"It's just a wall for me. Don't even know why I'm surprised after seeing the things you can do."

"Len! Jesus, help pull me out!"

Another explosion shook the door, crushing it further inward, nearly sending it off its hinges.

"How do they have explosives? Damn, why is all this happening now?" Atha cried.

Hays's taunting voice called through the door.

"Atha! Come on, just make this easy! We both know what the outcome here is!" He laughed as Atha flared with rage. Despite this, a calm seemed to fall over Len.

"I'm by no means a religious man, but I have faith in the wisdom they hold. I feel I am most comparable to Jephthah, given both a new child and a sword despite how unworthy he may be."

"What the hell are you talking about? Help me, Len!" Atha cut in as Len rested an arm on his shoulder.

"I truly am surprised how well you turned out. I know I didn't say it enough, but I love you, Atha. Now go, my son."

"No, Len don't—" Len's firm arm shoved him into the darkness.

Chapter 6

Free at Last, Free at Last,

Thank... God?

"What the..." Atha started, noticing his body was clearly visible despite the darkness.

"And so, the wayward son broke free of his shackles," a commanding voice that felt like warm water pouring into Atha's body called from behind him. Atha swiveled around to see an elderly man standing a few feet behind him. His white hair contrasted with skin so black it seemed to have a blue hue to it. He wore white robes that resembled armor and he smiled pleasantly at Atha.

"I'm dead, aren't I? Are you the devil or something? God?" Atha asked. The man shook his head, a white chair appearing behind him as he sat.

"You're not dead. I suppose in a certain sense one could compare me to God as I spur your universe back into creation once every eight trillion years. My official title is Universe Creator and my name is Xexon," he replied. A white chair appeared behind Atha. "Care for a seat?" he asked, but Atha ignored this.

"What do you want from me?" he demanded.

"Pardon me, I fear I have left you with many questions. You do seem rather composed though, being in a situation such as this."

"I've been hiding powers that can manifest whatever I think of. Not much of a leap to figure there was more out there. Figured something gave them to me, but I always had my money on aliens."

"Technically, to you, I am an alien, but I am not the one who gifted your power. As for my reason for bringing you here, I have certain boons of my own to bestow upon you to secure the future."

"It's strange," interjected Atha. "I have no reason to believe anything you say, but it's like... I don't know, like your words are *commanding* me to acknowledge them as the truth."

"That is because they do not speak to your ears but to your soul. Unlike a human, I do not speak in simple words, but your mind cannot comprehend their true form." Atha covered his ears, realizing he could still clearly hear him.

"I've met someone else who gave me this sensation of warmth when they speak. The lady in the library, way back when I was six. She—" Atha paused, a series of connections tying themselves together.

"You are such a brilliant child. Yes, she was the one who gave you this power to call forth objects. She is another creation of higher being. Gavreel is her name, and in terms that you can understand, she is a child of mine. I created her to watch over a world, the one you are heading toward, in fact."

"Yes, I knew it!" Atha exclaimed, clapping with joy as he finally sat down into his chair and scooched it up closer to Xexon. "Melinda's there, isn't she?! I knew she was alive, I knew it!"

Tears welled up in his eyes.

"Yes, she is, and yes, she is in this next world," Xexon replied. He watched in silence as Atha held his face and cried.

"I started to wonder if maybe I was just insane. These powers, how she vanished like that... I wondered if this was just some fantasy my mind made up. I'm sorry, I don't usually break down like this." Atha sobbed as Xexon lifted a hand to rest it upon Atha's head.

"I know of all that has befallen you as if I'd stood beside you all along," he replied, the words cascading over Atha's body like warm water. "You're a favorite of mine to watch. Most don't experience a quarter of the vibrancy you've lived with in their entire lifetime, and far fewer who lived it beneath oppression."

"Why didn't you help me?" Atha asked aggressively, peering back up at the creator.

"I am forbidden from playing too grand a part in the fate of mortals. When you entered that portal, normally you would have appeared instantly at your destination, but fortunately it passes through my realm and I took that opportunity to intercept. I've spoken with other incarnations of you before, but it is a rare occurrence for a human to cross dimensions in this manner, so this is a treat for me."

"I'm not really sure what to say; only Len has ever held me in such high regard," Atha said. "Maybe G too, but I could never read him. And who knows if either of them are even alive now."

Xexon shook his head. "That is information that I am not allowed to divulge. Fortunately, you will be able to learn of their fate one day."

"Why can't you tell me? You told me about *Melinda*."

"Because giving you that information would change the course of the future. Regardless of knowing or not, you would have searched and located her with ease. Some things I *can* change but only to assure things that must come to pass, do."

"Don't know how I'm supposed to feel about all this. Almost feels like I'm regaining a family member only to lose others." He looked down at his palms. "Maybe I should have just accepted my fate. Even if I never got to find out Melinda was still alive, it would have been worth it to make sure the people who've done so much for me got to live out the rest of their days."

Xexon leaned in closer with a twinkle in his eye. "That is something you will have to place on the scale and weigh for yourself. I look forward to seeing how, and in what manner, you do."

"Nothing is worth selling out family. I don't mean to be rude, but can I go now? I want to see Melinda," he said. Xexon's smile widened.

"Blood boiling eternally of rebellion, I see. Well, dear child, allow me to gift you a few things, and I'll send you on your way." He touched Atha's hand and red energy erupted from it. "This red glow emitting from you is known as Agro energy. When released from your body, it enhances strength, speed, and overall bodily durability. Along with it, I bestow the knowledge of how to properly use it to the extent understood by a novice. You will need it to survive for the initial portion of your homecoming. And lastly—" He paused, tapping a finger against Atha's head. Glowing white energy rushed down the finger like a jolt of electricity and vanished into Atha's flesh. "Modulation energy. You can use it to alter the fate of others to a limited degree, but unlike Agro energy, your body cannot reproduce more. That's all I can speak of it."

Atha began to speak but was cut off as the creator continued. "I can give no hints as to why you will need modulation energy, but you will figure it out. You are so very clever after all." He winked.

Atha extended a hand out to him, which was the first thing that had taken Xexon by surprise, notable by the fact the Creator's mouth opened a fraction of an inch. "Thank you, sir. I'll be sure to properly thank Gavreel as well for giving me the power that saved Melinda."

Xexon grasped his hand. "You are very welcome. Oh, and I should mention that you will not be able to speak of our encounter or of the modulation energy. We will meet again, Atha," he finished as Atha's eyes suddenly blurred. Intense light blinded him as he forcefully fell to his back upon the ground.

"Ugh, what the hell?" he exclaimed. He painfully gasped for air as his lungs struggled to rise. It was as if gravity had been amplified in this new world. His eyes slowly adjusted and he realized the blinding light was coming from not one, not two, but three suns in the cloudless blue sky above him. Lined up one above the other, they could have been the solar twins of Orion's belt had they been from Earth's system.

Toto, I have a feeling we're not in Kansas anymore, Atha thought, as he forced himself up enough to look around. He was resting in the middle of a grassy clearing filled with blades of thin, needle-like grass. Massive trees with purple leaves stood in a half-circle and stretched toward the sky. It was windless, yet their branches swayed up and down like waves. Atha focused the red energy now flowing through him. It sputtered out of his body, but even a small quantity was enough to get him to his feet.

I see why I need Agro energy. The gravity here must be at least twice what it was on Earth, he thought, a smile creeping over his face as he took in a long, deep breath of freedom. He glanced down at himself, the sickening bright orange clothing glaring back mockingly. Red energy filled his heavy arms and, like Superman tearing off his shirt, he ripped them from his body.

In just his boxers, Atha drew the image of jeans, boots and a white T-shirt in his mind. They dropped into his hands, and he began to pull them on.

"Shakka's desha!" a peeved, masculine voice yelled from behind him.

Atha flipped around and nearly fell as he was literally caught with his pants down. A figure wrapped in a purple robe that shrouded his face beneath a black hood frantically dashed around the circle of trees toward him.

"Ana laken abunze! Busel laken shuk alanda!" it continued, coming to a stop a short distance away and flailing its arm in the air like a preacher begging for God's mercy. Atha could only stare in disbelief, pausing in his effort to pull up his pants.

"Uh... I come in peace?" said Atha.

"Booka del marsha! Balmac magury vel seldando!" it screamed as if chagrined by the intruder's incomprehensible response to the words. Atha slowly continued to pull his pants up, keeping a wary eye upon the unknown figure.

"I don't understand you! Hey!" said Atha, pulling the shirt and boots on. "I do not understand you!"

The thing appeared puzzled by the strange language. It pulled its black hood back, and Atha lurched back with surprise as he realized this wasn't a human. Its face was scarlet with completely black eyes, which stared at him with a recognizable expression of confusion. Short black horns covered its head and shorter ones lined the space normally designated for eyebrows. Atha had thought himself prepared for anything, but after his mind autonomously drew the conclusion that a figure of this shape must be human the shock of the actual unveiling of its face caught him now metaphorically with his pants down, and he stumbled back and fell on his buttocks.

The creature reached a red hand down to him. Atha hesitantly grasped it, and the strange humanoid lifted him back to his feet before beginning to make gestures. It pointed to Atha, then itself, and toward the direction from which it came.

"I kick ass at charades. You want me to follow you?" Atha asked. He repeated the signals and formed a set of legs with his fingers, walking the pointer and middle finger through the air. The creature nodded, smiling to reveal fanged teeth. "And then you're gonna use those obnoxiously carnivorous teeth to eat me, right?" Red continued to smile and nod as he waved for Atha to follow. "Oh man, I'm probably walking my stupid ass straight into some sort of cult sacrifice ritual but eh, no clue where else to go." Atha followed behind, listening as the creature pointed to the trees and spoke more perplexity.

"*Oshta ba shosh. Shakka landes has de shosh*! *Les elda mey oy*!" Red said in seeming pleasure.

"What, you're gonna hide my body under that tree right there?" Atha teased as Red smiled back, flinching as Atha's red glow vanished, sending him crashing back down to the ground yet again. *My reservoir is empty. Well, now I know how long I can keep it sustained.* Atha groaned as most of the air was crushed from his lungs. Atha's new acquaintance fell to his knees beside Atha.

"*Oshtad belonk desh und?!*" Red asked hysterically, giving Atha's shoulder a shake.

"I'm fine," Atha said to him, but mostly for his own benefit as his concern grew with each painful difficult breath.

The creature looped one of Atha's arms over its shoulder and helped him up. They continued to walk. *Gotta keep practicing with it. Those instructions Xexon put in my head say Agro works like a muscle and mine's brand new.* They turned past the trees to view a beautiful archaic building made entirely of white marble. A steeple rose up from it, reminding Atha of a church. It had no windows, only a set of white marble doors at the front that where carved with an image of the trees surrounding the area. The doors swung open as they neared. Inside, Atha immediately noticed a dull glow that filled the entire space.

His eyes adjusted once more, and he realized the floor was translucent and deep like a pool of water. Dancing balls of light contained within appeared to be the source of the glow. Atha's head, pulled by the intense gravity, remained focused on the floor, and he watched the lights dance and flash. *What is this world? This place?* Atha wondered, straining to look up at the red creature.

"What is that?" he asked, Red cocking his head with a look of uncertainty as Atha began to point at the floor.

"The floor, what is this?" he asked again.

"Heka?" Red asked. Atha chuckled at this, the language barrier growing painful.

He felt more hands grab onto him, and a second figure hidden beneath purple-and-black robes lifted his other arm over their shoulder. The two pulled him through the room toward a door in the back. He caught a few glances around the room, realizing there was at least a dozen purple-garbed people within, most with heads bowed to the floor, seemingly in prayer. They entered a stone hallway filled with doors and entered the first, which led to a humble room.

A bed sat in the middle and they lowered him onto it, propping him up on the headboard. Atha's Agro energy had recharged a bit, and when he glowed red, he managed to lean up.

"Ov dea shlanta?" the hooded one asked Red, pulling the hood back to reveal a more feminine version of her friend. Black horns rolled down the back of her neck smoothly like hair, a slimmer, dainty face filled with confusion as she spoke back and forth with the male. *They resemble humans a bit. Pretty sure they have basic male and female sexes as well,* Atha thought as the female turned back to him, pointing and gesturing at his hand.

"Kiales," she announced.

"You... want to hold my hand?" he replied as she gestured again.

"Kiales, shuto," she replied as Atha slowly stretched his hand out. She grabbed it, dipping her free hand into her pocket to produce what appeared to be blue paper adorned with hieroglyphs. She pressed it against the back of his hand, and the hieroglyphs oozed off the paper and into his skin with a sharp zing. Atha yanked his hand back fearfully.

"What'd you do to me?" he shrilled just as his Agro energy gave out, sending him reeling onto his back. The female spoke again, but now her mouth moved out of sync with her words.

"Be at ease. It was simply an item used for translation."

Chapter 7

The Best Kind of Advice

"You—you understand me? I understand you! How did you do that?" he asked with bursting enthusiasm.

"Surely you have seen something of a similar sort before," she started, turning her words to her male counterpart. "Perhaps he is disoriented."

"No, I'm fine. I just—"

"Have you any idea where it is you are?" she cut in.

"The mystical land of Oz? I got no clue, but I'm really not disoriented," Atha replied as she reached a hand down to invasively feel his pant leg.

"This area is known as Shakka Village. It was dubbed such due to the fact that this is the holy forest of Shakka in the middle of which you thought wise to unclothe yourself according to Elenzer's testimony."

"Oh...uh, sorry about that," said Atha.

"What is your name? How old are you?" the female asked.

"Atha Honorati. I'm seventeen."

"I am Zell Tenzata. Is there reason you find moving difficult, Atha?" she asked as Atha pushed his elbows down into the bed to push himself up a little.

"The gravity here. Feels like I got sandbags pressing down over my whole body," Atha wheezed.

"Where have you come from? These garments and language are completely foreign, so I assume you have traveled a long way to be here," she replied.

She's grilling me. I must have stumbled over something that would make what I'm telling them suspicious, Atha thought.

"Let's not start assuming things here, Zell," Elenzer, previously known as Red, said. "Atha, if you're in some sort of trouble or need help getting back home, we can give aid."

Atha contemplated the situation. *They give off the air of being genuinely good. I think I can trust them,* he thought.

"Well, you have magical glowing floors and scraps of paper that can translate languages," he replied, "so I don't think this will sound crazy. I just came from a different world through some sort of portal and popped up in that field Elenzer found me in,"

Zell sighed as Elenzer shifted closer to her.

"Can you check for drugs?" Elenzer whispered, but Atha's sharp ears caught it.

"I'm not on drugs!" he yelled, attempting to get up but crashing back down onto the bed. Stars dotted his eyes and for a moment he was sure he would pass out.

"I grow weary of this game you play. You claim to come from another world, fine. Surely you will not mind if I search through memory to find truth in such words," Zell replied, pulling off a glove and twiddling her fingers at him.

"You—you can do that?" Atha managed to ask, forcing long, deep breaths.

"The contract I hold allows me to view another's memory as if my own."

"Contract? Never heard of a contract that can let you go all Professor X on someone."

"I know not of whom you speak. A contract is a pact between oneself and a spirit that allows the use of the spirit's power for a price. Mine is quite versatile, holding a variety of abilities of which memory replay rests among. But you already are aware of this, aren't you?" Zell asked coldly as Atha laughed.

"Holy shit! I'm in a magical world! Oh, this is awesome! Do it, I wanna see!"

She placed her hand on his forehead. "Memory bandit," she said. Atha felt a slight tingle in his head. "Humans dressed in orange...metal bars, metal doors...other humans carrying metal sticks. This seems to be all there is no matter how far back I go. Oh, stars and a *singular* moon?"

Atha restrained tears. *I remember that. Len took me to the roof for my birthday one year and gave me my first drink of alcohol. Oh man, that swish was so nasty I wanted to throw up, but I didn't want him to make fun of me*, Atha thought as she pulled her hand back.

"Either he speaks the truth, or someone went through exorbitant trouble to erase and reform memory. The detail in them was impeccable," Zell told Elenzer as Atha groaned with disbelief.

"I'm telling you the truth," Atha calmly replied, a mental storm beginning to form within his head. *It seems like they're slowly warming up to condemn me for something I'm not even aware of. Worst case scenario, I'll have to fight my way out of here.* The thought of using his own power came to mind. She likely hadn't found out about its existence thanks to Len's insistence he not use it. Len was so thorough, he even protected Atha in ways he couldn't possibly have foreseen.

"The weight pressing down on him," said Elenzer. "Not a hint of mana surrounding him. How did I not notice this before? Has your appendix been opened to mana?!"

"Mana?"

"Keen observation! Not a single trace, unbelievable!" Zell gasped. "This is conclusive evidence, Elenzer! No newborn could possibly survive more than a few minutes without the appendix activated!"

"He is from a *different world*. Shakka's mercy! Zell, what do we do here?" Elenzer asked.

"Compose yourself. Let us concern ourselves with that later. His body must be taking quite the toll supporting itself without mana."

"Oh, yes! I can open him, hold him up," he ordered. Zell grabbed Atha by the shoulders and pulled him up to a sitting position. Elenzer pressed his hands against Atha's lower right stomach, grabbing hold of a roll of flesh. A sudden zing came from his hands and Atha felt the weight lifting.

"I can feel it!" Atha replied, leaping to his feet. "I feel so light! This is awesome! So that's what the appendix is for!"

"Apologies for casting doubt upon you. Please know that I did have fair reasoning for it," Zell said.

"Bygones!" Atha laughed, eyeing himself over.

"Atha Honorati, welcome to Oluceps." Zell smiled.

"Oluceps, huh? Weird name for a planet, coulda said it backwards and it wouldn't sound any better. Anyways, now that I can move, I can go look for my sister. Can you guys answer some questions for me?"

Zell nodded.

"A bit over a decade ago my sister vanished into a black portal, like the one that brought me here, and I need to find her. Her name's Melinda and she'd be twenty-four by now. Do either of you know about her?"

An orange hologram opened in front of Zell. It was large, reaching from her head to her knees and curved inward toward her. A series of symbols appeared on it and she began rearranging them as Atha's eyes widened.

"Whoa, what the *fuck*? That's awesome! Is this a part of your contract?! Some sort of magical object?"

She continued rearranging symbols. "The former. Contracts come in a variety, and the one I possess falls into the information category. Luck seems to be on your side in many ways."

"It's about time!" Atha started, drumming his knees. "Only been waiting all my life for it to kick in!"

"Oh my," Zell gasped.

"What?" Atha asked. She turned the orange screen to him.

The image of a woman dressed in a long green dress displayed across it, hair long and black, pale skin glowing under the bright sunlight. She sat atop a podium, waving to a massive crowd before her.

Atha was stunned. She was a woman now, not a trace of the terrified girl he'd known was left, yet he instantly knew. "That's her."

"This makes perfect sense. Why she suddenly vanished and appeared again to take the throne once the danger had come to pass," Zell noted out loud.

"Throne?" Atha asked.

"Yes. She is the Queen of this nation," Zell replied.

"What? *The queen*? Wait, does that mean she's married?" he asked, but Zell shook her head.

"She has yet to take a king at her side."

"Oh. Anyways, why does this all make perfect sense?" Atha asked.

"During the time she vanished, the royal family was under siege from a syndicate known as the Chameleons," Zell explained. "It seemed inevitable they would annihilate her and her kin until she was simply spirited away. From nothingness she went, and through nothingness she returned again ten years ago, at which time it became evident that the royal family had used a top-secret contract or item to hide her. If she was with you, we can now say with certainty that she was hiding on another planet."

"But she came back to nothing," Atha stated.

"And reformed void into excess. Let me start from the beginning. The name 'Melinda' must have been an alias used on Earth in case the

71

Chameleons could manage to follow, as her name is Elise here, family name Luxria. Queen Elise Luxria has made it her life's work to rebuild this kingdom, and nobody would dare argue that she hasn't," said Zell, reopening her screen. She scrolled through images of burning villages, piles of corpses and destruction that sent a shiver down Atha's back. "This was the general state of the lands before her return. This next compilation of images adequately describes the current situation." She rearranged the symbols again as new pictures of parades, feasts and a proud army were displayed.

"She always did love taking care of others," said Atha. "I need to see her. Do you have a map or its magical equivalent that I can borrow?"

"My ability can cement one within the confines of your mind, but I fear Shakka would frown if I left a stranger out of sorts in a new world. Would you like me to guide you?"

"Absolutely! I mean, that sounds great, but I don't mean to impose on you more than I already have."

"It is my duty as a monk of Shakka to give guidance to those in need," she replied. "Should you choose to accept it, we may leave tomorrow."

"In that case, I'll just go by myself. I want to leave immediately."

"Even in that case, I must advise against it. An evil has awoken, and it is currently reported to be exactly between our location and the Royal Capital. At current rate of movement, it is estimated to have moved out of our path by tomorrow."

"I'm prepared to defend myself. Can I have my map, please?"

"I know what you are capable of. You wield a mysterious power, but you are still far from being able to defend against what I speak," Zell replied. Atha's face fell. She *had* seen his ability after all. The woman before him was nobody's fool. "I recognize your reasoning for wanting to leave immediately, but should you not heed my words, then you may find waiting a day extended by a lifetime."

"Fine," Atha replied, disheartened, but Zell's face brightened.

"Then I will prepare to accompany you tomorrow. If you wish," Zell replied.

"Well, I'm not gonna look a gift horse in the mouth," he said.

"A...gift horse?" she repeated slowly. "On another note, these garments will draw unnecessary attention." She turned to a drawer and pulled out a set of robes. "Change into these. They are Shakka disciple initiate robes." She handed them to Atha and she and Elenzer exited the room.

Atha pulled the new clothes on, the black robes and a long-sleeved button-up shirt that fit a bit snugly on him. Not fancy by any standards, yet extremely comfortable. He pulled his geode and burnt meteorite from the jeans, placing them safely into an inside pocket on the robes. It also had a black cape that he pulled over his shoulders before eyeing himself over.

I feel like a superhero. He paused, eyes widening. "I'm technically an *alien* here!" He gasped out loud.

"Are you decent?" Zell called from the other side of the door.

"Not decent but clothed. For now, at least." Atha laughed. "Before we hit the road, I have a few more questions. You mentioned there's danger between here and the capital. Even after said danger has passed, will the way be entirely safe? More specifically, should we be prepared for combat on the way there, and if so, can you hold your own?" Atha asked Zell as Elenzer stifled a laugh and nudged her in the side.

"A fair question but difficult to answer. Overall, Oluceps is a peaceful and safe territory yet it still holds unpredictability. As for myself, I am quite formidable in combat," Zell replied.

"You said your ability was information based. Do you have weapons or something?" he asked. She nodded, pulling back a fold of her robes to display at least a dozen daggers.

"While I do carry weapons, they alone cannot divulge the extent of my abilities."

Well, if daggers could possibly be considered viable in combat, then my firearms should be more than enough. "What about your contract? What are the rest of its abilities?" Atha asked.

"In this world, information of an opponent's contract can be a death sentence," Elenzer cut in. "As such, it's considered bad form to directly ask about one unless a situation presents itself that would require it."

"It matters not in my case," said Zell. "Save a few aces, I am comfortable revealing more basic aspects. As I previously stated, it is an information type but compared to most has a wide variety of topics. Dubbed Grand Mastermind, anything from architectural blueprints to information on people can be found if the right hieroglyphics are aligned. Still, it is not omniscient, since information must be added by another with the same contract. With skin-to-skin contact any of the information can be imprinted upon another, a single page at a time. Last fact of small note is the ability allows me to commune with trees at an elongated space."

"Commune with trees? What do you mean?"

"As in converse. Within your memory, I noticed the occasional tree, so surely you have spoken with one before." She noticed Atha's jaw drop. "Well, that would be the easy conclusion to jump to. Taking note of the fact mana is the tool used to connect with one, perhaps you never even realized they are intelligent."

"Damn, this place just keeps getting better and better!" Atha jumped to his feet. "Can we go talk to one right now?"

"Certainly."

They made their way back outside, the massive trees before them continuing to shift in the windless light.

"Tell me, are you aware of a flower's ability to perceive spoken language?" Zell asked.

"Like trees? No, didn't know that one either," Atha replied.

"Not exactly as a tree might. They can understand the concept of a word but not a full sentence. Neither can they give a response more than a few words long."

"Ok, you lost me this time. How can they understand the concept of a word but not an actual sentence?" Atha chuckled.

"Say ugly," Zell instructed.

"Uh, okay. Ugly."

"Now say beautiful."

"Beautiful."

"Did you feel a difference when you spoke?" Zell asked and Atha paused for a moment.

"I actually did. I felt good saying beautiful and sort of crappy saying ugly."

"Precisely!" Zell smiled, giving Atha a short round of applause. "Either of those words would be lost upon a flower by themselves. It is that *feeling* that conveys itself to them. To elaborate a bit further, if you were to tell a flower it was beautiful frequently, it would grow and prosper. Alternatively, if you were to call it ugly, the feeling accompanied with the word would cause it to fall ill and eventually kill it. Take for example our tenebris flowers nestled in the shadows beneath our trees."

Zell gestured to dainty little flowers Atha had missed on his way in. Petals a deep shade of black with likewise stems, they were unlike any Atha had ever seen. "They're gorgeous!"

"Their name translates directly to *darkness*. Normally, they are of a grey color, but when they are told they are beautiful begin to turn a healthy shade of black."

"Then why are they called darkness?" Atha asked.

"To survive they require just a single hour of light a day. Any more than that and they begin to overproduce glucose. As you could imagine, this is a difficult thing to accomplish in a world with multiple suns, and as such they are nearly extinct. The trees of Shakka actually shift their limbs to keep them in the shadows for the necessary time."

"So, getting back on subject then, these trees can *move?*" Atha replied.

"In a very limited sense. Their branches can shift vertically and horizontally very slowly."

"Can they see?" Atha asked as they walked. Elenzer shrugged at the question.

"In a limited sense. To put it more appropriately, they can feel surroundings through their roots," he replied.

"Then why didn't you just ask them if I popped out of a portal instead of questioning me?"

"Teleportation isn't common here, but it's not rare either. There are a variety of portals that can be categorized by the color of their energy, and roots cannot detect color. They wouldn't have been able to tell if you just came from the other side of the world or a different world altogether," he replied. They neared one of the massive grey and purple trees, and Atha started to become a bit flustered.

"What should I say?" he whispered to Zell.

"Take conversing with a tree as you would with an elderly family member. They are kind, knowledgeable, and immensely wise, but even then, addressing the trees of Shakka is a pinnacle of sorts. They were planted by the spirit Shakka over 8,000 years ago and have seen the rise and fall of many empires."

"Now I feel even more nervous. Been here for maybe an hour and I'm absolutely blown away by this world. Everything about it is so drastically different, I'm beginning to wonder if the label 'science fiction' should be renamed 'yet to be discovered.'" He stopped in front of a tree awkwardly as Zell nudged him forward. He wondered what to say to a tree when a stream of sparkling blue energy swirled out from its trunk and a human voice rang through his head.

"Hello, child! Such a dainty young man, I thought surely you were a female until I heard your voice," the warm feminine voice chuckled.

Okay, ouch. Man, this tree is talking shit to me, Atha thought as the voice laughed.

"Apologies, I did not mean offense. Please allow me to revoke my 'shit talk' and tell me what brings you beneath my humble branches this day."

"You can hear my thoughts? Sorry, this is all totally new to me." He gasped, the tree reaching a branch down to stroke leaves across his head.

"My mana has connected our consciousnesses, so yes, I can hear your thoughts. Tell me, you are not of this world, are you?" she asked.

"Did they already tell you or is it just that obvious?" he asked back, glancing across areas of the bark, unsure where to look.

"To me, it is obvious. I have spoken with travelers of other dimensions before. From where do you hail?"

"Earth. How many travelers have you met?"

"Seven. Counting you, eight. You are the first of Earth. Have you ever seen a tree before?"

"Yeah, but never spoken with one. We actually chop you guys down and use your wood for things like houses and paper. God, it's really sad when I think about it."

"And what did you do when you learned of our intelligence?"

"I wanted to speak with one. I like to understand things, know how they work. Kinda a habit from all the spare time I had. Being here has been— I don't know—like major culture shock for me, I guess. Every little thing is totally blowing my mind. Gotta say though, being able to talk with a tree currently takes the cake." Atha chuckled as the tree's calming voice came back into his head.

"Understanding is the doorway to union, and through union, elevation. Over my life, I have borne witness to many divides caused by the abyss of misinterpretation. It is peculiar that while you seek to understand things, I can also divulge that you tend to destroy them. Do you recognize my words to be true?"

"I do. Honestly, that's just how I was raised," Atha replied, rubbing his weary head in a vain attempt to clear it of sickening memories. "Now I guess the question would be is that the right mindset to maintain. And I don't think it is, but I also don't know if I can change. I'm corrupt; I'm ruined."

"If you are smart enough to realize your own shortcomings, you can be wise enough to change them."

"You just have the perfect response for everything, don't you?" he quipped.

"I do take pride in my ability to give advice. Taking advantage of it would be beneficial for you. Together we could dispel some of the darkness you keep bound within your heart."

Atha's head jerked up, realizing that if she can hear his thoughts, she probably also witnessed his memories. "Are you digging through my head?"

"I have no such ability. Regardless, to me, it is obvious. Every aspect, every characteristic of you, however well you hide it, points to a life forged through pain. You keep an eye on your surroundings, seeing danger as not an *if* but a *when*. You put little thought into your words, yet instinctively keep them blunt in case the next moment is your last. The image of who you are cannot be blurred. Your demeanor is rare, but I've spoken with a terminally ill soldier who acted just as you do. I have no knowledge of your past, but I suspect it was one close to this."

"Damn. You're good," he replied, stunned. "What's your name?"

"Cybele. And yours?"

"Atha Honorati. Nice to meet you," he replied, glancing up to the sky and realizing two of the three suns had already sunk bellow the horizon. A few white orbs glowed dully as innumerable dots began to appear. "Stars! And—holy shit! Are those...*moons*?"

"They are indeed. We have seven here. May I ask how many Earth has?"

"*Seven*? And the stars—oh my God, look at them! It's still daylight and you can already see them so clearly!" he roared, glancing back to the tree. "On Earth we only have one moon! I was in the middle of nowhere, which was perfect for stargazing without any light pollution, but these are already just as clear!"

"Night is but a handful of breaths away. If you'd like, I can tell you of all the constellations in the heavens above," she proposed, his head spinning at the very thought. "I can provide a better vantage point."

Atha first glanced to Zell, who motioned for him to go, and then he set off climbing up to the airy top of the tree. The branches beneath his feet tightened together, providing him with a leafy platform. He laid down and stared up into the sky in the lingering rays of daylight. The stars were already clear, and blue mana sparkled just in front of his face as lines began to connect the stars.

"The brightest star in the sky, Kita," said Cybele, "is used to help form the most prominent constellation known as Vakusu, depicting Queen Vakusu with an outstretched arm." An imaged formed from the sparkling blue, a dainty woman stretching out her hand with fingers clasping the bright star. "Kita is used to emphasize the contract Vakusu wielded known as 'Guiding Light of the Heavens,' making it appropriate as the crown jewel of the night sky. Queen Vakusu ruled the lands far to the east 2,178 years ago, and the constellation was created in her honor after her passing in a battle against a terror known as the plague of darkness." Cybele went on for hours, dozens upon dozens of constellations flashing before Atha, who listened in wonder.

"So many. Earth only had eighty-eight," Atha said.

"These are but the ones currently used. To list all that have existed over just my lifetime would take quite some time. Now, I have shared with you, yet feel myself wanting," she replied. Atha's stomach had been grumbling at him for over an hour, yet he hadn't wished to pause the conversation to seek food. *Oh! Wait, I can use my power whenever I want now! Len had me so trained to hiding it I almost forgot.* A can of soup fell into Atha's hands and he pulled the lid off, tipping the can back and taking a quick slurp.

"What, you wanna know about Earth?" he asked.

"Tell me of your experience with it. I want to know Atha Honorati's story," Cybele replied.

"Talking about the stars is one thing, but my life ain't been no fairy tale. I've done a lot of bad things and a lot of bad things have been done to me."

"Spare not a single gritty detail," Cybele replied.

"All right. When I was six, I woke up late one night to find my father choking my sister to death. On Earth we have weapons that can shoot shards of metal at thousands of feet per second, and I used one to blow his head off before he could kill her," Atha stated smugly, waiting for the tree to regret its question.

It was silent for a few moments, seemingly out of disgust, until finally prompting him. "Continue."

"What? You really want to hear more? Trust me, I haven't even gotten to the really dark shit yet," Atha scoffed.

"I don't mean to pester you," the tree's sweet voice seemed to smirk inside his head. "If you don't wish to speak of it, you need only say so, but believe me, none of the darkness expunged from heart comes from pits new to me. I am an ancient grandmother and have witnessed the worst this world has to offer."

"Got me feeling like Pocahontas sitting up here talking to you about my problems like this."

"I am not familiar with that name."

"Never mind. All right, let's start from the very beginning then..." And he did. He spoke for hours, smiling about the good, frowning about the bad. He frowned more than he smiled. Finally, he came to the part where he escaped prison and the portal opening.

"Len pushed me through. Next thing I knew…" His words slowed, Xexon's memory dripping away like water held in gapped fingers. "Next thing I knew the sunlight was blinding me," he finished, completely forgetting where he was going with that. "I'm happy that I'm free. I really am but—I don't know—the way Len forced me out like that left this *stain* on freedom and it hurts. I left the man who saved me behind to die and I didn't even get the chance to say goodbye."

"While I understand why you feel the way you do, I don't believe it's warranted. Would you like my opinion?" Cybele asked as Atha rubbed his face.

"Sure."

"Lenny Honorati was correct with his decision to fall upon the sword in your place. Forcing your departure was the best course of action in the given situation, despite the chance that you could have manifested items that would have ensured his safety."

"How can you say that? I owe him everything, I'd have been dead years ago if it wasn't for him!"

"We both know this has nothing to do with *repayment*. You wished to stay and fight to the last with him and nothing more," Cybele continued.

"So what? That's the way it should have been. I would rather fight and die beside my family than leave them behind to die while I scurry off like a bitch!"

"And how do you suppose Lenny would have felt watching you, his redemption personified, dying in front of him?" she asked. "He may have rescued you from a horrible fate, but you saved him as well. From

Lenny's perspective, protecting you was absolute victory, yet you would have seen even this taken from him with your own pride clouding reality. Protecting your sister was wholly a different situation, yet you seem to blur the lines between them and see the fact that Lenny perished on your behalf wrong. In part, this is due to you putting others before yourself despite the situation, which is a beautiful thing, yet still a misguided path.

"There will always be more factors than your own opinion drawing a verdict on whether a situation was handled appropriately or not, and you would do well to broaden your ability to understand them. If you can manage to do as I say, you will realize that not only is your freedom not stained, but the fact that you wallow in self-pity thinking that it is does stain *Lenny's* greatest triumph."

"You're right. I'm taking away from what Len's given me," he replied, running his hands through his hair.

"Yes, you are. Now we have covered the past and present, so let's examine your future. This new world can either be a continuation of the old Atha or a new beginning. Either way, you are not known here as you were on Earth, and whomever you present as in this world will be accepted as legitimate. You should take this chance to reinvent yourself," she finished.

A sun peeked over the horizon to greet Atha with light.

"My internal clock is all messed up. It should only be about eleven p.m. How long is a full day here?" Atha asked, rolling to the edge of the tree to glance down at the monks who began filing out of the monastery.

"Twenty hours and eight minutes."

"Oh, wacky. Where are they going?" he asked, his eyes focused upon the silhouettes of the monks.

"To farm. In addition to protecting the local village from threats, they sell crops to remain self-sustaining."

"How close is the village?"

"A mile to the north," she replied.

"Oh man, I gotta see this!" he said as he rolled off the edge and began climbing down. "I've still got plenty of time 'til we leave, so might as well go on an adventure!"

"Will you take my words into consideration?" she asked.

"I really appreciate you taking the time to show me the stars and talk with me, but I like who I am, for better or worse. I think I can let go of abandoning Len, but I'm gonna keep being Atha Honorati." Atha smiled, tossing his soup can into the woods.

"Pick that up!" Cybele's voice commanded. Atha complied, retrieving the can and sheepishly hurrying into the empty monastery to place it in a trashcan.

"On this planet exists a term for those who litter. We call them 'garbage plagues,' and you'd do well to not embody such a nasty jargon," Cybele scolded.

"Sorry, habit from prison. Wasn't really worried about desecrating a shithole, you know?" Atha chuckled.

"All the more reason to see these lands not reflect it. Oh, and watch that mouth. Truly, the manure spilling from it is atrocious," she called through his mind, making him laugh.

Atha was no athlete, and after barely running around the bend he came to a gasping halt. As his lungs took in precious air, he found his eyes fixated upon his feet. Beneath them, most people would only see dirt with the occasional stray blade of incredibly thin grass, but for Atha it was more significant. *This is freedom. I can just...walk,* he thought. He slowly reached down, grasped a handful of dirt and lifted it up, letting it dribble free from his grasp as his eyes watched. *Is this really happening?* The concept of freedom had become so strange to him, such an anomaly, his mind couldn't yet fully accept reality.

Next, he glanced around, recognizing the rest of the trees around him as familiar cedar and pine, one of few similarities but still strange. *Didn't pay it much mind before, but it's kinda weird there are humans and tree species here the same as on Earth. Maybe the worlds are more connected than the occasional traveler.*

The village was medieval, hardly living up to Atha's expectations. He saw only the slightest traces of magic about. A humble town, small blue buildings lined in rows beneath a canopy of trees. There was an abundance of recognizable farm animals, most fenced in behind the buildings. A massive bull penned up in a stable caught his eye. He walked down the dirt road, drawing little attention, but he noticed an additional two races. One was a blue humanoid, completely hairless with blue eyes and tentacles stretching from its head like dreadlocks waving lazily. The other was almost exactly human except for large black wings upon its back. But even with these amazing discoveries, only one thing about this place surprised him.

Again, despite his best attempt to keep his eyes from shifting down, he found himself glancing down at his feet as they trudged along the dirt road. He next peered up at a sign, unable to read it, but overtop of the words, English letters began to form. *Hanzel's Shoes,* the sign read, with an image of a pair of boots.

Well, I got no money but if I can get a glance at the local currency, I can probably manifest some, Atha thought slyly as he pushed the door open.

A human child crashed into his waist and tumbled down as he entered, and Atha glanced down to stare in stupor. He hadn't seen an actual child in years.

"Excuse me!" the child exclaimed, standing again and exiting.

"Sorry about that, he's late for school," a voice called from across the shop. As Atha turned toward it, he noticed the room. Unlike the monastery, it was rather ordinary. Leather and material shoes lined atop tables with price tags beside them.

"It's no problem. Just took me by surprise," Atha replied, pulling the door closed as he entered.

"Name's Hanzel. Feel free to look around and let me know if you need anything." The speaker was a bald, slightly overweight human sitting behind the counter, working on something out of sight.

"I'm Atha and actually I could use some help," he said, nearing the counter in hopes of catching a glimpse of currency but seeing none.

"Well, what can I do for you, Atha?" the man replied with a smile, eyeing his attire. "Oh, a monk initiate! I thought it strange to hear an unrecognized name in this town. Welcome!"

"No, they actually just gave me these because I had nothing else to wear. Your monks are good people." Atha smiled back as Hanzel nodded.

"That they are. I sleep well at night knowing they keep a watchful eye over this town."

"Watchful? What, are they like the local police or something?" Atha asked.

"More comparable to the guard. You don't know?"

"No, I'm not really from around here."

"Oh. I thought they were famous, especially that war hero, Zell," he replied.

"Oh, I met her! She's really nice. Didn't realize she was a hero," Atha said as the man's mouth practically dropped.

"Where exactly you *from*?"

Atha chuckled awkwardly. "Not from anywhere around here."

"Well, I don't mean to pry. Now, what can I do for you?"

Atha lifted a foot that still wore his battered prison work boots.

"Need some new shoes. Got any *magical* ones?" he asked, hoping to prompt the incredible as the man eyed his shoe over.

"What a strange dying style. Seen shoes from all over the world, but nothing like this. And I'm assuming you mean a contract-enhanced shoe, right?"

"Yes! Exactly! That's a thing, right?" The man stood, motioning for Atha to follow him into a back room.

"I'm small-time, but I have a few of the more generic models. Speed enhancing, hoverboard, basic models like that," he replied as Atha gasped with such intensity he jumped a bit.

"That's considered basic?" he said as Hanzel pulled out a few wooden cases of shoes in Atha's size.

"Please, you're pushing the boundaries of what I could possibly believe you haven't heard of," said Hanzel. "Would you like to try them out?"

"Absolutely! I don't wanna damage them, though," he replied.

Hanzel smirked, drawing a knife from his waistband and stabbing a shoe. He held it up in front of Atha, and a slight blue glow of mana emitted from his hand, repairing the ripped material.

"Most contract-enhanced items come with a self-repair feature. So, feel free to go as hard on them as you want."

"Can I try the speedy ones?" he asked.

"Sure. They double your natural speed and are the most expensive pair I have at 5,200 xen." He handed Atha a black shoe with a long red stripe down the side.

Not sure how much that translates to in dollars. Need to get more references, Atha thought, putting the shoes on and standing to walk. He eased a foot forward, feeling the shoe yank on it.

"Whoa, that's crazy! They really work!" he exclaimed.

"Feel free to run up and down the street a bit. Let yourself back in here if you would like to try a different pair." *He's very trusting of someone he just met,* Atha thought to himself

"Will do, thank you so much!" Atha replied, hustling toward the door and out into the street.

He zoomed up and down the street a few times, roaring with laughter and amazement. He tried two more pairs. One formed a blue hoverboard so he could glide above the ground, and the other formed a translucent blue walkway beneath his feet. He walked up into the air, high above the town into the sky to peer around at the surrounding area. Mountains sat far across the horizon, and endless forest stretched off in every direction, practically hiding the town beneath it as he gained altitude. He came back to the shop completely blown away and returned the shoes to Hanzel.

"Not interested?" Hanzel asked.

"Oh, no, they were *literally* the *coolest* thing I've ever seen. I'm just kinda broke is the problem." Atha chuckled sheepishly, hoping he wouldn't anger the shop owner with wasted time.

"Just hold on a second now," Hanzel replied, grasping a box from beneath his counter. "Take them, kid. On the house." He smiled, pushing the air-walk shoes toward Atha, who stared in disbelief.

"I couldn't possibly. I don't have a single xen to my name, sir," he replied, flabbergasted. Hanzel pushed them into his hands.

"Never seen anybody so enthralled by them before. These were a risky investment for me that didn't pan out. Everybody around here bases big purchases off practicality and took no notice when I put them out in my display window. At this point, they're just wasting space. Now, take them or I'm gonna go out back and burn them the second you leave."

He smiled, and Atha graciously accepted them, tossing his work boots into the trash and placing the new ones on his feet.

"I *will* come back here one day and pay you for these. Thank you so much. You really don't know what this means to me." Atha extended his hand out to Hanzel, who grasped it.

"Really, son, my treat. Just keep enjoying them like you were before and that'll be enough for me," he replied, walking around the counter to eye them proudly on Atha's feet. Atha admired them as well. They were a pale grey with two blue symbols on the side. "They have some extra features that you can use by pressing on the hieroglyphs. The one closest to your heel is used for simple walking and the one by your toes can be used to create a wider path for something like a carriage."

"Seriously? How fast can the path for the carriage form?"

"Max speed is five hundred miles per hour."

"That's one fast-ass carriage."

"A horse-drawn one, yeah, but taking into account contract enhancements, it's about as fast as you'd need unless you have a high-tier transportation type," he replied.

"Oh yeah. That makes sense."

"Well, go enjoy them. I expect the occasional update on how they're treating you." Hanzel smiled as Atha nodded and rushed out the door and walked straight back up into the sky.

Chapter 8

Creation and Disease

The third sun was beginning to rise above the horizon, signaling the time for departure was nearing. Giddy with cheer that had been so rare in the past, he dashed across the blue path his shoes formed through the air, going to straight overtop of buildings and heading toward the forest. It all seemed too good to be true, and he could almost sense the other foot beginning to drop. And there it was, a thud followed by a shrill scream, the type of scream Atha had heard just before a man was stabbed to death. Turning toward the source, he looked down upon the many animals stabled through the town. Seemingly all of them were going insane at the same moment.

He lowered himself to the ground and could see the animals thrashing about. Cows, horses, and pigs had fallen into a state of insanity. Blood began to ooze from the animals' mouths and eyes.

"Hey! What's going on?" Atha yelled to a passerby.

"It's a plague! Come, the monastery will have a protection field up!" he screamed.

"A what?! I don't understand!"

"Just run, man, run!" he screamed back, hustling off.

The massive bull he'd seen earlier crashed through its wooden fence, its face oozing blood as another group of escapees screamed and attempted to run past. *AK-47 ball-round load,* Atha thought, drawing the image into his mind. The gun fell into his hands, and he unleashed a blast of fire and metal to down the beast.

A blue woman grabbed him by the arm, pulling him along with her. "No, don't try to fight! It's the Red Sheep, it'll be on us any moment!" she screamed in a panic, but Atha pulled away.

"I'll be okay! Where's the school? I'm gonna check on the kids!"

"Two blocks over! The monks should be evacuating them!"

Atha nodded, red energy pulsing into his legs as he shot off. Animals had flooded the streets. Atha evaded them easily with Agro energy enhancing his speed until a scream from an alleyway stopped him in his tracks. Hanzel's son was fleeing from a thrashing horse drenched with so much blood its head had turned entirely scarlet. Atha exploded toward them, snatching the child before using his shoes to run through the air to a rooftop. He set the child down and pelted the beast below with rounds until it fell in a bloody mess.

"Do you know what this is? How do we stop it?" Atha asked the shaking child, who only stuttered back.

A voice, deep and powerful, came into Atha's mind. It sang a song with reverberating vibrato that was familiar to him.

"Oh where, oh where, could *Creation* be? Oh where, oh where could he be?"

A massive shadowy arm tore through houses a few blocks over, chunks of building and bodies flung through the air.

"Shit's hitting the fan," Atha mumbled, lifting the child up in one arm and materializing a pistol in his free hand.

"I *will* find you. I can *feel* your presence," the voice boomed again, the shadows ripping straight through the buildings a few blocks away and closing fast.

"Oh Jesus! Oh fuck!" Atha screamed, running across the rooftops until Zell landed in front of him, a plethora of monks on her heels.

"Here!" one of them called, snatching the child from Atha's arms before both began glowing white, vanishing.

"Atha, return to the monastery!" Zell yelled to him, beginning to run past him toward the destruction.

"Wait! I can help!"

"No! I have not a moment to waste monitoring you!" She dipped down off the roof.

Atha glanced back at the fleeting crowds below and back to the destruction ahead. Red glowed from his legs, jolting ahead toward the shadowy arm that continued to near. The monks blocked it off, Zell barking out orders to the rest as she opened her orange screen.

"Red Sheep, plague of disease confirmed!" she yelled into a ball of glowing orange light beside her head as she to rearranged symbols on her screen. "Weaknesses—none! Repeat, no weaknesses! Use quick hit-and-run tactics. Slow it down!"

A barrage of attacks blasted toward the out-of-sight opponent. Atha landed on the roof not far from Zell and stared down at the chaos. The sick animals flooding the road were easily dispatched by the monks— except one.

A lone sheep was leaking blood across its whole body, turning its white wool red. A dome of shadows twisted and swirled around it, distorting the image of the world around them like a black hole. Atha looked down at it with curious horror, noticing a pair of eyes, each as large as Atha's body, floating around within the shadows just above the mutilated animal. Wisps of darkness began to swirl out from the main dome of shadows, forming a massive arm. In an instant, the arm stretched out, lashing like a whip through the animals and a monk that was too slow to evade.

Tactical shotgun, buckshot load. Atha drew the image of the weapon into his mind and it fell into his hands as he leapt from the roof, unloading a blast into a pig.

"And finally, we meet." The deep booming voice echoed through his head as the bloody sheep turned toward him. It eased forward slowly as Atha thundered the shotgun again and again to no effect, pellets pinging off the shadow encasing it. *That dark area surrounding it deflects buckshot?! Don't freeze up, just try something more powerful! Grenade!* Atha pictured it, and the metal canister fell into his hand. He pulled the pin, tossing it and ducking behind a wall. A cataclysmic explosion sent shrapnel roaring across the area.

Glancing around the corner, he stared in disbelief as the sheep continued straight through the dust cloud, the shadowy arm reaching slowly for Atha. "No! Why won't you die?!" Atha screamed, falling completely into panic. *AK-47,* Atha pictured again, spraying the shadow hand with rounds that pinged off it harmlessly.

"Through my slumber the nightmares were endless. Now, I have reawakened and recall that the nightmare is me." The voice laughed, a shadowy finger curling back as the arm shot forward, flicking Atha in the chest with enough force to send him crashing through a large window behind him. "I owe you a debt of gratitude for returning dreams to their rightful owners, but it grows short-lived with these miserable assaults." Atha gasped for air, forcing himself back to his feet, watching the monks unleash another barrage. A monk climbed through the window after him, snatching Atha up by the arm.

"We must flee! The villagers have been ev—" he started, but the shadowy hand ghosted up through the floor and crushed the monk in an explosion of blood that soaked Atha. Atha screamed, falling back to the floor as the hand wiggled a finger playfully at him.

"Now, now, I have come all this way to greet you, and you would be so rude as to turn your nose up to me?" The voice laughed as Atha screamed with rage. An RPG fell into his hands as he turned back toward the sheep, unleashing the missile upon it with an explosion that sent a shockwave of dust across the area. Atha stumbled back to the floor, slicing his arm across of shard of glass. Blood pulsed from his arm in rhythm with his heartbeat, a trademark he recognized as arterial bleeding.

"Have I caused you offense? Very well, I will take my leave but do trust that we will meet again." The voice laughed, the bloody sheep utilizing the long shadowy arm like a catapult, bending it down before launching itself far off into the horizon.

Zell crashed into the shop after Atha, lifting him up and pulling him out as voices carried across the orange ball beside her head.

"It's exiting the village! Did that human scare it off?!" Atha heard someone ask.

"We have no evidence that would suggest it had reason to do so! Stay on guard and make for the monastery!" Zell yelled back as Atha pushed off her to stand on his own feet.

"I'm okay, I'm okay!" he gasped, shell-shocked and pale-faced. "What was that? The *devil*?"

He tripped and fell, but Zell caught him and aggressively looped his gushing arm over her shoulder. *She's using the pressure of her shoulder against my forearm to stop the bleeding and even has my arm elevated above the heart. She's incredibly levelheaded and intelligent.*

"The Red Sheep. A mythical monster that has slumbered for over a century. Its awakening marks the return of the ten plagues," she replied with stunning calmness. Atha's blood leaked down her front. The monk that had taken Hanzel's son materialized in front of them, and Zell shoved Atha into his arms.

"Him first;—he is wounded! Seven monks in the east block after, and then myself last!"

The next thing Atha knew he was sitting back in front of the grassy pasture of the monastery with the rest of the few hundred villagers. A light blue shield encircled them as people cried and scrambled about, searching for loved ones. Atha crashed down feeling lightheaded, slowly fading into unconsciousness as his arm continued to pulse blood.

"Atha, can you hear me?" Zell's voice called to him as he blinked, realizing he lay atop a sheet.

"What happened?" he groaned, everything hurting as he sat up.

"Blood loss rendered you unconscious. Cybele took notice and pressed you to top of the critical patient list. Here, drink," she continued, pressing a glass of water to his lips that he gulped down. He paused, spitting it out in shock as his memory returned.

"The—the sheep thing! The Red Sheep! Where'd it—"

"Worry not, you are safe here. It cannot enter the shield rendered by the trees of Shakka," Zell interjected as he began to panic.

"Oh my God. Oh fuck," Atha gasped, realizing he was still covered in the dry blood of the dead monk. He swiveled his head to eject the contents of his stomach across the ground as Zell thumped his back.

"There you go, just let it out. I think you should know that people have proclaimed you a hero." She smiled, brandishing a handkerchief to wipe Atha's mouth.

"W-why?" he stuttered.

"There is not a single circumstance upon which the Red Sheep simply left during the middle of an attack. It seemed as if those weapons you wielded forced its retreat."

"Didn't you hear it? Said something about not wanting to cause offense," he huffed back. Zell's face had remained composed through the entire attack, and yet at these simple words that composure fled.

"What? You heard it *speak*?" she said, forcefully snatching him by the front of his shirt to pull his face up.

"Zell, you're hurting me," he replied. She released her grip.

"Apologies, I did not mean to cause discomfort."

"You couldn't hear it?" he asked. She shook her head and rose to her feet.

"We will delve further into this topic at a later time. I must coordinate separating the infected from the injured and find a way to send message to the royal capital of the Red Sheep's awakening." Zell hurried off into the mass of casualties as Atha blinked. *Infected?* Pain flaring through every inch of his body, he took notice of a familiar face sitting close to him.

"Hanzel!" Atha smiled, thankful for a friendly face in the chaos. He sat with his son and a woman Atha presumed to be his wife. They were traumatized, yet had that air of calmness about them only possible when having just narrowly escaped death.

"Glad to see you're finally awake. You were out for a few hours," said Hanzel. "My son told me what you did. Said he got cut off on his way to school and that he'd be dead were it not for you."

"Thank you," his wife said. "If I'd lost him, I—I don't know what I would have done."

"I happened to get there in time thanks to these fresh kicks. Karma came back for your husband's generosity, I was just the vessel." He smiled back as she turned to Hanzel with teary eyes.

"Gave away another pair, didn't you? I'll never have words about you handing out stock again." She sobbed, burying her face in his shoulder as he held her.

A pair of monks strode by, a strange white box in the leader's hand that he held down beside Atha's head. "Clear," he announced, heading next to Hanzel and his family. "Clear," he announced again, holding it beside

Hanzel's wife. "Clear." This time beside the son. When he reached Hanzel, the white box turned black. "Oh, Shakka's mercy. Hanzel, I need you to come with me," he sighed, motioning for Hanzel to stand. Hanzel gave his wife a kiss on the forehead and hugged his son. As he stood to go with them, Atha saw bestial teeth indentations deep upon the flesh of his left arm.

"What? What are you doing?" his wife cried, bursting to her feet but was held back by a monk.

"He's infected. He's going to turn soon. This is for your own protection," the monk explained as Atha leapt to his feet.

"What the hell are you doing?" he yelled, grabbing the monk who pulled Hanzel along, but the kind shoe seller rested a hand on Atha's shoulder.

"No, they're right. Once an infected animal bites a human, the infection gets in you. It was just a scratch, so I hoped I needn't say anything before knowing. It's selfish of me to ask a stranger something like this, but you seem like a good kid. Keep an eye on my family for me, will you?"

"What? I don't understand! This can't be happening!" Atha gasped, the world beginning to spin around him as he felt sick again. "This isn't right! It's a mistake! We—we won, we drove it off!" Atha continued. Hanzel kissed his wife and gave his son a long hug and a few quiet words before following the monk. Atha watched as they continued off, a sudden thought occurring to him. *This is what Len was preparing you for. A world of pain and evil. You assumed that because you were in a different world that suddenly evil wouldn't exist anymore. Really, despite everything, only a single aspect is completely different—I'm free here.* Atha looked down at his hands. There was an unexplainable sensation nagging at him, as if he had forgotten something.

I'm the difference. I'm the only real *anomaly, and I know I can change this, but how? What am I forgetting?* A dull glow began to emit from his hands, a certain memory returning to him. *Modulation energy. You can use it to alter the fate of others in a limited sense.* A loud pop reverberated through Atha's head like a snap of the fingers. Every single wound on every survivor vanished as the cube the monk held beside Hanzel returned to white.

Was that me? Atha wondered, glancing the crowd. Nobody was taking credit for this, and nobody proclaimed that Atha was responsible, either.

"What?!" the monk gasped. "Just—hold on one second!" he whispered to Hanzel, hurrying off to speak to Zell as a cheer carried through the clearing. The cheer quickly turned to a roar and chaos broke out, people clamoring to return to their families, monks struggling to keep the groups separated.

"Silence!" Zell's voice cut through the clamor like a hot knife through butter. Chaos instantly vanished, replaced with undivided attention upon Zell. "Those who were designated infected, continue to isolation! None have ever healed from the infection and we have *no reason* to believe it has started now! We will send for a more conclusive infection reader, but until then, please, stay apart from your families if you value their lives!"

And they did. An hour later, an elderly woman came with a slightly different infection reader and thoroughly re-examined every infected. One by one, she cleared them all.

"What did you give me?" Atha mumbled, glancing up to the darkening sky. He'd changed into clean robes, but Zell's were still bloody. She came to Atha and fell down beside him, exhausted from the day.

"Might I be so bold as to request we leave tomorrow?" she asked.

"Of course. I couldn't hold my head up if I came to her knowing I left these people to die," he replied, a bottle of water falling into his hands. He stretched it toward her and she graciously accepted. She struggled with the lid, and Atha retook it to twist the cap off before extending it again. "So now that things are settling down, can you tell me exactly what in the *hell* that thing was?"

Zell chugged the whole bottle, releasing a refreshed sigh before turning to him.

"In Oluceps exist beings known as *Plagues*, which number ten strong. That was the fifth plague, the plague of disease, who has slumbered since long before my generation. Dubbed the Red Sheep, it is considered the most formidable of the lot in terms of combat, despite the fact that typically number ten is the strongest and each number lower is less so. A few others have come about recently as well to fill in for the gaps left by fallen plagues who, unlike the Red Sheep, perished in combat."

"So, there's even more of those things. Where do they come from?"

"Nobody is quite sure. Copious speculation, yet none backed by solid evidence. The one I tend to agree with is the idea that a higher power created them to stop the increasing lifespans of generations long ago. Once upon a time, it wasn't unheard of to meet a person over five hundred years of age. Then the plagues came about and seemingly targeted them."

That's a major difference from Earth. Is Zell old? She looks young, but there's a good chance that elongated youth goes hand-in-hand with elongated life.

"A little off-topic, but how old are you?" Atha asked.

"Thirty-four. Now if I may ask a personal question of my own. Have you any idea why exactly you were able to perceive a plague to such an extent?"

Atha shrugged at this. "Dunno. I've come to expect strange things for myself, and this isn't even the craziest."

Zell tapped a finger into his palm. "I assume you refer to this power you use to manifest items. Have you no guess as to its origin?"

"Actually, I kinda do, but I can't say. They may be linked."

"Cannot or will not?"

"Literally can't," Atha replied as Zell slapped his chest.

"Perhaps I can shed some light. I have a theory." She opened her orange screen and began rearranging symbols. "Here it is. An old myth some say, but I believe in all legend rests some truth. The legend states that long ago arose a woman with the ability to trounce these very plagues with abilities that allowed her to see through their dark power. Her name was Vakusu, or in modern tongue simply Solar Eclipse." She closed the screen again.

"Oh, Granny Cybele showed me her constellation. Is that what you think I am? Like her?"

"Perhaps. Tell me, how long have you had this power and what is the extent of its strength?"

"'It's bad form to ask another of their ability if the situation does not require it,'" he replied, mocking Elenzer's voice as she frowned. "I'm already starting to fit in!"

"Would be far more appropriate to say you make nuisance of yourself upon every given opportunity," Zell replied.

"Oh man, if I had a nickel—or in this case a xen!" He laughed while Zell stared, unamused. Atha finally calmed and continued. "Had it since I was six. Don't know its extent. Circumstances didn't permit me to get too bold with it often, but I did manage to draw up a few rules that limit the things I can do with it. Wanna hear them?"

Just then, a voice called for Zell and she sighed, returning the empty water bottle to him.

"Again, it seems we must finish this conversation at a later date," she replied, standing to chatter amongst the monks. *She commanded a mass panic as if it were easy. That woman's a force of nature.* Atha hurled the bottle toward a nearby trashcan, surprised at his own aim when it went straight in.

Atha was exhausted. The adrenaline of a new environment and his newfound freedom were the only things keeping him standing to this point. He wobbled to Cybele, who helped him up to the treetop where he could lie down upon the leaves once more. "I've never even seen something like that in prison. It was like something out of—I don't know—a war movie, the way chaos erupted like that." Atha sighed, resting his head back as leaves stroked across his face.

"Every world has many differences, but all share certain aspects. War is one that is exactly the same throughout, making..."

Her voice drifted off as he quickly fell asleep.

Unlike in prison, Atha slept peacefully, safe in both body and mind, resting fully in Cybele's protective grasp. His internal clock kept perfect pace to the second, awakening him at what would have been exactly seven minutes until four a.m. Earth time, breakfast chow time in prison.

"Up so early? You were sleeping so soundly I began to wonder if you would awaken at all," Cybele's voice chuckled into Atha's head as an energy drink fell into his hands. He took a swig, rolling over to the edge of the tightened leaves, and glanced down below toward the grassy pasture that had vacated while he slept. Atha already knew the crowd had left; he'd sensed the shifting of bodies below. Giuseppe's random awareness tests had instilled a heightened sleep awareness within Atha. He could be fully asleep and still be able to tell the exact number of guards that passed by outside his cell through the entire night. Yet here, his mind had additionally sensed the watchful presence of the tree and fallen into a slumber deeper than he'd ever known.

"Where'd everybody go?" he asked, chugging the rest of the drink before crushing the can and beginning to hurl it off into the forest, then pausing and slipping the can into his pocket.

"To bury the dead," she replied.

"Where? I feel like I should pay my respects after they've been so welcoming."

"Head back toward town. Halfway down the road is a dirt path on the left. Follow it, and eventually you will find the sapling nursery."

Atha headed off, briefly slipping into the monastery to deposit the can into a trash bin. Not a single sun had begun to crest on the horizon, but the lunar glow provided ample reflection of their counterparts. Atha's eyes could even detect faint traces of color hueing the black-and-grey landscape of night. The whole village was gathered there, all of them connected in some way to the many bodies that were wrapped in white linens on the ground beside their assigned grave. Hanzel sat toward the back of the large crowd, his family beside him. He waved to Atha as he trudged up.

"Atha! Where'd you get off to?" He smiled with a shine that a man could only have he had defied death. Atha came to a stop beside him as whispers broke out, several sets of eyes turning to him.

"I was sleeping in one of the Shakka trees," he replied, glancing around at the crowd. He leaned in to whisper, "Why are they staring at me?"

"You've become a bit of a hero here. While you were asleep, word spread of what you did. Nobody's ever pushed the Red Sheep back like that before."

Atha felt his chest puff out in a vain attempt to match his inflated head. The eyes shifted back toward the monks in the middle of the mass as they began to speak. Through the gaps of breathing bodies, Atha could see the frame of one breathless figure being lowered down into a shallow grave at the foot of a young pine tree. For a moment it seemed the gathering's breath had been stolen right along with the one sinking down into the grave. The brief mass apnea ended as the family members of the deceased strode forward, each gently hugging the thin tree that sat at the head of the grave. The last came to it, an elderly woman who held it for a long time, whispered words into the tree.

"What are they doing?" Atha asked Hanzel.

"In these lands the dead are buried beneath young trees so that the saplings may reap the nutrients and have a long, prosperous life. The head of the family then tells the tree the deceased life's story and for the rest of its own life the tree will remember it, spread it amongst other trees, and tell all who ask that story. The tree fills the gap left by the deceased, effectively becoming a member of that family until the day it too passes from this world. When that occurs, the family is entitled to its wood and uses it as they see fit with the tree's name engraved upon all the creations."

A shiver ran down Atha's back.

"That's beautiful. Poetic even," Atha whispered, watching the elderly woman finish her inaudible words of the deceased's life, kissing the tree as if it were a long-lost grandchild and placing both hands beneath a pair of parallel branches as if holding the cheeks of her newfound wooden relative. Her old face, wrinkled by time, became a mix of sadness and joy that Atha had never perceived, an emotional paradox unknown to an Earthling. Eyes filled with unfathomable despair not mixed with but solutioned by a genuine smile as brilliant as the light of the first sun and equally impossible as the fact that blades of light weathered treacherous pilgrimage through the dense forest to reach them. In time, Atha would come to learn a term existed in this foreign world for such an emotion. *Luxbris*.

"It is through this that we find connection to nature that normally wouldn't exist," Hanzel continued.

Atha watched more families lower wrapped bodies down into shallow graves, the members one by one proceeding to hug the trees. Hanzel patted him on the shoulder, moving forward with his family to join a group that wept over a wrapped body. *I know what I want to do now,* Atha thought, looking down at his open palms. *I'm sick of feeling so helpless all the time, but at least now I can do something about it. I need a plan.* He pulled his black meteorite from his pocket, tumbling it around in his fingers, feeling his mind sharpen. *My ignorance of this world is overwhelming, and even with years of experience it'll be difficult to change that. I need to balance it out with experienced people, start a new branch of the Honorati family. Don't exactly have the main body's blessing for this but the situation permits it. Already have a recruit in mind too, but it's a long shot.* Atha glanced between the crowd toward Zell.

The second sun had begun to rise as he headed back toward the temple with the monks, taking a spot beside Zell. "So, when do we leave? Can I get some new robes?" he asked, glancing down at his Earthy clothes.

"Within the hour, and what did you do with the set I gave you? They bear a self-repair and cleaning function," she replied as Atha winced.

"I kinda threw them away with the water bottle when y'all were collecting trash," he replied apologetically as she palmed her face. "Anyways, I wanted to ask you something. There's somebody else I want to find in this world who goes by the name Gavreel. Can you check for leads?"

She opened her orange screen, rearranging symbols for a few moments until she closed it and shook her head. "My information pool stands dry. Have you any other specific details that might see search watered?"

"Well, she's about my height. Probably wears white clothes, has long blue hair down to her knees."

"Such a description would lead me to assume you speak of an Antarie," she replied.

"Maybe. What's an Antarie?"

"You pry upon topics I find myself lacking answers in. A race shrouded in mystery equal only to the unmatched power they wield. As in most cases, puissance paired with the unknown leads to the belief they are evil."

Atha entered the monastery, dipping into an empty room and removing the Earthly garments to put yet another new set on. *Self-repair and cleaning? Must be like my shoes.* He eyed the handsome black robes before stuffing the Earthly set into a bin. He smiled at his rocks, slipping them back into his pocket as a rumble shook the room.

Chapter 9

Leaving and Escaping

Atha rushed out into the main hall, noticing Zell heading casually for the door despite the ruckus.

"What the hell was that?" he asked as Zell pulled the door open for him, sunlight from all three suns beaming in through the stone doorway.

"Our transportation has arrived." She smiled back. Atha walked outside, gaping openly at the sight before him.

Seven massive griffins, all head and shoulders taller than Atha, stood in the grassy pasture. Dazzling feathers covered them like swords. Sharp beaks and talons glistened in the light. Cables leashed them to a carriage. Six stood parallel to one other, a single griffin at the lead covered in black feathers with dashes of gold. Atha approached slowly. The lead griffin sniffed the air curiously until its head cocked toward him. Zell caught his robe with a quick hand, pulling him closer to whisper the faintest of words into his ear.

"Griffins are intelligent beings," she said. "Mind your tongue, for they are prideful and will take offense to ill-placed words." Atha nodded at this and noticed the lead griffin watching him. A commanding and masculine voice burst into his head.

"What is your name?" it demanded, almost in a panic as Atha's feet halted.

"It's uh…Atha. Atha Honorati," he stuttered back as the Griffin's voice continued.

"I see. Please excuse me then," the Griffin replied.

What was that about? Atha wondered as a man exited the carriage door, speaking in a gruff voice.

"Good afternoon, I'm here to retrieve a pair of unnamed guests," he announced.

"Both are accounted for," Zell replied, giving Atha a push forward to get his frozen feet moving once more. The man held the door for them, and Atha scoffed as he climbed up into the windowless carriage.

Well that's a buzzkill. My first time flying and not a window in sight, he thought as the attendant followed them in, pulling the door closed.

"My name's Blener, and I shall be your conductor this day. I must insist you make use of the seat harnesses until we're coasting smoothly in the air," the man announced before shuffling toward the front of the cabin to pull the door open to his own small, windowless room.

The seats were red and Atha could feel himself sink comfortably into his, pulling the harness over himself to latch himself to the seat. He sat back and glanced around with detest.

"My, what an expression. One might mistake it for ungratefulness." Zell smirked and Atha made no attempt to hide his displeasure, turning the look of disgust to her.

"We're in a *box*. A *flying* box, but still a box," Atha replied and Zell laughed.

"Not fond of nectarous words, are you? Perhaps next time you can secure both transportation and payment to see them sweetened."

"What, was a box with a window out of your price range?" Atha replied, unamused as the conductor popped his door open to call back to them.

"Would you like to make use of the Lanarian cab?" he asked. Zell nodded.

"Yes, thank you," she replied as Atha raised an eyebrow.

"The what?"

"A thing of no concern," she assured, quickly wiping the trace smile from her face. "Now that we have a moment, tell me of the restrictions your ability has." Atha nodded, thinking back to the experiments Len lead back in prison.

"We found seven all together, and—" The wooden walls vanished from around them. Atha, surprised, paused as he watched the seven griffins crouching down, their wings flexing. He had expected the griffins to be quick, but like one of his guns firing a bullet they burst forth in to the sky. Atha, shifting from surprise to a state of absolute panic, couldn't comprehend his critical underestimation, let alone what was happening.

"FUCK! OH JESUS! GOD! SANTA!" Atha screamed as Zell did a horrible job of muffling her laughter. The conductor swung his now invisible door open.

"Hell's gotten into you, man?" he asked as Atha's temper flared. Zell buried her face in her hands.

"Ooooh, you punked me pretty good," he spat as the conductor spoke up again.

"What you screaming for?" he asked.

Atha took a few deep breaths and composed himself, leaning close and setting his eyes firmly on Zell. "I saw a rat," he growled.

The conductor glanced across the invisible cab. "Uh...huh," Blener replied slowly. He eased his invisible door closed again as Zell erupted into laughter, stomping her feet and holding her stomach as if it would explode. An excessive cackle couldn't escape her mouth quick enough.

"Had your fill of pleasant views?" she wheezed between cachinnations.

"That was just... *dirty*. Like, I feel defiled," he replied.

"I had mind to tell you that a Linarian cab signified invisible walls, but you were being rude and disagreeable." She smirked.

Atha meant to continue arguing, but as the cab pulled up above the trees his mind quickly changed focus. Atha's eyes flitted from place to place as Giuseppe's had for all those years, the invisible cab providing a perfect 360-degree view. The sea of green trees raced by bellow them like they were looking down from a balcony overlooking the running of the bulls. Distant mountains surrounded them in all directions like building walls keeping the runners on course—and away from danger.

"Ok, this is *totally* awesome so I'm gonna let you off for now, but you got payback coming for this." Atha smirked back, pulling his latched restraints off to stand against the back wall. "Man, it's beautiful here! Completely opposite from the desert the prison was in!" A digital camera fell into his hands, and he promptly began snapping pictures of the scenery, the mountains, and anything else that caught his fancy.

"You were saying your ability has seven restrictions," Zell spoke, prompting him to continue.

"*Oh no*, you lost your turn to ask a question. So now tell me, exactly how many different intelligent races live in this world?" he asked, turning back toward the landscape to snap more pictures.

"Ah, well, let's see… Not counting the innumerable varieties of spirits that come here through a contract, or the Antarie who are more comparable to spirits anyway, only a half dozen," she replied as Atha looped his cameras lanyard over his neck, taking a seat beside her.

"What're they called? Back on Earth the only species with intelligence comparable to humans would be trees."

"Beings such as myself are known as Denata. Our main characteristics are scarlet skin, black eyes and horns," she replied, brushing a hand over the smooth black horns that ran down the back of her neck. "The Shelando are the blue-skinned race with tentacles protruding from atop the head. Kentantos share human appearance but bear a set of black feathered wings, and obviously humans, griffins, and trees." Atha stared into her dark black eyes.

"Interesting. Where did all these races come from?" Atha asked. Zell opened her orange screen and began shuffling symbols around.

"Denata are the product of human crossbreeding with demonic spirits."

"That explains a lot," Atha teased, but Zell paid him no mind and continued.

"Kentantos are the product of experimentation upon human race using illegal contracts. Nobody is quite sure where exactly the Shelando originate from. Some ancient lore states they fell from the heavens. As

114

for humans, griffins, and trees, they have been here since the beginning of recorded history," Zell finished as Atha pulled his geode from his pocket to dance it around his fingers.

"How exactly did a human hook up with a demonic spirit? I'm gonna take a guess and say they aren't like horror story ghosts from Earth."

"I believe the translation spell has struck a term that is *similar* to what you refer to as a spirit, but the definition is different in my language. The way you phrase it suggests you believe a spirit is like a human soul, which is completely different in from. 'Spirit' is a general term for beings from different dimensions who, in most cases, form contracts with us in exchange for things like mana or services. Some are biologically similar to humans, making hybridization possible."

"Ohhh, okay. I get it now. As for Kentantos, they were created with contracts that possess genetic modification abilities?"

"Yes, a sub-type of the enhancement category known as Ghoulish. Contracts such as these are illegal due to the innumerable nefarious ways they can be abused and because their main purpose is to cause harm through permanent disfiguration." Zell opened her orange screen, displaying images of horribly mutated figures that were so distorted that Atha couldn't discern their race or tell if they were even alive.

"Gross. Aren't there contracts that could reverse these effects?" he asked.

"Yes, there are. Unfortunately, while causing this disfigurement is easy, reversing it is difficult and perilous."

"How so?"

"Think of it as a puzzle. Removing pieces is simple, but attempting to place them back in the correct location is difficult. A wrong placement could spur a concatenation of events ending with a mana implosion powerful enough to crush steel," she replied. "My turn. What restrictions lord over your ability?"

"Let me give a little context to how it works first. Objects I picture in my mind can appear if I will them to. So, if I just think of something, it won't pop up. To do it, I really have to concentrate and go over the details of the object in my head before it will appear, like drawing a picture from scratch. I have a photographic memory, so that's easy for me. Len ran a test one time to see if I was taking literal, physical items off of earth, and hid a paper with the letter A written on it. I manifested it, and when we went to check on it, the one he'd hidden with gone. We concluded I can take specific items, or just a random one if I just draw the standard image into my mind, like a blank piece of paper in the scenario I mentioned. Even so, certain things can still prevent an object from appearing, and hence, the seven rules we've found so far. I can't summon anything that someone will notice is gone within forty-eight hours; can't summon anything that's alive; only one object per second, unless they are parts of a whole like a clock with all its gears; no gases unless they're compressed; nothing like pure fire or electricity; nothing that won't fit in the provided space, like manifesting a hat inside a water bottle; and lastly, I can't manifest items into a place outside of my vision. The last rule's kind of a two-parter, 'cause it also means I can't manifest anything smaller than the naked eye can see, so you can almost say there are eight all together. There's probably a maximum size limit too, but that was too risky to figure out. The biggest thing I ever conjured was about the size of my arm. Is it completely unheard of for an ability to exist without a contract providing it?"

"Not unheard of, but extremely rare. They are known as contract-less abilities—or, to spirits, they are known as glitches and exist at a ratio of about one in a billion. Never have I bore witness to one in person, but of the few known to me, none is comparable to yours, though some have been known to be quite outlandish. Still, a contract-less ability does not hinder you from forming a contract."

"Oh, so I can get a contract? I get the basic idea of what they are, but exactly how many of them are there?" he asked as Zell opened her orange screen.

"Currently there are 730,172 listed. Surely there are more that are unlisted too."

"Holy shit! I was guestimating like maybe a thousand! What's the point in there being so many?"

"Contract abilities fulfill every necessity and luxury, from simple farming all the way to manipulation of space and time. Contracts come in twelve different variations: agriculture; transportation; communication; enhancement, which is the kind used to make your shoes; combat; information, like my own; medical; supportive; time and space; illusion; defense; and unique. Unique is the only non-self-describing variation and is simply a contract that possesses characteristics of multiple other categories or abilities that fall under none of them. On top of this, every category has several sub-categories that more specifically annotate its ability, such as the ghoulish subcategory of enhancement that I mentioned a few minutes ago." Like looking into a shattered mirror, the image was distorted, but the overall idea of a world much like his own was shown clearly across her words.

"I get it. Everything my world does through technology Oluceps does through contracts. It actually makes perfect sense when you lay it out like that."

"Each contract is also given a grade for its respective category to give a grasp of how it stacks up against brethren," she continued. "From G, the lowest, all the way up to Triple S, which is the grade given to contracts that can reshape the world. Despite this, a grade is not to be confused with the contract user's actual skill at wielding it. It is not unheard of for a lower grade to trounce a superior one."

"It's not about the ride, it's about the rider!" Atha replied as she nodded.

"My own is class A, ranking it bellow S, double S and triple S, yet I am considered one of the most formidable contract users of my generation. In some cases, I'd even suggest that a contract's ranking is downright wrong, diminished by user's incapable of utilizing the ability to its full compacity."

"How is a contract formed?" Atha asked.

Zell whisked her screen back away before replying.

"Typically, there is a checklist that must be completed, like performing a ritual, but sometimes you need only call the name of a spirit you wish to form one with. The means to form one are just as diverse as contracts themselves. Once successfully called, you negotiate terms with the spirit, such as requesting a specific time period for which you wish to hold their contract, but negotiable terms have virtually no limit.

An example of a negotiable term would be something such as 'The contract wielder must help all those in need.' That is actually a term placed upon my own contract. The last thing of note regarding contracts is that only one contract may be possessed at a time."

Oh, so you can only have one superpower at a time. Good to know. But I wonder if she's been helping me so much because her contract's terms make her. "You're really smart, aren't you?" he asked.

She smiled at this and shrugged.

"This is but common knowledge in this world."

Atha shook his head at this.

"No, I meant just in general. You seem like a very intelligent person. Besides, it's one thing to blurt out the basics, but it's another to comprehensibly teach someone with no prior knowledge about intricate things like contracts. Can I ask you a more personal question?"

"Give voice and see an answer considered," she replied as Atha stared into her black eyes.

"What's your plan for the future? Are you gonna keep working—if you want to call it that—at the monastery?"

Zell sighed and straightened her purple robes.

"It is a service. And I suppose so," she replied as a smile edged onto Atha's face.

"Suppose? That's a weak response coming from someone so well-spoken." He hadn't meant to say that aloud, and the moment the words came out he placed a hand over his mouth.

"To an extent I enjoy it, but I do yearn for grander ventures." She sighed.

Without warning her expression became that of horror. She erupted to her feet and looked out the back of the translucent cab.

"Whoa. You okay?" Atha asked, watching in confusion. "Hello? Zell, you good?" Atha asked again, snapping his fingers a few times, but she ignored him. Instead, she flipped around and pulled open the conductor's door.

"Master Blener, there is something I must make known. Can I trust that you will remain composed?" Zell said in a calm tone that mocked her expression.

"What troubles you, good monk?" Blener replied breezily. Atha looped the lanyard holding his camera around his neck and listened. If something worried Zell, it was a safe bet it was something worth hearing. Zell took a deep breath and composed her expression to match her voice before replying.

"The trees have sent a warning of nearing danger. The Red Sheep is approximately half a mile behind and gaining on us." Blener's face went white and turned toward the griffins. Atha felt panic creep over him, the bloody memories oozing into his mind. He glanced down at the forest beneath them and caught flicks of shadows ghosting through the trees without so much as ruffling the leaves.

"It's beneath us! Its already here!" Atha screamed, feeling the carriage lift all too slowly as the shadows shot up. One long arm extended back down into the forest and snatched a boulder. The arm bent back and then snapped forward again to send it flying like a catapult at the carriage.

"Hard left! Hard left! Hard—"Atha screamed to the conductor, but the rock smashed against the carriage, completely ripping off the back half where Atha stood. Stunned, he knew only that he was falling. A long blue tendril encircled his waist and snatched him back into the remaining half of the cabin and into Zell's arms. Blood gushed from a gash across his head, but he quickly stumbled back up to his feet as adrenaline kicked in. "Why's it chasing us? What do we do?" Atha asked her in a jittery panic. The deep, reverberating vibrato voice crept into his head, singing an ominous tune.

"Baa, baa, Red Sheep have you any souls? No sir, no sir, *stolen* they were." It paused. "I know what you did, boy, healing those corrupted by my plague."

Zell grabbed him by his robes, pushing him back into the conductor's room.

"It's in my head! It's fucking pissed, Zell—" Atha began but stopped as the voice overpowered his mind, clawing at the inside of his head. It was as if it was screaming directly in his ears.

"What manner of remedy did you use?" the voice asked. "Don't feel the need to answer that just yet. I prefer *face-to-face* conversation. Come, let us palaver."

The voice stopped and so did the clawing sensation within Atha's head, leaving in its place a sense of terror.

"What do we do?" Blener screamed. "We don't have a defense for a threat like this! I don't know what to do!" Zell latched her hands onto

121

either side of the conductor's arms, steadying him before his tremoring legs could give out.

"Breathe and listen. Start gaining altitude and switch directions, or the beast may follow us straight into the capital. I shall disembark and slow it down for as long as possible." Blener's face brightened a tad. Atha glanced up in disbelief.

"Are you out of your *fucking mind*? That thing just tossed a small mountain at us like it was a whiffle ball!" Atha forced himself back up and shoved past the conductor to latch onto her arm.

"Release me!" she demanded. "If I do not slow it we will all perish." Zell twisted her arm to lose the restraining hand, but red Agro energy pulsed through Atha's arm, turning his grip into a vice.

"Let her go, boy! The Denata has made her decision!" the conductor screamed, grabbing her other arm and yanking her back toward the opening. Atha became livid, stepping past Zell and grabbing the man's arm, flinging it off her with enough force to almost send Blener onto the ground.

"Fucking coward!" Atha thundered, yanking Zell back by accident. "I don't leave people behind and if you jump down there, I swear to God almighty I'll go down right after you! Now stop wasting time and let's come up with a plan!" Atha released his grip as he caught a glance of the shadows shooting up from beneath the trees and grasping another boulder. *RPG.* Atha drew the image in his mind and the rocket launcher fell into his hands just as the boulder was loosed. Xexon's instructions had been planted in his brain, guiding his path: *Agro energy, when released from the brain, can slow the user's perception of time.*

Red energy pulsed out of his head and time slowed to a crawl as he set the iron sights on the nearing rock. With a burst of fumes, the rocket went screaming out, knocking Atha off balance. A massive explosion ripped across the stone, sending rubble scattering through the air, propelled by a bloom of smoke streaked with flames.

"Holy fuck, that was loud!" Atha gasped as he stood back up.

Zell's mouth fell agape as she stared down. Atha hurled the spent launcher down at the falling shadows, wiping at his eye as blood from his wound trickled over it. "That slowed him down a bit! Zell, is there any way we can lose it?"

"No, it seems driven to catch us and is completely immune to attacks of all magnitude. It slows only from the folly of its own hasty assault. Gaining altitude will prevent further attacks, but it will follow still, probably until we lead it straight into the path of the unsuspecting." Atha grimaced, pulling his geode from his pocket to roll it around in his fingers.

"Yeah, I got nothing too. Maybe if we weren't over a forest I could try manifesting a bomb, but who knows if it would even appear, let alone slow it. How far away are we from a clearing?" She opened her orange screen, a map popping up.

"A hopeless distance," she replied.

"My lead griffin, Shun, says he has an idea!" said Blener.

"Atha, let it attack unhindered," the black-and-gold griffin's voice rang through his head.

"What? Why?" he asked, but the griffin gave no reply.

Shun snapped free from his harness, flipped back around, and flew past the carriage to eye his prey.

"So, this is the Red Sheep? Aye, a horror indeed," he noted sarcastically, not a trace of fear in his words. He angled down toward the shadows.

"What's he doing? He's headed straight at it!" Atha said, jolting forward, but Zell reached an arm to stop him.

The shadows burst up toward Shun, yanking up the largest boulder yet.

"You may terrorize the lands, little sheep, but you now enter my domain. Aye, the skies belong to griffins, and you will learn your place!" Shun's voice boomed. The massive stone was flung at him, but Shun's talons dug into it and spun it like a tornado before releasing its grip, casting both the rock and the shadow clutching it off into the distance.

"He did it!" Atha burst, watching the griffin swing back around as the other distant shadows remained in place.

"Scum!" the deep voice roared, losing all the singing and taunting in its voice. "These offenses will never leave my mind until you and the bird are ground between my shadows! I'll flay the very skin from your bones! When you least expect it, I will be there, boy, bringing wrath and annihilation down upon you and all you hold close to your heart!" The voice screamed through his head, but Atha just laughed. Stepping toward the edge and lifting his hand up toward the distant shadows, his middle finger sprung up to declare war.

"Fuck you. You caught me with my pants down, but next time I'll be ready." He smirked as Blener burst with laughter.

"Not even a plague can stand against the mighty Shun! The legend of the gold dust of death stands firm!" he exclaimed as Shun swooped up behind the carriage, his eyes focusing on Zell.

"Aye, these old wings still have plenty of fight in them. Now, if I might trouble Lady Zell with a question. Just how exactly does your ally hear the plague's voice?" he asked.

"A query lost upon an unknowing recipient," she answered. "Much about his existence is a paradox that I am unable to reason with."

"Jesus, is there anybody who doesn't know who you are?" Atha asked as Shun's piercing eyes flipped to him.

"Aye, I recognized her scent as soon as we'd landed. It has been many years since I encountered it upon the field of battle, but I'd never forget such a great warrior." He turned back to Zell. "I know not why you wish to hide your identity, but your secret is safe with me," he finished, flapping back up to the front of the Griffins as his cables snapped back into place over his harness.

"You're like the Audie Murphy of Oluceps, *everybody* knows you. Who are you, Zell?" Atha asked. Her face saddened, and instead of answering she pulled a handkerchief from her pocket to wipe away blood that had reddened Atha's short brown hair. *I know that look,* Atha thought to himself as he closed his eyes so Zell could wipe overtop his eyelids. *Seen that mix of pain and shame plenty of times.* "You don't gotta tell me if you don't want to, I was just curious. On another note, I had one other thing I wanted to ask." Zell pulled the material back, folding it bloody side in and placing it in her pocket.

"I would prefer to not speak of my past," Zell replied quietly.

"Well good, 'cause I actually wanted to ask you about the future. I don't know exactly what I want to do in this strange new world, but I don't want to be a passive observer like I was back on Earth. I'm gonna start forming a new Oluceps branch of the Honorati family and I wanted to ask if you'd join." She recoiled, apparently surprised by the question.

"To what end?" she asked. Atha sat back onto the floor. He noticed that a large chunk of rock had caught his camera's lens, so he pulled the memory card out and tossed the rest of it into the trash bin beside the conductor's door.

"Well, that thing you said about Vakusu was really interesting," he said. "If I am like her, I should use this gift to stop that Disease plague. Wanna team up and take it down?"

She sighed, taking a seat as well.

"These objects you manifest—your arsenal—do you believe one holds the power to strike it down?"

"Dunno." Atha shrugged. "But I do know that even if nothing I have can, I'll still find a way. Len taught me that a man with enough will can do anything."

"Wise man," she replied as Atha pocketed the memory card and turned to her.

"So, what do you say?" he asked.

"May I think upon it for a time? The Shakka village deserves honest consideration."

"Of course. I know it isn't fair to ask a crazy question like that out of the blue," he replied as Zell cocked an eyebrow.

"I am not sure what the color blue has to do with it, but my answer will be given once you have been reunited with your sister," she replied.

"Oh, uh, it's a saying from Earth. Fair warning, if you do say yes, I'll probably blurt something out every now and then that'll make people think I'm high—and I'm gonna tell 'em you're my dealer."

Chapter 10

Locked Up Abroad

A single sun had set by the time they neared their destination. Atha flipped around in his seat to take in the sight of massive walls surrounding a sprawling city of tall blue buildings.

"Whoa! The capital's so much bigger than I imagined! Look at those towers!" he exclaimed. Three massive black structures reached high into the sky, looming large above the other buildings. The top of each came together in a three-sided spike, similar to a famous monument from Earth. "The black buildings look like obelisks. What are they?"

"They were given no name by their architect but they are commonly known as the Peace Towers," she replied. "They were built just over seventy-seven years ago by a single S contract, which utilized a quantum manipulation technique to enlarge handcrafted buildings from a 1/10,000 scale. Take note of the hieroglyphs etched upon the sides. Your shoes have a similar sort placed on the inner sole. Enhancement contracts normally utilize hieroglyphs."Atha took a closer look at the distant structure, noticing the intricate symbols embellished upon its walls before pulling a shoe off to find more hieroglyphs.

"Sure enough. I wonder if there's a certain amount of actual science behind these sorts of things."

The carriage neared the wall and a hologram screen appeared in front of Blener. On screen was the live image of a Shelando man who stared at them.

"Blener! I thought that was you! What happened to your carriage?" the Blue Shelando asked in a deep, raspy voice.

"You're not going to believe it, Borg," Blener replied. "The Red Sheep is awake. It hurled rocks at my carriage, but Shun fought it off."

"There was a rumor it had awakened." The Shelando's face fell. "This is troubling news. I'm sure the Royal Guard would like a report on. Your carriage and two passengers are cleared to enter. Set her down in lot Y-15. I'll send up a report. Be prepared to meet with the guards upon landing."

"Magical air traffic control." Atha chuckled to himself. The carriage passed over the wall, giving him a better look at the city. He realized that the buildings weren't quite as large as he'd originally believed. Instead, a second level of buildings was actually hovering above the ground. The ground itself was mostly occupied by trees, green leaves covering every inch of space in between the ground-level buildings, hiding all the bustling activity below from Atha's prying eyes. "This is unbelievable! It's like, I don't know, a totally different world from the Shakka village!" Despite the canopy hiding the ground from his sight, he noticed lines of traffic in the air, ant-sized dots far beneath them flying just above the tops of the second layer of buildings.

"Indeed. Higher ranking contracts tend to flock to populated areas, such as the royal capital, which in turn means it is more advanced in every aspect to a rural location," she replied as Atha knelt over the edge of the shattered carriage to get a better look.

"I thought Earth was more advanced, but this totally flips the script," he said, catching the occasional glimpse of flashing lights and crowds of people bustling beneath. They flew past, heading to a more desolate area before coming down for a graceful landing. When they touched down, dozens of people wearing green uniforms advanced on them. A black human male led them, black circlets covering the majority of his arms like armor. He approached the carriage's side. He was young, probably in his mid-twenties, with short hair and a blue-screened pad in his hands.

"Blener?" he called up. The conductor nodded and stepping out ahead of Atha and Zell. Zell pulled her hood up over her head before exiting, remaining quiet and virtually ignored by the mass of green uniforms.

"That's me," the conductor replied.

"I'm Captain Garo Malic. Please, follow me and I'll take your report on the encounter you had." Blener nodded.

Zell nudged an elbow into Atha's side.

"These people are of the Royal Guard. If you speak—" she began but one of the guards gasped, thrusting a finger up at Atha before pulling a picture from her pocket.

"Captain Malic! It's him, Atha Schneider!" she announced, and Garo spun toward him.

"Good eye, lieutenant! Queen's mercy, Atha, we've been looking all over for you!"

"Oh. Really?" Atha smiled back despite being flustered at sound of the last name from what seemed a lifetime ago.

"I know your situation. We've been canvasing the entire kingdom in a mad search for you. The Queen's orders are to bring you directly to her," Captain Garo said as Atha's smile stretched across his face.

"Melinda, or Elise, whatever you call her, has been looking for me?" he asked, barely able to contain his excitement.

"Yes! Every guard in the land has been looking for you nonstop since she summoned you here days ago! Look, I need to handle this report personally, but—" He paused to snap at a pair of men.

"Barka, Telcatta, escort him directly to the tower," he barked before slapping Atha on the shoulder a few times and stepping back. "You must feel overwhelmed with all of this. Please, keep the situation involving the Red Sheep to yourselves for the time being. We don't need a mass panic on our hands. If you didn't catch it, I'm Captain Malic. I'm sure we'll meet again, Atha." He smiled. Atha burst with laugher, turning to Zell as he threw an arm over her shoulder.

"This is it! God, I can't believe it! After all these shitty years!" He laughed and the two guards Malic had pointed out stepped before them.

"Follow me, please," Barka, a red Denata, requested.

Atha nodded and pulled Zell along with him as they headed toward the buildings across the runways.

The city was even more mesmerizing from the ground. Trees took up most of the ground level, shading them from light of the last sun while dull white lights glowed upon their trunks to provide the light they blocked from the dwindling daylight. Every building except the three black towers were entirely blue, with the occasional exception painted with what Atha could only speculate to be the equivalent of billboard ads. Strange words coursed across them, too fast for Atha to read. The fragments he caught told of some sort of festival, which explained why the streets were absolutely packed.

Storefront windows enticed him to enter, the magical goods that lined their spaces calling to him. In the streets, vendors had set up booths that offered an assortment of foods. He even noticed a shoe shop, but unlike Hanzel's humble store, well over a thousand pairs were visible through the window. Dazzling mystical creatures flickered about, some walking between the crowds with dozens more flying overhead.

"What is that thing?" Atha asked Zell, pointing to a winged cat the slowly glided by just over his head.

"Contract spirit. Most likely performing some manner of task for its wielder," she replied. Atha all but foamed at the mouth from the sensory overload. *Talking trees, mystical spirits, new humanoid species, floating buildings... The Shakka village was already crazy enough, but this city is almost completely different. It's like another world within a world. The weirdest part is I'm accepting it so easily, I just can't believe...*

A surreality crept over Atha as the plethora of sounds around him seemed to diminish. He stared down at his feet, covered by the shoes that had been gifted to him. *I can't believe this. I'm literally just walking around with nobody telling me I can't.* He glanced up at all the unnoticing passersby. *None of these people know who I am. Not a single look of disgust, no words of hate.* Coming to a complete stop amidst the hustle and bustle, he was bumped lightly by passing shoulders.

"Is all well?" Zell asked. Atha turned toward her, snapping out of his trancelike state as he remembered what he was doing.

"Oh, yeah. Sorry. I'm still just totally tripping out about this. It's so weird." He smiled back, catching a short frame bump against Zell's hip in the corner of his eye. Atha's arm instinctively shot out, catching a young Denata child by the arm and pulling him back. "That was a smooth technique, kid. Quick, nimble fingers with a small bump for distraction." The child quickly became distraught as tears welled in his eyes.

"What are you doing?" Zell asked in surprise that quickly fled as Atha yanked her pouch of coins out of the child's hand before tossing it to her.

"Aw, come on, kid. No need for tears. What makes you feel like you need to be out here pickpocketing?" Atha knelt before the child who'd frozen like a statue.

"Got a little thief, eh?" the Denata guard barked over the crowd as he pushed closer to Atha who nodded.

"Yeah, but I handled it. Nothing you guys should bother with," Atha chuckled up to them as a few words crept out of the shaking child.

"Money, f-food. Tella hungry. Please, sir," the youngster replied, a tear loosening itself from his eye. But the guard pressed on, grabbing hold of the child by his shoulder.

"That's not your decision to make. I know this one, a repeat offender," he said. Atha glanced at Zell for aid.

"No harm was incurred. My possessions were returned," Zell said, flashing her bag to the guard. He still didn't release his grip.

"I've come to realize that if you don't pull a weed when you notice it, six more pop up the next day," he spat back, yanking on the Denata child as Atha's temper began to flair.

"It's Barka, right? Look, I told you I have it handled, so you best back off." Atha stood to leer up at the tall guard.

"You threatening me?" the guard replied, veins protruding from his face as if they had been waiting to rear their ugly form.

"Take it however you want," Atha said. "This is your last chance. Let the kid go or I'm gonna lose my temper." Atha remained as calm as he could, not backing down an inch from the man who stared down at him. This surprised the guard, but a smile crossed his face.

"Have it your way. He goes free, then." He raised his free hand, a short green sword appearing in a flash as it swung down on the child's arm. "Not all of him though!"

Red energy glowed from Atha's arm, leaping up to connect a glowing fist with the guard's face. Atha could feel his teeth and jaw shattering as bits spewed from his mouth in a burst of scarlet. He crashed back into the crowd, completely motionless as Atha's temper hit its breaking point. The crowd roared with surprise, a clearing opening around them as voices called out across them. "He's fighting the Royal Guard!" The rest of the unnoticing crowd quickly turned as well, releasing a long "Oooohhhh" like the sound of wind gusting against a building.

Atha caught a glimpse of the second guard in the corner of his eye as a green sword swung for his side. A rock attached to a long tentacle of mana swatted him in the face, knocking the partner to the ground as Atha realized Zell had been the one responsible for it. A second Denata, a young girl even smaller than the first, slipped through the crowd, hobbling toward him as tears streamed down her face.

"Big brother!" she sobbed, latching onto him as he stared fearfully up at Atha.

"I warned him!" Atha spat at Zell who smiled and shrugged.

"You need not explain yourself to me," she replied as Atha sighed, doing his best to calm himself as he stretched his hand out to her.

"We should give them your money. They're hungry," he suggested as she smiled. She pulled out her coins and handed them to Atha, who in turn swung back to the children and held them out.

"You're a good big brother, aren't you? Very strong and brave." Atha smiled down to the boy, dropping the coins into his hand. "Where do you live? Do you have a place to stay?" The area quieted as a bright green glowed through the treetops down onto the street. "Here comes the paddy wagon. Hey, you kids go on and go get some food. I'll be back to see you later." Atha patted the boy's horned head.

"Thank you. Tella, let's go," the boy replied, pulling his little sister along after him into the crowd.

"Are we gonna get arrested?" Atha chuckled to Zell.

"Yes, I suppose we will."

"Oh man, I'm just a regular old jailbird. Sorry for dragging you into this. Oh, and for giving away all your money. I'll pay you back." The images of the coins were etched into his mind now.

"An inconsequential sum, unwarranted for fret." Zell folded her arms as the green light stopped overhead. A massive human came down, bald with a long white beard. He was covered in heavy armor and lofted a massive green battle-axe over his shoulder as he eyed the scene.

"Smart enough not to run at least. All right, put your arms behind your backs, don't activate any contract abilities, and we'll make this quick," he boomed. Atha laughed at the irony of the situation but complied, a bit surprised to see Zell disobey his orders. Instead she pulled out a black fold that resembled a wallet, opened it, and flashing the contents to the enormous man. He paused and took it from her.

"An all-exemptions pass. Never actually seen one of these before. All right, were your actions justifiable?" he asked. Zell nodded. The man extended the item back to her. "You're free to go then. As for you...I feel like I've seen you somewhere before." He shrugged it off and grasped Atha's arms to place a black paper over them. It stretched out, entangling around his forearms and pulling his arms together behind his back.

"Hey, what the fuck?" he spat but the guard pushed him forward.

"That pass only applies to her. You're still under arrest."

"Fear not, Atha," said Zell. "All will work itself out shortly." She smiled, but he grimaced and turned to the large man who pulled him along.

"This is bullshit! Your snoozing buddies over there are a couple of psychos!"

"Pipe down, you'll have a chance to explain yourself. Hollering at me in front of a crowd of festivalgoers isn't going to help either way." A green cloud swirled up beneath them to lift them above the trees. "Destination jail. Moderate speed," the large man commanded the cloud as it pulsed forward. Atha gasped as he bounced on the light and fluffy texture beneath his feet.

"Whoa, ha-ha! Okay, this was totally worth it for the ride." Atha smiled, peering over the edges at the crowd that glanced up at them passing overhead. "And you said festivalgoers, right? What's the occasion?"

"Today's the first day of the weeklong contract festival," he replied as Atha bounced happily.

"I actually just got here, had no idea anything fun was going on. I'll be sure to check it out."

"Well, you've got a bit of explaining to do before then," the guard snorted.

"I got a feeling I won't be held up too long." Atha chuckled as they came to a darker section of the massive town, a large black building standing before them. The cloud stopped, dropping through an opening between the trees straight down to the ground.

The huge man pulled Atha up through the doors. Outside were a pair of guards wearing green uniforms. The inside was empty except for a secretary sitting behind a desk.

"This the assault case, Vork?" the man behind the desk called. Vork nodded, pulling Atha down a short hallway to a set of stone stairs leading downward. They stopped briefly at a container. Atha's pair of rocks and memory card floated off him and into a bin.

"Better not lose those," he warned.

They descended the stairs until they reached a corridor lined with recognizable cells, a few with a translucent barrier in front of them that contained other detainees.

"Get in," Vork instructed, stopping in front of an empty cell. He pulled on Atha's arms and the bindings returned to the form of black paper. He removed the paper handcuffs before pushing him in.

"Magical handcuffs and a magical cell. A very lavish magical cell at that." Atha smiled, hopping onto the white bed rack stretching out from the wall as a translucent barrier blocked his exit.

"Sit tight. A guard will be down to talk to you in about half an hour," Vork said and set off down the hallway.

The cell was entirely white. A steady stream of water fell from a faucet onto a grate in the floor next to the toilet.

"Home sweet home," he said with a sigh. Atha leaned back onto the bunk but snapped back up as a voice from the cell across the hall from his spoke up.

"Hey, human, what you in for?" a Shelando called to him. Like Atha, he was dressed in all black, with only his blue face visible. His tentacles swirled above his head lazily. His blue eyes stared attentively at Atha as he stood and stepped in front of the force field that locked him in. *Ah, the simple pleasure of inmate comradery,* Atha thought.

"Beat up a guard. You?" he asked, not receiving the look of surprise he'd desired.

"I am held accountable for simple petty theft," the Shelando man replied, but Atha noticed the telltale signs of a liar.

"Don't bullshit a bullshitter. What you really in here for?" he asked, this time getting the look of surprise he'd hoped for.

"Oh, good eye. You a member of some part of the underworld?" the Shelando asked as Atha proudly folded his arms.

"You could say that."

"Round here either you are or you aren't. Who do you work for?"

"The Honorati family. You've probably never heard of us, but I've been tasked with raising a new branch, so that'll change pretty soon," Atha replied as the Shelando's smile darkened.

"I'd advise against that. The only group that claims turf around here is the Chameleons." Atha's interest perked.

"The Chameleons? That's the group that killed off most of the royal family, right?"

"The very same. Be warned, they don't take kindly to others moving in on their stomping grounds," he replied.

"I don't scare easy, but thanks. Out of curiosity, what are you really in here for?"

"Got caught in an off-limits area. Well, *caught* isn't really the right word. I needed to come into jail and this was the easiest way in."

"You wanted to get arrested?" Atha asked, seeing no trace of a lie this time.

"Yep. We needed to do some recon in here and I volunteered because I wished to see how formidable the jail system is."

Atha laughed. "Oh yeah? How's that working out for you?"

"Quite the letdown. I'd heard it was formidable, but they rely on nothing but contract abilities to contain offenders. There are no guards standing at attention. I figured I was already here, so I'd enjoy the atmosphere a bit. I spent a long time in a place like this up into my late teenage years, but this is dreadfully lax in comparison." Atha's smile slowly fell. *I'm getting really bad vibes from this guy. Same as the serial killers on death row.*

"What's your name?" Atha asked, a bit taken aback by the seemingly true story.

"Harmer. My friends call me Harm. You?"

"Atha Honorati. Who do *you* work for?" he asked. Harmer took his time answering.

"Well, I guess telling one kid in jail won't hurt nothing. The Chameleons." He smiled back as Atha's blood went cold. A sudden sense of overwhelming bloodlust flowed out of Harmer as he stared Atha down.

"You grew up in a similar situation to me, didn't you?" Harmer continued. "Not many people can naturally feel killing intent like you clearly can."

"What are you doing in the capital?" Atha asked. All his senses had sharpened and his instincts were kicking in.

"Dunno yet. The boss put out an order to meet in the capital. I was tasked with doing recon on the Queen's guard and jail system. Haven't been told why."

"You here to finish what you started, aren't you? Killing off the royal family?" Atha replied.

"Oh no, most of the old members died after that plan failed, including the old boss. That was before I joined. We have strict orders to stay clear of her. Fairly certain I know why, and if I'm right then she's completely safe from us."

Atha calmed, a sense of relief creeping over.

"I didn't know the old members died. Why would you work for a group like that?" he asked as Harmer smirked, his bloodlust growing.

"I enjoy the things we do. I'm not a complicated person. The only thing I love is killing. Well, that's not the right way to put it. Killing in and of itself is enjoyable but not comparable to facing down a worthy opponent. That moment when you stare down at someone who could just have easily been staring down at you and watch the life slowly dribble out of their eyes that..." He paused, taking a long lustful groan as he clasped his arms around himself. "Oh, look at me, a total mess at the mere thought."

"Pretty fucked-up in the head, ain't you?" Atha replied as Harmer laughed.

"That's true, but don't sell yourself short. A mere glance into those nasty little eyes and I can see a similar pleasure in you."

"You're wrong. I only ever did what I had to do to survive."

"Whatever the reason was, you enjoyed taking those lives. You have the clear eyes of a killer. Not a single trace of regret shares that space. I can also tell that you favor yourself to be quite a force."

"Hard to be remorseful for killing monsters who deserved much worse than a quick death. And yeah, don't think I'm tooting my own horn when I say I'm no punk."

"What does tooting your horn have to do with this?" Harmer scoffed.

"It's a, uh, it's a saying from where I'm from," he replied, kicking himself a bit at letting another slip.

"Never heard a saying quite like that. What would you say to joining the Chameleons?" Harmer asked. Atha recoiled for a moment, completely shocked at the question.

"Why the fuck would I ever do that?"

"Keep your enemies close. If you really aim to start your own gang around here, you could do it while keeping an eye on your biggest competition, and I'd be interested in keeping an eye on you as well. I got a pretty good knack for finding unknown talent and I feel a good whiff of it coming from you. Win-win."

He actually does make a fairly decent point, Atha thought as Harmer continued.

"Boss wouldn't even mind you openly aiming to start your own thing if you were honest about it. He likes a psychological challenge just as much as I like a physical one, and I bet he'd find a way to convince you to stay."

"You put together a pretty good pitch, but I have to decline. I'm Honorati through and through."

"I've never heard a whisper of this Honorati you speak so highly of. But seriously, a word of advice from one who would like to see you grow and develop—the Boss don't share my enthusiasm with letting enemies grow. He's more of a 'kill them all, take no prisoners' kinda guy. If he learns about you building a force that could potentially challenge his own? Oh, he'll come for you."

Atha huffed with laughter. "Let him. It would only save me the trouble of finding him when I'm done with the Red Sheep."

"The Red Sheep? What business do you have with a plague?"

"He attacked a town I was staying in but left halfway through for some unknown reason," Atha replied. "After that he popped back up and chased me on my way here."

Harmer took his turn at skepticism. "Not just any plague, but the five-thousand-year-old monster rumored to be strongest of the lot attacks you twice and yet you draw breath?"

Atha nodded, his snobby side shining through.

"Yep. Don't believe me if you want, but it's the truth," he sneered back over the sound of Harmer's laugh.

"No, I believe you, Atha. I feel I have misjudged you. You're not becoming strong, you already are. Are you having a difficult time growing into a powerful contract?" he asked but Atha remained silent, a bit taken aback by the on-point conclusion despite a lack of actual information.

"Your face tells me all I need to know. The Chameleons have a member who's a plague. A human lass, she's totally psycho—even by my standards, which is really saying something. We Chameleons have thirteen members and rank ourselves in strength based on our number within it. She's number seven, putting her in the middle in terms of combative prowess. As for myself"—he paused, holding up just a pair of fingers in a strange fashion with the pinky and index finger just above the top of his face—"I stand far above her. You can—what did you call it, toot your horn?—but believe me when I say this: no matter who or what you are, there's *always* someone stronger."

Atha was already busy processing the last piece of information.

"So, you work with a plague? How do you reason with something like that?" he asked as Harmer agitatedly thumped his head against the clear wall.

"I say all that and that's what you take away from it? Isn't it obvious? Plagues are like anything else: they come in all sorts. And while she might be a bit unorthodox, she is still an invaluable member. You don't really seem too know much about anything, do you?"

"Is it that obvious?"

"Very." Harmer paused as a blue portal appeared on his wall and a dainty feminine voice called through it.

"Hey, Harm, we're getting ready to begin the operation. Boss wanted to make sure you're set," the voiced said cheerfully.

"Understood. Yeah, just finishing up at the jail. Everything is set. I'll use my exit when I'm done," he replied.

Must be another Chameleon using some sort of contract ability.

The portal closed and Harmer raised his hand. The translucent door vanished and he stepped out. "Well, we're all out of time," he said, walking toward Atha's cell. "Wanna have a friendly little test before I go?"

Atha lurched backwards in his cell. "You get any closer and I'll cap your ass. Best just leave while you got the chance," Atha spat, but Harmer only laughed, waving a hand to dissipate Atha's translucent door. He

144

kept that same hand raised up like a declaration of war. Atha continued backing up slowly.

"Last warning, motherfucker. Next one's gonna be a hole!" Atha yelled, a .45 caliber pistol falling into his hands, but Harmer strode forward. Atha raised the pistol. A flash and *BANG* and the reaching blue hand lost a pair of fingers. Now Harmer stopped and pulled his hand to his face in astonishment as Atha raised the pistol again.

"Ha! Not so hot now, huh? Want another? I've got seven more of his buddies!" Atha yelled, but next thing he knew he was slammed onto his back with Harmer's hand clasped around his neck.

"That's not a contract power you wield. Tell me, Atha, what manner of ability is this?" he asked, his face darkening as Atha gasped for air.

"S-screw you!" he replied between gasps. Harmer's face lowered closer to his own, his hot breath tickling Atha's neck as a shiver went down his spine. Agro energy pulsed from him, but Harmer continued to hold him in place with unfazed ease. Now that Harmer was so close, Atha realized his own tactics were being used against him. Harmer was reading his face for the signs of a liar.

"You don't even know what this power is, do you?"

Atha's throat was completely cut off from air but it made no difference; he knew his flustered facial expression was answering Harmer's question.

"Interesting. I find myself completely enthralled by you, Atha Honorati," Harmer replied, releasing his throat but continuing to pin Atha to the floor. "I may know of a Chameleon who could remove the shroud from this mysterious force you wield. Can't say for certain if my hunch is correct, but when next we meet I will know for sure."

A large blue portal opened beside them and Harmer sighed, glancing angrily to it. "Can't even wait six more minutes without giving me grief. Ah well, I suppose I've had my share of fun. I'm going to release you and you are going to let me leave unhindered for sparing your life. Sound fair?" He smiled down to Atha, who only glared back. "Oh, I do so love those eyes. Attack if you wish, but I won't go so easy again if you do." Harm stood up as Atha watched. "Can't leave those behind," Harmer mumbled, pulling a small red button from his black robes. Clicking it a few times, a second, smaller blue portal opened and sucked up his fingers and blue blood.

Agro energy burst from Atha. He yanked the pistol up and took aim, but Harmer moved like a ghost and slammed a fist into his chest, knocking the air out of him. He rocked back against the wall. "Can't say I didn't warn you." Harmer laughed, staring down for a moment before stepping through the blue portal that closed instantly behind him.

Atha gasped in pain for a few minutes before finally catching his breath. A green light illuminated the hallway, the sound of nearing guards further angering Atha. He stepped out into the hallway, the nearing light blinding him as he folded his hands behind his head and laid face down. *Just like the good old days. Fucking helpless and weak.* Hot tears welled up in his eyes as the light came to a stop. A feminine voice on the verge of tears spoke up only to whisper a single name.

"Atha?"

Chapter 11

Dearly Beloved

Atha's head snapped up. The image of the woman Zell had shown him now stood before him in the flesh. A beautiful green dress covered her body and long black hair flowed down her back. Green-gloved hands covered her mouth as she gasped. Tears streamed down her face as Atha burst to his feet.

"Melinda!" he screamed, slamming into her so hard the two nearly toppled back onto the stone floor.

"Atha! Oh, Atha!" she sobbed, clinging to him as his own tears dribbled down her neck.

"Melinda, I thought you were dead!" he cried, pulling his face back to stare at her.

"I'm so sorry. I wasn't given any choice, and we didn't have the means to bring you right away," she replied, her pale face growing red from emotion. Several guards had come with her and one approached, clearing his throat to get her attention.

"Ma'am, we should really give him a quick once-over. Who knows what—"

She flipped her head, cutting him off.

"I appreciate your concern, Dimitri, but that is unnecessary." The guard bowed his head, stepping back slowly as she returned her sights to Atha. "You must have so many questions," she started, reaching her shaking hands up to his cheeks. "And there are so many things I'd like to ask as well. Come, let's move our reunion to a more appropriate location."

Atha could only stare, completely overwhelmed by sight that stood before him. "Look at you. You've gotten so big."

She smiled, their eyes at equal height to the others. "I've missed so many things." Her tears started right back up again as Atha pulled her face back onto his shoulder.

"I'm here now. A lot of things have changed, but you're still the same old lobster face." He laughed, feeling her nod against his dampening shoulder.

"And you're speaking in full sentences," she said, her voice muffled. "I guess it's easy to figure which of us has grown up. Now come on, I really shouldn't be doing this here." She pushed away and grasped his hand, pulling him along.

"I need to get my stuff. They took everything I had and put it in a box," Atha replied. She nodded and pointing at a guard.

"Please see that his items are brought to my quarters," she instructed, and with a bow he headed off down the hallway.

"Wow. So, you're really the Queen here, huh?" Atha asked, the green-uniformed guards surrounding them on all sides as they headed back up the stairs.

"I am," Melinda responded. "It's part of the reason why we were sent to Earth."

"I know. I heard about the Chameleons and what they did. Actually, I met one right before you showed up," he replied as she looked to him in surprise.

"Here in the jail? That shouldn't be possible. I have a protective field up around the capital that prevents those with ill will from being able to cross its threshold."

"He left in some kind of blue portal," Atha replied.

"I will have a team investigate it. Let's just enjoy our reunion now. I've missed you, my dearly beloved," she replied, stretching an arm up around his shoulder and planting a kiss on his forehead as they reached the lobby he'd first entered the jail through.

They stepped outside and Atha noticed the suns had set. The street lights provided pools of light on the ground.

A green cloud formed beneath them and the others, lifting them off the ground. They continued to rise high into the air, well above the rest of the city. The city below shone with light and activity, thousands of beings bustling through it.

"Where are we going?" Atha asked, unsure of how high they were going to climb into the starry sky.

"That black tower. The middle one," Melinda replied, pointing at one of the massive black obelisks that he'd noticed upon arriving to the capital.

"What? Your quarters are in there? That's so cool!"

"Actually, I own it. It was part of my inheritance." She smiled back as Atha nearly fainted. "I originally owned all of them, but I donated the extra pair because it seemed a tad ridiculous for me to keep things I could never hope to make good use of. As for the last, I only use the very top portion. The rest are for the families of my Royal Guard."

"Okay, I get it, Mother Teresa," he replied.

"Oh, don't get me wrong, it benefits me as well! I literally have hundreds of guards in the same building if anything were to happen."

"Oh yeah, I guess it would make sense you'd get my reference. Sheesh, I've just been a mess since I got here." Atha laughed for a moment as she nodded understandingly.

"I had trouble adjusting too. You'll start to fit in over time," she said.

As they neared the middle tower, one of the sides slid open like an automatic door. The cloud floated through it and came to a stop in a room bursting at the seams with potted plants and Royal Guards. They all took a knee as the Queen landed. One of her guard entourage announced, "You may rise," before leading Atha toward a door in the middle of the massive room. A pair of guards stood on either side, a man to the left and a woman to the right.

"Ma'am," they announced in unison as she neared. The woman tapped the wall behind her and the extravagant door swung open. Melinda's room wasn't anything like he'd imagined. It was insanely spacious, which was emphasized by the emptiness inside. The ceiling was high, and an elaborate system of lights lit the room, which was easily the fanciest feature. A lonely couch sat in the left corner beside a small shelf of books. Beside that was another door and a small desk to the right. Over a dozen screens floated around the desk. At the far end of the room was a wall of glass that opened up to a balcony. Through the glass, Atha could see seven winged guards floating about.

"It's so empty in here," Atha noted out loud accidently as Melinda twirled her finger. Green fog encased her body and her dress shrank into a green tank top and shorts. "Whoa, magic wardrobe! Not worried about the Kentantos outside the window seeing a little leg, huh?" Atha chuckled.

"Oh no, that wall is mirrored. All they can see from the outside is the black exterior of the tower." She laughed, grabbing him and sitting him down on the couch before taking a seat as well. "Oh, and my name isn't actually Melinda. That was an alias used for Earth if anybody managed to follow us across dimensions. My real name is Elise Luxria. Your first name is accurate, but your real last name is Lamkos."

"No, it's not, it's Honorati. And sorry, I already heard of your real name. It just seems more natural to call you Melinda," he replied as she cocked an eyebrow.

"Honorati?"

"Yeah. It's a long story."

"I have the feeling we will be sharing plenty of those with one another. Would you like to get the ball rolling?" She smiled but Atha's expression fell.

She doesn't know I was in prison, he thought to himself before shaking his head.

"Let's come back to that. Tell me what happened after you vanished! God, I want to know so bad."

"All right, we'll start with me then." She paused, reaching a hand up to her neck and grasping her skin to pull it back. Atha realized it was synthetic. Her throat was a clear tube system, pumping up and down with her lungs.

"Paul Schneider was the alias of Dako Luminar, the man tasked with accompanying your pregnant mother and myself to Earth, a duty given to him by your real father. Oh, just to clarify, we are not actual brother and sister. When he attacked us that night, Dako crushed my throat, which set off an emergency alarm here in the capital. They were waiting for the day I would be old enough to take up the royal contract blessed upon my family. It's known as Ruler's Right."

"Whoa, whoa, slow down! Let me get this straight—we're not really brother and sister?" Atha asked.

"Biologically, no, but I believe we are both in agreement with the fact we are family, no? To me, it changes nothing, and is little more than a side note," she replied, already knowing the answer before Atha nodded.

"Yeah, I know, but still. I'll just throw it on the growing pile of facts that contradict everything I thought I knew. Sorry, keep going." Atha replied, rubbing his temples in a vain attempt to help his brain process this newest information.

"I was supposed to be brought back a year later on my next birthday, but they had to activate an emergency summoning, known as a hasty portal. It doesn't have a full charge and brings you within a certain vicinity of the central summoning area. I did the same thing for you. I received a report you were in imminent danger and activated your summoning early, which is why you popped up over a hundred miles away in the Shakka village." Atha reached forward, pulling her fake skin back again as the horrific day replayed in his mind.

"I knew it was bad, but…" Atha paused, huffing with anger and sadness.

"I have come to terms with it. After all these years, the only thing that still bothered me was leaving you behind like that," she replied, her eyes getting glassy as Atha's anger dissipated.

"Aw, come on, don't cry again. Keep going, I won't interrupt." He smiled. A light knock on her door sounded and she stood and twirled her finger. A green bathrobe covered her dainty PJs, and she pulled the door open as a Shelando extended a box to her.

"Atha's possessions, ma'am," the Shelando announced as she grasped it.

"Thank you, Dimitri. Please make it known that I am to receive no further interruptions unless they are of the utmost import." He bowed his head, pulling the door closed. She handed it to Atha and he pulled out his rocks and memory card.

"Oh, is that what I think it is?! You still have that thinking rock your teacher gave you?" She laughed, pulling the sparking geode out of his hands to admire it in the light.

"Some habits never die. Moving it around in my fingers still helps me focus," Atha replied as she placed it back in his hand.

"I can hardly believe you still have it! It is a beautiful rock, though." She smiled, pausing in surprise as Atha got on one knee and bowed his head as he held it up to her.

"If her majesty finds herself so enthralled with a commoner's possession, he should humbly offer it up to please her, if for but only a moment," Atha replied in mocking exaggeration as she laughed.

"God, who are you and what have you done with my brother? And fine, I will keep it, then!" She snatched it from his hands as he huffed with laughter and got back on the couch.

Green fog pulsed around the geode, green chains forming from nothing to pierce it and turn it into a necklace that Elise looped around her neck.

"Oh, you don't have to make me feel special by wearing it."

"I think it's beautiful! This will be a splendid addition to my daily wardrobe," she replied, eyeing it around her neck before turning back to him. "So anyways, after I ended up back here I didn't automatically become the Queen. They'd appointed a distant cousin of mine as the acting Queen and kept my return hidden until my birthday. Once that occurred, I was of age to accept my contract and was officially placed upon the throne."

"So, wait, you have some sort of special contract?"

"Yes, Ruler's Right is what actually put my family in a position of power. Triple S contracts such as mine are practically, if not literally, considered holy. Every ruling family in this world has one that's tied to their specific bloodline."

"Zell told me about contract power grades. So that means you're like, super overpowered right?"

"In a sense, yes. To put it in an easy comparison, I am the nuclear weapons of my nation," she replied, another knock coming from her door.

"Enter, Dimitri," she called.

"Apologies, ma'am," Dimitri said after entering. "Senator Carlille will be arriving soon for your meeting."

"Send her a message stating I must reschedule for tomorrow. Clear the rest of my schedule for the night while you're at it. Don't give specific reasoning, and make them know this isn't negotiable. Thank you."

"Yes, ma'am." Dimitri backed out and shut the door.

"I'm not holding you up, am I?" Atha asked as she sat again, shaking her head.

"Don't be ridiculous. This has been long overdue, and the only inconvenience would be postponing it any longer. Now, where was I?" She sighed, twirling her finger again as green fog looped her long black hair neatly into a tight bun atop her head. "Oh, so yes, my contract is the only factor that distinguishes me as royalty. There are a few contracts that are tied to specific bloodlines and can't be formed by normal means. All royal contracts share this fact. The Chameleons were hell-bent on overthrowing the royal families, but with the ensuing war most of them where killed along with many of the Royal Guard. Your father was a Captain of the Guard and your mother was the acting admiral. Your real dad gave his life while helping us escape. The loss of so many figures of power left a terrible gap in the structure. To this day it hasn't fully healed, but with every passing moment things come closer to being as they were. It was difficult at first to get used to this strange world. The most common of things vexing me to no end."

"Oh man, I'm totally on your level with that."

"But I slowly started to see the method to the madness. Ruling actually came easier to me than figuring out contracts and the like. My first year was rough, especially with the acting Queen, Erida, attempting to start a civil war, but after that I had a firm grasp of what needed to happen and when it needed to be done."

"Whoa, whoa, whoa, slow down. *Civil war*?" he repeated.

She nodded. "She believed herself entitled to the throne and, having been fairly successful with its duties, many agreed with her. That was my darkest time after arriving here. We had grown close or—at least, I thought so. Perhaps it was just my wish to have family clouding my mind, but I still hold out hope that she will come around."

Atha patted her knee.

"Well, you have family now. And I promise I won't ever start a civil war!" He laughed.

"How considerate of you. Too bad I have other plans," she taunted back, twirling her finger in the air as green fog pulsed around him, tightening down to restrict his arms and legs.

"What are you doing?" Atha chuckled unsure of what to make of his predicament. A sense of terror crept over him as she twiddled her fingers, slowly easing them toward his ribs.

"Shouldn't make rude jokes to the one person who knows all your most ticklish spots. Time for you to get a taste of—"She paused, lunging forward as Atha attempted to stand and hop away. "Tickle war!" she screamed, yanking him back onto the couch with malicious fingers that dug into his tender ribs.

"AAAAAAAHAHAHAHAHAHAHA! No! Stop, I'm sorry, I'm sorry, I'm so sorry! Come on, I'm tapping, this isn't even fair! This is abuse of power, I tell you!" Atha screamed, twisting and turning fruitlessly as Elise's assault continued. By the time she stopped, his ribs were completely red.

"Jesus, that was borderline child abuse," he groaned, pulling his black robes up to eye the redness.

"Oh, you're such a whiner. I barely touched you. Besides, you're practically an adult. Your eighteenth birthday is in two weeks, you know," she replied as his smile returned.

"You kept track after all this time?"

"June 7. Of course I did. Do you know how old I am?" she teased back.

"Twenty-four. You're not-—" Atha began, but one of the screens over her desk began to flash red, and she sighed irritably before getting up.

"Hold that thought. This'll be quick," she told him, once again having a green bathrobe fall over her as she reached the desk. She snapped a finger at the screen, bringing it to life, and the face of an elderly woman popped up as Elise forced a smile onto her face.

"Senator Carlille, I assume Dimitri has passed along word of my need to reschedule our meeting," she announced as the older woman nodded.

"Yes, ma'am, he has. Please, it is imperative I speak with you. Time is truly of the essence," she replied.

"Apologies, but this is not negotiable. If rescheduling is a problem, then I could send Captain Garo in my stead," Elise replied as the woman sighed, resting her face in her hands for a moment.

"No, this is something I really must discuss with you. Is their truly no chance you will rethink this?" the conflicted Senator replied but Elise shook her head.

"No, there is not. Come now, Carlille, of all the times you've insisted to speak with me, have I ever asked to reschedule?"

"No, you have not."

"Then please leave me in peace just this once. I give you my word I will see to you before any other business is attended," she replied. The senator paused for a long moment.

"As is your will, my Queen," she finished, the screen clearing back to an empty white as Elise groaned.

"Is everything all right? Really, if you got things to do, I can wait," Atha called to her as she sat back down on the couch for yet the third time.

"That's the problem, Atha, I always have things to do, and despite how monotonous those things may be, people *always* insist that they are of the highest priority." She laughed, glancing back once more to the desk before looking back at Atha.

"Now, please, I want to hear about what's been going on with your life."

He hesitated. He didn't want to talk about it, knowing it would ruin the mood, but knew he couldn't keep this from her.

"Okay, but before I say anything I want you to know you were in no way responsible, okay?" he started.

"What do you mean? Did something happen?" she replied as Atha reached his open palm up in front of her.

"Well, let's start from the beginning. I have this ability. Zell said it's called a *contract-less ability*. Here." A plastic rose fell from thin air into his hand as Elise recoiled in surprise. "Just about anything I can picture clearly in my head just appears."

He handed her the rose as she looked at it with utter disbelief. "The first time I ever used it, I manifested a gun and used it to shoot Dako in the head. You were already unconscious when it happened."

"Oh—oh my God. I knew he had passed but Atha—I had no idea." She reached forward to rest a hand on his shoulder. "I don't know what to think about all this. It's a lot to process."

"Since I killed Dako and you vanished, the Feds charged me with double homicide and chose to make an example out of me. The government removed laws that restricted children from being placed in prison, and I was the first child ever to be sentenced to life in prison with the caveat that on my eighteenth birthday I would be put to death. Nothing like that had ever been done before. Pretty messed up, huh? Letting me rot like that 'til I could legally get a lethal injection."

She gasped, shaking hands covering her mouth as tears began to well up.

"I'm not gonna lie to you and tell you it was fun, but I had good people looking out for me inside. I was actually adopted in an official capacity by another inmate, Lenny Honorati. He and a few other guys made sure nothing ever happened to me. Kept me safe and taught me a bunch of stuff." He stopped as Elise became hysterical, burying her face in her hands. Atha pulled her head against his chest.

"I never gave up looking for you. All those years, I searched for any sort of answer, from black holes to aliens, magic to conspiracies." Atha chuckled, doing his best to hold everything together but his voice cracked as he talked. "It was really hard. I looked and looked, and nothing ever helped or gave me even the tiniest clue. I actually started to think I was insane and that you really were..." He paused, a screen over her desk flashing red. She burst to her feet and flung the plastic rose down, snapping her fingers at the screen without bothering to put the robe on.

"My Queen, I—"

"Has Dimitri not told you I am not to be disturbed?!" she screamed at a guard who quickly became flustered. He attempted to stutter back a reply but she shut the screen off, leaning over the desk as tears began dotting it. Atha got up as well, resting his hands on her shoulders as she continued to cry.

"Do you want to hear the rest? It doesn't get any better." She flipped around, holding his face with delicate hands.

"I need to hear it," she replied as he nodded. His head sagged as the memories came back to torture him.

"I got romantically involved with a nurse who started working at the prison. She was all alone like me. Yellowstone Park blew up and killed her family. I was selling drugs, but our prices went up and some tweaker couldn't pay. They kept begging and begging me for fronts 'til I cut him off completely. He—he…" Atha huffed, breaking down as Elise sat on the desk, taking a turn holding him as he sobbed. The image of a substance that provided him with confert in times like this popped into his mind.

A small bag of white powder appeared from thin air and dropped onto Elise's desk and Atha quickly grasped it and flung it into a nearby trash can before she could notice.

"When I was about to escape, the guards turned on us. Me and Len, we were trapped and that's when the portal showed up. I got stuck in it and Len, he—he pushed me through." Atha sobbed until an explosion lit up the window with a resounding boom.

Without thinking, Atha twisted, yanking Elise to the floor beneath him and covering her body with his own as she gasped. "What the hell was that?!" he huffed shakily, glancing over his shoulder to the window where the guards flapped lazily.

"The contract festival is going on. That light was just a synthetic sun being activated." Elise pushed herself up and back to her feet.

"Oh, Jesus, I'm sorry. That just totally took me by surprise," Atha muttered.

"Forever my protector, my dearly beloved." Elise smiled, whipping her tears away as another flash and boom lit the sky. He glanced over, admiring the massive ball of light that now rested a few stories bellow the window. It provided light for the dances and celebrations upon the layer of buildings that hovered above the ground.

"Magical sun," Atha added. "I'm glad I finally talked about Emilia. This was the first time since she passed." Atha sighed, looking down into his palms.

"I'd love to hear all about her."

Atha shook his head.

"No, I think that's about all I can say right now. I've never been good at talking about my problems." Atha's words halted as he glanced toward the trash can, where a bag of white powder, no larger than a golf ball, sat. "And it brings me back to a dark place." He stepped to the window, Elise following slowly. Atha stared down with mystified eyes, watching more artificial suns bursting into existence above every section of the city through the massive window.

"Man, they're really turning it up out there. What's with this festival everybody keeps talking about?" he asked, desperate for a change of subject.

"It's the yearly contract festival. A two-week long occasion featuring a specific contract category each day so that people can come and experience the one they're interested in. Today's the first day. The featured category is agriculture."

Atha cocked an eyebrow. "Two weeks? That would be fourteen days. I thought there were only twelve categories. "

"Well, yes, but the last two days are dedicated to the Combat Contract Tournament. Learning about contracts is just a fraction of the ordeal. There's also carnival games, food stalls, shows, sporting events, and so forth," she replied, noticing the vibrant twinkle in Atha's eyes as they widened.

"Can we go?!" he burst as she smiled.

"Of course. Let me get changed and get an escort," she replied, dipping back through the door beside the couch. She came back out in a festive sleeveless green dress that reached just past her knees.

"I better not have to remind any stray eyes that you're the Queen, eh? But did you even change or do your little fog wardrobe change thing again?"

"The fog thing. I just went back there to get these." She held up a pair of golden rings in her hand.

"Oh. Why?" Atha asked, watching her push one onto her finger. He suddenly realized he didn't know the lady before him.

"Who are you?" he asked, reeling back.

"Elise! You don't recognize me?"

Atha blinked a few times, realizing it was in fact her. "Whoa, what was that? Anti-recognition magic?"

"Exactly! With these we can enjoy the festival without my status bothering us!" She placed the other ring in Atha's hand.

"That's some strong mojo. Jeez, I was literally looking at you and then it was like you just vanished."

"It stops your brain from making connections about certain things. The only way to break the spell is to state your name out loud. It can also turn off if the area isn't rich with mana. Since this whole world is bathed in mana, I doubt that could happen, but it's not crazy to imagine a contract with such a power existing."

"Zell mentioned how many different contracts there are. If that happens I shall risk life and limb to protect you, my fair lady!" Atha replied, throwing a few jabs into the air.

"Settle down, karate kid. There'll be plenty of Royal Guards about for that very reason. Now come on, I need to let Dimitri know so he can prepare a detail." She exited out the door and back into the room teeming with plants and guards. A tall Shelando was standing in front of her door with a cold, stern face. His tentacles where wrapped neatly in a bundle atop his head and his green uniform held a number of red dashes down the arm.

"Atha, this is my second in command, Admiral Dimitri. He's taken care of me ever since I first returned," she stated proudly and Atha extended a hand to him.

"Nice to meet you," Atha said.

Dimitri extended his blue hand.

"Well met, Atha," he replied, his voice as cool and empty as his face.

Atha noticed Zell in a far corner, her purple robes giving her away even though the black hood hid her face.

"Oh, I didn't realize Zell was here!" Atha smiled as Elise's eyes widened. She put a hand up to her mouth and shushed him.

"She's trying to remain incognito!"

"Oh, whoops! Probably should have been able to figure that out by myself." Atha winced apologetically, rubbing his head and stepping around Dimitri to go say hello to Zell.

"Hey! Didn't realize you were hanging out over here. Were you here when I came through earlier?" Atha asked as her hooded face glanced up to him.

"Indeed, I was. After your arrest, this was my first stop. You are adored, Atha. I need only mutter your name and found myself before the Queen herself."

Elise came up behind him. "He certainly is. Please, allow me to see you to a room, master monk."

Zell bowed her head.

"Queen Elise. My accommodations are already suitable for my needs. Pay me no thought and enjoy reunion with your lost brother."

"Please, Zell, I would not abandon you in the lounge area after you have traveled so far to bring him here. Go rest in my room or I will take personal offense in this matter." Elise gave a slight tug on her arm.

"As is your will, ma'am." Zell smiled, letting Elise lead her over to the pair of Guards that stood at her door.

"Tap the bottom left screen over my desk and a guard will respond to fill your needs," Elise said as the doors opened for Zell.

Zell entered the room as a team of Guards dressed in black robes instead of the traditional green came in through the entrance. Elise and Dimitri stepped to Atha's side as they approached.

"My Queen," a male Denata started, the whole group bowing their heads before he continued.

"A pleasure as always, Captain Deldora. Thank you all for coming on such short notice. Has Dimitri already given you a brief? If any of you

165

have questions, please ask them now, for I am to remain completely undisturbed during the festival."

Atha watched in surprise. *All this just to go out?* he wondered as Elise began to answer questions.

"Do not come within thirty feet of us and stay completely out of sight if possible. If you get too close it could blow our cover and the night will be lost. Anything else?" she asked again as Deldora stepped forward.

"I have not so much another question, but a few extra words for Atha," he started, stopping in front of him and staring down with a pair of steely black eyes. "If anything does go awry we will move into action with haste, but you should consider yourself the first line of defense. Stay vigilant of your surroundings. Also understand that we aren't here to protect or watch you, so consider yourself on your own if she leaves your side. Should the worst come to pass, we will remove her and her alone away from the scene unless it's determined your life is in danger, but even then, you are second priority. Do I make myself completely and utterly clear?"

Atha smiled and nodded.

"Wouldn't have it any other way."

"Good. Then, ma'am, if you two would put your rings on and state your names we'll be off." They did just that.

"Elise."

"Atha." They cleared their identity to the guards who pulled into the air atop a green cloud before shooting back out the exit.

"Oh, and don't use my name while we're out or our cover will be blown. From here out refer to me as Elly and yourself as Atty. Now, come on, let's go!" She smiled, yanking him toward the exit as a new cloud lifted them up into the air.

"Oh man, I can only imagine what this is going to be like. How many times have you gone?" Atha asked as they gusted out into the cool night air. Between the synthetic suns above and dazzling lights below, it was the brightest night Atha had ever experienced.

"This is actually my first time attending. In the past I've made quick appearances but never actually went incognito and participated."

"What? You gotta be kidding!"

"I've always been so busy I couldn't justify putting things off for a few hours of fun. I may have belittled the matters I'm constantly presented with earlier, but in truth most things cannot progress without my approval. Even so, I'm glad I waited. Now I can enjoy it with fresh enthusiasm, just as you will!"

The cloud vanished beneath their feet when they landed in an empty part of town. Atha caught a few glimpses of guards atop roofs but quickly lost sight of them as they began to walk toward the roaring crowd. "And let's not act as if I deserved to enjoy myself. With what you went through—"

"Stop it. I don't want to ever hear you blame yourself for what happened to me. Let's just party it up and forget our woes!" Atha cut in, wrapping an arm over her neck as they neared the first set of stalls.

Atha paused at the first one, where a spider that was encased in a glass box was wrapping webs around a blue stick in a mesmerizing fashion.

"What's this?" he asked, but his question was answered as the vendor retrieved the web-coated stick, handing it to an eagerly awaiting Denata who, to Atha's dismay, proceeded to take a bite from it. "Oh...magic spider cotton candy. That's...gross. And we're walking." He started to go, but Elise pulled him to a stop.

"This stuff is actually really good! It takes a high-level agriculture contract to get this breed of spider to weave in gratuin—the stuff that makes it sugary tart, that is—so this is a rare opportunity!" She pulled a pouch of coins from the side of her dress.

"You can get one, but I'm good," Atha replied as she spoke with the vendor. The spider sprang into motion to produce another white ball of web. Elise retrieved the stick and, to Atha's repeated disgust, took a hearty bite before sticking it in his face.

"Come on, just give it a try!"

"Oh, I know what this is. I'm the foreigner presented with some sort of delicacy who's supposed to see the error of my ways once I find out how good it is. Except that's not gonna happen 'cause there's no way I'm putting a ball of spider webs in my mouth!" He laughed. Elise pulled the mess of webs away in disappointment. "Look, I'll fall for the next cliché, okay? Oh! Are those games?"

He pulled her toward a set of booths with a large gathering of children strewn about. A holographic screen above one displayed a stick figure falling through narrow cliffs, and Atha came to a stop in front of an excited vendor. The Shelando paused, her blue eyes rolling over Atha, who had forced his way past a group of kids with Elise in tow.

"Can I help you?" she asked, her tentacles swirling vibrantly atop her head.

"Yeah, we'd like to play! What kind of game is this?" Atha blurted out as the group of children whispered and pointed at him.

"This is the free-fall collision experience. Its recommended for ages *seven* and up," she replied, giving little effort to hide her disapproval.

"You had me at free-fall! How do you play?" he asked, giving no mind to the obvious shade she was casting on him.

"It's easy. You just fall and steer yourself through the obstacle course. You gain points until you hit something. Then it's game over."

"That's awesome! Can we both play?" He pulled Elise up beside him.

"One player at a time, but you can both play individually."

"You're welcome to go first," said Elise, pulling a coin out and handing it to the lady as Atha bounced with pleasure.

"Put your palm on the cube and you'll be transported to the course's plain," she replied as Atha blinked.

"Is this like some sort of virtual reality thing?" he exclaimed, slamming his hand onto the cube and vanishing from site. He glanced around in surprise, realizing he was sitting atop a hovering platform. Patches of clouds stretched off endlessly beneath him, while jagged, rocky cliffs lined either side of him. To make matters worse, spinning saws bounced throughout the air. Atha screamed as he glanced over the edge.

"Oh my God, this is real! Get me out! I don't want to fall!" he yelled as the platform began to dissolve beneath his feet. A sense of pure terror creeped over him as his feet met air. He fell, his scream growing louder as the first saw came toward him. He covered his face as he collided with it, toppling back onto the street. A group of children laughed as Atha sprawled out on the ground, screaming with fear as the vendor snorted with laughter.

"I've never actually seen anyone get knocked out at the first obstacle!"

Atha realized he was back at the festival.

"Come on, you're going to blow our cover making a scene!" Elise whispered, yanking him to his feet as sweat dotted his forehead.

"What the f-fu-fudge?! That's a *kid's* game? I got hit by a *buzz saw*!" he gasped, latching onto Elise's arm as she led him away. "Jesus, eating cobwebs and a masochistic kid's game. What is this place? The twilight zone?"

"Don't be silly, you can't actually get hurt in that game. Why don't you just try something a bit more simplistic?" Elise replied, pointing a finger to a booth where a chubby Denata sat. "That one's pretty basic. It's like the knock-down carnival game on Earth except the pins fly around."

Atha's eyes sparkled as he pushed forward. The chubby Denata glanced up as he approached, putting down a book he was reading as a coin landed on the table before him.

"Bit old for this game, aren't you?" he chuckled. Atha was beginning to grow tired of the mocking words.

"Bit old to be running a game booth too, but I don't hear anybody judging you. Give me seven balls," Atha spat back as the Denata's eye twitched. He snatching the coin from Atha's hand and placed a rack of balls in front of him as Elise tugged on his sleeve.

"Oh, look at the stuffed Dratch!" she said, pointing a finger up to the top of the booth where a plush dog with smoke coming from its mouth sat.

"You want it?" Atha asked with added vigor as Elise nodded. The pins sprang to life, growing wings and flying about as Atha grasped a ball. *Okay, they're not actually moving all that fast. This should be pretty easy.* He threw the first ball, smacking a pin square in the center. Its wings vanished and it fell to the ground, but the remaining ones sped up. He got the next three fairly easily as well, but the last two flew through the air with incredible speed. *Fuck it, time to cheat.* Agro energy pulsed through Atha's head, and time slowed down as he knocked another down. The last pin went ballistic, but Atha still had the edge, hurling the last ball at it, surely catching at least its edge. But it didn't fall.

"Sorry kid, not this time." The chubby Denata smiled, pulling his book back up.

"Gimme another seven," Atha growled, plunking another coin on the counter. The Denata sighed but reached a red hand over to accept it.

The pins sprung to life again, and Atha easily dispatched of all but the last one. Atha payed close attention to it. He used Agro energy to slow time down, and he clearly saw the last ball catch the pin's top. Yet it passed by without a trace of a hit. *It's rigged. This motherfucker.*

"Oh, so close!" Elise groaned.

"I feel sorry for the lady having to watch you lose twice. Best to cut your losses and move on if you ask me," the Denata taunted him, running a hand across his spiked head, but another coin fell in front of him.

"Well, funny thing, nobody asked you. Run it again."

"Really, Atty, it's not that big of a deal. Come on, let's wander some more." Elise smiled sheepishly as the Denata paused to glance at him.

"Run. It. Again," Atha rumbled, and the pins sprang to life. Red energy pulsed through his arm. The first ball smashed the pin to pieces, slamming so hard into the back of the booth it left a crack in the wall.

"Hey, what the—" the vendor cried, but Atha paid no mind, continuing to destroy the pins as Elise stared in surprise. The last pin remained, and Agro energy pulsed through Atha's mind, sending the ball straight through the entirety of the pin as it continued to bobble in the air. The ball continued so hard it finished off the booth's back wall, sending fragments of it falling back onto the ground as Atha sneered at the vendor.

"You—you cheater!" cried the Denata. "I don't know why the contract sensor didn't go off, but you were clearly using one!" The crowd's attention was now firmly on them as Elise flung her head around in dismay.

"The pot shouldn't call the kettle black. Think you can sit there and rob me?" Atha yelled back, reaching up and ripping the stuffed toy down before extending his hand. "Give me two coins back."

"Leave it," Elise ordered. "It's pocket change! Come on, we—"

"No! He's been laughing in my face over a rigged game! I'll pay for the toy, but I want the money for the game back!" Atha yelled, slamming a fist down onto the booth's counter as the Denata reared back in distress.

"Stop it! Come on!" Elise groaned, yanking him away.

"This isn't over! I'll remember your face!" Atha screamed as he was pulled away, sticking his finger out like a declaration of war. Elise pulled him through the staring crowd and into its oblivious mass. They made their way to a series of tables spread in between carts of food. "I'm sorry, Elly, I didn't mean to blow up like that. I just, I don't know. I get so mad sometimes."

Elise found an empty table and sat down. Atha quietly followed, fearfully anticipating the scolding to come, but Elise began to laugh, growing in vibrancy as he blinked.

"That's not the reaction I was expecting. I really am sorry I flipped out like that," Atha assured her sheepishly.

"Did you see the look on his face? I thought he'd have a heart attack when you threw that ball and cracked his booth's wall!" She slapped her leg as Atha began to laugh.

"He did look pretty horrified, but I think it got worse when I asked for the money back," he added as she banged her hand into the table.

"Yes! After the way he was thumbing his nose at you and then it was like a downward spiral!" she replied, pulling up her stuffed animal. "And thank you for this. It's absolutely adorable."

"You don't have to lie to me. I know you can have whatever you want."

Elise frowned at this, setting the stuffed animal on the table.

"Not everything has its worth decided by the price tag hanging from it. To me, this sparkling rock, this stuffed animal—I have no other possessions that I would secure before either one if I had to leave in an emergency. These are irreplaceable relics I will cherish for the rest of my life."

Atha hid a smile.

"It's really not that serious, Elly. You want to hold the table while I get us something to eat?" he replied, getting to his feet and glancing around at the selection. *Those kids should have been right around here somewhere.* His eyes scanned the surrounding area. Back in an alleyway, he noticed the young Denata child he'd seen earlier. *There's one. I bet Tella is ducked off in the alleyway.*

"Oh, go get some of the jemboly steaks! Here, take a few coins." She pulled out her purse as he reached behind her ear and pulled back a coin.

"Oh, look at that! I already have one!" he replied as she stared in disbelief.

"When did you get that?" She chuckled as he held an open hand out in front of her, another coin dropping from thin air into it.

"Anything I can think of." He winked.

"Oh, who's abusing power now, eh?" Elise smirked as Atha winked again and headed for the nearest food stand.

He bought the first thing he thought he recognized and returned with massive portions of sizzling steak that glittered with seasoning along with sauce, some drinks, and two extra plates.

"Here, I got some meat dish and a few drinks. I didn't know what was good, so I got a variety," he announced, setting everything down.

"And as for this dinosaur carcass…" he continued, pulling up one of the monstrous steaks with a knife and slicing it into thirds. He slid the extra cuts onto plates with additional knives, stood up, and headed back into an alleyway.

"Where are you going?" Elise called after him, but her question was answered when two tiny Denata children popped out from the shadows near Atha.

"Figured the pair of you would still be here. Little Miss Tella, and I didn't get your name yet, kiddo." Atha gave plates of steak to the children, who gratefully accepted them.

"My name's Janster. Thank you for helping me earlier," the boy whispered, setting his little sister down first and cutting her steak up into small bites.

"My name's Atha, which isn't as cool as *Janster,* but I make due," said Atha, handing a pair of drinks down to them. They ate for a few moments as he watched, finally bringing up the topic he'd come to discuss. "So, what are you guys doing out here? Are you homeless?"

Janster paused, setting his plate down before turning up to Atha. "We are. We were in an adoption home, but they wanted to split us up, so I took Tella and we ran."

"Refused to leave your sister behind?" he asked.

"She's all I got. Wish I had just let it happen, though, putting her through all this…" Janster huffed, his tiny black eyes glossing over as Atha reached a hand down.

"You did what you thought was best. You're not in this alone anymore. We're gonna figure this out together," Atha replied as he felt a hand rubbing across his back.

"Remind you of anybody?" Elise whispered to him.

"Nah. He's got way more backbone than I ever did when I was his age. I need to say something to you about them real quick." Atha sighed, pulling Elise back. "One of the guards tried to cut his arm off for lifting a few coins off of Zell." A shiver ran down his back as anger flowed into her eyes.

"Who?"

"One was named Barka—he was the one who actually tried to attack Janster. His partner's name was Telcatta, and he came after me when I clocked Barka. Is that considered acceptable here?"

Elise replied with a sinister tone. "When I first came here, there was hardly a thing that was considered unacceptable, but I'm doing my best to spur reform. I assure you, these guards' actions against children will not go unanswered. They will be made an example of."

"Well, that solves one problem. But what do we do about them? They don't have a home and I'm not leaving them out here."

Elise reeled back. "Homeless? No, my single shining movement was abolishing homelessness in the capital. Remember how I told you I donated a pair of my towers? One of them is dedicated wholly to providing boarding for the needy until they can afford their own. The bottom portion is reserved for children and doubles as an adoption center."

"What? Elly, that's—that's awesome! God, I always imagined myself doing stuff like that if I ever became like president or rich or something."

"Aren't you already? You put yourself at risk to defend children. That was heroic," she replied warmly.

"Doing the right thing isn't heroic. I'm just trying to be who we needed when we were kids."

Elise's cheer faltered at this. Atha could feel her reading his expression, gauging the underlying pain that still twisted his mind despite all the years that had passed, and leaned in to whisper the one thing that had ever really made him feel better about it.

"You always have been." Before turning and pressing a finger against the lobe of her ear, speaking next to seemingly nobody. "You caught all the information about the situation with the children, Deldora? Good. No, I'm going to move farther into the alleyway, so you can pick them up. No, tell the treasurer it will have to wait until tomorrow. She said— okay, all right, tell her to just give me a few minutes." Elise sighed, rubbing her temples for a few moments.

"Everything good?"

"There is business I must attend to. I'm so sorry. I promise I'll be as quick as possible. Let's get the kids to the guards. I'll be off for a bit, but you should stay and explore some more." Elise smiled as Atha nodded, a camera falling into his hands.

"Okay, but just in case you can't come back, let's get a picture. Hold your stuffed animal up!" He laughed, pulling her to his shoulder before lofting the camera up in front of them and snapping a picture. "Oh yeah, that's a keeper. God, we look so grown up." Atha turned the camera screen to Elise.

"Oh, I look terrible, but I really need to hurry. Let's—"

"Well, here, you take one then." Atha smirked, pushing the camera into her arms before she could argue.

"Fine, one more. Look, the key is to get a good angle, so you hold it up above your head and look up to it and—" She snapped another picture as Atha twisted his face into a mess. "And voila—oh, you jerk!" Elise gasped, only noticing his deranged expression as she eyed the photos. She shoved the camera into his hands, hurrying forward to usher the two kids back into the alley and away from the crowd.

"What are you gonna do with them? You can't separate them," Atha whispered to her. She glanced back at him, looking insulted.

"You think I could separate such an adorable pair? I will personally oversee their adoption." Black-cloaked guards descended from the roof in front of them. Janster's eyes flipped back to Atha in panic.

"What are you going to do with us?!" he gasped, but Atha knelt in front of him before the guards could approach.

"I told you, kiddo, I got your back. Don't worry, I'm going to keep an eye on the adoption process and make sure you get a home that deserves you. Both of you, that is." He could see his words taking effect as Janster untensed.

"It's Janster, right? Come on, we're going to get you and Tella situated for the night," the guard beamed down to him, but Janster pushed forward to hug Atha's leg.

"Thank you for seeing us Atha," His voice was small and frail, yet Atha sensed a certain flair of greatness within it. Atha reached a hand down and patted the child's back before Janster fell back in with the guards and he and his sister were lifted into the air atop a green fog.

"I'll be back in no more than an hour, so find us something fun to do before I get back!" Elise called down to Atha as everybody but him was pulled up into the sky. Atha waited until they were out of sight before a grin pulled across his face.

This is it. I'm free, I'm making a difference. I'm earning what Len gave me when. Atha's thought halted as cold sweat dotted his forehead. Bloodlust gusted over him like a cold wind from behind. He flipped around and, despite the distance, instantly recognized the figure heading down the empty alley. Harmer.

Chapter 12

Something Wicked This Way Comes

He turned his eyes to the ground, heart speeding away like a runaway train, but he forced himself to rationalize the situation. *Calm down and think. He can't recognize you,* Atha assured himself, feeling Harmer's gaze burning side of his face like napalm.

"Move and you die. Utter a single word or use an ability and you die," Harmer called to him playfully as Atha's body froze in place.

Fuck! How does he know?

A pair of figures fell in tow behind Harmer, and Atha's sharpening senses detected a single person's footsteps behind him.

"Drop all the items in your hands and move your back up against the wall," Harmer instructed. Atha did, his camera clattering to the ground as he moved ever so slowly up against the wall. A young blonde—probably around Elise's age—dressed in a short, flowery dress stepped alongside Harmer. She wore a wrathful look on her face as she glanced at Atha.

"What are we wasting time for? We're done here," she groaned.

"Now, Jun." An enormous Denata with huge black horns protruding from his head striding at Harmer's opposite side cut in. "Let Harmer talk to his friend in peace. This success is thanks to him, so he deserves that much."

"Shut up, Zenta," she spat. "This is who you spoke so highly of to the boss? Looks pathetic to me."

Harmer continued to smile.

"Looks can be deceiving, Jun. Even if he caught me off guard, he still managed to take a few fingers off." He chuckled, flashing his now fully intact hand up.

"Just take care of your business, Harm, and stop riling her up," Zenta cut in again as a woman with short black hair pushed by, a scythe taller than she was lashed across her back.

"This is him? Stop fidgeting, child, let me get a look in your eyes," she instructed with a toneless voice, her eyes empty like dark pits. "Yes, he's got darkness and hate within him. Emphasis on the hate. Almost exactly like yours, Jun." She glanced back to the blonde who's face twisted with disgust.

"What—" Atha started, but with a flash the woman ripped loose her scythe and pressed the double-bladed metal against his neck.

"Nobody told you to talk," she said plainly. Harmer sighed and eased forward.

"I've already got dibs on him. Back off, Reap."

She pulled back, twirling her scythe for a moment before returning it to her back.

"Sorry, Harm. He's all yours," she replied as he stepped in front. Killing intent practically suffocated Atha as their eyes met.

"Fun bunch, aren't they?" Harm chuckled. Atha remained silent even as the bloodlust receded. "Thanks, Reapora. He won't even talk now," Harmer groaned back to the short woman.

Jun cut in. "Not her fault he's a little bitch. Locked up the second he saw you."

"Don't worry, the loudmouth blond is rather unruly in general," said Harm. "I just wanted to stop you and say I know the origins of your *contract-less* ability. Unfortunately, that news comes with the fact it could directly impact our mission if I told you, so we'll have to hold that thought for now. But, oh, is it big. Better than even I had thought. It's gonna cost you. Tell me, what exactly is your connection to the Queen? She holds you very dear to her heart." Harmer's smile darkened as Atha's anger flared.

"Leave it be, Harm," Zenta interrupted again. "You know better."

Giuseppe had extensively drilled Atha on how to proceed if he was captured by hostile forces. Step one was to throw your captors off, saying or doing something unpredictable, and in that moment of chaos find an avenue for escape. Harmer had set Atha up perfectly for this.

"We grew up in a different world together. We got separated over a decade ago and she summoned me here," Atha announced casually, awaiting the looks of shock and disbelief.

"Is that true, Reapora?" Harmer asked.

"It is." The short woman nodded. "We had suspected as much from the way she vanished without a trace. He would have been in the womb at that point, so it makes sense."

Atha's mouth fell open. His plan not only fell completely flat, he'd actually recoiled a bit from how easily they accepted this major reveal.

"Now that is interesting. So other worlds do exist. I fear I have attained more information than I intended and see that I've left myself in debt to you now. How can I even the scale?" Harmer asked, holding his chin in thought for a moment before snapping his fingers. "Ah, I know. Ask me a question. I'll answer anything except something pertaining to our mission." Jun snapped her fingers at Harm's words and lifted her slender arm and bashed it back into the wall, producing a huge crack.

"You're really pissing me off, Harmer. We didn't come here so you could play your fucking mind games," she sneered. Atha froze as Harmer's murderous rage flowed out.

"You're starting to try my patience, little girl."

"Oh, well, excuse the fuck out of me. I'm downright terrified. No, sorry, that was a lie. I will fuck you up, Harmer. Give me a reason," Jun said leering back at him. Zenta stepped in between the two.

"Jun, Harmer is the highest-ranking member—meaning he's in charge right now—so respect the chain of command. Harmer, stop letting her get to—"

"How did you know who I was?" Atha cut in, seeing another chance to surprise them as Harmer turned back to him. The revelation of different worlds was definitely his prime chance, but Atha had even more vigorously learned to improvise, adapt, and overcome.

"What do you mean by that?" Harmer replied as Atha lifted his hand and flashed the ring.

"This thing has anti-recognition magic imbedded in it, but you knew who I was right away. How did you know?"

Harmer's smile returned. "That's a very good question, and you'll gain valuable intel from it. My contract has the ability to shut off other contracts and items utilizing their abilities within a certain radius of it." *So that's why he was so surprised when I blew his fingers off. He thought I was using a contract and thought he could shut it off.* "It's like an invisible field around me that I can stretch and manipulate at will. It also actively keeps factors like anti-recognition from affecting me, even from a distance.

"I noticed you about thirteen minutes ago and I just trailed you and waited to catch you alone. I also notice you use translation magic like a few of the Chameleons do, so I have it deactivated for stuff like that. It has a few more aces, but I think that's about enough to return our balance to nil. We'll see you soon, Atha," Harmer finished, turning away and heading back down the alley as Reapora followed. Jun remained and Zenta kept an eye on her, speaking up as she began stepping toward Atha.

"Jun—"

"Shut up, Zenta," she growled over him, raising an arm and pushing Atha up against the wall as Harmer flipped back around.

She smiled at Harmer for a few moments before turning back to Atha, applying more pressure to his chest as her piercing green pupils met his. She moved her head up slowly toward his and planted a long kiss, running a hand through his brown hair. "That's for taking his fingers off. He squealed like a stuck pig when I reattached them. Bonus points for being decently cute." She winked at him and pulled her arm back as

Harmer twitched with rage. The tentacles atop his head lashed violently about. "Call me up in a few years. Harmer is a two-hundred-pound bag of blue shit, but he can spot potential with uncanny accuracy, and I'd be interested in working out some *anger* in more than a *few* ways," she said, whipping her blond locks across Harmer's face as she passed. His blue face panged with streaks of red and his eyes twitched. Zenta laughed and stayed beside Atha as Harmer stormed off with Reapora following behind.

"Jun acts crude, but is actually a very nice young lady. She's at her worst around Harmer. They have a bit of a past, so don't hold this against her." He chuckled but Atha remained silent. Zenta pulled a red button from his pocket, clicked it, and a small blue portal opened beside his head. "Hey, Blair, I need a curse of silence. Yeah, the one Harmer mentioned. Can you do it? Good, yeah, he's right here."

Black gas oozed out of the portal and shot toward Atha. He screamed and leapt back as it entered his throat. The reverberating echo of croaking frogs paired with a squeaky voice bouncing through his head.

"Hello, brother," the voice croaked. "It saddens me that this is our first encounter, but it pleases me nonetheless. From this point forward, if you share any information regarding a past encounter with any member of the Chameleons, your heart will explode. This goes for accidental or even unknowingly sharing with a mind reading contract, so do take care. I will be watching and will know instantly if this comes to pass. We will speak again soon."

Zenta strode past Atha, pausing for a moment to glance back at him.

"How's Zell doing?" he asked.

"You best stay away from her," Atha replied as Zenta smirked.

"Calm down. My words aimed to strike no threat. She's stronger than me, anyways. Nonetheless, keep an eye on her, would you? She's been through a lot." The massive Denata finished speaking before heading down the alley and into the crowd after his comrades.

What in the mother fuck just happened? Atha wondered as he slunk down the wall down to the ground. *Those people are monsters. The vibes I got from them were worse than anything I ever felt in prison.* He grasping his camera and eyed over the picture he'd just taken with Elise. *Why can't I ever just have fun? Why do I always attract these situations? I can't even tell them there are Chameleons here. They're probably still hanging around this area. I'm going to have to blow our cover to get her out of here,* Atha thought to himself, boiling with anger. He jumped up and swung the camera into the wall, shattering it before pulling the memory card out.

He stepped back into the packed street, found an empty bench, and sat to wait for Elise to return as the crowd swirled around him.

She had said that she would return in no more than an hour, but that mark came and went. Atha hardly noticed. He was good at letting time slip by after all the practice he'd had. Another two hours passed. The crowd had lost its younger members, as it was mostly just adults now enjoying the festivities. Finally, Elise came dashing out of the alley.

"I am so, so sorry, Atty. We had an emergency and I swear I absolutely had no choice but to see it through," she said, stepping in front of him and straightening out her short green dress as she caught her breath.

Here goes nothing. Atha sighed and looked up to meet her eyes.

"It's fine, Elise," he replied, and suddenly every set of eyes flocked to her with absolute shock. She just blinked, unsure of her own ears.

The crowd exploded and clamored, but before anyone could react, the guards shot down and surrounding her. They restrained the festivalgoers until a green fog pulled the guards and her into the air. Nobody paid Atha any mind, and he continued to sit on the bench, watching sadly as the festival crowd continued to follow beneath the fog. *God, she looked so betrayed.* Atha buried his face in his hands for moments that felt longer than the hours he'd waited.

The walk back to the tower was long too. He replayed the incident with the Chameleons over in his head. His meteorite danced in his fingers as he walked, mostly to calm him down and sharpen his mind as he contemplated his next move.

What do I do now? If they ask me about my run in with Harmer, I won't be able to answer. Even if I feign ignorance, they may try to check my memory with an ability like Zell's, and then I'm dead. Well, really, with so many unknown factors about this world, trying to figure out a plan is impossible. There are too many variables. If they try to question me, I can try to explain my situation, but even that's grey area. Zell would know what to do, but I can't risk bringing her in on this either because she's likely to catch on. Fuck it.

Atha stuffed the rock back into his pocket and came to a complete stop in the middle of the empty part of town. A large stretch of open sky above him displayed the glimmering moons and stars. A pair of eyes shimmering, maybe glowing, in the moonlight met Atha's. A massive winged figure rested lazily atop a roof. *Is that a griffin?* Atha thought.

"We meet again," a familiar and commanding voice called through his mind. Massive wings stretched out as it stood and gracefully glided down to the walk before him.

"Shun! Hey, what's up?" Atha replied in cheerful surprise. "What're you doing here? Get the day off for the festival?"

"No, after learning of the cowardly human's treacherous scheme to lose a passenger so that he might flee, I resigned. I feel shame at the simple fact I ever breathed the same air as he."

"For real, what a piece of shit. The way he burst at the idea of Zell jumping out to stall the Red Sheep makes me sick," Atha replied.

"Aye! Well said, little man. Had I known of the rising plot, I fear I would have thrown the knave down in her place. I took great pleasure in learning of you standing firmly against it." Shun

Atha puffed out his chest.

"I'm not the type to sit back and watch an asshole have his way. Sorry, I gotta keep moving," Atha replied and continued forward. Shun was massive, but he moved with an eerie silence beside Atha.

"Aye, after the good Queen," Shun said. "Seek me out upon a time, then. There is much I would tell you of your mother."

"You knew my mom?" Atha replied, briefly halting his steps.

"Queen Elise has not yet broached the subject with you?"

"No, but that's my fault. We chatted for a bit, but I begged her to take me to the festival since the conversation was getting pretty sad. I'm not good at dealing with mixed emotions and even less with sadness. I'm more of a—I don't know—either I'm up or down, you know?" Atha replied as Shun's telepathic voice snickered.

"Aye, yet another characteristic mirroring the image of Desmona. I would greedily seek to steal an opportunity to tell you of the great woman myself, since it has yet to be reflected upon." Shun stepped along beside him but paused, noticing Atha's face darkening with anger. "Does something trouble you?"

"I don't want to piss you off," Atha replied, but Shun's head lowered down to his own.

"You speak with a friend. Let your words be heard and accepted no matter the weight they carry."

"All right. I don't give a shit about my biological mom or dad. My real dad's name is Lenny Honorati,, and even if he wasn't actually my father, I still don't want anything to do with some people who shipped me and Elise off to Earth with *Dako Luminar*."

"Dako? What is your quarrel with him?" Shun replied as Atha scoffed.

"You knew him, too? Then you should know he's the scum."

"I don't understand. The Dako I knew was a good man. Like anyone else, he had his flaws, but nonetheless his heart was true."

"The hell he was! That motherfucker beat the *shit* out of us every day. Things got really crazy one night and I shot him in the head. That's why Elise came back early—she almost died when he crushed her throat!"

Shun's eyes widened. "His death was a known fact to me, but of this I was unaware. I'm not even sure what to make of this, to think he would commit such atrocities."

"That's why I don't care about my 'real' parents. They died before I was old enough to know them, but I'll never want to," Atha replied. Shun fell silent for a few moments.

"Aye, you will hear nothing of them from me, then. To say we were as family would be an understatement, your mother having undergone the ritual of partnership between a griffin and rider with me, but I do not wish to push you away. The past should stay buried with all its failures and glories to protect the future."

"Griffin and rider? You two worked together?"

"Aye, to put it in the most basic of ways. A pact between a griffin and a rider is holy. It is a union formed in a similar manner to a contract. It connects the senses and heightens combative abilities beyond what a pair of unpartnered warriors could ever dream of. She and I were partnered until death, as is customary."

"Learn something new every day, or in my case, like, at least eight mind-blowing things. You know, I don't want to hear about them, but it sure would be cool to hear about you." Atha smiled, slowing his pace.

"Shouldn't you make haste?"

"Yeah, but I need some time to figure out what I'm gonna say to her. I really jacked things up." Atha sighed, rubbing a hand over his weary eyes.

"Hmm. I suppose I can entertain you for a few moments, but this will be but a glance into the past. I dare not ramble on and lower my guard with such a yearning for blood upon the air tonight." Shun ruffled his feathers, adjusting his mighty wings to sit on the ground.

He must be talking about Harmer. Probably seen a lot of bad shit in his time to be able to sense it.

"I was born in a land far to the east of here in an unnamed and unkept region full of lawlessness. Despite my upbringing, I craved order and power, so I took out a mighty contract that allows me to manifest, manipulate, and disperse high volumes of gold." Gold flakes appeared from the air around him and swirled around Atha for a few moments before vanishing.

"Whoaaaa! Holy shit, you're like King Midas except better! Or—or the golden goose except cool! *My god*, the things you'd do to the stock market on Earth!"

"None of those references are known to me."

"Oh—uh, yeah, never mind. Keep going!" Atha urged, leaning onto the edge of his seat in anticipation.

"Now I had power, but still sought order. I traveled here, to the kingdom of Luxria, and joined the Royal Guard. Now, don't misunderstand, the guard of today is a force to be reckoned with, but during my era..." Shun paused. He had no mouth to smile with but Atha could tell he was. "It wouldn't be an overstatement to call it the *golden* era of this proud and storied kingdom, but I don't wish to take all the credit."

"Oh, I see what you did there! Double entendre, I can dig it!" Atha laughed.

"Aye, just as eloquent with words as you are formidable on the battle field. The gods must feel foolish for crafting a being so short on flaws." *And a hell of an ego to go along with them.* "Not long after I arrived did

191

I begin searching for candidates to partner with. Alas, it was no close call, as it was as if your mother and I were originally purposed to be parts of a whole yet born apart. Individually, we were already at the pinnacle of combative forces in a land that was at the pinnacle of the world, but together we were gods."

Shun continued, staring up toward the stars, "The few flaws I bore she not only mended, but so appropriately reversed that they became yet more strength. None dared challenge us. The only obstruction in any sky we flew in were the mountains of medals and accolades amassed through our glories! They grew so numerous that they began to obscure our view and damper our senses. That's when the Chameleons came."

Shun paused again, this time for nearly a minute until his head lowered back to meet his piercing eyes with Atha's.

"We'd mistaken strength with invincibility, and this they exploited. During just their first attack, they annihilated half the royal family and the entirety of our pride. On their next, just a single member of the royal family survived, Queen Elise. The chain of command was all but annihilated and at this point many considered all to be lost, but not me and not Desmona. In our darkest hour we found a contract user who held what is regarded as the highest tier of transportation contracts, a doorway to different dimensions, and through it went your mother carrying you, Elise, and a powerful Royal Guardsman.

"This was the closest to victory we could hope for, yet it left both sides feeling defeated and seeking resolution. As the closest thing remaining to leadership, I led the final assault against the Chameleons and, despite all the horrors we'd seen, the worst had yet to come. It took the deaths of seven Chameleons and innumerable guards for the war to end, and it only did when both their leader and your blood-father perished. The Chameleons took everything from me, including a glorious death, and now here I sit before you, a weary old griffin with nothing left but stories of failure."

Even Atha's boisterous attitude sobered in the silence.

"Even the Chameleons paled in comparison to the greatest foe we faced. Hubris. You need not remember me when my time comes, but do not ever forget the weight of this word that brought a kingdom to its knees."

"You're wrong, you know," Atha finally replied as Shun tensed up. "I'm here because of you. More importantly, Elise is here too. We owe you everything. By process of the domino effect, I think it's safe to say the whole kingdom is only what is now because of you!"

"Do *not* think you can counsel me. I share tales to sever the repeating cycle, not for attention, and certainly not for pity," Shun's commanding voice growled.

"Damn, chill out. I'll keep my opinion to myself next time," Atha grumbled irritably as Shun sighed.

"Apologies. The mood has put me on edge this night. Had your mother been present she would have seen it canceled out with playful banter. Alas, the scale is permanently left uneven."

"Hey, hold on a sec. Can I ask you a question, Uncle Shun?" Atha asked, Shun cocking an eye down at him.

"Uncle?"

"Yeah, you said y'all were like family, right? That makes me your nephew! Sucks I didn't get a big-ass set of wings to go with it, 'cause that's kind of what I need to ask you." Atha's feet halted, and he pointed up at Elise's tower. "I got left behind. Can you fly me up?"

"Oh, did a squabble cause the good Queen to abandon the little man?" Shun chuckled.

"Okay, look, I'm five feet seven so I don't know where you're getting this 'little' thing from. At any rate, I have the same feeling you do. Bloodlust is in the air, so I blew our reunion because I was getting worried. Now come on, let me get a lift!"

Shun shook his head.

"A griffin to allow an unpartnered rider is sacrilege. But…" Shun paused, a sly look in his eye as he raised a clawed front leg at Atha. "Even a human with a little man complex is worthy of talons."

"Oh yeah, that sounds safe. Let me just fly through the air held safely in the claws of a degrading griffin," he scoffed, reaching for a button on his shoe. "I'll just walk my happy ass up, then. Thought it would be cool to fly but—" Atha's words where halted as Shun burst forward, snatching him up in his talons and rocketing up into the air.

Atha screamed, surprised and afraid, the ground quickly fleeting as they rose with insane speed. "Jesus! Santa! God!"

Shun almost instantly reached the tower's peak, the side popping down to allow Atha entry as they hovered a long distance away.

"So, you wish you had wings?" Shun asked playfully.

"Don't you—" Atha started as the massive hind legs pulled back like a catapult latching into position. Shun thrusted Atha's body airborne toward the entrance, the ground below receding further into the distance. "Dareeeeeee!" he finished as he came to a sliding halt across the slick floor of the plant filled entrance room.

"It was a pleasure to meet you officially, Atha. Watch over the good Queen in my stead," Shun said to him as he turned to fly off. Atha scrambled to his feet and ran back to the entrance.

"Wait! I still had another question!" he yelled. Shun paused in the air and flipped back. "Come work with me! I'm gonna build a team and could use your help, Uncle!" Atha yelled to him. Even without being able to see his eyes, Atha could sense the sadness that filled them.

"My time has passed. Aye, it is your generation's turn to carry the burdens to come. However, should you find yourself in a troubling time, you need only make it known to me and I will be there. Farewell," Shun finished, his image fleeting into the night as Atha smiled.

"Fuck. He's cool as hell."

Atha sensed fast, heavy steps behind him and turned to narrowly dodge a fist. He grasped the arm is was attached to and twisted it behind the back of the body of his attacker. The lead guard from the festival outing, the Denata Captain, glared painfully at him. "Better watch it. My first instinct was to smash your teeth in like your buddy's," Atha sneered at him. Dimitri burst forward to force himself in between the squabbling two.

"Have you lost sense, Deldora? Stand down," Dimitri instructed. Deldora straightened his black uniform as he stared Atha down.

"Better do as your boss says before I wipe that look off your face," Atha taunted. The guard burst forward and reached an arm over Dimitri, who forced him back again.

"What is wrong with you? Saying the Queen's name added pointless danger to a simple operation! If she had been injured it would have been on you, boy!" he screamed and Atha's sneer morphed into full-on anger.

Atha paused, feeling his anger starting to take the wheel. Instead, he took a long breath and muttering back, "Don't ever call me boy."

"Explain yourself!" Deldora roared as Dimitri pulled him away.

"You're a fucking captain, right? Sure took you a long couple of seconds to swoop in and snatch her up! I don't feel confident knowing a loser like you is watching over my sister!" Atha yelled back, not meaning a word of it, but his sense was now fully replaced by anger. Deldora was livid too. Even Dimitri glanced back in surprise at the harsh words.

"Find out for yourself just how capable I am! Let me duel him, Admiral. You know he deserves—"

"Enough! Both of you!" Dimitri screamed over him. Atha roared with mocking laughter.

"You wanna fight?" he asked, red energy pulsated over him as he slammed a foot into the floor. "Bring it, then! Let him go, Dimitri!"

Deldora's face lit up at the challenge.

"He accepted! Please, Admiral, let me teach the brat a lesson!"

"Please reconsider," Dimitri whispered to Atha. "I don't think you fully understand what a duel consists of."

Zell had been watching and rushed over to the pair.

"Cease this senseless argument, Atha! You would see time wasted when it could be spent alongside family?" she cut in, but Deldora's smile taunted him from across the peacemakers, fanning the already erupting flames.

"No! Who knows if she'll even be here next time with a scumbag like this hanging around!"

Zell snatched the front of his black-and-purple robes.

"You go too far!" she growled, but Dimitri rested a hand on her shoulder.

"Let's allow the children their scuffle. Perhaps they will knock some sense into each other," he said and released his hand from Zell's shoulder. Dimitri pulled a small white cube from his pocket. Deldora placed his hand on it and vanished.

"Uh...what?" Atha asked as Dimitri lifted it toward him.

"It will send you into a sparring area where a deathblow is impossible. When there is a victor, it will send you back here. Be warned, injury is still entirely possible."

Dimitri glanced back to Zell.

"I can win, right?" he asked.

"He stands a captain of the Royal Guard. To be victorious would be to overturn unfavorable and unprecedented odds," she replied as Atha rolled his eyes. "This is but the fate you have sewn with rash actions and ignorant words. Reap it."

"Whatever," Atha spat back. "Where I come from, a duel is life and death. But hey, thanks for the vote of confidence."

"Would you have me give false tongue and leave you unaware?" she replied, but he ignored her and placed his hand on the cube. An empty world of white surrounded him. Dimitri, Zell, and a small gathering of guards appeared overhead, resting in a clear room that hovered high above.

"The price of your insults will be a high one. Ready to pay the toll?" Deldora smiled at him from a short distance away.

"Oh, wow that was original! Hope you're ready for the *unemployment* line after I kick your ass. Or the *morgue* depending on if this place is really as up to snuff as your boss man thinks it is." Atha's smirk was met by a burst of laughter from Deldora. What appeared to be red wax oozed out of his hands, covering his black robes. An AK-47 fell into Atha's hands.

"Begin—" Dimitri started, but Atha had already lofted the weapon up, squeezing the trigger as a blast of fire and lead ripped across the Denata. Blood covered the white ground behind Deldora as he flew backwards, crashing down hard as Atha paused.

"Oh fuck. Did I really kill him?" He glanced up to Zell who jabbed a finger toward his opponent. Blood oozed across the ground like scarlet snakes, reentering the wounds as the destroyed flesh mended itself. Deldora sighed and returned to his feet, the red wax thickening and tightening down like scarlet armor overtop his green uniform.

"That actually wasn't half bad. You use an interesting weapon," he said from his crouch. Red wax exploded beneath his feet, shooting him forward as Atha lurched back. Red Agro energy glowed from him as he raised his arms, protecting his chest as Deldora smashed a fist into Atha's AK, completely shattering it. Atha left his feet, but Deldora caught a foot and slammed him onto his back before pressing a forearm into his neck. "Had you gone for the head or heart you might have won. Get ready to learn your place." He smirked as Atha, filled with rage, twisted his legs up and wrapped them around Deldora's neck and flipped him onto his back. Agro energy covered his arms and he began to hammer at Deldora's face, the wax absorbing blow after blow until a kick sent him flying back.

All right, this guy really is no joke. I'd be dead if it wasn't for Agro energy and it's gonna run out in a few minutes. Time to kick it up a notch. A grenade fell into his hand and he hurled it toward the Denata. A massive explosion ensued as Atha covered his face and ears.

"Just what manner of power does the child have?" Dimitri asked, turning to Zell.

Okay, that had to have put him down. Please, please be down, Atha thought, the smoke slowly dispersing. He released an exasperated sigh at the sight of a red face now darkened by soot.

"All right kid, I admit it. You're a theat. But I think it's time to put an end to this."

"Holy shit, you're like the Terminator! With overused one-liners too!"

"I don't know who the Terminator is," Deldora scoffed.

"Yeah, that makes sense."

"Let me tell you a few things I *do know*. My contract is known as Masochist's Dilemma and it works by reversing damage taken to my body and storing it as energy that can be returned to the dealer. For half of the stored amount, it can be dealt to another target—"

Atha yelled over him. "Shut up! You think I need a handicap?"

"No, exactly the opposite, so let me finish. One of its aces is that its power quadruples when the target knows the details of the ability. When stated out loud, Masochist's Dilemma switches from defensive to offensive mode."

The red wax covering his body reshaped, forming artificial muscles over his legs and two long blades from either arm. He crouched down, the muscles tensing before erupting forward, reaching a blade for Atha's face.

Atha screamed, flinching as it neared, and fell back into a table holding potted plants that went crashing down with him. "Dammit," he mumbled as the rest of the viewing party appeared in the open spaces around him.

"Atha, that was extraordinary!" Zell was pulling him back to his feet.

"How? I lost," he replied, feeling disheartened as she gripped his shoulders.

"You gave a captain of the guard a legitimate scare! For a moment I thought you might actually *win!*" Zell patted his cheek and, despite his best efforts, he felt a smile forcing itself onto his face. It was short lived, falling back into a grimace as Deldora stepped before him. Atha couldn't even rationalize to himself what was fueling this anger; it was almost as if it didn't even belong to him.

"It is as she said. That was a fine match," he announced, raising a hand to shake Atha's, who raised his own, balling it into a fist at the last moment and smashing Deldora's face.

"Yeah, how you like your own medicine?" he screamed at the stumbling Denata. Dimitri groaned and stepped in between them again.

"No, I deserved that," said Deldora. "We both showed the worst of ourselves this day." He sighed, stepping past Dimitri and re-extending his hand. Atha stared in shock for a moment, his anger beginning to dissipate as he grasped it.

"Whatever, dude. I still don't like you," Atha replied as Deldora leaned in.

"Well, do not think I have forgotten your ignorant comments. What say we settle this officially at the Combat Contract Tournament?" he asked, his hand tensing down on Atha's, whose own glowed red.

"You're on. Oh, by the way, I've never practiced with my ability before. Don't pat yourself on the back for defeating a newborn." Atha smirked, crushing the hand a bit before turning toward Elise's door. Zell followed behind, coming to his side before he could make it to the door.

"I have come to a decision pertaining to your proposition," she announced. Atha came to an immediate stop and faced her, already fearing the answer.

"And?"

"I agree to your proposal. Joining the Honorati family seems the best course of action at the current time."

"Really?" He blinked.

"Yes. This surprises you?"

"Well, yeah," he replied. "I'm not so stupid that I don't realize I'm a bit headstrong. Len always told me it was my biggest flaw."

"When wisdom speaks, it would be sagacious to listen. Luckily, you are young and still have time to see wisdom not just heard but embodied."

A smile creased Atha's face.

"Don't hold your breath. Welcome aboard, Z. You're the first ever half-human to join the family, so this is a historical moment! Since it's settled, I'd like to commemorate this moment by asking a favor."

Zell cocked an eyebrow. "Quite an original way to receive such news."

"I want you to train me until the contract tournament. I still don't know much about you, but it's obvious you're some big-time hero, somebody capable of being my Mr. Miyagi. Also, can you be the acting leader? Until you think I'm capable and knowledgeable enough to take the reins."

"The placement of your thoughts aligns with my own," she replied with a faulting smile. "But, Atha, I think it fair you know I am no hero." Pain eclipsed her the usual cheer on her face but he only chuckled.

"I knew tons of veterans in prison, sad to say. Got a few stories out of them over the years too. But you know what? Every time somebody called them a hero they denied it. Hell, I'd even say some of them took it as an insult."

"Atha... This is not a comparable situation."

"They all had that look on their face too." Like a horse broken of its spirit, Zell hung her head. "Maybe you'll tell me about it one day. I gotta go talk with Elise."

"Sort your business out, and we will reconvene in the morning." She patted him on the cheek before stepping away, vanishing behind the mountains of potted plants.

Atha headed for Elise's door, easing it open slowly to find the sight of her chatting at her desk into a multitude of hovering screens. She noticed his entrance and gestured for him to wait as she continued her conversation. He took a seat on her coach. It was almost an hour later when the screen closed and she sighed, moving to sit beside him.

"Sorry, that couldn't wait. Heard about the bad feeling you'd gotten during the festival. Why didn't you just say something?" Elise sighed as Atha turned to her.

"Look, let's just skip this part and get back to talking, okay?" Atha replied but paused as Elise's eyes became glassy with tears.

"Oh, come on, El." He sighed. A handkerchief popped into his hand to dry the tears before they could fall.

"I-I thought you had gotten upset with me. I know I took much longer than I said I would and worried about it the entire time I was gone, but Atha—"

"Okay, look let's just skip that part too okay? It didn't bother me one bit so go ahead and throw that thought right out." Elise whimpered for a few more moments but collected herself, chuckling sheepishly.

"I'm sorry, I haven't cried this much in years. Really, I'm sorry for leaving you sitting there. I'm always this busy, if not more so. Being

Queen is an honor and a privilege, but it is paired with personal sacrifices. I do appreciate your acceptance in this current situation, but what about the time after this? The next? It's an endless cycle." Elise sighed as Atha tossed the handkerchief into a trash bin.

"We'll worry about the future as it comes, okay? No point in stressing it now. Besides—" Atha lost his train of thought and glanced around the room.

Elise took instant notice in the sudden change in temperament. "Are you feeling all right?" she asked as Atha blinked a few times, regaining his sense.

"Yeah, sorry. I get a little tripped out every now and then."

"About?"

Atha took a moment to collect his thoughts. It wasn't easy putting the glorious word *freedom* into words for someone who hadn't shared his experience. "Everything. I mean, don't you think it's crazy how we can just walk around, and nobody tells you that you can't go somewhere or do something? Like, I could literally walk out the door right now and go *anywhere* I want to."

As he finished he noticed something unexpected on her face: understanding.

"It is a blessing. But on that note, there are a few questions I need to ask you," Elise said, her face hardening. "This contract-less power of yours is incredible, and there are those who would seek to take advantage of you because of it. Can you tell me all you know of it?"

"Len figured the same thing. I got it from—" Atha paused, beginning to mention the woman from the library but his words cut off as a zing shot through his body. He forgot where he was driving that sentence toward. "An unknown source."

"I...see. Well, what exactly do you know?" Elise replied as Atha cleared his throat and gave her the same information he'd given Zell, to which she stared at him, equally bewildered. "That's it?"

"Yeah. There are probably other rules, but like I said, Len was wary about getting crazy with it and kept the tests small. There's probably a max size limit and maybe a few more."

Elise shot to her feet and moved to her desk. She tapped on a red screen a few times until it began to flash. Zell's familiar voice eventually entered the room.

"Do you require something, ma'am?" Zell asked.

"Yes, I'd like to make use of your information contract. Can you procure an image of the sword Shooting Star?" she asked.

"Yes. Do you intend to use toward the purpose I suspect?" she asked as Elise glanced at Atha.

"I do. Please use the button beside your right hip to transfer the image to me," she replied. A moment later the red screen flashed, displaying the image of a chained sword. The hologram screen floated across the room to stop at Atha, who eyed it over. Its sheath was entirely white all the way up to the black handle, archaic hieroglyphics covering both portions that he suspected signified enhancements like on the towers and his shoes. Despite this, the most peculiar feature were the black chains that wrapped around it from top to bottom, leaving only the handle exposed.

"Thank you, Zell," Elise finished, and the line went dead. She stepped back to the couch.

"This sword is wicked! You asking me to conjure it?!"

"Yes. Can you do it?"

Atha drew the image into his mind. The sword fell from the open air, and he reached out his hands to catch it. It was much lighter then he'd anticipated.

"Well, there's your answer," he chuckled as Elise's mouth practically hit the floor.

"With such ease! Atha, this is a legendary weapon that was lost during the Chameleon war!" she gasped, pulling it from his hands to eye the hieroglyphs etched into the white sheath.

"Found it," he chuckled with unshared enthusiasm. She smiled and handed it back to him, Atha taking a turn looking it over. "What's with the chains?" He pulled at them in hopes of getting a better look at the symbols beneath, but realized they didn't just cover it but were forcibly holding the sword into the sheath like a powerful magnet.

"They are a precaution to ensure the sword is not drawn by accident," she replied. "This sword is known as Shooting Star because however hard it is swung, it multiplies the speed and power of said swing by 1,000, typically ripping either a whole body—or, well, just an arm— through the air, and the blade glows white with vividness matching the swing. While in the sheath its ability is null, hence the need for the chains."

"Definitely named appropriately at least. Shooting Star. So, what are you gonna do with it now? Give it to a guard or put it in a museum?"

She shook her head. "No, it is rightfully yours."

"Why? All I did was manifest it."

"That is not my reasoning. You see, when I said it was lost in the war, it already had an owner. That owner has passed, but he does have a sole heir for which its ownership may pass to."

She glanced to Atha, whose eyes widened.

"It was my dad's?"

"Yes. And on that note," she said, pulling a large clear gem bearing tiny hieroglyphs from her robe pocket, "your mother left you a message. Would you like me to leave you in privacy to listen to it?"

"Nah, just pitch it. I'll keep the sword because I'm feeling it, but I don't want to hear anything either of them has to say."

Elise's face fell.

"Atha, that's not fair. I know you hold animosity for them because of their choice in guardians, but the situation is not so cut and dry. Dako was in fact a good man before Earth, and to this day I cannot rationalize his behavior. I've actually investigated what provoked him but found nothing, suggesting either PTSD or another underlying mental illness."

"You have my answer. Chuck it," he replied coldly.

"No, if you insist on being stubborn, then I'll hold onto it for now. When you're older, you may find that you wish to hear it." Elise pocketed the gem again. A screen above her desk began flashing red, begging for attention. She glanced to Atha.

"Don't look at me, go do your thing," Atha said. "Do you got a bed I can lay down in until you're done? I'm exhausted."

"Certainly, it's already quite late. My chambers are through there, rest as long as you please." She smiled, pointing to the only other door in the room. She sprung up, hustling over to the desk and tapped a screen. Atha made his way to the door, pushing it open to find yet another bare room, a massive bed hardly filling the sprawling space. Sheets decorated with waves crashing across a shoreline covered it. Ocean sounds flowed through the room in soothing white noise.

Whoa, magical white noise bed sheets. He noticed a bookshelf covering most of one of the walls, and sifted through it to find reading material. One stuck his curiosity, a book titled *Current Bounties Bingo Book,* and he pulled it from the shelf. *Cool, I could be a bounty hunter.* He browsed through the pages, noticing that bounties went by smallest to greatest. Instantly, he flipped to the final page. *Let's see who the biggest fish is.*

The bounty between the last two entries was astronomical, jumping from 350,000 xen all the way to 1,500,000.

Name: Harika Teldon Marsh. Crimes: Mass murder. Head count: Greater than 10,000. "It's over 9000?!" Atha gasped out loud before glancing to the bounty's mugshot. He paused, seeing the face of a young Shelando child. An asterisk beside it informed him that the image was out of date. *Actual age: 22. Due to volatility of criminal, updated image cannot be captured. Contract: Unknown. Mana particle count: Unknown. Location: Capinilal Mountains AKA Glowing mountains. Dead only.*

Yeah, no shit dead only. Atha smirked, closing the book shut and returning it to the shelf. He crashed down onto the bed, the name engraved into his mind. *Harika Teldon Marsh. I wonder if his head count is because of his own doing or a collective count from some organization. I'll ask Zell about it later.* He didn't really mean to fall asleep, but the soothing sounds of crashing waves lulled him instantly to slumber.

Chapter 13

Learn to Forget

Seemingly only a moment later, Atha awoke with a snort. Glancing around the room, he realized that Elise had never come in. Atha rubbed the sleep from his eyes as he stood, heading back for the door and pressing it open to notice she wasn't at her desk. Atha was starting to get worried, and headed toward the door that led to the main room. He thrust it open to the sight of Zell chatting cheerfully with Deldora.

"Zell! Where did Elise go?" Atha burst, hurrying to her side.

"Ah, good morning, crystallized princess!" Zell chuckled as he cocked his head.

"Who?"

"Tis a recognizable icon. How does it feel to be on the receiving end of a reference you do not know?"

"Ha-ha. Wow, you really got me. Where's Elise?" Atha asked, and eyed the smiling Deldora. "Stop eyeballing me, fuckface."

"Child, take a breath. She had business to attend to and wished to leave you resting," Zell replied.

"Damn, does she ever sleep?" Atha replied, turning with displeasure to Deldora, who saw a prime chance to jump into the conversation.

"She receives artificial sleep supplements. Now if you're curious about me, I just sleep a healthy seven hours. As opposed to your dozen, that—"

"O captain, my captain, please shut your mouth or you're gonna find out how that poem ends," Atha replied with a roll of his eyes before Zell yanked him to a corner of the room away from Deldora where Shooting Star was propped against a wall. Zell grasped it and pulled a section of the chains loose, the majority still restricting the handle.

"When did you get Shooting Star?" Atha asked.

"Queen Elise left it in my care upon departure. Hold still," Zell replied, tugging the chains around Atha's waist to hook them together. She pulled back, admiring the beautiful white sheath hanging from his side. "Very handsome. You know not to attempt using it, correct?" Zell asked as Atha nodded. "Good. Fear not, its use shall not remain foreign. Under my watch you will learn its power."

Atha ran a hand over the black chains.

"Yeah, about that. I want to start training today. Do you know somewhere safe we can go?"

"You wish to begin so soon? It has been nary a day since you have been reunited."

"Yeah. I wish I could relax a bit longer but learning how to defend myself in this world isn't something to put off. God, it feels so good to have found her after all these years, but I need to be ready for the next threat." *Not to mention I'll die if they force answers out of me about the Chameleons.*

"Very well," she replied. "Our destination is quite a distance, mind you, so far in fact that the utilization of teleportation will be necessary."

"Wait, if teleportation is common, then why did we fly here?" he asked. "Seems like any other form of transportation is irrelevant when you add teleportation into the equation."

"Of course, but no such contract was held in the Shakka village. As I stated before, more potent contracts tend to flock to cities where their abilities can be used to turn a profit. Here, we need only find a user whose cost is within our purse limit."

"Ohh, okay. I get it. That makes sense. Well, I want to say goodbye to El before we hit it, do you know where she is?"

"Of course. Let us make haste."

They exited out of the main as green fog wisped into existence at the edge of the tower. Acting as an elevator, it lowered them to the ground, and they headed just a block down a pleasantly breezy road, shaded thickly by the trees that grew across every space not occupied by a building. Coming to a stop in front of a large blue hall, they headed up a flight of stairs toward doors heavily patrolled by Royal Guards. They took quick notice of him as he made his way up the steps, seemingly unsure of how to handle him as none said a thing until he began to reach for the door's handle.

"Apologies sir, the council is currently in session," a human female announced, nervously adjusting the bun of black hair wrapped tightly upon her head. Her body language and hesitance to halt him suggested to Atha that she had no intention of attempting to stop him if he continued on.

"Sorry, I promise I'll be quick, okay?" Atha smiled apologetically. The guardswomen's mouth twitched but she remained silent, watching

Atha pull the door open. The inner chamber was far more occupied then he'd anticipated. Hundreds of faces turned toward him from around a long table that stretched all the way through the expansive room. Despite this, locating Elise was no daunting task, as she sat atop a massive green throne at the head of the far end of the table. The dull roar from the crowd picked up as they took notice of him and Elise erupted to her feet, green fog lifting her up and levitating her over the table to land in front of Atha.

She whispered frantically, "Atha! Please, now is not the time! You need to leave!"

"Sorry, I just wanted to say bye before I took off," he replied, noticing all the disapproving eyes of whispering councilmembers staring at him.

Elise lost her cool at this. "You're leaving?"

"Yeah, I'm gonna go learn how to use my ability, 'cause right now I feel like I'm back in my first year of prison." He chuckled, but Elise's face fell. She turned back to the council.

"We—we will reconvene in seven minutes."

She yanked Atha into a private room, Dimitri following and closing the door behind them. "Is this some sort of joke? I don't find it humorous," Elise said, but he shook his head.

"I'm completely serious. I haven't even been in this world a week yet and I've already seen terrible, horrible things that are even worse than what I saw in prison. At least here I can actually do something about it."

"No, you don't need to do that! I'm not the weak little girl I once was, so don't use me as an excuse to run off. Can't you just let me protect you?"

Atha gritted his teeth. "Even as a newbie I understand that you've got some big-time contract in this world, but what about me? I'm nothing. Nobody. Just that quiet little *boy* who can't finish his own fights. I literally feel sick to my stomach admitting that, but it's the cold hard truth and—if I'm being completely honest—I hate the fact that you openly acknowledge it and offer to protect me."

"You know that's not what I meant."

"Yeah, I know. But that's how it is when you shave off the sugar coating you put on it, sis," Atha replied.

"Is this really what you feel you must do?"

"Yeah, it is. I'm not ever going back to that place we were stuck in."

She sighed. "Oh, baby brother, I know we won't. But it's time to let that go and stop letting it control you."

"I'm sorry, but I'm just not a courageous person like you. If I can ever hope to move on, I gotta do it my way," Atha replied as Elise eyed the sword on his hip.

"Shooting Star looks handsome on you. Is Zell going with you?" she asked. Atha nodded. "Then you have my blessing. Go, do what you need to, but be *careful* and come back to me in one piece, okay? And take this with you." Elise held a hand up as green fog swirled from it, tightening down to form a small green dagger.

"This looks like the weapons your guards have," Atha noted, stretching a hand up to it. Upon contact, it vanished, sending a zing through his body.

"With that, I can track your movement and will know if you become injured. In case of an emergency, stretch your hand out and roll your thumb across your fingers." She gestured for Atha to follow her instructions, and as he did, the dagger appeared back in his hand. "Tap it seven quick times with your opposite hand." He did, and a small red screen appeared beside her head, Atha's location and a health bar showing across it.

"Whoa, magical low-jack dagger." Atha chuckled.

"Exactly. Now just release your grip on it, and it will return to your body."

Atha did, and with another zing through his body it vanished again.

"Well, now I feel bad. I got a magical dagger and all you get is a sparkling rock."

"I suggest you afford my prized jewelry more respect than that."

"Or what, is it gonna be 'off with his head' time?" Atha laughed, dramatically flopping to his knees. "Please my Queen! I am but a humble peasant and meant no offense! Please, spare me!"

She laughed, grabbing onto an arm to yank him back up.

"Oh, you goofball, this again? Get up! Get up!" Finally managing to get him back up, her laugh calmed, and she stared at the young man before her. "You know, I had envisioned how you would be when I finally got you back, but never once did that image have even an inkling of the cheer and attitude I see before me now."

"Was I at least tall?" Atha stretched his back out to get a hair over Elise's height.

"Oh, yes! Head and shoulders over me!" She held his face. "But I would never dream of trading any of those visions for the reality I have standing before me. Now go, continue to be the best version of you I could never hope to write." She pulled him in and hugged him tightly. "Someday you will realize the stars you are chasing shine bright inside you. I love you, my dearly beloved."

"I love you too, El. Come watch me in the contract tournament when I get back, okay?" Atha finished, kissing her on the cheek before heading past the silent Dimitri for the door.

"I wouldn't miss it for the world. Again, please be *safe* and heed all the words of instruction Zell gives you!"

Atha swung around to give her a janky smile and thumbs up before pulling the door and walking through it. Atha hurried through the crowded streets searching for Zell's face in the meeting spot they'd set, noticing her hooded figured backed up against a wall.

"All set! Now come on, I wanna teleport!"

A sly smile creased her face.

"What?" he asked, but she shook her head.

They made their way through the churning crowd, reaching a more desolate part of town lined with the usual blue buildings yet not sharing in the strange shine the rest had. They entered one on the end of the row, a dirty room filled with dusty orbs and lit by a dim shine from a large central orb. A chubby, old human man snored audibly from behind a counter, remaining asleep even as Zell cleared her throat a few times.

"I got this," Atha whispered to her, a small red firecracker falling into his hand followed by a lighter.

"What manner of contraption is that?" Zell asked as Atha lit the explosive and tossed it behind the desk.

"A wakey-wakey charm. Watch, he'll snap right up." Atha smiled and Zell cocked an eyebrow, turning back to the sleeping man. With a *bang,* he farted and shot up. Zell screamed and recoiled back for a moment as Atha roared with laughter.

"Atha, are you—"

"Hey, hey, remember that time you let me freak out in the carriage?! Let's just call this payback!" Atha jabbed a finger into her forehead as Zell's eye's narrowed.

"Um, can I help you two?" the chubby old man asked.

Zell snapped her attention to him, having completely forgotten another victim was present.

"Oh, yes, apologies! We require teleportation either directly to the destruction training grounds or an area within a few miles of it," she replied. The man nodded as he stood and made his way around the counter.

"A favorite destination among the Royal Guard. I have a waypoint set about a mile just off the reservation. The price is one hundred and fifty xen a head for teleportation there," he replied, picking out a small orb with a frozen image of a dirt path surrounded by trees.

Zell pulled a few coins from her pouch, handing them to the man.

"That suits our needs."

"All right, let me just open the gate and I'll send you on your way," he replied, grasping the orb in his hands for a few moments until he motioned for Atha's hand.

"Oh man, this is gonna be sick," Atha said and smiled, noticing Zell stifling a laugh as he extended his hand.

The man grasped it and Atha was instantly on the dirt path with trees stretching down on either side of it into the distance. His stomach instantly churned, sending him to his knees, gagging and puking as Zell appeared beside him, bursting with laughter.

"It appears the universe is once again in balance. For future reference, you should hold your breath while teleporting," she taunted as Atha recovered.

"What's your problem, Zell?" he gurgled, pausing as Zell's red finger jabbed into his forehead.

Mocking his voice, she laughed back. "'Wakey-wakey charm."

"Well, ha-ha, you got me."

"Our destination lies to the north," she said, pointing down the path. "Come, the first sun will be rising soon." She started ahead as Atha trailed.

Eventually the path widened, revealing a massive stony canyon stretching out across the horizon. The first sun's light began trickling over it, revealing scorch marks scattered about. Zell pulled back her hood to take a breath of fresh air.

"And here we are, the destruction contract training grounds. As the name would suggest, it is a spacious area where the use of powerful contracts is safe. For secrecy's sake, we will continue in a few miles to ensure stray eyes cannot take notice of your abilities."

Atha nodded.

"Sounds good. Lemme try something real quick," he replied, drawing the image of a four-wheeler into his mind. It crashed down in front of him as he burst with excitement, hopping onto its seat and twisting the key to spur it to life. "Check it out! I got us a ride!" Atha patted the passenger seat behind him.

"What is this?!" Zell asked, eyeing it over as Atha yanked on the throttle a few times to rumble the engine.

"It's called a machine! This specific type is known as an all-terrain vehicle, a 1000cc beast capable of traversing even the worst mud!"

"A machine...How does it work?" Zell replied.

"It's powered by an engine that creates energy from combustion. So, what's up, girl, you working or walking?" Atha laughed. Zell scoffed but got on the back nonetheless. "All right, hold on!"

Shifting into first and with a hard yank on the throttle, he screamed as they shot forward, then slamming on the brakes. "Jesus Christ! This baby's really, *really* got some power."

"Just how much experience do you have with machines?" Zell asked.

"Well, I've operated a sewing machine before, so I guess you could say none. Actually, hold on." He held his hands up, a black helmet falling into them before handing it back to Zell. She forced it down over her short black horns and Atha conjured a second for himself. "I'd try using the self-generating path, but let's see how well I drive first." He

219

chuckled a bit fearfully, this time tugging slightly on the throttle to ease forward. They went for a few miles and he began to get more comfortable with driving, finally coming to a stop as Zell pointed to a small clearing just on the outskirt of the massive canyon.

"You weren't kidding, there's really nothing out here. Didn't even see a blade of grass," Atha noted as Zell struggled to pull her helmet back off. "Sorry, these aren't really designed for a head with horns." Finally, she succeeded and set her helmet on the ATV beside Atha's.

"Of little note. Come, let us begin," she replied, walking off into the open portion of rocky canyon as he followed. "Before we start any actual training, let us review what I hope we can accomplish. We shall begin by learning as many details of the mysterious ability you hold as possible, even to the point of it taking up all our time if necessary. Once we have a firm understanding of your capability, we can apply this to how it can be used against actual contracts in terms of combat."

Atha interjected. "I'd like to do that even if we can't completely figure out my ability. I want to be ready for the tournament."

"No, as I said our highest priority is taking away the unknown factors of your ability. Right now, I would go as far as to say it is a threat to you and anyone around you due to how little is understood about it. With so many questions could come just as many troubling answers, and before anything else I must urge that they are erased."

"You think my ability could accidently hurt someone without me meaning to?" Atha replied.

"Of course. Having seen its destructive power firsthand, that is a clear cause for concern. If we can manage to do this—to my satisfaction, mind you—we shall move onto actual theoretical combat situations. Lastly, we will practice with Shooting Star and perhaps find a contract that can intertwine with these factors suitably."

Atha's face lit up. "Oh, I hadn't even thought of that! I want a contract. Let's do that first!"

"Again, our priority is to erase the many questions hovering about, not spur more. Besides, it would be wise to know which will fit alongside what you already possess most appropriately," Zell replied.

"But I want a kick-ass power."

"Do tell what you have in mind."

"Hadn't really thought about it. I don't know. Something super powerful, I guess. Something with lots of firepower."

"Like your handheld explosives?"

"Yeah, like my grenades, exactly!" Her face fell further as he said this. "What?"

"Does it not seem redundant to you to have a contract that can do exactly what you already can?" she asked.

"When you put it like that, it sounds kind of stupid."

"Deafeningly so. Come, we have wasted enough time," Zell insisted, pulling off her hood and cape to suit the increasingly hot temperature. "Attempt to summon an object larger than anything you have before. An object slightly bigger than current record and from there something larger than that. I stand ready to pull you away should an item appear above you."

"What an icon of safety. I see why the first thing Elise asked me was if you'd be coming with me. All right, let's see." Atha drew the image of a car into his mind, the nondescript coupe crashing down beside him.

"I can conjure a whole fucking *car*!" Atha gasped, slapping the hood like a proud father. "Okay, let's go with an SUV next."

Atha drew the image into his mind, a slightly larger car plopping down beside the first. "Yes! Oh man, I'm so overpowered!"

"Have you felt any fatigue?" Zell asked.

"No, nothing," Atha replied. Zell motioned for him to continue. "Let's go bigger, then."

Atha mumbled to himself, drawing the image of a school bus into his mind. It crashed down beside the car and SUV, Zell's mouth falling a bit open as she stared. "What?"

"Assuming you can manifest any manner of object either equivalent or smaller than this, it would hardly be reaching to say this ability falls into A, possibly even S category," she said.

"So, I'm kind of a big deal then, right?" Atha laughed, puffing out his chest.

"You jest over a serious matter. Power of this magnitude is not to be made light of."

"Whatever. Let's kick this up a notch, eh?" He smirked and drew the image of a C-130 plane in his mind. It slammed down, metal creaking across the ground. "Whoa. Didn't think it would actually work." Atha smiled, his excitement growing alongside the size of every new manifestation.

"Do you feel anything? Any amount of energy exertion whatsoever?" Zell asked in utter disbelief.

"Still nothing. Let's try the AN-225 next. Gonna need material for this one." Atha first drew the image of a magazine filled with pictures and information of the largest vehicles in existence. Len had instructed Atha to memorize the covers of hundreds of magazines for this exact reason. If needed, he could conjure magazines illustrating weapons, clothing, food, electronics, vehicles, and just about any other imaginable topic of mass-produced Earthly items. Scanning the magazine, he located the desired plane, and drew the image of the massive machine in his mind. Larger than a 747 at over a football field's length, this was the largest plane ever to be produced.

With a boom, it thundered down beside the C-130, its huge metal body a testament to his power. "This is insane! This is so much more than I ever expected! God, if Len could see this, he'd flip!" Atha laughed, closing his eyes to go over more titanic images his photographic memory had stored in his mind. "Okay, this is the biggest single object in *existence*. Ready for the grand finale?" Atha called to Zell who paused, pointing to the massive plane.

"Larger then *this*?" she scoffed as Atha glanced at his magazine.

"Oh yeah, way bigger. Heavier too, over 350,000 tons," he replied, reading information from the magazine.

"Such a thing exists?"

"Yeah, they transport things across the ocean. Drum roll, please." Taking his own recommendation, he began drumming his knees, the ship's image popping clearly into his mind. With the force of an apocalyptic explosion, the massive metal ship crashed down across the whole canyon, causing rockslides across the entire area with the shockwave. Atha was sent flying from his feet by a blast of air as dust eclipsed the area. His magazine was torn from his hands and sent flapping away into an oblivion of dirt. Zell hit the ground beside him, shielding her head as rocks skipped across them.

"Holy shit, it worked! You know Len had a crazy theory about me, said I might be a god or something. Ain't so crazy now!" Atha laughed, regaining his footing in the swirling dirt as Zell did the same.

"Come," she instructed plainly, yanking on Atha's arm as they headed clear of the dirt.

"So, what would I rank as now? Or do I even need to ask?" Atha smirked, slapping handsome amounts of dirt off himself with pride. Zell's face, to Atha's surprise, became grim.

"That is exactly what we must speak on. This power has trumped my most radical estimation, a tireless and possibly even endless ability to manifest anything." She sighed as Atha raised an eyebrow.

"Why do you say it like that? This is amazing! Not trying to sound repetitive, but look at me, I'm a god!" Atha brandished his arms toward the mass of metal.

"This is power the likes of which no being should be able to possess."

"Oh, I see what this is. The whole 'with great power comes great responsibility speech.'" He chuckled but stopped as Zell's hands yanked on the front of his robe.

"Take this matter with the utmost seriousness!" Her voice rose, irritating him.

"Fuck, all right! What's with you?" Atha retorted, pulling free of her grip.

"What you can do, manifest objects with enough sheer size to decimate an entire town, is dangerous!"

"You don't think I realize that?"

"In your mind, I am sure that you rationalize so, but you do not, not as I do. I have seen warriors with just an inkling, a mere *shadow* of the force you control, make bad calls, and the aftermath of those will bow to your own should it come to pass. I have watched helplessly as a monk who forgot to check a target's background sent devastation ripping across both foe and ally! Now you will be silent, and you will absorb every word I say as sponge to water. Am I understood?" Zell finished like a calming blaze. "At this time, we cannot establish if a limit to size exists, but in absence of such a restraint we must create our own. I will take time to pen a list of secondary laws for use of your ability. Before we leave this wasteland, you will come to see them stand just as adamant as the regular rules to which it abide.,"

Atha eased his hand into the air.

"Yes?" Zell asked.

"I wanted to bring this up at some point, so I guess this is a good time to do so. There was this incident in prison. I got into it really bad with another inmate. We argued until he finally went to leave, but by this point I was beyond pissed. Drew the image of a hammer into my mind. I was gonna clock him over the head with it but instead of popping up in my hand it went hurling through the air and cracked him right smack across the dome—"

Zell cut in, her expression becoming grim as she glanced to the massive ships.

"To sum up, you think it plausible anger caused it to manifest with velocity. What a terrifying power."

"Len found out and freaked. He never let me try doing that again, said it was too risky." Atha glanced toward the creaking ship, a slight smile creasing his face as Zell sat contemplating his words. "We should figure it out, right?"

"It would be in our best interest to do so here, in a controlled environment, rather than anywhere else, so yes," Zell replied, glancing toward the ground and grasping a rock. She turned, hurling it a fair distance before flipping back to him. "That is your target. Make an attempt to hit it squarely. And Atha"—Zell paused, her red face leaning in closely to his—"Small. Objects. No larger than the size of a fist."

"Let's go with a baseball," he sighed. Closing his eyes and taking a long deep breath, he recalled his memory of Dako choking Elise. His face twisted with rage as the image of the baseball filled his mind, plopping down in front of him.

"Try again. Are there any other details that might have affected the ability in prison?" Zell asked.

"None that I can think of. Obviously, it's not as simple as getting angry. Any words of guidance?" he asked as Zell opened her orange hologram screen.

"You are already familiar with my ability Grand Mastermind, but you do not know how exactly it operates. See these symbols on the left side?" she asked, pointing a finger toward the hieroglyphs. "Using practically any type of contract takes practice, but mine in particular can be used as a perfect example for that point. To find the exact information I need, these symbols must be assorted appropriately. The wrong combination and the outcome will be dissatisfactory. It took years to figure out the order they should be placed. For example, moving into the que box the symbols signifying liquid and consumables"—a list of beverages popped up—"gives me quite the list. Now if I add in age and set it to eight and up"—she paused again, this time a list of alcoholic beverages filling the screen—"it displays information of drinks that require aging of eight years.

"Take an example and apply it to yourself. To get the result you desire you need to first know what must be aligned. Anger is likely the first symbol, but now you must find the rest."

"So, I should try adding in different things until I figure out what triggers it. You're a good teacher, you know that?" Atha replied.

"Rare words of praise yet still appreciated." Zell's sly grin creased her face, a clear sign to Atha that treachery was soon to follow. "I would do well to stay in the good graces of such a powerful deity."

"Oh, gonna go straight to throwing that in my face, eh? Be warned, I've smote better men for less." Atha snickered.

"I tremble. Now give it another go," Zell replied, gesturing to the rock. Atha returned his focus to it.

Several hours passed along with a brief break to eat. Well over a thousand baseballs covered the ground and Atha grew increasingly chagrined with every addition to the pile.

"Why? What do you want from me?" Atha screamed, another ball falling from the air onto the ground. "Fuck! I don't get it! I've tried everything!"

"Perhaps the error is not with you but with the situation. Regardless, keep trying for now. We need certainty before changing the scenario, which will force a full restart," Zell replied as Atha groaned with exasperation.

"This shit looks like the outfield after Babe Ruth cleaned house and you want me to keep going?"

"Breathe, as previously stated, I mean only to attain certainty before moving on," Zell replied smoothly.

"Whatever. Already wasted a whole day, so we might as well finish it off," Atha spat. Another baseball fell to his feet. "Fuck!" he screamed, focusing on the taunting rock again. Again he failed. Anger reached the breaking point as he tried again. "Little rock bastard. Don't think you're gonna survive this. If the next ball doesn't hit I'm gonna go over there and smash your ass," Atha mumbled under his breath as the next baseball fell to his feet. Screaming with rage he slammed a red glowing foot through the baseballs. The baseball's image drew back into his mind and hurtling through the air, smashing the rock. He took a long pause, glancing at the rock and then back to the equally surprised Zell to reaffirm the damage before bursting with excitement. "Oh! I did it!" He laughed but Zell's face grew grim as he slowed to a stop.

"Anger is not the only element necessary. You must have a specific target, crippling rage, and an absolute desire to see the victim laid waste."

"What's with the look? That's a good thing, right?" Atha asked, but she remained silent. "Look. I'm sorry for being a jerk, okay? I just get so angry sometimes."

She shook her head, practically scoffing at the apology.

"Irrelevant. My mind lays conflicted with itself, not mere words."

"What's that supposed to mean?"

"That I find that my will to continue helping you piece together your ability may be hindered by my own fear of what it could be capable of. My inner conflict might stunt understanding rather than spur it for fear of what else may be discovered."

Atha smiled at the bluntness.

"Thank you for being honest with me. I'm right there with you. It surprised me too, and if you don't wanna help me I understand," Atha replied, but Zell shook her head.

"No, the aim of my words misses the true target. To rephrase, I simply mean let us take pause from this course for the time being and venture into other endeavors that will help you grow. Once I can say for certain that I can help you with this course with unclouded mind, we will resume it."

"You're a good person, Zell. Really, thank you for being so honest with me. I'm glad I have a friend who can just say it how it is."

"And I, you, for continued acceptance understanding of my dissonance," she replied. Atha's smile began to grow and he drummed his knees in anticipation.

"So, we're moving onto contract warfare for noobs! Damn, what a shame!"

Chapter 14

Infamous Hero

Atha and Zell set up camp in the form of a pair of tents, a small fire pit surrounded by chairs and a portable shower. Despite the tent, Atha rolled his sleeping bag out across the rocky dirt, the endless array of stars lulling him to sleep as he gazed at the constellations Cybele had shown him.

They were up before the first sun's rising. Atha put together a rainbow of overly colored wheat cereal, directing words splotched with the dull crunches to Zell, who cringed at his lack of manners.

"Hey, something occurred to me last night," he started, setting the empty bowl down and swallowing his last bite before continuing. "The main constellation is a female, and my sister is the sole ruler and holds a triple S contract, which I gather is the equivalent to nuclear weapons. It actually seems like most of the prominent figures here are female."

"What of it?"

"It seems like a pattern. Like females are the dominant sex here. On Earth most of the prominent constellations are male and practically every figure in power is male," Atha replied. Zell blinked for a moment.

"Oh, I grasp the basis of your question. The lack of awareness of mana's existence in your world renders such logic sound." Zell stood and motioned for Atha to follow as she began walking. "Women are considered superior to men here for a simple reason: mana superiority. A perfect example of this is male and female twins. Despite having numerous comparable features, the female would have a higher amount of mana than her brother, and it's mana that powers a contract, displacing the skill factor of wielding it."

"Oh, I didn't realize mana powered a contract. How does that work?" he asked.

"We will revisit that question in depth later this day when it fits in my syllabus, but answering original question will in turn answer a portion of it. Theoretically, if those twins wielded the same contract with the same amount of skill—or even if the male held superior skill up to a certain level—the female would still be more formidable with the elevated mana. Virtually every function of a contract comes with a mana cost, so the female could simply outlast, if not overpower, the male. But, even mana is not the most substantial difference between the sexes. Females, when pushed past desperation points in a situation—such as defending their children—can forcibly raise the power of their contract past the normal ceiling."

"What do you mean, like an adrenaline surge but for a contract?" Atha asked.

"A splendid comparison. Such is an extremely rare occurrence, and I have only bore witness to it once before. Tripe S contracts are typically only possessed by females, and here combat power is viewed as a desirable aspect for a ruler. Often, a powerful woman doesn't take control by force but rather is simply handed it. Queen Elise was."

"That makes sense. Yeah, back on Earth men are typically physically stronger than women, so the opposite is pretty much true for everything you said. Guess might-makes-right is a universal thing."

"Do not misunderstand; there are male rulers who hold triple S contracts, but female leadership vastly out numbers them. Centuries ago, men were even considered sub-par citizens to women, unable to hold positions of power or high-placed jobs," Zell replied, coming to a stop in a clearing some distance from the baseballs and massive vehicles, the creaking metal echoing lightly through the canyon. "Having already had a taste of a combat contract, you have a vague idea of the concept, but as I stated previously, the sheer number of contracts is overwhelming. Combat contracts are not as common as other categories, but the selection stands equally vast."

"Yeah, I noticed that most people actually go for necessity over firepower."

"A quality you would be wise to emulate."

"Again with that?" Atha sighed, rolling his eyes.

"Well there are just so many you could improve. Like rolling your eyes. Such a childish action, unbecoming of a young man."

"Whatever."

"So, you already know of the basic ranking system of contracts, which is G, F, E, D, C, B, A, S, SS, and SSS, from weakest to strongest. However, since some contracts utilize multiple categories, such as transportation and combat, the ranking system goes a bit more in depth. Queen Elise's Ruler's Right, for example, has combat, defense, transportation, *and* communication, but only the combat and defensive rank in the triple S level. Transportation is A and communication is B. By this standard, it's known as SSS category two."

"Oh cool. What would mine rank as?" Atha asked.

"It is a difficult task to place an ability I have so little knowledge of."

"But still at least triple S, right?" Atha pressed.

"While the applications could theoretically be endless, at this point, going purely of what you have displayed, I would rank it at S. Triple S is a designation reserved for power that could bring ruin to the entire planet," Zell replied.

"Are you saying Elise could destroy the *world*?" He chuckled, sure something had been lost in translation, but Zell nodded.

"Precisely. It would only be so easy as speaking the words, if no other Triple S contracts stood against her, but that's exactly what keeps nations from waging war against another."

So, she literally *is like this world's version of nuclear weapons,* Atha thought, returning his attention to Zell who spoke up again.

"Only you do not consume mana to wield your power, making it devastatingly formidable. Mana is the same as currency to spirits, and a contract wielder exchanges it for the use of the abilities. Myself for example..."

Zell drew a small black screen from her pocket and pressing it against her wrist to display the number 3012. "My mana particle count is 3,012, which is a healthy number. Mana particle count increases depending on the physical strain the body endures by simply moving about. If muscle is increased, that strain lessens and alongside it, mana, which acts as a counterbalance to the density of mana filling the air."

"That makes perfect sense! Since men are stronger, our bodies are less strained by the crazy gravity here, which means our mana is constantly lower!"

"But even with a physical capability equal to a female, it's rare for even the most adept mana count of a male to match that of an average female. Take yours for example," Zell paused, pressing the black screen against Atha's wrist to display the number 807. "Hm. Even lower than I anticipated."

"Are you kidding me? I'm weak, though. That's not fair!" he groaned as a sudden thought occurred. "Wait, do you think my Agro energy could cause the low mana? The red glowing light? It makes me way stronger and tougher than normal."

"That would actually make perfect sense. As opposed to being strained by gravity, if a body were to be too strong, then mana particle level would be harshly stunted. Increasing levels takes time, but lowering it is a quick process."

"So Agro energy cancels out mana. That sucks," Atha grumbled, but Zell shook her head.

"Not at all. It is a powerful energy. Considering you already have excessive versatility I would go so far as to say a contract is obsolete. I have no knowledge of this Agro energy, but let me see what I can find." Zell opened her orange screen and shuffled around images.

"Hm. Inconclusive," Zell noted. "Perhaps this topic of information has a reasonable price."

She shifted to a new section of the screen he hadn't seen before.

"Purchase? Like someone knows and you're seeing if you can pay them xen for it?"

"Not precisely, but close. My contract's basic information search does not cost mana, but for a set amount of mana particles I can buy the information from the spirit whom I formed the contract with. This is a secret function of my ability, so please do not share it."

A series of Agro energy related topics popped up, mana particle prices beside them, as Zell picked through them.

"Hm, unfortunately most are out of my range. Price is based upon how many living people know the answer to the query but simply examining the purchasable sections of a topic gives answers too. See here where it says *advanced level Agro energy blasts*? This would suggest there are more possibilities for wielding it than simple bodily enhancement. None of the options in my price range would help us in any way, and would leave me exhausted for the remainder of the day, so let us leave it at that." Zell's screen vanished.

"So, I got superhuman strength but if I keep using it I won't be able to use mana?" Atha asked. Zell shook her head.

"It will hit a bottom point, but you will always have mana since your pores have been opened. I would estimate around 300, which is still an acceptable amount for lower end contract selections."

"Oh well, glass half full, I guess. Hey, what would you rank my Agro energy as?"

Zell thought for a few moments.

"Roughly in the class C enhancement or combative classification. It certainly makes you quick and durable, but many contracts could trounce it."

"Figured as much. Oh well, I like it." Atha smirked, flexing his skinny arms as red energy spiked from them.

"What exactly is this Agro energy?" Zell asked. Atha paused, not entirely sure himself.

"I don't know much about it. I know mana is drawn from the surrounding atmosphere, but Agro energy actually comes from within my body, but that's about it. Kinda makes sense they don't work well together; jack-of-all-trades, master of none. And before you ask, no, I don't know how to teach it."

"Seeing as how it affected you, such was not my intent. Regardless, it will pair well with your sword once we delve into its use, but for now let's stay on topic." Zell chuckled, running a hand across her black horns. "To learn the best way to counter a combat contract, you first need to learn which categories it falls into, which is a difficult thing to do. Some contracts can even lead you to believe that they fall into a completely separate category, such as an extremely high-speed contract that appears to be teleportation. Both are forms of transportation, but if you string a wire you could manage to decapitate a speedster, not a teleporter."

"*Whoa*, okay, I just totally visualized that. Thanks, Zell."

"The point is, different categories have different counters. Experience will help you decipher what you face, but there will always be situations where you must go off a simple hunch. If it comes to that, the best option is to simply run. Or, if you cannot flee, to assume a fully defensive front. Having no need of mana, you could simply exhaust a foe's supply."

Atha pulled his black meteorite from his pocket, bouncing it around between his fingers to help absorb the sudden influx of information. "Giuseppe taught me something like that once. You mean to say that if I can't determine what the basis of their ability is, or exactly how powerful it is, to automatically assume it's superior to my own, correct?"

Zell faltered for the briefest of moments. Atha was now fully aware of her body language, realizing he'd not only summed up exactly what she was trying to convey, he'd divulged what she'd meant to lead into.

"The interpretation paired with accuracy of your statement begs that I find the source for such rare brilliance. That stone of yours; perhaps madness has but temporarily passed onto myself, but I do believe I find myself convinced it is the source of heightened intellect," Zell said. Atha chuckled, tossing the rock to Zell, who caught and eyed it over.

"It's not some magical rock if that's what you're asking. It's just easier to focus when I have it bouncing around. You're not the first to notice, either. That award goes to my old teacher, Miss Morry."

A bittersweet smile came upon his face at the memory. "She was the first to ever realize there was more to me then a mumbling kid," Atha said with a half-hearted chuckle and caught his rock as Zell tossed it back to him.

"I find difficulty in imagining you ever a mumbler," Zell laughed, and the sweet left Atha's expression, leaving only the bitter. "She must have been quite the teacher to discern intellect through far fewer words than the many it took me to notice it."

Atha tucked the rock back into his pocket.

"She was. I've been blessed with many great teachers. Even so, you're the best I've ever had." Atha's eyes met Zell's, and he realized his words had actually taken her by surprise. For the first time since the met, the woman with a word and a plan for everything was silent. "Miss Morry helped me forget my pain. Len made me embrace it. You're like the perfect medium between the two. Just enough light, and just enough darkness. Why did we come all the way out here?" Atha finally felt the need to prompt Zell, who simply stared off for another moment.

"Oh—yes, I wished to show you another method of manipulating mana for combat. Observe." Blue mana steamed out of her, tightening and forming translucent blue tentacles from her back.

"Oh, so that's actually mana? I'd assumed it was like a contract-enhanced item."

"No, this is an advanced application of mana, completely possible with neither item nor contract. It is rare to see mana used this way, for it takes extensive training, but it gives you fair grasp of an alternative use," she replied, the tentacles drawing daggers out from underneath her robes.

"O-kay? And that required you to take me all the way out here?" Atha asked again, a sly smile crossing Zell's face.

"What better way to help you see the error in your way than to be defeated by a foe who wields an information contract?" she replied.

"You're kidding right?" he scoffed. "You saw what I could do, and you want to come at me with a handful of fucking *knives,* Freddy Krueger?"

Zell nodded.

"I'm not doing this! I'll crush you to, I don't know, *death!*"

"Then let words give way to action," she replied as Atha shook his head.

"Okay, bad joke, but seriously, Zell, I'm not doing this."

"You cannot harm me. Now come," she replied as a flustered Atha groaned.

"Fine, but I'll go easy." He drew the image of a mailbox in his mind. It fell over Zell, but with ease, a knife slapped into the wood, the tendril pulling back before whipping forward to throw it at Atha, knocking him down. Zell leapt over and pressed a boot into his chest.

"Congratulations, you perished. Care to try again?" she taunted before moving her foot and reaching a hand down toward him.

She's way quicker than I thought. All right, maybe she can take the heat, Atha thought, regaining his footing.

"Start a few yards back. It will give you higher ground," Zell continued coolly. Atha scoffed but did as she suggested.

"I'm gonna bring it for real this time. You ready?" A shiver ran down his back as Zell's face darkened. He drew the image of a bus into his mind, sending it crashing down on top of her, but she was too fast, shooting out from beneath it and bursting toward a backpedaling Atha. A car crashed down in front of her. She smoothly vaulted it, closing in on Atha as red energy pulsed from his feet. He began to shoot back farther but a long blue tentacle shot out, catching the back of his heel and sending him crashing down. Once again, Zell was on top of him with a foot pressed into his chest again.

"You're a beast, Zell!" Atha gasped as she helped him up again. "I mean, Jesus, I only had time to crank out a pair of vehicles! I was trying to get some distance to have time for another but damn, a single second never seemed so long." He brushed the dust from his messy brown hair.

She replied as Atha's face fell, "I used a compilation of your weaknesses against you. I could practically have trounced your obvious plan while blind."

"Well, I didn't use guns or explosives."

"A wise decision. I would have had to cause you injury if you did," Zell replied matter-of-factly. "Information is my weapon, and I have an ample amount on you. How do you think a battle is won?"

"Lots of different ways. First and foremost is firepower."

"No, firepower is simply most recorded. The most spoken of in grand tale. For every prominent battle won through sheer fire superiority, eight are quietly ended through information. Perhaps seven through simple strategy. When either of these fail, *that* is when a warrior falls to brute strength. Information, strategy, and firepower. Mixing at least a pair is adequate, but true warriors focus on them all."

"Back to being a jack-of-all-trades. I don't think trying to take me out of my forte will help anything."

"And yet you were defeated by someone without using an actual contract, so you have no further distance to fall. All it took was a basic mix of information and strategy and your pure firepower fell at my hand."

"If being a monk ever falls through, I think you could be a world-class debater. How do I gather and apply information and strategy during an actually battle, though?"

"How one learns to do anything: practice. We will continue to skirmish until you can decipher the obvious flaws I reveal. Once you can do that, I'll increase the difficulty."

"Oh, like a video game!" Atha replied. "Hell yeah, I'm down. Give me a taste of master level first to give me an idea of how far I need to go!"

"You would ask that I go all out?"

"Yeah, for demonstrative purposes. Come on, I wanna see big bad Zell at—" Atha's words halted, his blood running cold as sweat prickled his brow.

Zell hadn't moved but, despite the three suns blazing down, he felt cold bloodlust pouring over him like waves of an icy ocean, freezing in place as his senses began to sharpen. He could barely breathe, let alone move. Every part of his body screamed at him to stay still, that this battle couldn't be won, to present no challenge and hopefully just some broken bones would come from what inevitably would happen. Zell eased slowly forward and with a finger, tapped him in the forehead. The feeling immediately receded, his body untensing as he fell to hands and knees, gasping for air.

"Be careful of what you ask," Zell warned.

"Who are you, Zell?" he asked out loud by accident. Zell paused awkwardly as Atha realized what he'd said. "Sorry, that slipped out. I know you don't wanna talk about it." He wiped off the cold sweat before getting back up to his feet.

"No, we should discuss the topic before word is given by another's tongue." Zell sighed, leaning back onto a nearby boulder.

"No, really, it just slipped out."

"Gratitude for making an attempt to accommodate my insecurities, but I assure you this is for the best. So, to start, just how much have you learned of my past?"

"Uh, well, I know you were in the war with the Chameleons. I'm not sure exactly how you played into it, but I figured you were either a Royal Guard member or a freelancer."

"I was in the war but fell beneath neither of those options."

"Huh? Okay, you lost me. How could you have been in the war if you weren't—" Atha stopped. Zell's next words came as he began to connect the many dots.

"I was a member of the Chameleon syndicate."

Atha waited a few moments for her to continue but she didn't. "Well? Go on."

"That is all? Go on?"

"Your announcement sounds crazy without context, but you must have had a good reason," Atha replied.

"Why do you hold such *faith* in me?"

"You're Honorati now. I don't give a shit if the whole *world* hates you, if you did what you thought was right, I'll always have your back."

"You have a good heart, Atha. I am honored to have joined you."

"Oh, stop it. I'm not good with touching moments. Now get on with the story, it's killing me!" Atha drummed his knees with anticipation and Zell nodded.

"Yes, I fought for the Chameleons, but not consciously. With the royal family being slaughtered and the lands in chaos, a plan was formed to infiltrate enemy forces. Myself and another Denata by the name of Zenta Zukomura"—*Oh, I met him!* Atha thought. *The huge Denata who was with Harmer*— "had our memories completely erased and filled in with memories that would complement our banding with the Chameleons' cause. That dissolution of old memories was so completely thorough that to this day I cannot recall several details of my past, such as my parents or even my true name."

"Why couldn't they be restored once your mission was over?" Atha replied as Zell poked a finger against her temple.

"The process causes permanent damage to the medial temporal lobe. But as in all wars, sacrifices were necessary, and we gave up our identities to become Zell Tenzata and Zenta Zukomura. I will spare you the horrors of what followed this transition, but the final effect was that we leaked vital information about enemy attack strategies, contracts, communication, safehouse locations, and even specific plans that led to the eventual downfall of the Chameleons."

"Whatever happened to Zenta Zukomura?" Atha asked, flawlessly feigning ignorance.

"Once our true personalities where restored, I transitioned back into civilian life and became a monk of Shakka, but Zenta..." She paused, lowering her head toward the ground as Atha leaned in closer to catch her whispers. "The man was haunted by what he had done. The duality of his reality was not so easily severed for him, and eventually he delved back into the darkness and rejoined the Chameleons. We have not spoken since."

Atha remained silent. He had experienced rock bottom himself and could tell this was Zell's. He knew there was nothing he could say.

Zell changed the subject. "Enough of the past. Let us return sight toward the brightening future. There is still much time left in this day and I plan on seeing it put to good use." Zell smiled at him. Suddenly, mana glistened around her, tightening down into tentacles that procured knives from her robes once more.

"Look, I get it. I can't hang with big dog Zell yet, so can we just move on to the next lesson?"

"Not until the 'yet' in that sentence is omitted for 'never.'"

Several hours came and went as Zell's foot came and went from Atha's chest dozens of times. The three suns were replaced by seven moons and millions of stars in the pitch-black canyon. They gathered around a dainty fire that smoldered between the tents and ate slices of pizza doused with assortments of meats.

"Hey, so I had an idea, something we could do for a little extra practice before the tournament," Atha started, taking a swig of soda.

"Oh, do tell. What madness rings of utmost sanity through this swirling void of conscious?" Zell replied as Atha recoiled.

"That was a bit excessive. But anyways, while I was hanging out in Elise's room I started reading this book."

"Oh, he can read! I had wondered."

"Fuck you. So anyways it was basically a bingo book for criminals, and my natural instincts forced me to find the biggest and baddest, and that was some dude named Harika Teldon Marsh with an insanely—and I mean astronomically high—bounty on his head. It had a little info about how he had got such a big bounty, but nothing on how he managed to do it. Not even a contract name is listed, so I thought, 'Well, I'll just ask Zell! She'll know, though I'm not sure her snarky comments along the way will make it worth it.' And here I am, asking and regretting it already."

Zell finished the last bite of crust, her orange screen popping up in front of her as she began to shuffle its many symbols around.

"While I favor myself a scholar and approve learning of a new subject, allow me to both swiftly and decisively tell you with certainty that this is a target beyond our collective power," she noted, flipping her orange screen to Atha. It was filled with far more detailed information than he had ever seen. Atha pulled it in closer to get a better look.

"So according to this, the guy just has a shitload of mana and no contract?" Atha started, nudging a provocative elbow into her side. "What where you saying before about women being superior?"

"The term *incongruous* exists for a reason. It would be more accurate to say his impossibly high mana amounts to more of a contract-less ability. To put this concept into form you can understand, mana particle counts have known limits of around 5,000. For a count to rise to high past that ceiling literally rends flesh from bone. At the age of eight, Harika released a blast of mana particles that measured well over *a million,* and with it he rewrote what our world knew as fact and fiction. The sheer scale of the blast radius covered a mile, and due to the location of its release, it obliterated a village. It was so mind-boggling that a team was dispatched to search for a contract user capable of releasing explosions. Here, there is a video recording from them."

The video started with the sight of a sprawling forest far below.

"Recon, this is overwatch, the bomber isn't in this grid, nothing but trees. Do you copy?" a scratchy female voice asked. A second, a much more dainty female voice responded after a few moments as the video continued to pan around portions of the forest from high above.

"Good copy. Check surrounding grid and move on. No breaks until target is located. Stay frosty, overwatch."

"Roger that. Progressing to check grid 92 for heat signatures," the scratchy overwatch replied, the recording turning a quick 180, gusting over the forest. Suddenly the camera focused, the image of a tiny Shelando child fleeing through the woods showed across the screen. "Recon, I've got a child in the danger zone. Awaiting further orders, copy."

"Copy, stay on task, overwatch. Dispatching rescue team now," she replied. Overwatch released a happy sigh as a Denata shot across the sky, landing between the trees beside the child. Without warning, a gust of blue light ripped through the forest, flattening the trees to the ground for the split second before the glow became blinding. The explosion sent dirt and bits of trees scattering through it, and the clear wall of a shockwave rocked the recording.

"Recon! Recon! Rescue team down! Repeat, rescue team for child is down and no sign of bomber! Awaiting further orders!" Overwatch screamed in a panic, the recording refocusing on a devastating gap in the ground barely viable through the flying dirt.

"Copy that, pull up higher into the sky and focus on the center point of impact," recon replied loud and cool, clearly hoping to instill a sense of calmness over the now hyperventilating overwatch, the recording distancing from the forest yet still displaying a clear image. The dust began to clear, the image appeared of the Shelando child running through the crater with an eerie blue glow resonating simultaneously in and out of his body.

"Recon, are you seeing this? The child is alive. I think we have our point of origin! Mana count 1,560,000?! What the hell is going on? what are we dealing with?"

The recording ended and Zell whisked her screen away.

"Did you see how pure mana particles devastated the area? Now, to put that into a form of relativity you can understand, my mana tendrils each consist of exactly 200 particles of mana. That explosion was telling us Harika Teldon Marsh is not to be disturbed."

"In that video he was running. It seemed more like he was doing it by accident than willingly blowing up the place," Atha countered. "He was just a kid."

"True, his intent was not malicious, but that does not mean he is not dangerous. He recognized that danger and hides within the Capinilal Mountains to ensure accidental contact never occurs," Zell replied. Atha fell silent for a few moments as he gazed up to the stars.

"So he's actually a good guy?"

"Perhaps, but again, dangerous. Power that great can destroy all that surrounds it despite intentions," said Zell, her words falling on deaf ears as Atha noticed a shooting star flicker across the sky.

"I think I can help Harika," Atha said.

"How?" she asked.

"I can't tell you. Can you trust me on this?" Atha replied, the memory of Xexon and his gifted modulation energy leaking back into his mind.

"If you choose to try, I support that decision," Zell replied.

Atha clapped. "We have our first mission! So where exactly are these Capinilal Mountains?" Atha asked. Zell pulled her orange screen up and began shuffling symbols around until a map appeared.

"The center point is the capital. To the north, this grey area represents the destruction training grounds. Further to the north you can find the Capinilal Mountains."

Atha glanced up to them.

"On here it calls them the Glowing Mountains. What's with that?" he asked. Zell rearranged symbols, an image popping up of mountains glistening with blue light.

"Over the years, his mana has grown to an estimated seven million based upon our estimations of his progress since the age of seven. The sheer volume of mana being pulled from the surrounding area causes something called the Marsh effect. Named in his honor, the Marsh effect causes the glow that lights the mountains through the night. Due to the increased mana volume in the air, the gravity is considerably increased and can cause death to an unprepared body."

Atha's body glowed with a red hue. "I've got that covered. So when should we go?"

Zell whisked her screen away. "This is your plan. I shall leave the details to you, including just how you plan to transport us all the way out there.".

"I don't think I can drive the four-wheeler all the way there. Y'all don't got any magical teleportation items, do you?"

Zell nodded. "Yes, but I think it's reasonable for you to learn to figure something out for yourself."

"Fair enough. I'll figure out a plan. We'll reconvene in the morning."

"Goodnight, Atha." Zell stood and disappeared into her tent as Atha sank down onto his sleeping bag to look up at the sky.

"Fuck, I love stars," Atha mumbled pleasantly to himself as the soothing crackle of the fire lulled him to sleep.

Four a.m. Earth time rolled around and, like always, Atha awoke with a snap, popping up to the sound of Zell's light snore. *Judging by how my internal clock has gotten further off kilter, Oluceps has about a twenty-five-hour day. Good, this will give me a little time to practice.* Atha headed out into the clearing, the daunting metal objects blotting out most of the horizon to the north, but if his idea worked, they wouldn't be there for long. *Street bike, 1000cc, black color scheme.* Drawing the image into his mind, the machine landed in front of him, the kickstand giving into the dirt under its weight as Atha sprung forward to halt it. Red energy glowed from his body and he yanked it back upright, taking a few moments to admire the powerful machine glinting in the moonlight before him.

He reached down, pressing the button on his shoe to create an open-air path. A blue trail led a few meters into the air in front of the bike. Sitting on the seat, he studied the switches and pedals on either side, deciding this was far more complicated than the simple ATV he'd manifested before. Popping open the trunk beneath the passenger's seat, he located the instruction manual and glanced through the expansive table of contents. Unfortunately, he only possessed one X chromosome and decided he had no need for instructions and stashed the manual back in the trunk before commencing a long series of trial and error.

Twenty-seven minuets, fifty-two attempts, and innumerable expletives later...

The bike came roaring to life. He tugged back on the throttle a few extra times for added effect as a smile crossed his face. *All right, let's see how long it takes to either paralyze or kill myself on this thing.* Pushing his foot down, he shifted into first gear. He pulled up into the air, a subtle wobble to his balance as the trail began to stretch forward while simultaneously vanishing behind him. He swiveled through a few rocks to get a firm understanding of how the path would climb or descend based on his movements, flipping into higher gears until he was blistering through the air.

"This is bitching!" he screamed, angling up over the massive tanker ship and roaring back down the other side.

He instantly lost control as the bike skipped roughly over the adjusting path and toppled over. The bike went crashing toward the ground as he slid across the blue path, rolling to a stop just in time to see it explode across the wing of a plane.

"Holy fucking shit!" he gasped, feeling over himself to check for injury but surprisingly found none. "I can't believe that just happened!"

"Shakka's *mercy*!" a bewildered Zell screamed up to him from far below.

"Oh! Good morning, Zell!" he called back to her. "Just getting a little practice in before we head off. Hey, so funny story that, uh, fiery ball over there actually had a mechanical problem and had nothing to do with the fact I found out you can't hit a jump off a magical pathway that glues itself to the bottom of your tires."

"Down here *now*!" she yelled up to him.

"Yes, mother," he mumbled before clicking his shoes off and falling onto the deck of the ship.

A few jumps later, he was listening as Zell strode back and forth, spewing a long lecture at him.

"Have words managed to strike reason in suicidal mind?!" Zell finished, coming to a smoldering stop in front of him.

"Hanging on every word," he lied.

"Now do you hold your skill at operating your machine in high regard?" she asked as Atha chuckled awkwardly.

"What *is* skill anyways? Come on, we'll live." He paused, glancing at the black smoke trailing up into the air from his first attempt. "Probably."

A new black bike appeared, and Zell snagged the helmets from atop the four-wheeler, forcing hers down before handing Atha his. Atha hopped onto the bike, Zell getting on behind him and grasping his waist as the bike roared to life.

"Okay, hold on!" Atha hollered back, pressing the button on his shoes to summon the blue path. He pulled up onto it, speeding up until the bike began to rattle back and forth.

"Oh shit! I'm losing control!" Atha joked back to Zell who instantly formed her blue tentacles, yanking Atha back off the bike and sending them both sliding along the path. The bike slid beside them for a few feet before toppling off the side and down across the rocks. Gravel and portions of the bike scattered across the terrain.

"Jesus Christ, I was kidding!" he gasped.

Zell snapped to her feet and pulled him to his own, giving him a shake.

"Are you *mad*?!" she yelled. Atha scoffed, tapping a finger into her forehead.

"Yeah, remember that time you—oh, I don't know—let me puke my guts out after teleporting?" he said as Zell paused, releasing her grip and waving a hand at the path.

"This yet stands in poor taste. Well, go on, manifest another, but no more jokes," Zell scolded almost sheepishly as a new bike fell onto the path.

"Oh, trust me, I won't. I'm afraid I'm gonna die when you prank *me*, and I'm afraid I'm gonna die when I prank *you*. Maybe we should just call it even."

Chapter 15
Power That Is Too Great

Keeping a steady eighty miles per hour, Atha and Zell glided above the treetops with the full force of all three suns beating down on them. Far on the horizon, daunting mountains spiked high into the air, completely filling the horizon with snow-capped stone, yet there was not a trace of the blue glow.

"Zell! Hey, is that the Capinilal Mountains up ahead?" Atha roared hopelessly through both his helmet and the wind. An orange ball of light entered his helmet.

"What was that?" Zell's voice buzzed through the light.

"Whoa! Magical walkie-talkie, wicked! How'd you do that?" Atha replied, the orange ball reverberating with his voice.

"Part of my contract consists of communication. I added you into its function, which allows me to monitor your physical health. To dismiss or manifest the comm, simply state the command word 'contact.'"

"Oh, so now I got both you and El keeping tabs on me." Atha groaned. "Anyway, are those the mountains? I don't see a glow."

"During the day mana thins, hanging at high altitude. Look up."

He did. He could clearly make out streams of blue glow flowing through the sky. They converged atop a distant mountain, creating a light so bright it was visible despite the radiance of three suns.

"That's all mana?" Atha gasped.

"Harika's mana acquisition level is beyond comprehension. We will begin to feel elevated pressure paired with relentless gravity approximately a mile out from his location. With Agro energy at your disposal, this will cause you little distress. Unfortunately, without protection of my own, this is a trial you must face alone."

As they drew toward the mountain range, having not even hit the mile marker yet, Atha began to struggle with his breath and a weight pressed on his entire body.

"I can definitely feel it. I'm trying to wait to use Agro in case something happens. I can only use it for about eight minutes. Let me know when you can feel it and I'll set you down," Atha spoke into the orange ball, feeling Zell nod her head into his back.

"The pull of his reservoir is so great it will sap particles straight from my contract function, rendering it useless. Expect the same effect to sap the energy from pathway rendered by your shoes, so have a plan ready. Set me there, in that opening." Zell pointed a finger past Atha's head to a wide, flat space between two of the rocky peaks.

Atha guided them down and Zell hoped off. Atha gasped for air as he took a quick gauge of the nearby peak, where the blue energy was focused. *Shouldn't take too long to get there if I haul ass, but I gotta be careful of my path vanishing. This is way more dangerous than I thought it would be.*

"Easy peasy, lemon squeezy, I'll see you in a few, Z." Atha smiled back to the red woman. Zell was busying herself with an orange screen.

"Should you succeed, we must leave with haste. Bounty hunters are surely in the area," Zell replied. Another factor Atha hadn't planned for.

Red energy pulsed from his body as he yanked the throttle back, zipping up into the air toward the peak. Just as Zell had warned him, the blue path began to show up spotty and thinned, nearly vanishing all together as he pulled up to a stop upon a rocky ledge. Glancing up the daunting mountain, he realized he still had quite a way to go and forced more Agro energy through his legs. He burst high into the air to the next closest ledge.

This was a bad idea. Giuseppe would go ballistic if he knew I was going forward with this with hardly no planning. He paused atop a ledge, drawing the image of a digital wristwatch into his mind and quickly setting the timer for what he estimated to be his last four minutes of Agro energy. Mana now hung thick in the air, running across his skin like sandpaper.

Conditions got worse as he reached the top. The crushing pressure became almost unbearable. The point where mana streams converged was only a few boulders away. Forcing himself forward, he hobbled past the rocks to find a naked Shelando with long blue tentacles swirling lazily atop his head. The crushing mana flowed straight into his body as he sat with folded hands, praying silently.

"I'm gonna go out on a limb here and say you're Harika," Atha said as he chuckled uneasily. The Shelando's eyes turned and focused on him.

"It is not safe for you here. Please leave," Harika replied in an empty, almost droning voice that paired well with his expressionless face.

"Well, that's probably why my dumb-ass wobbled all the way up those cliffs to talk with a living bomb. My name's Atha Honorati by the way." He extended a hand down to shake Harika's.

Harika ignored it, slowly getting to his feet and heading away as Atha followed behind. "Hey, sorry, I know my jokes suck. I really need to talk to you. I'm actually running on a timer here."

"If you have come for revenge, allow me to deter you," he replied slowly, moving past the edge of the boulders to a vast open view.

Atha paused in shock upon realizing that the mountains ended abruptly past this one. There was nothing but a massive crater as far as he could see, scarring the face of the planet. Like the raging storm of red upon Venus, this too would surely be visible from space.

Atha rarely found himself at a loss for words, but in this moment his mouth fell open to match the gaping hole upon the planet.

"This occurred when another came to confront me. He did not survive," Harika noted emptily, turning to Atha.

Zell's words came back to him in that moment. *Power that is too great destroys all that surrounds it.* Horrifyingly literal in this case.

"This is way more power than I expected. I mean, I saw a recording of— of the previous incidents, but Zell said that blast radius was around a mile. This is the horizon." Atha was stunned, finally managing to pull his eyes away and back toward Harika.

"Yes. Please, just go," he replied.

Atha pulled out his blackened meteor to bounce it around his fingers. His mind cleared instantly, allowing him to check his watch to see the amount of time that could very well signify his remaining lifespan. Two minutes and seventeen seconds—and counting.

"I wish I had more time to make a better decision, but I don't so I'm gonna have to count on your honesty to make a good decision. Can you answer a few questions for me?" Atha asked.

"I will if you agree to leave once they are done. Be warned, my emotions are currently under control, but should that change, I will release a burst of mana," Harika warned.

"What do you mean by that?" Atha asked, trying to find any telltale signs of a liar but seeing nothing in Harika's eyes.

"Emotion is directly linked to my mana," he replied.

Atha waited for him to continue, but he didn't.

"So, are you saying you blow up by accident when you feel happy or sad?"

"Yes," Harika replied, again leaving Atha waiting for words that did not come.

"Then would you say you've never intentionally hurt anyone before?"

"Yes."

"Is that why you moved up here? To keep from hurting anyone?"

"Yes."

"All right, last question. Hypothetically speaking, if you were able to control your mana, would you want to leave here?"

"Yes," Harika replied and Atha nodded, his watch beginning to beep as he stuffed his rock back in his pocket.

"All right, I'm all out of time, so I'm gonna try something," *Come on modulation energy. Do your thing or else I'm screwed.* White glowed from Atha's hands, streaming from them and into Harika. The mana flowing into him slowed to a crawl. "I think it worked. Do you feel any different?"

Harika paused, eyeing himself over for a moment. "No."

"If what I think I did worked, then your mana should be"—Atha started, but his mouth suddenly finished the sentence for him—"reduced to a millionth of its original amount." He clasped his mouth in surprise for a moment. The streams of blue mana dissipated almost on cue, thinning before vanishing from the air.

"Is this a trick?" Harika asked. Atha shook his head.

"No, you should—" His words halted as Harika whimpered. A blast of blue energy ripped across Atha and flung him across the mountain's top just as his red energy died.

"I'm sorry. Are you okay?" Harika asked slowly, hobbling after Atha who groaned as he rubbed his head.

"What the hell was that?"

"I felt happy. I'm sorry, Atha," Harika replied, a slight smile creeping over his face.

A set of pants fell into Atha's hands and he tossed them to Harika. "It's all right. Put those on, can't have you running around butt-ass naked. Now come on, we gotta get you out of here before the bounty hunters arrive."

Harika slipped into the pants. "I thank you for what you've done, but I will turn myself in," he replied.

"But—but why?! I reduced your power. You can go anywhere now! Why would you choose to use that freedom to switch your figurative prison to a fucking literal one?" Atha spat.

"I have many crimes to pay for," Harika replied.

Atha groaned with irritation.

"I came up here to help you, so you could make up for what you've done, not so you could rot in a cell! Your answer isn't going to solve anything!"

"I'm responsible for much death. Nothing could make up for those who have been lost," he replied slowly as took a long, deep breath.

"I get where you're coming from, but it was an accident. Look, all I'm saying is don't fix one tragedy with another. You've got a fucking ton of mana and last time I checked that's what this whole world revolves around. Could you even imagine what you could do with, I don't know, a healing contract or something?" Atha replied.

Harika mulled the words for a few moments, eventually droning out, "You really think I could do that?"

"Absolutely! Now I was gonna do this later but let's go straight to my pitch. Join the Honorati family. I am-- for lack of any better ideas-- putting together a team to help people and hopefully combat forces like the Red Sheep," Atha declared.

"Who's the Red Sheep?" Harika asked.

"You don't know? Oh, well you have been living on a mountain for over a decade, so I guess that makes sense."

"I'm sorry but I could never hurt a living creature. All life is precious," Harika replied.

"That thing has it coming," Atha replied.

"All life is precious."

"We'll have to agree to disagree, but I'll work to accommodate your beliefs. Imagine what we could do together, all the lives we could save! If you really believe what you're saying, then you know your own life is precious too! Why waste it?" Atha burst, jabbing a finger into Harika's chest.

"So how 'bout it?" he finished and extending his hand again. This time Harika slowly extended his own to grasp it. "Welcome to the Honorati family. Now come on, we seriously gotta get outta here."

Atha clicked his shoes on, materializing a bike and hoping on it. "Get on and I'll fly us out of here."

A blue glow emitted from Harika's feet as he eased into the air.

"I can fly."

"You're fucking awesome, dude! All right, follow me!" Atha laughed, pulling up over the edge and down the mountain.

Atha rolled to a stop beside the awaiting Zell, both screaming as Harika slammed into the ground with enough force to leave a crater.

"You all right?" Atha yelled, hopping off the bike and hurrying toward Harika, who climbed slowly from the crater.

"Yes. I overshot the distance down," he replied. Zell stepped beside Atha.

"So, this is Harika Teldon Marsh. Unfortunately, we must save introductions for another time, We must make haste."

Atha nodded and hurried back onto the bike as Zell pulled her helmet back on and got on. Atha revved the engine and they were beginning to gain altitude when a bolt of black energy smashed the back tire, causing Atha to instantly lose control. They slid across the pathway, which cracked then shattered, sending them flying down toward the ground.

"Bounce house!" Atha screamed out loud, the last of his Agro energy slowing time as he flipped over to grab Zell. He held her to his side as they slammed into the plastic building.

"What the fuck was that?!" Atha screamed, digging himself out from the deflating structure as Harika slammed down onto the ground beside them.

"We were too late. They are upon us!" Zell yelled. Atha pulled his rock from his pocket to concentrate.

"Harika, put this on and whisper your name to us!" Atha called out as he pulled Elise's anti-recognition ring from his pocket and gave it to Harika. Atha, and Zell blinked for a few moments, forgetting who the glowing Shelando was.

"Harika Teldon Marsh."

"Whoa! That gets me every time. All right now just be quiet and we'll handle this!" Atha yelled back as three streaks of blue crashed down around them. A pair of female humans and a male Denata surrounded them.

"This them, Jako?" the tall blond female called to the Denata, who nodded.

"That's the human who went up. Harika was with him until a few moments ago," he replied as the second shorter female stepped forward.

"Ok, boy, how'd you—"

"Don't call me 'boy,'" Atha spat.

Zell's orange screen popping up and she blitzed symbols around faster than Atha had ever seen.

"H-hey! Stop that!" the tall blond shrilled, a black bow dropping through a red portal to fall into her groping hands, but Zell burst into action. Her mana tentacles stretched out and with a swirl she swept the legs out from beneath every assailant. One tentacle wrapped around the male Denata's neck and then slammed him onto the ground. He went limp.

"Holy fucking shit!" Atha gasped, eyeing the groaning party as the blond female paused in shock.

"Orange screen, mana vector extensions—oh shit, your *Zell Tenzata,* aren't you?" she asked, her partner's eyes widening at the name.

"I am. Now let me tell you how this is going to play out," Zell said as she motioned to Atha.

"The pair of you will do battle with him. Should you be triumphant, I will divulge the location of Harika Marsh and I will not obstruct you from acquiring him. Are these terms acceptable?" she asked. The two paused and glanced to one another as Atha moved close to Zell to whisper to her.

"What are you doing?" he said. "We shouldn't assume they're alone!"

"Be at ease. The unconscious male acts as both tracker and communication source with their main party. I assume they broke off alone after perceiving opportunity to capture Harika for themselves," she replied as Atha glanced over at the knocked out Denata.

"You figured all the out in seven seconds?" Atha asked.

"We accept your terms," the blonde spoke up, standing to her feet.

"Very well. Begin whenever you wish," Zell replied.

Atha glanced to her in surprise as the two female humans sprang into action. The blonde's bow ripped a shot off. Atha ducked to no avail as an arrow with a hefty tip not much different from a bowling ball slammed into his side. It wasn't a heavy blow, but with barely recovered Agro energy, it felt like a bowling ball. Glancing up, he realized the other was hovering above him, one hand glowing green while the other shined an eerie red, tapping the former into her body before beginning to fall straight down. Atha barely had time to roll, her body slamming down into the ground and crushing straight through the hard rock.

"Zell! What the fuck?" Atha screamed, leaping back as another shot toward him. A car popping up in the way, but with a quick veer, the arrow easily avoided it and nailed his shoulder.

"You struggle against mediocre opponents because you still fixate on simple firepower. The blonde uses a targeting ability that causes her arrow to never miss the point she focuses on with her eyes. Her ally wields ability that can double objects' weight if touched with her right hand, or halve it with her left hand. Now find the difference information can make."

Atha pulled his rock from his pocket to dance it around in his fingers as the blonde's face fell.

"That wasn't part of the deal!" she screamed. Zell shook her head.

"We set no specific terms," she replied as Atha pocketed his rock, sneering at the blond.

"Game on, bitch," he called to her.

Her face turning red with anger and she shot a black arrow toward Atha. This time he watched where she was looking, and released a small glow of red from his head to that spot. The arrow shattered harmlessly across him. The blonde paused in disbelief as the second woman climbed up out of the ground and floated up until Atha caught her leg. Yanking her back down, he snatched her red hand, slapping it into her body over and over as she slammed back onto the ground, struggling to reach the green hand over.

"I coulda whooped them on my own," Atha said with a smirk for Zell. A quick spark of red glowed from his shoulder as another arrow shattered across it. *12-gauge, rubber buck-shot load.* Atha drew the image of a black shotgun into his mind, catching it from the air and unleashing a flurry of blasts at the blonde. She screamed in pain and fell backwards onto the ground.

"This was just a test! You go too far!" Zell screamed at Atha, but he shrugged.

"She's fucked up, but she ain't dead." Atha chuckled, the not-so-subtle screams of the blonde almost blocking his voice out. Zell yanked Atha by the shoulders, thrusting him back toward the bike before hurrying to the blonde. She pulled a vial from her pocket and with a flash of white the blonde's growing welts began to recede.

"Thank you," she stuttered to Zell, who nodded and headed toward Atha.

"Go," she ordered coldly, pulling her helmet back on.

The trip back was quiet. Harika flew beside them and Zell's orange ball popped up beside Atha's face, carrying her words to his ear.

"That was excessive force," she growled.

"Yeah, you're right. But the way she talked to us, calling me 'boy.'" Atha felt his anger beginning to surge again despite his best attempt to smother it.

"I know you hold disdain for the term, but you must learn to control your emotions," Zell explained. Remember how I told you a battle is won through a multitude of factors? Information was a mere piece of the puzzle, and once added, did you not see how quickly their advances failed? Emotion stands as its equal, but unlike the other I cannot simply speak and have it understood." Atha took a few deep breaths able to bottle his growing anger.

"Yeah, so you keep saying, but it's not that easy. Let's just change the subject. What should we do with our newest addition?"

"Posing such a question to me causes my own to beg answer. You are wanting of a plan?"

"Oh no, I got a plan. I plan to drive a big greasy cheeseburger smothered in bacon into my gut tonight," Atha replied.

"Again? The insatiable way you hunger for grease, the unheard cries from arteries—no, never mind that! Your contagious stupidity has grown to such boundless proportion that it breaks thresholds and compromises my own mind."

"Don't fight it. It only makes things worse."

"Atha, what do you plan to do with Harika?" Zell chuckled, thumping a fist against his back.

"I don't have a clue. He's with us now and that's all that matters. We'll figure everything else out as it comes. Obviously, we need to keep his identity a secret."

"He possesses the anti-recognition ring, so there is little else we can do."

Harmer's contract could shut the ring off, though. "Yeah, but what about contracts that could stop its effect?"

"True. Strange, you are not normally so thoughtful. What made you consider such a possibility?"

Atha's eyes widened. *Zell doesn't miss a thing. Make up a believable excuse that she can't disprove or this is gonna go south.*

"It was just something that easily compared to trying to stay hidden on Earth. Even if you change your appearance, a facial recognition system can still see through it," he lied.

"So past experience did the thinking for you. To be blunt, if that were the case, there is nothing we could do. But it matters not, an ability of that caliber would fall to at least an S grade, thus making it anomalous."

So, Harmer's ability is rare.

The last sun had long since set by the time they returned to the barren canyon, a massive cheeseburger in Atha's hands before they even sat down, greasy bacon dangling from the side.

Atha slumped down in a seat next to Harika, slurping up the bacon like a noodle. "I'm gonna set up a tent for you. Do you need anything else right now? Food? A drink? A psychological examination?" Atha smirked but Harika did not join him in the humor.

"I do not require food or sleep. I do not recognize the terms used in the last question."

"No food or sleep? How?"

"It is quite possible," Zell cut in. "In theory, mana can substitute for any bodily necessity, including the REM sleep cycle in high enough quantities."

"Theory? How is it a theory if we got an insomniac and a—I don't know, there's no word for someone who doesn't eat other than dead—sitting right here?"

"A simple answer. Nobody has ever reached high enough levels to fully sustain a functioning body without traditional nourishment," she replied as Atha glanced back to Harika.

"Dude that is so cool, you're like a machine! I mean, a horrible curse at the same time 'cause just look at this burger!" He laughed, stopping as Harika remained silent. "Look man, first thing you gotta know about me is that my jokes are usually borderline offensive. I don't mean nothing by them. Well sometimes I do, but not this time." He smiled but Harika again showed no signs of amusement or any other emotion whatsoever.

"What was the joke?" he asked.

"The—the food thing. Never mind, I'm gonna hit the hay before you hit *me*. We'll make a plan tomorrow," he replied, giving Harika a pat on the back before ducking off behind a rock where his sleeping bag awaited.

He awoke with a snap a few hours later to the sound of whispers. He peeked around his rock, noticing Harika sitting in the dirt muttering quiet prayer.

"For the loss of a life is a loss to the world. A loss to the world is a loss for me and everyone I will ever know. Each individual provides the world with warmth that cannot be taken for granted despite the inability to grasp it, for only when the warmth is gone do we truly realize the cold that surrounds us."

Atha slowly made his way toward Harika, coming to a stop beside him. He quickly realized Harika was paying him no mind and yawned exaggeratedly to gain an audience.

"Apologies, did I awake you?" Harika asked.

"Not your fault, I'm just an insanely light sleeper," Atha said. "Grew up with the idea being if someone was in my cell in the middle of the night, it was never good news. If you don't mind me asking, what was that prayer? It was beautiful."

"It's called the answer," Harika told him.

"The answer, huh? And why is that?"

"It is an intercessory prayer that simply states life should never be taken for any reason," Harika explained.

"Eh, I always stayed away from religion 'cause of ideas like that. I don't agree with most of the ethics. I noticed you pray a lot though."

"I do." Harika nodded.

"Does it help you keep your cool? I got a quirk kinda like that where I dribble a rock around in my fingers. Helps me think."

"That, and because I have much to pray for," Harika replied as Atha's smile whisked away. "May I ask why you believe some people don't deserve to live?"

"Because some people deserve to burn in hell," Atha replied. "Back at the capital I met some guy who tried to cut a kid's arm off for stealing pocket change to get something to eat. If the kid wasn't right there, I'd have knocked his head off."

"What if he was to discover the cure for a disease that infected you?" Harika asked.

"I'd rather die."

"What if it would save the child he tried to hurt?" Harika replied.

"Fuck, dude, I don't know. I just go off what I see in front of me without worrying about what *could* be," Atha replied.

"You have little empathy, don't you?" Harika observed.

"I wouldn't say that. Just low tolerance for bullshit."

"In my religion, those who dismiss abstract ideas of current existence are considered enlightened. No good, no evil, just life and with it, the hope that the future holds bountiful gifts from all. Those who weigh too heavily upon the merits of a person's past are considered the lowest level of within it."

"I don't worry too much about what random extras think of me." Atha shrugged. "What do *you* think, Harika?"

"I don't agree with that label. You say harsh things, but you helped me, and I think actions speak louder than words," Harika replied.

"Well, at least you got a little faith in me. But is that the whole point of your speech? Being sonder?" Atha asked.

"Sonder? I'm not familiar with that word," Harika admitted.

"It means to realize everybody around you is living a life that's just as vivid as your own. It's probably the most exotic word I've ever used without the aid of my rock." He chuckled.

"That is an accurate description for it. Apologies, I don't have a very broad dictionary," Harika replied.

"That's fine with me. I got used to not using very big words back in prison 'cause most of the time people didn't know what they meant. So, a little off topic, but how much do you know in general? Would you say you have a firm grasp of how this world works?" Atha asked, leaning back into the dirt for a better gaze of the stars.

"No."

"All right man, gotta give me a little more context. How much would you say you know?" Atha replied, beginning to pick out constellations in the clear night sky.

"I attended school and church regularly when I was younger, but I have forgotten much since."

"Oh, well that still makes you a few years ahead of me! Everything is so confusing here."

"How is it that you know less than I?"

"I'm not from this world. I grew up on another place called Earth. Been here for less than a week and having a pretty difficult learning curve so far."

"I see."

"That's not the reaction I was expecting. The last person I told who didn't know my backstory straight up called me a liar and thought I was on drugs."

"You have given me no reason to doubt you."

"I'll make sure I never give you reason to. Looks like it's almost wake up time," Atha noted.

As if on cue, Zell exited out of her tent to release a long yawn, showing off the pointed fangs in her mouth. "Just FYI, Zell seems like a hard-ass but she's actually really cool," Atha whispered to Harika.

"She uses many words I don't understand," Harika responded.

"Yeah, that's kind of her thing, I guess. She uses an information contract and being excessively articulate is a way of constantly demonstrating her knowledge superiority. Actually, when I say my theory out loud it kinda makes her sound like a bitch. I don't know, I like her."

"Seeing as we have a new addition to our forces, I thought it best to broach a subject that could aid you both of us—divulging contract," she said as she walked over to them.

"Damn, this day just gets better and better!" Atha burst to his feet with joy. "Not to look a gift horse in the mouth, but didn't you say we should figure out my other abilities first?"

"Yes, but we'll skip ahead for Harika's benefit. I doubt we will find a contract suitable for you," Zell responded.

"Ok, Buzz Killington, where do we start then?"

Zell popped open her screen. "We start by ascertaining which varieties are of most use to either of you and selecting from them. Considering you both have a decent grasp of the main types, give voice to the ones you desire and why. *If* deemed worthy, we will discuss and pursue the notion."

Atha instantly spoke up. "Combat! And because-"

"No. Harika?" Zell cut in, turning her attention to the blue Shelando.

He paused for a long moment, the blue tentacles atop his head swaying slowly in the breezy, warm air.

"Medical. I would like to make up for some of the pain I've caused," Harika replied, turning his void blue eyes to Atha, who gave him a thumbs up.

"*Medical,* you say? Interesting. Motivation is also well placed, personal reasons solutioned adequately with desirable practicality," Zell replied, moving a few symbols around on her screen until a list popped up. With a flick of her wrist the screen moved in front of Harika, who stared plainly at it.

"Hermes healing factor?" she asked.

"Hermes? Like the Greek god Hermes?" Atha asked, shifting to stand behind Harika to look with him. The recognizable caduceus symbol hung beside it, a pair of snakes wrapping around a staff. "A direct connection to Earth! Is Hermes real?"

"There exist many spirits who claim themselves a god and, considering they freely traverse plains of reality, it is not a reach to assume one may have visited Earth," she replied.

"Holy fucking shit! I've made the discovery of the century! This could explain so much of Earth's past!" he continued as Zell moved to a seat closer to Harika.

"It is a double S contract, ranking it amongst the most potent of healing abilities. You are certain this is the candidate you wish to propose a contract to?" she asked.

"Yes."

"Very well. The next step is to discern the details of the contract and number of years you wish to hold it for," she replied, tapping a finger onto the caduceus symbol to pull up more information. "Contract-specific abilities are listed as well. Able to perfectly replace damaged portions of the body, excluding the brain; blood can be replenished but not drawn out; and unable to heal sickness or flush toxin from blood. Shakka's mercy, quite the list of puissance followed by little debilitation."

Zell gasped before continuing to read off the information. "Spirit typing demonic, basic mana transaction-based use via familiar. Here it is, the contract forming method. To call a term-setting representative spirit, subject must write name upon sika paper in their own blood, burn it, and await contact. If you are sure this is the optimal choice, then we can begin the ritual immediately."

"Yes," Harika replied.

"Then let us begin. Atha, manifest the sika paper," Zell continued, shifting a few symbols around until the image of a green sheet of paper shown on her screen. It waved lazily through the dry air into his palm. He handed it to Zell.

"Thank you. Next we shall need to prick your finger." She pulled a knife from her robes as Harika extended his hand.

Atha glanced over curiously, unsure what the color of the Shelando's blood would be. He screamed in surprise as Zell slammed the knife down onto a finger.

"What are you doing? You trying to take a finger off?" Atha screamed, stopping as he realized Harika was not only bloodless, but he'd taken no damage whatsoever.

"Mana reinforces the normally frangible bound of flesh. I estimated Harika's would require force far beyond the norm, but it appears that even now it shatters common reality," Zell replied in shared surprise, returning the first knife and securing another made of black metal.

With another forceful slam, Atha involuntarily yelped again, peeking open an eye to the absence of blood once more. Zell sighed with distaste, drew back again, swinging her knife down with all the force she could muster.

With a loud *ping* the knife snapped, the blade whirring past Atha's head.

"Inconceivable!" Zell gasped, holding up the lonely handle.

"Apparently not, Vizzini. Your fancy little knife 'bout took my eye out. What now?" Atha asked.

Zell reached a hand over to tap the sword at his side.

"Seeing how ineffective the best weapon in my arsenal proved, our last resort rests with Shooting Star. It is made of the highest-grade metal in this world."

"Is that a good idea? Elise said it's dangerous."

"An unavoidable risk. Fear not, my guidance is at your disposal," she replied, standing up to move behind Atha.

"Draw the blade slowly," she instructed. "Any movement you make with that arm will be amplified a thousand times." Atha reached a hand down onto the plain black handle, easing it up as the chains encasing it began to shift. Ever so slowly, they untangled from the sheath and wrapped up over his arm and hand to lash him to the handle.

"Whoa, that's awesome!" Atha laughed.

"Focus. Gradual, slow movement," Zell said. Atha rolled his eyes but gave no retort.

The blade was perfectly straight and glossy with a dull white glow brimming from it. The chains continued to tighten on his arm until it was fully drawn. Atha admired it for a moment before Zell continued.

"Ease it above target. Use an equal amount of force you'd put into crisply pressing a button."

Atha was becoming nervous and actually felt comforted by Zell's micromanagement as he held the glowing blade over Harika's hand.

"Hope you trust me," Atha whispered to Harika.

"I do."

"That makes one of us. Here goes." Atha took a calming breath before jerking his arm. The blade's light pulsed, chains tightening around his arm, multiplying the force and slamming down onto Harika's finger. Atha was sure the finger would be gone, but just a spot of blue blood dribbled free.

Zell smiled. "Well done. Now ease it back into the sheath."

Atha eased the blade back over the holster, and with a swift click and rattle of retracting chains, it returned to its home.

Harika drew out his name on the paper and a lighter fell into Atha's hands.

"I thought El had exaggerated a little, but damn that sword is crazy," Atha noted, taking the paper from Harika and flicking on the flame.

The green paper had barely a corner darkened to ash before a massive red portal opened high in the air above the camp. A massive white pole thicker than a tree trunk slid out and lodged into the ground, leaving the tail end hidden within the still-open portal. Atha pocketed the lighter and stared up at the massive pillar.

An enormous snake came through the portal and swirled down the pole. A set of massive black wings hung from its back, yet surely not enough to carry the hefty body that continued to curl out of the portal.

Atha's eyes widened in shock. He had expected a Roman god but was now greeted with a living nightmare.

"What in the hell is that thing?" he asked Zell, noticing a look of shock on her face as well.

"I assume the overlord of the hierarchy from which it comes," Zell replied.

The snake ran out of pole so it remained partially hidden in the portal. It stretched its massive head high into the air as slitted eyes stared down on the Shelando.

"Harika Teldon Marsh," it said in a deep, reverberating voice, angling its head down until it came to eye level with Harika. "Ah, the joy I feel having the magnificent power I offer chosen by one so gifted with mana as you. I am Renshut and have elected to personally deal with this transaction."

"Hello," Harika replied as emptily as ever.

"Lord Renshut, if I may be so bold," Zell said as she stepped forward and bowed at the waist.

"Granted, half-demon." The snake flicked its eyes at her.

"Gratitude. I am Zell Tenzata, and I shall deal with negotiations regarding Harika's terms based on the premise that he holds little knowledge of such transactions. Is my proposition acceptable for you, Lord Renshut?"

"Terms accepted, but know that he alone must finalize the exchange," he replied coolly.

"Certainly, my lord."

"So very well-mannered," he replied. "My opening offer is as follow: a lifetime contract, six million particles of mana up front, an additional million every hour and two million every time the contract is used."

Pangs of blue streaked Zell's face. "M-millions?! My lord, his body would perish."

"*Perish* you say? You know far less than I had assumed. Harika's body holds *billions* and every moment that number increases. Normal users have an average of ninety-five percent of daily mana intake exchanged for the use of my contract, yet I ask for less than one percent of Harika's," he replied with a sly chuckle as Zell's mouth fell open.

Zell froze like a deer in headlights. Atha could practically see the gears slamming to a halt in her head as she attempted to stammer a response to these unforeseen facts.

"Apologies, Lord Renshut, I find myself lacking sufficient information in this matter."

"I assure you my terms are quite fair, so what say you, Harika?" The snake turned smugly back to Harika as Zell's head flipped between the two.

"Are you done?" Harika asked the panicked Zell.

"This—the matter at hand is beyond my council," Zell stuttered back. Atha stepped forward as his rock juggled around in his fingers.

"I can take it from here, Zell." He smiled to her but the snake's tongue lashed out and slapped him like a whip across his face.

"She was appointed negotiator! You would do well to know your place, boy!" the snake roared. Atha filled with rage at the remark.

"Don't *ever* call me 'boy'! I see why snake is a synonym for swindler now!" Its tongue lashed out again, but Harika's hand snapped up, shielding Atha's face as his empty eyes looked up to Renshut.

"Please don't hit him again," he announced plainly as he released the snake's tongue.

"You would name a negotiator then allow another to take the title? You waste my time!" Its roar rattled the ground, but Harika remained unfazed.

"Oh, Ren, fucking shut it!" Atha sneered "You know you had Zell spazzing out and you wanted to take advantage of it! Now you gotta deal with me." He pulled his meteorite from his pocket, bouncing it around his fingers to size up the situation. "The way I see it, you're getting a hell of a deal but leaving us high and dry. Simply comparing mana percentages doesn't justify inflating your price to astronomical heights without some type of compensation." He continued to juggle the rock as the snake's mouth curled.

"And what would you propose?"

"Information. From what I understand, every contract has a harsh learning curve and higher-class grades get it the worst. Give Harika a detailed guide to the ins and outs of Hermes's healing," Atha replied.

"Absurd. Spirits are not permitted to give out information that a mortal is not aware of."

"Oh well, you know what they say, there's always another contract. I'm sure we'll find a spirit willing to bend the rules for millions of mana particles," Atha replied, turning back to Harika. "Sorry buddy, this option's a bust—"

"No!" the snake screamed in a panic. A sly grin appeared on Atha's face that quickly vanished before he turned back.

"I want all the best learning methods, a detailed guide of all the strengths and weaknesses, a list of all secret abilities it possesses, and lastly, I want a fucking fresh pizza! The best Earth has to offer!" Atha demanded.

Zell stared in shock at the demands. The snake's head sagged for a moment, slowly bobbing back up in a recognizable nod before returning his slitted eyes to Atha.

"I accept your terms," he replied, Zell's mouth dropping at the words.

"Obviously, if your learning methods don't pan out too well I expect another form of compensation to be determined one week from now based upon Harika's growth with the ability. Based on my own judgment of course." Atha smiled up to the snake whose face snarled with rage.

"You overstep, human," Renshut hissed.

"Many times every day, but I think we both know this is fair." Atha smirked. A blue hologram popped up in front of Harika. Atha hurried back to his side, peering over at a set of well-written out contractual agreements. "Oh, so a contract is *literally* a contract. Hold on, let me read it over before you sign."

Harika nodded and stepped back.

Atha read through for almost an hour, the expansive contract illustrating details in minutiae.

"Yeah, everything's there. Go ahead," Atha instructed.

Harika stepped forward and slowly scribbled his name at the bottom as Renshut released a long sigh.

"Then our accord is finalized," Renshut said. "I look forward to the business we will do, Harika Marsh. As for the human, may we never meet again."

The pole retracted back up into the red portal before it vanished with a loud *pop!*

Zell gasped, falling to her knees as Atha rushed to her side.

"Hey, you okay?!"

"Renshut—mighty king of the spirit realm came to us to deal personally with terms—and you thought it wise to *insult* him?!" she screamed, yanking on Atha's shoulders.

"Hey, calm down! Remember, 'I find myself lacking—'" Atha started, mocking Zell's stuttering voice but stopped himself when he realized actual distress was on her face.

Zell scoffed, pulling her hands down her face as if to wake herself from a bad dream. "Oh, the tempest now screams for the breeze to *calm* itself."

"I was just looking out for Harika!" Atha retorted. "Spazzing out like that was exactly what Renshut was hoping you'd do!"

Zell covered her eyes for a moment before nodding slowly.

"Your words spray blissfully with ignorance yet strike true. I found myself in a panic and had not considered the possibility of a spirit of that caliber appearing. This went well, but for future reference a spirit, regardless of status, is not a force to taunt," she replied.

"Noted. Not saying I won't do something dumb, but noted," he said with a chuckle.

"Unfortunately, I expect no less. Might I inquire how you managed to negotiate that deal? I have never seen someone trade something so well when they knew so little of it, let alone its worth," she asked as Atha beamed with pride.

"Len taught me how to make a trade with anybody for anything. It doesn't matter how much what you've got is worth, you just gotta know how badly the other party wants it. He made the opening offer, which is a huge mistake in any negotiation, but he even freaked out when I dropped the whole *let's go look somewhere else* line, which is a *major* no-no. Honestly, I didn't think it would be that easy considering he obviously had experience in trading, so it really showed just how badly he wanted Harika. He left the door open for me to make any demand I could think of." Atha pausing when a small red portal opened beside Harika. A much smaller winged red snake slithered through, flapping in the air for a moment until he reached Harika's arm and curled around it.

"Hello, Mister Marsh! My name's Healix and am the familiar assigned to you from this day
forward!" it squeaked in a high-pitched, peppy voice.

"Hello," Harika replied flatly.

Atha began to protest the absent pizza but smiled as a skinny square box fell out of the portal onto the ground at Harika's feet.

"Never mind! There's what I was waiting for!" He laughed and reached down to retrieve the box. He gazed at the glories hidden within and snatched a fresh slice and took a monstrous chomp.

"Oh my God, this is my new favorite food," Atha said around a mouthful of pizza. "Healix, bro, you gotta tell your boss man that I take back half of the mean shit I said. This pizza is *fucking amazing*!"

The snake glanced dismally at Atha before turning back to Harika. "What a charming human. So, would you like to get right to it?"

"Yes," Harika replied.

"Allow me to accompany you. I find myself eager to learn of Hermes's healing factor," Zell added, smiling and bowing her head to the snake.

"Oh, you must be lady Zell! We could use your aid while I bring Harika up to speed. Before I do, I must inform you that adding any of the tips I divulge onto your contract's information system will directly breach the terms of our agreement," Healix noted. Zell nodded. "To begin, I'd like you to procure an assortment of injured insects for us. They are the easiest patients to operate on to get a feel for repairing a damaged body."

"Easily procured from foliage." She gestured toward the distant forest.

"What am I supposed to do?" Atha asked of Zell, who shrugged.

"Pretend you do not exist," she replied hopefully.

"Screw you, Mrs. Dursley. Oh, can I practice with Shooting Star?" Atha exclaimed, setting his pizza slice down to slap his sword.

"I would prefer you awaited my supervision," Zell replied.

"As if I needed any more reason," he replied.

"Do as you will, but keep your Agro energy at full strength, stop when it runs out, and use no more force then what it took to draw blood from Harika. Now come," she said to Harika, motioning for him to follow.

Atha leapt at the words. Red energy began to flit off his skin. Setting the watch on his wrist to ring in eight minutes, he grasped the handle. With a slight tug, the black chains shifted, untangling from the sheath and pulling up over his arm. The blade mixed two opposite colors splendidly, the black chains and handle attached to the white blade, which glowed a dull white that brightened with movement.

Atha found a target for it, a large bolder directly to his right. With a quick flick, he slammed the blade into it. He'd barely twitched, but

Shooting Star pierced smoothly into it like hot butter, coming to a harsh halt at the center.

He gave a light twitch on the sword but found the rock's grasp to be quite firm. "Oh, I've got a classic sword in the stone situation! Yeah, we'll see about that," Atha mumbled tauntingly to the rock, propping his foot up beside the sword and giving a slightly harder tug to no avail. Growing frustrated, he yanked it up, the rock shattering from the force of the sword that burst with a blinding white light, ripping Atha up high into the sky behind it.

"OH SHITTTTTT!" he screamed. Coming to a slow a few dozen meters in the air, he reflexively twisted his arm again to the right, yanking hard down toward the ground. He skidded across the rocks and dirt before coming to a rolling halt. He quickly scanned his body, checking for damage.

"Shakka's mercy! Are you injured?!" Zell dashed over to Atha's side.

"No, but I need some fresh drawers," he wheezed, carefully sheathing the sword as Zell buried her face in her hands.

"Alas, I find that the claws of stupidity yet clench firm."

Chapter 16
Meet the Boss

Atha clicked his shoes on and hopped on the all black bike, pulling his helmet down over his head before ripping up into the air. Zell and Harika had already disappeared toward the forest, so he was once again left to his own rights. He ripped through the canyons on the screaming bike.

"Is this real?" Atha mumbled to himself, glancing across the dazzling horizon set ablaze by the three suns. "Extra suns. Probably how my mind rationalizes the super bright light the doctors are shining in my eyes 'cause I'm in a coma right now. Or in the loony bin.

"Or maybe I died in prison and the portal was really my soul moving on. Or maybe I never actually went to prison! Yeah, if it isn't real then I must be dead. No way my unimaginative mind could have made this world up."

A bright flash flashed in between a set of distant canyons. *The doctor's got a new pen light. Time to go poke my nose where it doesn't belong.* Atha pulled to the left and headed for the spot the light had come from.

He came up over a rocky cliff. Below a group of green humanoids encircled a black-winged man, kicking and jabbing at him. Atha twisted down the path, rocketing toward the scene.

He was nearing the group but paused in surprise as the green monsters vanished, leaving the winged man to dramatically wave his hands at Atha, who pulled up to a slow stop before pulling off his helmet.

"Hey, you all right?" Atha asked. "I saw those things ganging up on you, where'd they go?"

"My apologies, I did not mean to startle you. They were illusions manifested by my contract," he replied as Atha studied the man.

His hair was black and well maintained, slicked back and down his neck. His skin was ghostly white, and everything but the face of this tall, slender man was covered by the recognizable uniform of a Royal Guard member.

"You're a Royal Guard, right? What're you doing all the way out here?" Atha asked, clicking his bike off and pulling a leg over to stand in front of him.

"Proudly so. I came here to just sharpen my skills," the man replied in a smooth voice, smiling down to Atha, who was head and shoulders shorter than he.

"Out here? But this is the *destruction* training grounds. Why come all the way to the middle of nowhere just to practice with *illusions*?" Atha asked, eyeing him over suspiciously.

"I keep my techniques a secret. A friend today could be a knife in the back tomorrow," he replied, a fact that Len had reiterated hundreds of times over.

"Point taken. Oh, my name's Atha, by the way." He smiled and extended a hand up to the man who grasped it.

"Alkibiades. Just call me Al. And I am very much aware of who you are, Mr. Honorati," Al replied pleasantly, giving a firm shake. A like-minded fellow who'd even used Atha's proper last name. It was rare for Atha to warm up to others, and yet here he was beginning to think he liked Alkibiades.

"Oh no, please, just Atha. I don't think I'm some big shot 'cause of who my sister is. Well, I do think I'm a big shot, but just 'cause I'm a badass. Can I ask you a question?"

Al cocked a curious eyebrow at this. "I have no issue with any query you may pose," he responded.

Atha raised a finger up to the massive set of black wings on the man's back.

"The whole winged race thing. Kentantos. I know a little but not really enough to call myself a novice of the topic, so this *might* sound offensive. Did a contract actually do that to you or were you born with wings?"

"How strange this world must seem to you. I was born with them. The original set of humans who distorted into Kentantos had both their DNA and genes altered. Now they pass these wings down through bloodline."

"How did your mother give birth to you, then?" he asked, growing increasingly curious of the topic.

"C-section. Wings are considered a complication and require a contract to operate on the womb once the child is determined to be Kentanto."

"Okay, that does make sense. It must be cool to have wings. If you went to Earth you'd be a huge hit, like, people would line the streets to catch a glimpse of you!" Atha exclaimed, causing Al to chuckle.

"Perhaps I shall visit it one day. I suppose now would be a good opportunity to pose a question of my own. Please don't take this the wrong way, but as is mortal nature, the guard chatters, and rumors spread. Recently most of that has been upon the topic of the past between you and the good queen." Atha leered up at him, backing aggressively off the bike.

"The fuck you mean by that?" he asked as Alkibiades rubbed his hair apologetically.

"When too much is left to speculation, rumors form. It has been circulating that you dispatched the caretaker sent to Earth to protect her," he replied. Atha calmed back down upon hearing this.

"Got what he deserved," he replied.

"So it is true! Might I inquire as to what prompted such an event?" he replied. Atha paused.

"What the *fuck* is it to you? And why do you even care?" he spat. Alkibiades raised his hands in that ironic no-offense way somebody who knows full well they were offensive would.

"Apologies, I mean not to pry."

"Well, you're doing a shitty job," Atha scoffed.

"Again, apologies. It's just that a few of the *children* Dako wronged before leaving for Earth are in the guard now and wished to attain conformation of his demise," he replied sadly. Atha was taken aback by the statement. *What? I thought Shun said he was a decent guy here. Well, he hid what he was really well on Earth, so I guess it's not a crazy discovery.*

"My bad. I get snappy about touchy stuff like this. Well, I'm pretty snappy in general, but even more so when it comes to personal issues," he replied as Al nodded.

"I won't press, I just thought it would be nice to present them with the facts straight from the man himself."

Atha straightened up at the masculine title. "No, it's for a good cause, I guess. So here it is: about a decade ago I woke up to a crash and came in to find Dako choking Elise. I used a weapon from Earth known as a gun to shoot him in the head. He suffered in his last breaths," Atha didn't notice the smile that crept over his own face.

"You are such an interesting young man, not at all what I had expected," Al replied before taking a few steps back and ruffling his open wings slowly.

"You headed out?" Atha asked.

"Duty beckons. I eagerly await our next encounter, young Atha," Al replied with a warm smile. His black wings lurched him into the air with one fell swoop before giving Atha a wave. Once again alone, Atha kicked his bike back to life and rode in silence for a few more minutes.

Pulling back into camp he propped the kickstand down before heading over to where Zell and Harika sat. Healix was curled around Harika's arm, eyeing a twitching insect that sat on a rock before him. Atha came to a silent stop behind him, watching as Healix gazed at the bug.

"I detect seven life-threatening injuries," Healix announced, his fanged mouth opened, a red portal opening within it as tiny metal instruments began to ease the bug's body apart. Atha gasped in amazement. Harika closed his eyes and more red portals began opening above him, allowing seven white cubes to pop out before shrinking down to the bug's size. In a split-second, portions of the bug's body snapped into

Healix's mouth portal, and the newly created white figures shot down to take their place before the tiny body popped back into place.

"Ah, so close. The intestines were a hair off that time, Mister Marsh," Healix said with a sigh.

Out of nowhere, Zell lunged for Atha and knocked him onto his back before covering her own face.

With the force of a bomb, mana erupted from Harika as he sobbed, blasting the ground around them to pieces.

"Harika! Harika calm down!" Atha screamed. The blast stopped in an instant.

"Sorry," he gasped.

"You seemed to be prepared for that. Not the first goner?" Atha asked Zell, who nodded.

"Had we not already experienced an outburst I would not thought to move from cover of forest." Zell's grim expression matched her words.

"Yeah, I was actually thinking about that while I was out riding. Can't have him walking around waiting for something to set him off, so I think it's only right that I take up a contract that can control his emotions since he's my responsibility," Atha replied, glancing over to Harika who hobbled slowly toward Zell's distant chair.

"Intentions are well placed and received. I will look into the matter," Zell said. "For now, Harika and I must return to the forest to procure more insects. Could you manifest some manner of containment?"

Atha drew the image of Tupperware containers into his mind. He manifested a stack and handed them over to Zell.

Harika found more success with the next batch of bugs. The suns exchanged for moons, yet he continued under their light.

Zell motioned for Atha, who was busy finishing off the rest of his pizza. "I found a contract that fills the criteria you have designated paramount. But also..." Zell opened her orange screen, shifting the hieroglyphs upon it to bring up information. She turned the screen toward Atha to read for himself. A smile slowly brimmed across his face.

"This is perfect. With this I could control my *own* emotions as well as Harika's," he noted.

"With this you can adjust the level of anger you feel, allowing manipulation over contract-less ability," Zell replied as Atha looped an arm up over her shoulder.

"This is everything I asked for and a bag of chips. You're awesome, Z. Thank you," Atha replied, giving her a good shake before releasing his grip. "Can we do it right now?"

Harika came over slowly and placed the last empty container upon the stack.

"I have finished. Can we get more patients?" he cut in with his empty voice.

A dull sob sounded from Healix at this request. "Please, no more. I'm exhausted," he whined, dramatically flopping his tail across his own forehead.

"A shared sentiment. To answer both questions, we will continue tomorrow," Zell said before vanishing into her tent. Harika glanced to Atha, who shrugged.

"Boss lady has spoken. I'm pretty—" Atha paused mid-sentence, glancing around the surreal camp, expecting the lucid dream to wash away at any moment. He knelt to grasp a handful of warm dirt, letting it trickle through his fingers and turn to dust as the lazy breeze caught it in the open air. *Is this real?*

"Are you well?" Harika asked.

"I have these moments where it just strikes me that I'm free. It's like, I don't know, a revelation, except that makes it sound too biblical," he replied and drew a long, deep sigh. Shaky breath chased his sigh and tears started falling from his eyes as he began to sob. Atha covered his face, attempting to hide the sudden stream of tears.

"Freedom brings you to tears." It was a statement, not a question.

"You know, when I got here, I thought it was the trippy magic stuff wigging me out, but it's more than that. I wondered if Elise was dead for over a decade, and now that I know she's alive I've seen her just a single fucking time since I've been here."

"I understand what it feels like to miss family," Harika replied.

"You have a family?"

"No. They lived in the city I blew up." Atha forgot to breath for a moment, his tears stopping as easily as turning off a faucet. What right did he have to cry about hard times while standing before an even more crushing loss?

"I'm sorry to hear that. Do you wanna talk about it? Or—well, you're not going to send out a blast of mana, are you?" Atha asked.

"My emotions are under control. If it would please you to hear of them, I have quite a few stories," Harika offered.

"I absolutely would," Atha said. "Did they know about how strong your mana was?"

"They did. It was so high as a child that they were forced to take special precautions to ensure I would not be taken away from them."

"How?" Atha prompted.

"Originally they both had contracts that pertained to their jobs. My father was a mana theory specialist and my mother a botanical nurse who cared for trees. After I was born and both their contracts had expired, they switched to ones that could hide mana particle levels."

"I've never heard you talk so much. They sound like they're worth the extra words, though," Atha replied as Harika paused again.

"They gave up everything for me," Harika continued. "My mother was diagnosed with a disorder that should have prevented her from giving birth. Father would say that it was such a blessing to receive news of his baby boy, which spurred my name, Harika. In my language Harika means miracle child."

Harika sagged his head. "Miracle child. A curse disguised as a blessing."

"Well, now you're changing that curse into a blessing." Atha stood to face him. "Your mom was in health care, so could you even *imagine* how proud she would be to know her son is gonna be the best healer ever? How proud your dad would be?"

"You should see your sister more. Tomorrow is not promised," Harika replied.

Tears welled up in Atha's eyes again.

"I'm gonna go for a walk. I'll be back in a few," Atha said, heading off toward the cliffs.

"Contact," he announced and an orange ball appeared beside his head and Zell's grumble rang out.

"Mark my words, child, if there is not blood, broken bones or impending death at hand…" Her words trailed off into a series of mumbles that Atha was unsure were actual words or a series of gibberish. If he could see her mouth moving out of sync with her words he'd know for sure.

"I was wondering if you know of a magical device that I could use to contact Elise. I just…I haven't talked to her since we came out here," Atha explained.

"A common trinket. I will forward an image into your mind," Zell replied and a sudden vibrant image popping into Atha's head of a small statue of a lizard. "Heed my words and do not mention Harika's existence or the extent of your ability. Either could put her in unfavorable position."

The ball vanished as the statue fell into Atha's hands. No sooner did he grasp it than the tiny figure sprang to life, vanishing into a red portal that remained open as Elise's welcoming voice could be heard.

"Atha?!"

"Hey, El!" Atha replied.

"Has something happened?" Elise asked, sounding panicked.

"No, I just...I—" Atha paused, feeling tears well up in his eyes again. "I just missed you."

"Oh, my dearly beloved, I miss you too! I'm so sorry I *really* must go. There has been another attack by the Red Sheep, the worst yet. It was close to the destruction training grounds, so please be safe. Use the dagger to signal me if you find yourself so much as unsure of a situation okay? I love you."

"I love you—" Atha started but the portal vanished mid-sentence. "Too."

***

The next morning Atha prepared a monstrous breakfast. Zell watched in disgust as he consumed plate after plate, the suns finally rising as he finished.

"Gluttony will see you placed beneath the trees," she announced as a toothpick fell into his hands and he began picking his teeth clean.

"Gotta make up for all the time I spent eating the same menu every week," Atha said, pulling his lighter out of his pocket and playfully burning the pick before hurling both away.

"If you are satisfied with your feast, then perhaps we could begin preparations for your contract," Zell said and Atha perked up.

"Oh shit. I was so busy eating in self-pity that I forgot! Come on, let's do this thing!" he replied.

Harika's empty eyes turned questioningly toward Zell.

"I have not forgot about your insects. We will go once this business is in order."

She smiled to him as he nodded. She flipped her orange screen open, reading over the instructions. "The contract is known as Cortex Control and it allows the user to freely adjust their own emotions or those of another with permission freely given. Unlike Harika's, it has a frugal mana particle exchange cost, as well as a negotiable usage time frame starting at a minimum of a year." Zell paused, turning her black eyes to Atha. "I implore that you sign for a year. Should it not suit our needs, then it is preferable to ensure a minimal loss."

"A year it is," Atha agreed.

"Good. Unlike most contracts that offer selective time-spans, Cortex Control is particularly favorable. Most charge extra mana and some even take away certain functions all together, but in this case, the only lessened factor accompanied by the minimal signing period is the total number of beings that you can hold emotional dominance over, which is seven." Zell turned to a page titled Contract Registry. "Contacting the spirit to set terms appears simple enough. You need an electrical jolt coursing through your body while hopping around on a lone leg and simultaneously laughing. Do you need the image of an electrical item?"

Atha shook his head. A Taser fell into his hands and he looked upon it with fear, imagining the soon-to-come jolt. He'd forced a screwdriver into a socket during shop a few years back, resulting in a scolding broken by laughter from Len and a permanent fear of electricity.

"Fuck, why couldn't I get a prick on the finger like Harika? You know, this whole ritual sounds whacky," Atha replied, getting to his feet and beginning to hop. He forced out a booming laugh and flipped the switch on the Taser, which crackled with foreboding electricity.

"Hahahahahaha oooghhh-hahahaha!" The shock almost brought him off his legs. As he came full circle, he noticed Zell doing a poor job of suppressing her laughter, and came to a stop. "I've been bamboozled. I really should have seen that coming."

She extended a finger, pressing it into his forehead.

"Just desserts for feigning loss of control!" she roared.

"I'll *show you* a loss of control. Come on, I want to get my contract!"

Zell stifled her laughter and turned back to her orange screen.

"Such a poor sport. Manifest a serulminon stone and use it to draw out this hieroglyph in the dirt," she said, flipping the screen around to display a shiny rock and a symbol.

Atha hurled the Taser toward the camp's trash bin, and to his surprise it went in. Then he drew the rock's image into his mind and caught it out of the air. The simple symbol only took a few seconds to draw out, and he stood back up to admire his work. "All right. So, where's the spirit?"

Over an hour passed as the two sat and waited, Atha working on a Rubik's cube to pass the time. "Okay, what the actual shit? Harika barely finishes his little ritual and the head honcho comes screaming down out of the sky, but I sit and wait for over an hour?" he whined.

"The value a spirit would place upon you pales beside Harika's," she replied.

He finished the cube and red energy began glowing from his hands as proceeded to crush it.

"This is bullshit! I ain't gonna sit here all day, waiting for some—" Atha stopped, perking up and jumping from his seat as a tiny red portal opened in front of him. "Finally, some damn service!"

A tiny woman no larger than a fist buzzed out carried by tiny translucent wings.

"Greetings! My name is Dulcina, and I will be the spirit dealing with you today." She beamed. She wore an extravagant blue dress that matched her sparkling blue skin. Her eyes slanted upward and her long purple hair hovered weightlessly in the air behind her.

"He gets some big-ass snake to talk to and I get some fruity fairy?" Atha scoffed.

Zell's face fell as blotches of blue streaked her cheeks. Bursting to her feet, she yanked Atha's head down, bowing her own next to his as she spoke.

"Apologies for the behavior of my comrade, Dulcina. He knows not of proper dealings with spirits," she replied. The tiny woman stared, wide-eyed, just as surprised as Zell.

"Why I never! Fairy?! I am of Luminine heritage, a proud race! I insist you take that back!" she squeaked. "Do not make me repeat myself!"

Atha pulled his watch up to his face.

"I will, but you gotta wait an *hour*. Just like you made me do you little—
"

Zell wrenched her arm over his shoulder, turning a previously unseen shade of blue that nearly eclipsed her red face.

"This ends *now*! Apologize, you fool!" she screamed as he groaned, rolling his eyes and stopping them on the hovering figure.

"I'm sorry for calling you a fairy," he said flatly.

The tiny woman folded her arms as she buzzed irritably.

"I accept your apology. Do we have business to attend to or should I take my leave?" she asked as Atha slid Zell's arm off.

"Just give me your pitch."

She flitted down in front of his face, meeting his wrathful stare with one of tranquility. "Well, mister—"

"Atha."

"Well, Mister Atha, I do *not* think we can do business," she replied, the last trace of her smile fleeting from the tiny face.

"After you made me wait now you're gonna turn me down?" He felt his anger beginning to grow.

"No, I misspoke. The standard fee per emotion adjustment is twenty mana particles. For thirty I will accept a year contract," she said as Atha took on the shade of red missing from Zell.

"You brought this upon yourself," Zell told him. "You desire something she has but have little to return."

"What a splendid young Denata! Had you a trace of the bountiful virtue inside her, you would have reaped a generous deal. I don't need my empathy equipment to see anger guides your narrow path," she replied, yet her smile returned. "Fortunately for you I am in pleasant mood. A year, twenty mana per use. Say yes."

Atha's eyes burned with a rage that was eclipsed only by the fiery stare he was receiving from Zell. Through gritted teeth that wanted to say so much more, he growled out, "Yes."

A contract made of blue paper floated out of a red portal before him. He caught it and read over it carefully before using his finger to sign.

"Very good then. To the Denata, I bid good day. As for you, Atha, I do believe you will find yourself quite...*happy* with the contract," she said with a wink before grabbing the blue paper and flitting back through the red portal that snapped closed. Another red portal opened over Atha's arm, a black bracelet with intricate markings springing out of it before latching to his arm.

"Lost to a bitchy little fairy, gained an ugly ass bracelet. Still an improvement." Atha chuckled.

Zell stepped in front of him.

"Look at me. Have I not already warned you of what speaking to a spirit in such a manner can bring?" she whispered. Atha's head sagged for a moment before she lifted it back up.

"I know I make an ass out of myself."

"Be silent. The time for discussion has passed; now you will listen. Atha, you are intelligent—incredibly so, to be blunt. But this rage you allow to reign supreme smoothers and consumes the opportunities to show your talents, and the conclusion is you end up behind. As of yet, the fallout has been minor, but eventually it will get you, or Harika, or myself, hurt. Understand?"

"Yes," Atha whispered.

"Good. Let us not waste any more daylight, then," she replied, patting Atha on the cheek as he blinked.

"That's it? God, I thought you were about to work me over."

"I have made my point in as many variations as I know how. Next occurrence I fear it will not be simple words teaching this lesson."

"Fair enough. Let's get Harika set up. How do I use my contract anyways?"

"It is a low-level contract and fairly popular, so finding usage tips will come easy." Zell whisked her screen. "Here it is, to begin an adjustment begin by stating the command word 'control.'"

"Okay then. Control." The bracelet lit up, the symbols glowing as a life-size hologram of Dulcina's tiny body popped up over it, causing Atha's face to fall.

"Come now, don't give me that look. I am here to aid you after all. Now what are your commands?" She smiled up to him as he glanced at Zell, her eyes narrowing in warning as he sighed.

"Thank you, Dulcina. Give me a minute to figure out how to proceed," he replied as she nodded pleasantly.

Zell continued reading the instructions. "Now simply name an emotion and how much you wish to either increase or decrease it."

"All right, let's go with sadness then. Can you increase it by seven percent?" Atha asked as Dulcina held her chin.

"Sadness you say? No, let's put a *smile* on that scrunchy face," she said.

As if an extra three suns had appeared in the sky, the world brightened around Atha as an overwhelming sense of perfection lined every detail. A warm breeze sighed through the cliffs, carrying only a refreshing amount of dust as to not cause discomfort. Time had been kind to the many rocks, shifting them from miles beneath the ground to rest beneath the blazing suns. Every particle of dirt had been blown delicately across the area, and every detail of the scenery had been placed in an inexplicably flawless place, exactly where it needed to be.

I never even took the time to notice the beauty of this wonderland. Len always said I take everything for granted, and he was right. That time I got a cold meal for chow, I threw it down onto the ground. I thought Len would agree with me, but he got angry in a way I'd never seen. He told me, "There are starving kids who would have killed you for that meal." He told me, "Atha, this lack of appreciation stems from never having been in a horrible situation, a really sick *one." He told me that while I was on death row, and I believed it to be the single most absurd thing he'd ever said. I thought he was just blowing smoke, but he's right. I take everything for granted. No more.*

Taking a shaky breath, a smile pulled across his face and tears streamed down from his eyes as he turned around slowly to take in every last stone, every ray of light.

"How is it possible something so beautiful could exist?" he gasped, falling to his knees and grasping handfuls of dirt that dribbled tenderly through his hands. Over a dozen more epiphanies blitzed through his pondering mind, but one stood above the others, begging a single question be asked.

"Zell?" Atha sobbed, glancing up to her as she stared down in disbelief. "Do you have rainbows here? In—in prison I saw a rainbow out the window and I wondered how something so perfect could be real. Zell, do you have rainbows here?" She froze in place, unable to decide if she should laugh or be seriously concerned.

"All right, I think you've had enough," Dulcina said and sighed, the smile fading from Atha's face as the tears came to a stop.

"What in the holy hell?" He gasped and huffed for air as he picked himself up out of the dirt.

"I brought your sense of joy up to the maximum level you could feel without going insane. Now do you comprehend a little bit more of what your ally warned you of?" She smiled coldly as Atha's lip quivered with rage, his bracelet-bearing arm forcing itself up to bring her hologram level with his eye.

"I like to think of myself as a kind, loving being, but even so am quite capable of malevolent retaliation. As far as spirits go, I fall toward the lesser end of those capable to do so. Imagine what a *powerful* spirit could do."

Atha was now at his snapping point, trembling with rage and regret at his selection, but as he opened his mouth Zell cut in.

"Calm, she means only to reiterate the point I made."

Atha took a moment, closing his eyes and calming down.

Through gritted teeth he replied, "Thank you, Dulcina."

"You are very welcome!" she said. "Now please, let's move past this and never revisit it. Oh, and that adjustment was free. I can only charge when I follow instructions."

"Well, we know it works," said Atha. "And just so we're all clear, I stand by what I said. Rainbows are awesome."

"You are in luck, as we do in fact have rainbows. With those topics thoroughly covered—Harika?" Zell called, noticing the Shelando praying silently a few meters away, completely oblivious.

Atha crept to his side, resting a hand on his shoulder to get his attention.

"Come on, let's make sure you're taken care of," he said.

"In regard to?" Harika replied slowly, getting to his feet as Atha flashed his new bracelet.

"I got a contract that can keep your emotions sealed up. Figured we should take steps to ensure nothing happens."

Harika's empty eyes turned to him. "You picked a contract that would help me?"

"Of course. You're Honorati. This is what we—" A blue blast lifted him from his feet, hurling him through the air and crashing onto his bike before he could react.

"Atha!" Zell screamed, hurrying to him as Harika stepped slowly after.

"I'm good, I'm good." He laughed, hobbling back to his feet before slapping Harika on the shoulder. "Man, I'm gonna miss that. Like a free roller coaster 'cept you don't know when you're gonna be taking a ride!"

"Harika, grasp Atha's bracelet and state out loud that you willingly accept to yield control over your emotions." He nodded, reaching a blue hand out and resting it on the bracelet as Dulcina's image floated over top of it.

"I willingly accept to yield control over my emotions," he announced slowly as Dulcina spoke up.

"Are you currently under the influence of another contract that forces you to do so or in any way threated into this?" she asked, reading from a script.

"No." A ping sounded from the bracelet and a red portal opened over Harika's wrist. A chrome bangle fell from it and clasped around his wrist.

"You now reign over his emotions," Dulcina declared cheerfully before her hologram vanished.

"Thank you. I already have a debt I could never repay you for, and I owe another now," Harika said to Atha.

"You don't owe me shit. This is just what we do."

"Why are you so good to me?" Harika asked.

"Atha has formed a cathexis for your cause," Zell informed him.

Harika paused, looking unsurely to Atha for clarification.

"She's saying I feel emotionally invested in you," Atha whispered.

"Oh. Whatever the reason, I am grateful," he replied as Atha slapped him on the back.

"See, that's all I needed. We're square. So, what's next on the agenda, Z?" Atha smiled, glancing over to her as she adjusted her purple robes.

"Let us see how effective Cortex Control is at smothering rage." Atha nodded to this, already having thought the same thing.

"All right, let me get worked up real quick." Smothering his anger was like tossing a thimble of water onto a forest fire. Creating it, however, came with incredible ease. With a life like his, he need only put a certain memory on a loop in his own mind, his photographic memory recreating it with flawless detail. He closed his eyes, recalling the image of Elise being choked to death, the gurgle from her throat ringing in his ears, the cold tile beneath his feat, the sense of terror and helplessness in his heart.

His face twisted with anger, wishing Dako life again if only so he could kill him once more. "Control! Set anger level to null!" Atha commanded, and while the bracelet did ping, he felt no different. He repeated the command, another ping showing the order accepted, yet he still twisted with rage. "Enough games, Dulcina!" Atha screamed, and the tiny woman's image appeared above the bracelet looking quite puzzled herself.

"This is something even I cannot rationalize. Take pause, I shall speak with my superior," she replied, her image vanishing for a few moments until it appeared again. "I-I am sorry, but I can neither tell you why the contract cannot smoother your anger, nor tell you why exactly it is unable to do so." Atha noticed a slight tremble in her words.

"Why not?"

"Because to do so would tell you something that would alter the course of history. Spirits are forbidden from such revelations."

"So this power can't even help me!" Atha spat, turning to Zell, who was equally puzzled. She whisked open her orange screen, digging through panels of information for a few minutes before closing it.

"I cannot explain this. No other account of such an ordeal is listed," she informed him apologetically, and Atha could tell by her body language she was actually disappointed in herself. *She probably blames herself for whatever's happening.*

Atha took a long, deep breath, hopelessly attempting to calm the rage he'd taunted until it had reared its head. "All right, so it won't work on me, and because of the reason, you can't tell me why. Riddle me this, though: If I guess until I get it right, and your body language gives it away, would you still be accountable?"

Atha hoped to circumvent the issue but was already able to read the fear upon her face before Dulcina replied. "Then I won't." Atha sighed.

Dulcina paused, surprise now showing upon her face. She'd probably expected Atha to guess regardless. "Thank you. I have been instructed to offer you the lowered price of ten particles per usage as compensation. In addition, I am also permitted to tell you of the best methods of usage. I can only offer this if you swear silence on the contract's issue. It would ruin us if it became known to the world." *She's proven her strength and I'd like to have her as an ally.*

"Give me the original price of 20 and we'll call it even." Now Dulcina's face fell with disbelief.

"Why would you counter-offer with something of less benefit?"

Because you could be a powerful ally. "Because you taught me an important lesson already. You did it for free, hoping only to protect me in the future. Let's just call it even at that, eh?" Atha thought for a moment that Dulcina might cry. She beamed with joy, wings buzzing like a hummingbird.

"I feel I have misjudged you, Atha. I accept the revised terms and look forward to our future dealings." She smiled and gave him a drawn-out curtsy before her image vanished. Zell was at a loss for words, simply filling the void with a slow clap. Atha gave a comical bow like an actor, finally actually feeling his anger returning to sleep.

"For but a moment you fell, soaring next to unfathomable heights. What is lost in information and mana will be returned tenfold with having a spirit as an ally."

"Only time will tell. Still, I wish I knew why my anger can't be smothered. Honestly, no guesses?"

"None reinforced with structured evidence."

"Oh well, I'm not too worried. Harika's taken care of, that was really all I picked the contract for anyways. So what's next?"

"We acquire supple insects for Harika and then what say we give Shooting Star another go?" she replied and Atha lit up.

"Shit, you know me. If it ain't a bad idea, I ain't down. But I want to do something real quick," he replied. A camera attached to a tripod fell into his hands, pulling his memory card from his pocket and slotting it into place. "Picture time. Come on, sit down." He set a timer on the clock before forcing himself in between them atop a boulder. Rolling his arms over their shoulders, he put up a double peace sign and a small click sounding from the camera. "That's a keeper." He showed the camera to Harika, who nodded slowly at the photo. Atha pulled the card out again and smashed the camera before hurling it off.

"Such infatuation with memorabilia stunted dreadfully with destruction," Zell noted in an exaggeratedly monotonous voice as Atha nodded.

"Yeah. I always wanted a camera, but Len told me it was just asking for trouble. Making up for lost time I guess."

***

The day wore on. Harika began operating while Atha and Zell stood a long distance away on the flattest, most open portion of the cliffs.

"It should be brought to light that Shooting Star garnered a dark sobriquet. *The Ripper*."

"Because it would rip an arm out of its socket, I'm guessing?" Atha chuckled as Zell nodded.

"Mishandling a weapon of this caliber will lead to injuries regardless of whose hand wields it."

"Literally a double-edged sword. I got it, trust me. Remember me flying through the air? I would remember too, but I got a concussion from it." Atha smirked.

"Yes, well you seem to need to hear the same warning multiple times predating fraudulent memory loss. Now, draw Shooting Star and activate Agro energy. Hold it out in front of yourself and draw circles in the air following in the precise path of the last loop," Zell instructed.

Atha pulled the sword out and smiled as the chains lifted around his right arm. He then began to circle it in the air in front of him for a few minutes.

"Uh, how long am I gonna do this?" he asked, thankful for a few clouds beginning to dot out the blaring suns.

"All day," she replied as Atha's face fell. "In order to run, learning to crawl is a fundamental step. Erratic form even at this level portends problems later on. We will move onto the next when you can perform eight consecutive loops without a lurch."

As if on cue, Shooting Star jutted hard to the left as Atha groaned and returned to turning it in the air in front of himself. He grumbled irritably as Harika slowly approached Zell's side with a slew of empty containers held in his arms.

"I have not forgotten about you, Harika. Continue until Agro energy runs out," Zell called back to Atha.

Atha made subtle improvements in the few minutes before his energy elapsed. He treated himself to a few donuts before heading back to camp.

"Come, sit." Zell waved to him and sat down beside her as Harika continued to operate.

"He's getting pretty quick," Atha noted as he watched Harika repair the wings of a fly, which quickly buzzed off.

"In normal situation, a wielder of his contract could practice a single time a day. Between his inexhaustible mana and the instruction you bargained for, his improvement comes at prodigious pace."

Atha smiled at this, watching Harika pop open a new container as Healix's eyes scanned it over.

"Can you imagine what he'll be able to do when he can operate on *people*?" he whispered.

"Insect operations are hardly comparable to those upon actual people. Your optimism of him continues to cloud your mind."

"As opposed to what? Doubting everything I'm trying to do, Miss Pessimism?!" Atha spat back.

"A quote comes to mind on this topic. 'An optimist chooses a contract with thoughts of future grandeur. The pessimist chooses one that would allow him to keep eating. Lastly, the realist chooses based upon the fact he knows what will put coins in hands, and possibly quite a few.' I would firmly label myself the realist, which would you label yourself by this standard?" Atha rolled his eyes. "Ah, the infamous rolling of the eyes. Just mull my words over when next you draw an ideal of Harika into mind. As for next lesson, we will study the Plagues until your Agro energy revitalizes."

Atha perked up to this, eyeing the screen that showed information of the plagues.

"The fifth plague of Disease, known as the Red Sheep, is the only member of their ranks that you are familiar with. In numerical order, they are: Creation, Frogs, Lice, Wildlife, Disease, Boils, Thunder and Fire, Locusts, Darkness and, most formidably, Death. Consider also that they are ranked in order of how formidable each plague is."

"You said back at the Shakka village that Disease was the strongest."

"Many consider him such for a few reasons. All plagues wield powerful contract-less abilities, but just like any weapon, they must learn to use them. For a plague, this takes an excruciating amount of time. Disease has lived for over five millennia, allowing him ample opportunity to do so."

"That thing is over 5,000 years old?! How is that possible?!"

"Many a plague scholar would be appreciative of that information. The theory is that its power can somehow extend the normal lifespan of a typical sheep. It also wields a slew of terrifying abilities, such as an impenetrable space surrounding it, disease that instantly turns livestock within its vicinity into bleeding monstrosities, and another developed with the aid of the last plague, Creation—the ability for the infection to transfer to people with a single bite."

"Wait, so plagues can boost each other's power?"

"Not in most cases, but the Creation plague is characterized by an ability to bring new evils into the world. In this case, it could manipulate the genetic make-up of illnesses, and Creation worked alongside the Red Sheep. This type of being is known as special infected. Only trees are completely uninfluenced by a bite."

"Magical biological warfare. That's a scary thing to think about."

"Once bitten, the victim typically has a few hours of life until their past identity is erased, leaving a hollow body with a singular mission of causing further death and spreading the disease. No known cure exists, and the victim will exist in said state until a traumatic wound is dealt. A difficult thing to do, considering special infected are in all aspects three times more physically capable." She finished speaking and displayed the image of a human man on her screen. Blood slowly oozed from his mouth and the label "special infected" was at the top of the screen.

"Could they catch another sickness and die from that?"

"No, only *physical* trauma ends their suffering."

"So basically roided-out zombies with extra kill areas." Atha laughed uneasily. "Do they follow the Red Sheep around?"

"In some cases, but mostly they seem to act upon its orders. Typically, they move in groups free of their overlord." She sighed, whisking her screen away as Atha nodded.

"Why is it so smart, since it's literally a sheep? Some sort of magical breed?"

"While animals have been experimented on, no known outcome resulted in heightened intelligence. The only known fact of its origin is that it was owned by a wealthy businessman before becoming a plague."

"Do you think we could kill it the way we are now?" he asked, glancing up to the red woman.

"No, I do not. What you saw was the Red Sheep at its weakest. It gains more power with every attack, which grows the size of the protective shadow and number of arms it can form from it." Her words where cold but Atha smiled at this.

"So, it gets worse."

"You seem madly pleased by this news."

"I do my best work when the odds are stacked against me. And hell, maybe I'm the next 'Solar Eclipse' like you were saying," he replied, a small pulse of red coming from his hand. "Agro energy's mostly back. I need a lecture break anyways. My ADHD is starting to kick in."

"Take a pause. Let us put your theory to the test," Zell replied, picking up a rock and stopping a short distance in front of him.

"Of what?"

"That you work best against bad odds. This is the jog phase test, if you can pass this then we'll skip walking. Try to slice a stone from the air."

Atha drew the blade. "Well, look at you! You know, for somebody who talks about listening so much I think this is the only time you've worked off of what I said."

"Because typically you speak of what you know nothing about. You say you learn best under pressure and who would know better than you? Now, at the ready," she said, pulling her arm back.

It wasn't a hard throw, but the rock was no larger than a golf ball, making it a difficult target to strike. *Okay, I should be able to slow my perception of time to some extent with Agro energy. All I need to do is focus the Agro energy into my head.* With a red glow spiking from his head, time came to a crawl and the rock nearly came to a stop. *That was easier than I thought, but I can't move any faster than usual. If I just ease my arm up I should be able to correct the awkward movement enough to catch the rock.*

Shooting Star glowed a dull white as he slowly pulled the blade toward the rock's path. With another slight tug, Shooting Star came closer and closer to its target. Time sped back up as the rock crumbled against the blade. Zell stared in disbelief as Atha smiled and smoothly slid the sword back into its holster.

"How did you surpass a daunting task with such ease?" she asked as Atha smoothed out his black robes. "Your strokes were exceedingly direct compared to the sword's predecessors."

"I used Agro energy to slow time. Well, not so much time, but when I focus it in my head I can slow my own perception of time. I'm still just as slow as usual," he replied as Zell's mouth dropped. "Right?! Goddamn, I am like the definition of *overpowered*!" He laughed but paused as she recomposed herself and gathered a handful of rocks, her own mana oozing out and forming tentacles that wrapped around her arm.

"Run phase it is."

The clouds above continued to darken until night fell, blotting out the stars and leaving the world a dark void around Atha. He was thankful for this as a welt from one of Zell's rocks had started swell on his cheek. The three rode toward the distant forest with nothing but the bike's headlight lighting the darkness ahead.

"Let's hurry, it looks like it's about to rain. Couldn't wait 'til tomorrow to get some more bugs, huh?" Atha asked Harika through Zell's orange communication device.

"Sorry," Harika replied.

"No, it's fine. I'm glad you're so dedicated."

"If Healix didn't tire I would help patients through the night," Harika replied as Zell's finger stuck out past Atha's windshield toward a section of nearing forest.

Zell said, "The trees tell me a colony of yarper spiders recently scavenged that area. Bursting containers should come with ease there."

"Oh swell, a spider colony. As long as it's not a rat colony we're, well, not good, but not horrible either." Atha chuckled uneasily before angling the blue path down. Harika landed with a slight boom next to them as Atha set down the bike down.

"Oh, getting better at landing!" Zell teased. Atha smiled as rain began to drizzle down on them, creating a pleasant forest sonata as it rang on the leaves above. Atha paused his search, pulling down the top half of his robes as the cool rain dashed over him. Zell chuckled but even in the dark she noticed a long, deep scar across Atha's stomach.

"Battle scar?" she asked. Atha flinched, pulling his robes up over it.

"It's nothing."

"Apologies then," she replied, returning her eyes to the bushes as she continued to dig for spiders. A flashlight fell into Atha's hands, and he held it over her shoulder as she continued to search.

"Sorry, you've told me personal stuff and I'm acting like a bitch."

"Not out of desire to do so; I merely wished you hear it from me. As you said, if you wish to talk do so, but I will never press." She grasped a twitching bug and placed it in a container.

"I knew this girl while I was in prison. She worked in the infirmary as a nurse, so I saw her a lot and we kinda hit it off. Long story short, I got into it with this dude I sold cocaine to. I cut him off one day, so he"— Atha paused, his throat cracking for a moment—"I purposely used my ability. It was the only time I did it against Len's wishes. I used it to break out of my cell and into his and squared him up. I'm small and weak, but another inmate taught me to fight and I ended up getting him in a chokehold pretty easy. He had a shiv and sliced me pretty good, but it never healed very well." Atha felt the distorted flesh for a moment before pulling his robes back over his chest.

"Was she a romantic interest?" Zell asked, getting back to her feet.

"I'll tell you about her someday, but not yet. Thinking about it puts me back on the edge of a dangerous hole." Atha stared down at an empty palm. A small bag filled with white powder appeared in his hand and he promptly opened it and dumped the contents onto the ground like a quick flurry of snow.

"Come, the rain thickens."

They exited the forest and a backpack materialized into Atha's hands. He stacked the containers in them beside his bike as a quiet moan echoed through the cliffs.

"Did you hear that?" Atha asked Harika, who glanced slowly down to him.

"What?" he replied.

Atha lifted his flashlight on the rolling rocks.

"I don't know, sounded like a moan," he replied as a fleeting shadow darting across his light's path.

Chapter 17
Warning Shots

"I saw something! It was fast! Hey, who's up there? Show yourself!"
Atha hollered up toward the cliffs, flashing his light around in a panic as
Zell's blue mana began pulling knives from her robe. Atha listened
intently as another dull moan sounded, then another, but this time he
caught the source with his light. A pig staggered across the rocks, blood
gushing from its eyes and mouth as a pistol fell into Atha's hands.

"Infected!" Zell screamed as more poured over the rocks behind it.
Across the black horizon they came in innumerable swarms.

"They're everywhere! Zell, what do we—" Atha started as a figure
blitzed around behind them. It reached for Zell, who narrowly dodged
it. A bleeding human crashed into the black bike with devastating force.
Atha nearly froze in disgust at the sight of a special infected in the form
of a young woman, blood oozing from her mouth as she staggered into
view. Atha screamed and unleashed flashes of metal, sending the
distorted human flying back to the dirt. Squirting blood, she thrashed
and flailed for a moment before eventually stilling. Atha added a few
extra rounds to be safe.

"Contact the Queen! Use the knife she gave you, Atha!" Zell snapped
her fingers at the terrified human. "Quickly! Now!"

"Oh yeah!" he replied. The dagger fell into his hands and he began
tapping on it but was interrupted by more fleeting shadows darting

near with inhuman speed. He raised his pistol and blasted another as Zell's mana tentacles blitzed across another two.

"Harika! Cover me!" Atha yelled with a glancing over to the blue man who was staring blankly at the bodies on the ground. He ignored Atha as Healix popped out of his portal and rolled down his arm.

"We have a patient. Give me blueprints," he announced plainly to the snake, who stared uncertainly at the bloody corpse.

"Uh, she has long since passed, Mister Marsh," he replied, following Harika's sight next to the backpack Atha slung down.

"Harika, come on, they're getting closer!" Atha screamed, the main mass bearing down on them as he began to tap again. A special infected amongst the swarm grasped a rock and hurled it with blistering speed at Atha's hand, knocking the knife from it and sending the blade into the air.

"Fuck it! RPG!" he screamed, a missile launcher falling into his hands. He sent a brilliant explosion across the cliffs. It did little to slow the swarm, however, and Atha's anger began to stir. "You motherfuckers want some?!" He tossed the RPG aside and yanked Shooting Star from its sheath.

"No! Contact—" Zell's words were drowned out by the growing downpour.

Atha ripped forward with a pulse of red. Time slowed as a grenade fell into his free hand. Pulling the pin with his teeth, he tossed it blindly into the cascade of bleeding animals before him. An explosion lit the area up for a moment as he sliced a cow in half with Shooting Star.

Automatic shotgun, buckshot load. The weapon fell into his free hand and he began blasting away, ears ringing as a bus went hurling through the crowd.

Atha laughed at the effect like a child with fresh toys, drawing the image of yet another grenade to manifest in his spare hand. Already growing accustomed to the functions of grenades, his thump slipped cleanly into the pull pin and sent it flying, releasing the spoon and hurling the explosive into the descending horde. The blast split a goat down the side and Atha watched it wail for a split second until a hologram screen displaying Elise popped up.

"Is all well? I felt you begin—" She paused, her eyes rolling across the screen as she leapt to her feet. "Dimitri! Dispatch captains to the destruction training grounds! Atha, where's Zell?!" Elise screamed as his smile fell and he came back to his senses. His eyes floated back to Zell, who was currently cornered by infected, the desperation of the situation returning to him.

"Oh shit! I gotta go!" Atha screamed, bursting back toward Zell.

"Captains are inbound to your location, just stay close to Zell! I'm coming for you!"

The screen vanished and Atha rushed to Zell. He swung at an infected, but the human was quick, spinning and leaping away.

"Elise is on her way, captains too! What do we—" Zell grabbed him by the shoulder and flung him down as a green glowing sword narrowly missed him.

"What the hell?!" he gasped, turning up as a green glow illuminated the area.

"Oh, no," Zell whispered as Atha turned his eyes up to a figure sitting high in the air atop a cloud of green fog.

"That looks like El's fog. Zell, what's going on?" Atha whispered back.

"The White Queen, Erida, is before us," Zell growled back, pulling Atha behind her as the cloud lowered.

"Erida?! Elise's cousin that started the civil war?!" Atha replied as the darkened silhouette glowed green. She wore an entirely white dress that matched her white hair that fell to just above her shoulders.

"Take Harika and run into the forest," Zell ordered.

"No! I'm not leaving you."

"Do as I say! Go!" Zell screamed as hundreds of swords formed from the fog, launching forward like green lasers toward, Zell who parried them away with her knives.

Atha glowed red, hustling back to Harika, who was operating on a bug, and yanked him over his shoulder.

"Put me down. I have a patient," Harika replied dully, shoving with insane strength against Atha, who stumbled and released him.

"Goddammit, Harika, we gotta fucking go!" Atha screamed at him, glancing back to Zell who flitted closer to Erida.

"No," Harika replied, lost in the oblivion of his own misplaced good intentions.

An AK-47 fell into Atha's hands. He spun around and unloaded a long blast toward Erida, but the green fog swirled in front of her and formed a clear barrier. The rounds pinged off uselessly.

"Settle down," Erida said. "I'll see to you shortly, little boy."

Atha manifested an RPG and raised the barrel up toward her as she looked on with a mocking smile. The smile fled as a fiery explosion ripped across her shields, forcing her to topple back onto the cloud. A piercing scream escaped her mouth.

"Fuck, that weird fog is no joke," Atha sighed, staring in disbelief as more glowing swords formed in the air.

"You just placed yourself atop the list," Erida growled, regaining her footing and glowing bright green as she pointed a finger at Atha. A sword that could be easily confused with the mother ship of an invading alien race began to form out of the torrent of green fog swirling overhead. It trumped even the greatest of Atha's seafaring ships, halting the very rain that poured down having blocked out the sky. Despite taking longer to form, the colossal sword moved just as fast as the others, turning and firing down at Atha in one swift motion. Atha began to draw the image of a ship into his mind to act as a shield. Luckily he needn't even attempt such a futile effort. A new sword of massive size swirled into existence in the sky above him. The first sword shattered into oblivion and returned to the base form of green fog, stunning Atha, who glanced at the woman in white to find reason for this transgression. Erida's eyes were fixed on the horizon, and following her gaze Atha saw another green fog outlined clearly in the black clouds.

"Elise!" Atha exclaimed, relieved at the sight of the incoming calvary in the form of the mighty queen and a slew of Royal Guard captains.

"Stand down, Erida!" Elise said. "We can talk about this." She flicked her wrist to form a cage of swords around Erida.

"We are far past words. For now, continue enjoying my accomplishments, Elise," Erida replied. Green fog swirled around her, dissipating to reveal an empty cage.

"She can't teleport; she must be working with new forces!" Elise yelled to one of her captains as green swords struck down every infected.

Elisa glided to the ground and Atha burst toward her, his arms wrapping her tight when he came upon her.

"That was awesome! That lady got outta dodge fast once you showed up!" Atha laughed.

"You weren't bitten anywhere, were you?" Elise asked. She flipped her wrists again and swords appeared above and slammed into the heads of every infected.

"No, we're all good," Atha replied.

Elise kissed him on the forehead.

"I'm sorry, but I need to make haste," she said, stepping back and beginning to rise, but Atha caught her wrist.

"W-wait! You just got here! At least stay and chat for a few," Atha replied, watching Elise's rain-drenched face fall.

"I would like nothing else, but I just don't have *time*," she replied, noticing the distant bus. "Did you manifest that? It's massive!"

Atha nodded proudly. "Oh man, you should see what—"

"My Queen, that is the largest object he can produce," Zell interrupted. "We have also found quite a few extra rules."

"I see. Being able to summon something of that size could lead to terrifying possibilities. Please put together an evaluation of his power and deliver it to me when you return to the capital," Elise commanded. Zell bowed her head.

"Yes, ma'am."

"Thank you, Zell. Now really, Atha, I must go. Be safe and signal me again if something happens, okay? I love you." Elise released his grip.

"I love you, too," Atha sighed, watching her as she flew back over the forest.

"Why'd you lie to her?" Atha asked.

"Fear not, she will know soon enough. For now, we must take precautions to ensure this knowledge does not get out," Zell replied.

"Fair enough," Atha said. "Did you notice how the infected ignored me? I mean, I was right in the thick of it, but they targeted you and Harika."

"It was peculiar that monstrosities, with no other purpose then to spread disease, would ignore a prime target. Perhaps they were following orders? Even more intriguing, they seemed to be operating alongside a regular human, Erida. If that is the case, then she must be also working alongside another plague. The Red Sheep would not come to an understanding with a human, despite how powerful she may be."

An umbrella fell into Atha's hands. He snapped it open and held it over them.

"Well, that's a scary thought. The biggest, baddest plague working with not only another plague but also Elise's evil stepsister? And hey, why did she have the same contract as El's?"

"The White Queen wields a Unique category contract that allows her to copy the abilities of other contracts. The main reason she was dethroned upon Queen Elise's return was due to the fact she lacked the clout intertwined with possessing an SSS contract."

"So, she picked up a copycat ability and used it on El. If it's that easy, why doesn't everyone copy high-level contracts?" Atha asked.

"Some contracts require certain trials be completed before their power can activate. For Erida it would have taken seven or eight trials, with requirements along the lines of staying within a certain proximity to the target for a week or seeing their contract's different functions."

Atha glanced toward Harika, who was still operating on insects.

"She was in a good spot to do it, being close too Elise. Hey, did you see Harika during the attack? He was like, I don't know, having a mental breakdown or something."

"I believe he cannot rationalize the difference between living organisms. To him, an insect or even an infected is the same as a person and another insurmountable weight upon his conscience," she replied as Atha sighed, stepping away from Zell to hold his umbrella over Harika, who carefully placed the insect back inside its container.

"Come on, let's get you out of here before the guards start asking questions," Atha whispered as Harika collected the backpack and stood. Atha pulled his bike up into the air, heading back toward the camp. But they hadn't gotten far before Zell's orange ball brought her voice into his helmet.

"In that quarry, an infected!"

Atha's glanced down to see a shadowy figure scampering frantically across the rocks. He ripped down toward the ground, skidding in front of it and bursting off the bike as it doubled back away from them.

"Missed the party, huh?! Come here, I've still plenty left!" Atha yelled, glowing red and bursting forward to slam the figure down on its back. He drew his sword, raised it up over the figure but paused as a voice came into his mind.

"Mercy! Please, mercy!" a feminine voice begged as the figure held her arms up in front of her face. She was a small human, middle-aged and dressed in tattered grey robes with blood oozing from her mouth.

"Uh, are you sure this is an infected?" Atha called to Zell, who stopped at his side with Harika.

"Beyond a doubt. It is a paradox that it should act in such a way," she replied.

"Yeah, I can hear it in my head."

"Of what does it speak?"

"It's begging for mercy. Should I kill it?"

"Infected do not communicate or show emotion on any level," Zell replied. "It would be safe to assume the Red Sheep possesses the ability to manipulate an infected to a certain degree, so our best course of action would be to end it."

Atha raised his sword again. "Off with her head, then," he chuckled, but Harika's firm grip clasped his arm.

"No. Can't we just let it go?" he interjected.

"Goddammit, Harika! I gotta draw the line here with you. This thing needs to die," Atha said, even as the voice wailed through his head.

Harika pleaded as Atha's temper began to rise. "I understand that you were acting in self-defense before, but this woman isn't trying to hurt you. Please just let her go?"

"So, if we let it go and somebody ends up dead because of your decision, are you gonna take responsibility?"

"You have no proof that suggests that would happen."

"I don't need proof! That's just what they do and if you don't accept that as fact then you're in denial!" Atha retorted.

"Why can't you understand that you sound just like the people who imprisoned you?" Harika replied. Atha's anger vanished immediately.

"This is different Harika. I—"

"No, it's not. You think you know all the facts but you have nothing to back them," Harika cut in as Atha lowered his sword.

"Zell?"

"My words stand firm. Only when weighed against my pledge to support the decisions of Atha Honorati do they crumble," she replied. Atha sheathed his sword.

"She comes back to camp with us as a prisoner. If we can determine her consciousness is somehow intact, we'll go from there. But, Harika, if we determine otherwise…" Atha glanced at the blue man.

"I know. Thank you, Atha," Harika replied slowly.
***

Back at camp, Atha manifested a large metal cage, locked the infected woman in it and hung a tarp over the top to block some of the rain.

"All right buddy, I need my nappy time. Keep an eye on her while Zell and I sleep okay?" Atha smiled and slapped him on the shoulder before disappearing into his tent. He set the umbrella in the corner, pushing mana into his robes and screaming in surprise as they shot the water they'd absorbed out across his tent.

"Oh, come on, like you didn't think to warn me, Zell!" Atha yelled before slumping deeper down into his sleeping bag and quickly falling asleep.

Atha awoke perfectly on cue at four A.M. the next morning, popping his head out of the tent and glancing at the caged infected. She was locked in a staring contest with Harika.

"Any activity to report there, big brother?" Atha chuckled.

"She does not appear to have the need to blink," Harika replied.

"That's a little unsettling. How long have you been staring at her?"

"Since you fell asleep."

Zell sat down in a folding chair, motioning for Atha to do the same.

"We should call Guinness. I think they set a new record for staring contest," Atha joked to her as she flicked through orange screens.

"With the tournament drawing near, I think it's time to implement a list of self-imposed rules to guide contract-less power," Zell replied, flipping her screen to Atha who read it over.

"Never to be used to harm a noncombatant. Never to be used for monetary or personal gain. Never to be used out of anger. Never to be used for reason other than self-defense. Never to be used to *prank Zell?* Ha-ha thought you'd throw that in at the end to make sure I actually read them?"

"I mean only to say the idle use of such power must be monitored with elevated discretion," Zell replied. "From this moment forward, use ought not come save for when bodily harm is threatened. Banter aside, swear to me that you will do all within your power to see these rules upheld."

"I know you mean well, but I know myself too well to swear to that. I got big plans for the whole monetary/personal gain rule, so maybe we could just overlook that concept from time to time?" Atha replied sheepishly.

"Very well, view that as more of a guideline then an actual rule. I had only meant to instill it as such. Can you firmly swear to the rest?"

Atha raised his right hand. "On the Honorati name, I swear to abide to by the rules you have set before me. Happy, Barbossa?" Zell patted his knee and stood.

"My expectations fall just as short as the human responsable for their downfall." She smiled to him as his face scrunched at the remark.

"Wow. Only heard a million digs at my height in prison. What's the plan for today?" Atha said.

"You shall take Harika to procure supple insects when needed and proceed to practice with Shooting Star. I must focus my attention on discerning the allegiance of supposed heightened infected." She nodded to the infected woman.

"Come on, Harika," Atha groaned, motioning for the glowing blue man to follow. They hopped on his bike and shot off.

Atha zoomed over the cliffs, dipping up and down like a roller coaster. Beneath the slowly brightening skies, they neared the forest. Reaching the apex of a rise, he paused. Green-clothed figures stood out prominently against the drab, rocky background.

"Those look like Royal Guards. You got the ring on still, right?" Atha asked Harika through the orange ball.

"Yes."

"All right, you go on ahead to the forest. I'm gonna go keep them occupied. If anyone sees you, don't use your real name and call me right away, okay?"

"Okay," Harika replied, continuing to fly straight on as Atha veered off toward the figures.

Easing down before them, he pulled off his helmet. He immediately recognized a pair of faces.

"Captain Garo! What's up, man? And you're the guard who arrested me." Atha smiled, hopping off his bike and heading for the four guards who turned toward him. Captain Garo's white teeth practically shined against his pitch-black skin.

"A pleasure, Atha. What brings you back this direction?" he asked, shaking Atha's hand.

"I could ask you the same. Figured you'd all be gone by now," Atha replied, cleanly dodging the question as the mountainous human stepped up behind Garo.

"Out here wasting precious man-hours to secure the area surrounding your training area. Could ya guess why?" he boomed as Garo raised a hand.

Garo growled back to the huge man, "Enough, Vork. We are out here locking the area down on behalf of *Queen Elise's orders*."

"Not like you had anything better to do then small-time arrests anyways right, big guy?" Atha sneered up at Vork, who eyed him for a moment before quietly stepping quietly. "So, who are your two friends?" Atha waved to the other two guards.

"The female is Captain Shakkoo." A female whose entire frame was hidden behind either the green uniform or wrapped in black bandages bowed her head to Atha. *Oh jeez, a mysterious woman. God, I love—no, stay on task. Keep them occupied.* "And the male is Captain Inersha." A male with feathered blond hair held back by a set of goggles waved to Atha.

"Lots of captains. Aren't y'all the cream of the crop in the Royal Guard?" Atha asked.

Garo nodded. "The Queen wished this mission to be expedited. After we eliminated the threat, we stayed behind on separate orders," Garo explained, noticing Atha eyeing over the concealed female captain. *Not a trace of face to be seen. Bet she's super-hot—No! Stay on task!... Well, really, if you can keep them busy and check her out, what's the harm?*

"Well, if y'all need anything while you're out here, I'd be happy to oblige. How about some food?" Atha replied, a box of steaming hot pizza falling into his hands. *Come on, I know you've been out here in the blazing sun hurting for some food! God, I'm such a degenerate.*

"Hey, the boy's all right!" Inersha laughed.

"Don't call me 'boy,'" Atha spat.

"Did I say boy? I meant *man*! Please don't tell the Queen to fire me, I really need this job," he chuckled sheepishly as Atha sighed.

"Chill out, man. I was just kidding with you," he lied. "Come on, eat. Y'all want some drinks too?" Atha directed his words to the female captain, who secured a slice of pizza. To Atha's dismay, she pulled her hood down to completely conceal her face before removing a section of bandages and taking a bite. *Seriously? Who eats with their face covered?*

"Oh, I see your game," Inersha chuckled, looping an arm over Atha's shoulder before whispering. "If you just asked to see her face, I doubt she'd say no. Should she accept, take care to place your words carefully."

"Is she, I don't know, scarred or something?" he asked.

"She's been through a lot. Are you familiar with a ghoulish sub-category?" Inersha asked. Atha nodded. "During the war with Erida, Shakkoo was captured and tortured. She doesn't talk much anymore, but don't take that as a sign of weakness. She's stronger than every other captain here put together," Atha pushed the box into Inersha's hands before stepping forward.

"Uh, pardon me, Captain Shakkoo?" he called down to her as she stopped eating. "Uh, I was, uh, just wondering if—if you would like a drink?"

"No, thank you. Gratitude for the food, though," she whispered back so quietly Atha almost didn't catch it.

"Let me know if you change your mind," he replied with a smile before turning back to Inersha. Atha sighed. "I'm not good at talking to girls."

"Well, they love talking to you! That was the most I've heard her say in a long time!" Inersha laughed, holding the pizza box up to Vork, who grunted and turned away.

"What's Bald Hagrid's problem?" Atha asked, flipping between Garo and Inersha.

"Bald who?" Inersha asked.

"It's—oh, never mind."

"You seem to make a habit of directing questions to the wrong person," Vork growled as Atha turned to him.

"Well ten fucking points to Gryffindor—oh wait, you got *expelled*, didn't you?!" Atha retorted, laughing at his own joke.

Vork glanced at the other captains, searching for an explanation that none of them had.

"You looking for a fight?" He strode forward but halted as Garo raised a hand.

"Enough, Vork, we—"

"Actually, I am," Atha replied, beginning to stretch.

"He accepts. Lead Captain Garo?" Vork replied, turning to his ally as Atha roared with laughter.

"Not with *you*! Him," Atha replied, slapping Inersha's shoulder as the captains paused.

"Why me?" Inersha chuckled.

Atha had expected this response, setting himself up perfectly to insult Vork in a way he assumed would be considered a low blow in Oluceps. "From what I understand, males have less mana than females, and larger, muscled specimens have even less. I'm after a decent challenge, not a punching bag." Atha sneered at Vork, who turned a previously undiscovered shade of red.

"W-well, no, after Shakkoo, Garo is the next combatively inclined. Vork and I are too close to call," Inersha replied as Garo stepped in front of Vork.

"You think yourself better than me with your tiny wrists and nonexistent muscles?!" Vork roared as Atha's hands clasped his hands over his wrists to shield them. He didn't know what this meant, but he assumed it was another insult he was ignorant of.

"What's wrong with my wrists?" he whimpered, turning to Inersha.

"Oh right, you're from wayyyy out of town. See, womanly features on a man are considered favorable. Many a man would kill for your slender waist, skinny legs, and dainty figure," Inersha replied. He smiled brilliantly, thinking he'd given favorable clarification, but paused as Atha's mouth quivered, unable to decide between anger and insecurity.

"This is psychological warfare I wasn't prepared for. Look, let's just do some slap boxing so I can get a gauge of how far I've come, okay?" Atha replied as Inersha shrugged.

"Fine with me. Just to clarify though, I'm stronger than Deldora. We spar often, and against him I'm 15-2." Inersha smiled.

"Oh really? Do you mind me asking what type of ability you use?"

"Not at all. I wield a transportation/combative type mostly governed by my familiar, Roka," Inersha said. A red portal opened behind him as a human-sized wooden doll sans legs popped out and hovered a few feet off the ground. Colored both blue and red, its painted-on face moved and laughed as the strings coming off its hands wafted down and attached to Inersha's arms and legs.

"Whoa, magical reverse puppeteer!" Atha exclaimed before circling around to take in the sight of the familiar.

"Don't let his looks fool you. Roka's a bit of a sadist," Inersha grumbled as the doll cackled.

"Oh, fair master, your words cause me great pain! To scorn me before Atha who looks upon my wooden form with such wonderment will assure that I take his side in this duel." Roka laughed as Inersha shook his head.

"Both times I lost duels with Deldora it was due to Roka *sabotaging* my chances of victory!" Inersha yelled back to the marionette.

"Sabotage? Always blaming others for your own shortcomings."

"You slammed me into the ground seven consecutive times while he took cheap shots!"

"Well, you can make anything sound bad when you spend all day thinking of ways to blame me and have a knack for stringing words together," Roka retorted.

"Okay, this is getting old really fast. Are we gonna go or what?" Atha grumbled.

"Yes, we will continue this discussion lat—" Inersha began but was cut off as Roka yanked on his strings, lifting him off the ground and slamming him down onto the rocky ground with enough force to leave a small crater. "*Queen's mercy,* Roka! I nearly bit my tongue off!"

"My hand slipped. I get nervous when you talk to me in that tone." Roka cackled as Garo shook his head.

"Oh mother, why did I not listen when you suggested I become a chef?" Garo sighed, pulling a white cube from his pocket.

"What a shit show," Atha muttered, placing a hand on the cube and reappearing inside the endlessly white world. The other captains appeared within the hovering translucent room. Inersha stood about fifty meters before Atha.

"Would you mind if I pick the scenery?" Inersha hollered.

"Sure, whatever that means," Atha replied as Inersha snapped his fingers up to Garo. The white world blinked for a moment, and then a forest of massive trees popped into existence completely filled the empty white void.

"Whoa! Is this real?" Atha gasped, thumping a hand against the closest tree.

"No, this is a synthetic world. Feel free to go all out," Inersha replied, pulling his goggles down over his eyes as a countdown timer appeared and began ticking down from ten.

Atha drew his sword and pulled his meteorite from his pocket, rolling it around in his fingers. *Roka smashed him into the ground pretty hard, so it's safe to assume he can take massive amounts of punishment. Besides that, all I can gather is that he controls his contract in a partnership with a similar relationship to how I work with Dulcina. Now let's see just how fast he is.*

Atha drew his sword, slowly pulling it back until the timer hit zero.

Thrusting forward, Shooting Star glowed white and forcefully yanked Atha toward Inersha. Agro energy surging, time slowed in his mind as red energy glowed across his whole body. Despite creeping time, Inersha moved out of the way so fast that Atha couldn't follow his movements and it wasn't until he landed and glanced around that he noticed the captain twitching against the base of a cracked tree. Atha grunted with anger. A pistol fell into his hands and he unloaded a few shots, again to no avail. Inersha proceeded to avoid the shots with ease, the bullets ricocheting from tree to tree like a pinball.

"Roka, stop it!" Inersha groaned, coming to a sudden halt mid-air in perfect range for Atha's pistol. "Oh, I should have seen that coming." Inersha watched as Atha waved the pistol at him.

"Is this a fucking joke to you?" Atha screamed, popping a shot clear past the captain.

"No, no, it seems Roka favors you over his own master," Inersha sighed as Atha turned his attention to the puppet.

"What If I was really trying to kill him? You'd let him die because you like me better?"

"And lose my mana source? Of course not! But this is simple play time," Roka mused as Atha sneered.

"Just because you're a fucking doll doesn't mean this is playtime," Atha replied, spitting at the ground beneath Inersha. "This is the last line of defense that protects my sister? All you captains make me *sick*."

"Inersha," Roka growled, tensing down on the loose wires until they became taut, singing like guitar strings ready to snap, "let's eat the boy alive."

The pair vanished in a flitting gust.

"Control! Anger level increase!" Atha boomed, twisting with rage. He glanced around, catching branches flitting about every few moments until the captain pressed an arm into Atha's chest and smashed him against a tree before vanishing again. He picked a good place for his contract. I can't see him, I can barely follow his movements. I need to narrow his path to me, funnel him to where I can improve my strike chances, Atha noted before dashing toward a tightly set group of trees. He drew a steel rope into his mind and snatched it from the air. He wrapped it between a pair of trees to narrow it further. This stuff could rip through a car. He may be tough but his isn't getting through this.

Atha leapt back down to the ground. Inersha was still too fast, slamming a pair of feet into his chest and sending him back into the wire. He tried to push Atha into it, but Atha began to glow red and caught the captain's arm, twisting and smashing him to the ground. A pistol fell into Atha's free hand. He aimed it down, but Inersha rocketed up, lifting Atha a few stories into the air before launching him back toward the distant ground. Inersha had slowed and kept his eyes focused on the falling Atha, who in turn saw his opening and manifested a car that hurtled down toward the captain.

Despite being completely out of even his peripheral vision, Inersha shot clear of the danger and careened back, slamming down on top of the rising car, caving its roof in and sending it plunging down toward Atha.

Atha drew Shooting Star and blindly thrust it to the left and narrowly dodged the car. Instead, he crashed into a tree, firmly imbedding the sword in it along the way. He ripped it free with excessive force, and ended up being flipped and pulled in the opposite direction. Inersha brought a leg across his side, kicking him and sending Shooting Star in a new trajectory toward another tree that the blade imbedded in.

He's fast, smart, and a superior combatant, Atha thought. *To make matters worse, he isn't underestimating me. He attacks in quick bursts but doesn't press long enough for me to counter. My only move from here is to act unpredictably and hope for a lucky strike.*

Atha jumped over to the sword and ripped it free again, hurtling backwards as Inersha inevitably swooped in. A car appeared in front of Atha, shielding him from Inersha's view, swinging the glowing sword in the open space above himself where he hoped the captain would try to strike from. Despite guessing correctly, Inersha still cleanly evaded the blade and vanished back into the forest.

Atha barely graced the ground before an automatic shotgun appeared in his free hand. Pulling the trigger, he unloaded the full magazine unpredictably around Inersha, again to no effect. Another quick kick across the face sent the sword yanking him toward another tree. Stuck again, Atha manifested a grenade in his left hand and hurled it randomly before manifesting another and hurling it as well. He yanked the sword free, misusing it to shield his face from the explosions that pelted shrapnel across his reinforced skin.

He manifested a fresh grenade into his free hand and flicked the pin free of its slot with his thumb, barely catching the flickering image of the speedster out of the corner of his eye. Turning to hurl the explosive ahead of the captain's line of movement, Atha was the one surprised as Inersha landed a heavy kick straight into Shooting Star which promptly glowed white and snatched his body into the air. Fortunately, Shooting Star narrowly missed a tree, but unfortunately Atha head was perfectly in line with it. With crushing force he smacked straight into the base of a hearty oak. In the four seconds that the grenade was set to explode in, he realized all too late his hand had miraculously managed to hold tight.

Atha, still slightly disoriented, was confused by the sight of the synthetic forest vanishing, leaving nothing but rocks and canyons around him. "Control, negate previous command." His anger dissolved on cue as the captains materialized simultaneously with the cars he'd conjured. "Man, you're an asshole. To an onlooker, it would be hard to tell if I was fighting the trees or an actual person."

Inersha pulled his goggles back on top of his blond hair.

"Sorry, I was gonna give you some wiggle room, but you put Roka in a sour mood," Inersha replied. "For a sadistic evil spirit made of dead wood, he is quite sensitive."

"I was just trying to get y'all to fight. By the way, it may have been one sided, but I was holding back, so don't be too proud." Atha smirked as Inersha leaned in.

"So was I." He winked and stepped back as the whole group glanced to Harika, who landed softly a few meters away from Atha. He sprinted toward Harika, who patted the backpack.

"I have gathered patients," he declared dully.

"What the hell are you doing? I was over here talking with them to keep them from noticing you!" Atha whispered.

"A friend of yours?" Garo asked.

"Uh, yeah, but no time for introductions. We gotta get going," Atha replied, pulling Harika back toward the bike and pulling a helmet over his head.

"I see. Might I ask your friend's name?" Garo asked.

"My name is Ha—" Harika began, unable to finish as Atha smothered his mouth with his hands.

"His name is Miracle! Really, we need to get going. I'm sorry, but it was nice talking, eating, arguing, and fighting with you all—not necessarily in that order!" Atha chuckled, a chill running down his back as Shakkoo glided in front of him.

"Take a moment, please," she whispered. Atha gulped and assumed the worst. She pulled the black wrap off from over her face. She had gorgeous, flowing red hair that spilled out from beneath the bandages.

As her face came fully into view, Atha had to collect himself. Eye sockets covered her face. Some contained an eye, but most were empty.

"It's—it's not as bad as I imagined," Atha lied, stuttering a bit.

"Inersha spoke of your desire. And please, you need not lie. I am comfortable with my corruption," she replied, a hint of a smile creasing her lips as Atha flipped his black visor up. *This is perfect. A little situation redirection and they'll forget Harika was even with me.*

"Well, in all honesty, I think battle scars are sexy as hell," Atha said as Shakkoo blushed. "Match that with red hair and you have the perfect mix for a beautiful lady."

"I find myself at a loss for words," she replied.

"We should go on a date," Atha suggested.

"I—I am twenty-nine years old, more than a decade your senior."

"And I was incarcerated for the difference, so it's time I started catching up! Come on, what do you say?" he continued, but she shook her head.

"I must decline. Regardless of innumerable other reasons, the Queen would have my head," she whispered as Atha sighed.

"Ah well, maybe in a few years? See you around." He flipped his visor down and pulled Harika onto the seat behind him before kicking his shoes and bike to life. He waved and shot up into the air, rounding a bend and immediately slowed to pull off his helmet.

"What the hell, man?! Do you know what would have happened if you broke the anti-recognition spell?!" he yelled with a glance over his shoulder at the Shelando.

"I have nothing but my name left from my parents. Please do not ask me to abandon it too," Harika replied.

"You said your name means miracle child, right? I called you miracle. In my language that's the same as your name's meaning."

"Oh. So, it's my name in a different language?"

"Exactly! Except it wouldn't break the spell. Hell, we could even say your last name is Child, making it a perfect translation!"

"I see. I am sorry I ruined your plan. I meant only to see to the injured as quickly as possible," Harika continued, but Atha shook his head.

"I took care of it. That stunt I pulled at the end is gonna be the center of discussion, leaving you totally in the background. Just, please, be more careful, okay? I'll be damned if I ever let anybody lock you up." Atha reached a hand back and slapped Harika's leg.

"Oh, you used a diversion," Harika replied after a few moments.

"Yeah, Len taught me how to overshadow certain memories. People instinctively remember embarrassing or offensive events before anything else. So, despite the appearance of an unknown Shelando, when they talk about our encounter today they'll remember me flirting. It's just a simple mind game, but its practical uses are endless."

Pulling back into camp, Zell was gesturing for Atha to come to her.

"Your ally is a good woman," the voice of the infected called through his mind.

"And she's not bleeding out of her mouth with infection either, so maybe you are too," Atha replied, coming to a stop beside Zell.

"Portions of her conscious mind remain, yet so do many questions. This could end up being a revolutionary discovery, but with the appearance of royal forces, we must take measures to see that her existence is hidden until we have conclusive evidence. Elenzer moves to us. He will relocate her to a covert location and will continue the investigation with elevated resources."

Atha sighed. "And I was about to cut her head off."

"At my beckoning. I take responsibility for that, so push it from your thoughts," Zell replied.

"Thank God we had Harika with us. Speaking of which, some of the captains that came to the rescue with Elise were still hanging around by the forest. They're locking the area down after the attack, they said, but get this—Harika strolled right up to us and almost used his name."

"Another predicament. What is our move for him, considering the nearing tournament?"

"He comes with us. And I think we should enter him into the tournament. The way things are going, it's only a matter of time before someone figures out who he is, so if we enter him, we could show he's not the threat he once was."

"Your thoughts mirror my own," Zell said, a bit taken aback.

"Why do you seem so surprised?"

"You will know soon enough," she replied, stepping past him as his eyes fell down to the infected woman.

"Looks like the bleeding is starting to slow," he observed, taking a seat before her. "I'm sorry about yesterday. My name's Atha. Do you know yours?"

She spoke in his head. "Lunesella. Lady Zell found it within my broken memories."

"Zell's gonna keep working to help you figure this out, and there's nobody I'd rather have working on my case. Do you need anything?"

"I am content."

"Let me know if that changes, okay?" he said. As he was getting up to leave, she spoke again.

"That power of yours—what are its origins?" she asked.

"I'm told it's a contact-less ability. Why?"

"It feels strange to me. Different from the others. As if telling me to stay away."

"Not really sure what to make of that. I thought it was dangerous at first, but I'm starting to realize it's just a frog hopping into the big ol' sea. Not much to fear," he replied, stepping away toward Zell.

"So, what's on the agenda for today?" he asked, sliding down into a chair beside her.

"Prepare lunch and we will discuss it after."

"Now that sounds like a plan!" He laughed, drawing the image of a juicy cheeseburger into his mind, but nothing appeared. "What the fuck?"

He closed his eyes and focused on the image again to no effect. "Zell, my power stopped working," Atha announced, drawing several more images into his mind as she glanced at him.

A five-pound weight fell from the air, cracking him over the head as he roared with surprise and pain. Lifting the weight up, he suspiciously eyed it over. "What the hell?! Nothing's ever fallen in a way that could hurt me."

He tried again, and this time successfully manifested a box of pizza into his lap. "It's working again. That was the weirdest series of events I've ever had with this power."

"This occurrence could signify deeper meaning. Abilities that come and go seemingly without reason tend to be controlled by another, comparable to how Dulcina turned emotion control against you."

"After all these years I think I would have figured out something else was controlling it. Maybe I did something different with it, like I added in some factor that made it respond differently. Whatever the reason, this power's worthless if I can accidentally kill myself with it." Atha laughed, tossing the weight to the ground where it landed with a *thud-thud.*

Two thuds? He glanced down and noticed a grenade with its pin caught on a rock laying at his feet.

"Grenade!" he screamed. He kicked the grenade high into the air and leapt toward Zell, smashing her beneath him on the ground, Agro energy bursting from his back to act as a shield. Not a moment later the grenade exploded overhead, ringing Atha's ears and sending hot shrapnel across him. He rolled off her, stunned, holding his ears for a few moments. "Holy shit! There is something! It fucking tried to kill us!"

Atha glanced over to Harika, who appeared completely unaffected by the explosion.

"Drawing comparison to a simple emotional contract and taking into account the manifestation limitations, I would deem this no more than a warning," Zell noted, dusting herself off and returning to her feet before pulling Atha up.

"How can you say that? It dropped a fucking bomb at my foot!" Atha screamed back.

"Turn your head and see the answer given," she replied, gesturing to the series of massive metal boats that loomed menacingly in the distance.

"Okay, fair point. So, what do we do about it?"

"To begin, it seems angered by belittlement," she replied, but paused as she saw a shadowy image pulling up over the horizon, moving along at a relaxed speed.

"Who's that?" Atha replied.

"Elenzer. He comes to collect Lunesella."

"Did you find out anything else about her?"

"Only what a search on her name could supply. Having been a vagrant, sources citing her existence were short."

"Well, progress is progress."

Chapter 18
Royalty and Loyalty

Atha repurposed the backpack they'd used to carry insects, placing his short list of possessions into it. The day of the tournament was at hand and under the darkness of night they would begin the long journey back to the capital. Atha popped his head out the tent, glancing to the daunting machines that even the moonless night couldn't hide.

"What should we do about those?" he asked Zell.

"I shall weave a story to explain their existence. A tall task, yet it is far more practical than either moving or destroying them."

"Harika, do think you could destroy those?" Atha joked to the blue man praying quietly.

"I do," he replied. Harika's hand brimmed with pulsing blue light, expelling the shadows.

Like a missile, a ball of blue shot from Harika's hand, and with a rippling boom, the plane was vaporized.

"Jesus Santa God! Harika! Harika, I was *kidding*!" Atha screamed hopelessly into the cloud of ensuing dust, watching as countless more balls of potent blue light shot across the machines. In less than fifteen seconds, Harika completely decimated the gathering, taking the majority of the time to annihilate the massive tanker.

"He's gotten stronger," Atha whispered to Zell, who nodded. He turned to Harika. "I want you to enter the tournament with us."

"I would prefer not to," Harika said.

"Come on, buddy. You gotta get over this, I don't know, fear of combat you have."

"Is pacifism such a bad thing?"

"Oh, look at you using big fancy words. Did you learn that from Zell?" Atha chuckled.

"I did."

"I'm not saying it's a bad thing, but not standing up for and defending what you believe in is. Look, I'm not trying to pressure you, so can you work with me on this or not."

"I will. I owe you everything," Harika said, but Atha shook his head.

"Stop saying that. I told you, it's just what we do. Well, let's hit it, we still gotta clean up the pair of cars I left by the forest."

Atha had begun getting comfortable with his bike, cruising at one hundred miles per hour as they headed straight for the capital. By the time the city came into view all three suns had risen, and he gasped with relief.

"Finally! Damn, I knew it wasn't gonna be as quick as teleporting, but it took us over seven hours," Atha announced as he slowed high in the air. As he neared the wall, a hologram screen appeared before him showing the image of a woman clothed in the green garb of the Royal Guard.

"Atha Lamkos, you are entering Capital airspace. What is the purpose of your visit today?" she asked.

"Honorati! My last name is Honorati!" he yelled back as the woman's smile twitched. "I'm here to enter the tournament."

"Very good. Turnout numbers are quite low this year with the Red Sheep about. Only at five hundred so far. Sign-ups are in the fourth district inside the building with the combat contract symbol above it. They close in an hour, so make haste. The Queen is aware of your arrival and will meet with you upon first opportunity. With that, we conclude your welcome screening, and I bid you good day."

The screen vanished as Atha passed over top of the wall. Thousands of people crowded the streets below them and the skies nearly as packed. He weaved carefully through the air traffic, heading for the distant hovering combat contract emblem of a sword resting atop a scroll.

"Just out of curiosity, how many people do you think will be watching?" Atha hollered back to Zell, whose orange screen popped open.

"The arena where the live feed will be displayed seats 70,000, which is expected to be filled, while last year's viewers who observed from afar via contract numbered in the millions," Zell replied.

"Millions?! *Goddamn*, I was figuring like maybe a couple thousand tops!" he replied, easing down toward an empty alley and dipping off his blue path as Zell hoped off. He kicked the peg down and sat for a moment, staring off into the crowd as a sense of surreality crept over him. *Is this real? Am I free?* Zell paused and watching as he pulled his hands up to his face and stared blankly at them.

"Our time is short before entry closes," she noted.

"Oh—oh yeah. Sorry, I was having one of my moments there. It's just so weird being free, you know?" he said. Harika landed softly beside him. Zell glanced at the Shelando and pulled her screen back up, flipping to an image of a white mask with a pair of black dots over the eyes and a single flat line for the mouth.

"Extra precautions should be taken for Harika. This mask can hide his face and only be removed by his own hand once attached," she informed them as the mask fell into Atha's hand. He tossed it to Harika. "Affix it to your face. From this moment on you will be referred as Miracle," Zell advised. Harika nodded, bringing the mask close to his face. It snapped onto him like a magnet. The black line of the mouth began too morph, turning into a frown.

"Magical masks. It looks just like the tragedy drama mask. Well, I guess all our bases are covered," Atha said, pausing as Zell eased her purple hood down to hide her face. "Oh right, ex-Chameleon. Should we come up with a nickname for you too, Miss Assassin's Creed?" Atha chuckled, but Zell shook her head.

"A pointless endeavor. My combative style is quite unique, divulging the same information as my full name would. Using only my first name will keep errant eyes from taking notice until the tournament begins." Atha forged ahead through the crowd toward the combat building. When they arrived, Atha held the door open for Zell and Harika before entering himself.

The lobby was filled with chattering combatants who all glanced idly at them before filling their curiosity. As soon as he pulled the door closed, a sheet of paper fluttered in front of them, pulled along by a blue twig. Zell grasped it and began scribbling as Harika and Atha followed suit.

"Full name? Stage aliases permitted but given name must be listed. Not off to a good start," Atha whispered to Zell, snatching Harika's paper from him and filling it out first. "Birthdate, eh, we'll switch that up a bit as well. Contract isn't necessary so just leave that blank. Emergency contact? I'll just list El for both of us," Atha muttered, finishing both the papers and taking Zell's from her as he strode up to the nearest attendee, an older Denata male.

"Excuse me, sir?" he started, holding up Harika's paper to the man, who turned irritably to him. "I had to—adjust some of my friend's information. I just—"

"It must be accurate, or the contract that pairs combatants up for the first round will reject it," he grumbled as Atha's smile vanished.

"All right, let's try that again. My name's—"

"Atha Lamkos, yes, I know who you are," he cut in again as Atha's temper began to rise.

"Honorati, actually. I need you to make an exception for me. Stop wasting time 'cause I promise it's gonna happen with or without you," Atha growled back as the man scoffed.

"An *exception?* There are no exceptions. The rules for entries exist to keep criminals from participating and they don't bend because you're known to the Que—" His words halted as the doors burst open.

A Royal Guard entering and boomed, "Her Highness Queen Elise enters!"

Everyone in the room except Atha knelt to one knee.

"But what?" Atha sneered, holding a hand up to his ear and patting the kneeling Denata on the head before flipping around as Elise strode in.

She was encircled by Royal Guards but pushed through them and hurried toward Atha.

"Kneel and kiss my ring finger," she whispered fretfully. He complied, kneeling and grasping her reaching hand to kiss it as the guard addressed the room again.

"Stand but hold your position in room. Make no use of contracts until the Queen has left."

Everyone stood again and nobody moved from their spot. Elise smiled to them.

"A fine turnout this year! My heart fills with joy to see so many prominent and up-and-coming combatants participating despite the current circumstances. May you all battle with pride and honor while demonstrating this land's potency before the world." When she finished, the room roared with applause.

She returned her eyes to Atha. "How did training go?" She smiled, taking obvious precaution to keep the conversation formal in the public setting.

"It was good, thanks to Zell. I know you must not have much time to chat, but are you gonna be watching the tournament?"

"Of course. A booth is set aside for my use. And yes, my schedule begs feet to keep moving. I just wished to check up with you between meetings." Elise reached a hand up to grasp the geode hanging around her neck.

"Well, your timing is perfect. Can you help me out with something?" Atha asked, pointing a finger back to the Denata receptionist.

"Is something the matter?" Elise replied as Atha held Harika's paper up.

"My friend needs to stay incognito, so we can't fill it out accurately. Can you ask the receptionist to make an exception? He's giving me a hard time about it," Atha whispered to her as she cocked an eyebrow.

"I don't ask, per se, for anything." She smiled, pulling the papers from his hands and handing it down to the Denata, who almost banged his head against the table bowing to her. "Please see him accommodated with anything he needs."

"Yes, my Queen," he replied pleasantly, grasping the entries from her hands.

"Thank you. Keep up the hard work," Elise said as he bowed his head again.

"Your kind words humble me, ma'am.".

Atha bent in to whisper, "Look at you go, big shot!"

"Hush. Now I must go, we will speak again before the day's end," Elise said before reentering the mass of guards the accompanied her and shuffling out the door.

"Damn, I couldn't have coordinated her showing up better if I'd planned it." Atha laughed to Zell, who buried her face in her hands.

"Of all the lessons given, never did formalities and protocol when dealing with royalty cross mind?" she groaned.

"Was it that bad?"

"She stands Queen of this realm. Should a recording of this incident come to light, your actions could be used to discredit her standing to a certain degree."

"Seriously? Damn, I hope I didn't screw things up for her."

"Error rests on my shoulders. Fret not, I shall see it rectified with haste."

"Ha! You said rectified!" Atha chuckled, watching as three badges fell into the receptionist's hands.

"Atha Honorati, participant number 706. Miracle Child, participant number 707. Zell Ten—" He paused, his eyes widening before flashing up to Zell, who rested a finger over her lips. He rose to his feet, a sharper change in demeanor flowing over him as his eyes filled with joy.

"To be addressed directly by the Queen, only to meet a living legend of the Denata in the flesh moments later, I—" He dug a hand into his pocket and produced a crystal. He held it in his palm as a hologram of a young Denata female formed over it. "My granddaughter, Zell, is named after you. She might not be here if you had not sacrificed so much to keep our lands safe. I don't mean to press beyond my grace, but could I interest you in dinner? Only so that she may meet her namesake at least once in her life."

"The preliminaries end at seven tonight and I've never been known to turn down a meal," Zell said, smiling at the Denata.

"Ain't that the truth." Atha chuckled and then grunted as Zell's elbow dug into his side.

The receptionist scribbled frantically onto a sheet of blue paper before handing it to Zell.

"My address. Ask for me by name, Horzter Drezmod. We will be expecting you at seven, and again, thank you for all you have done for both the world and the Denata." He smiled as Zell bowed her head and turned toward the door. Back into the crowd they went, Atha's stomach begging for food as he followed behind Zell.

"All hail the mighty Zell, eh? That old bastard really has a thing for you." Atha laughed and received a cold glance from Zell.

"I take jokes made in poor taste in stride regularly, but do not assault such a topic again."

"Whatever. Where should we eat? I feel as hungry as I did the time I went on hunger strike. Ha, just kidding. I never did that. I did eat my chips right in front of guys who were though, that did happen." He laughed but his spirits quickly sunk as Zell shook her head.

"We are short of time. Matches begin in eight minutes," Zell replied as Atha groaned in despair.

"Eight minutes?! But I'm starving! Why didn't you warn me sooner?"

"I did not know myself until minutes ago."

"Oh, Miss Know-it-all didn't know when the tournament began? She's setting me up to weaken me so I don't win, Miracle!" Atha moaned to his glowing ally.

"The schedule was posted on the wall," Harika replied flatly.

"Oh, excuse me for not noticing it while I was busy forging your application," Atha retorted as a single slice of pizza fell into his hands.

"Want one?" he asked through grotesquely large bites. Zell shook her head.

"Arteries beg that I fast out the gruel pumping through them. Before we reach our destination there are a few more factors to go over. This tournament is of unforeseen scale and through the preliminary stage the usage of your Agro energy will mostly likely suffice. Even in the least favorable scenarios, manifest nothing larger than a large car, understood?" Zell asked as Atha leered at her.

"Gruel? This is greasy, unhealthy goodness, and I beg you take that back," he replied as her face sank.

"A whole speech on restraint and that is what you take away from it? In a sense, I suppose that reflects the cumulative efforts taken during training." She sighed and turned to Harika.

"As for you, a quick burst of mana of equal strength to that used in decimating the cargo machines will suffice. These matches will be staged inside of a contract-rendered dimension where lethal force will automatically end the match, leaving any foe you encounter uninjured."

"Thank you. I will do that," he replied as Zell glanced back to Atha.

"He makes it seem so easy, no?" She smirked.

"Well, if I get matched up against Deldora, you can bet I'm throwing the kitchen sink at him," Atha grumbled.

As they rounded a bend in the crowded road, Atha saw the massive arena stretching into the sky.

"A grave error. This is but a simple tournament and any combatant equal to the rank of private or higher in the Royal Guard would dare not show either best moves or key strategies. Fighting Deldora at full strength would prove nothing other than the fact you couldn't beat him unless you held the advantage," Zell replied coolly. "Is Atha Honorati the type who needs high ground to win?"

"I see what you're up to. I'll beat him without showing any of my aces. Damn, and here I was ready to drop a cruise ship on his head the second the match began," Atha said with a sigh as they walked through the front entrance of the arena and through a short tunnel. Upon exiting, they found themselves in the center of the arena. Rows of seats crept up into the blue sky around them.

"Good. An ability that remains unknown will force an opponent to keep their distance. Once facts of its usage are known, its potency is more than halved," Zell replied, leading them up a set of stairs toward a section filled with combatants. Atha noticed Deldora sitting in the first row. He hadn't noticed Atha, who had just manifested a jug of juice in his hand. Snapping the cap off and taking a quick sip, he caught his foot on the back of the other. With a gasp, he fell, flinging his jug with purpose across Deldora.

"Oh my goodness! I am so sorry, sir!" He smiled apologetically as Deldora shot to his feet, slinging the jug of juice down and stepping toward Atha. Zell stepped in between.

"Take anguish out in match," she muttered to Deldora, who was still leering at Atha.

"I'll see you soon, *boy*," Deldora growled as he sat back down.

Atha attempted to step around Zell, but she was quick to catch him.

"You had that coming. Now go," she spat at him, pushing him in the direction of the stairs. Atha gave Deldora one last snarl before striding up after Harika, who had paid the situation no mind and had already found his seat. No sooner had Atha and Zell sat down in their seats than a chubby old human man stepped out before the group.

"Kinda expected more chicks to be here," Atha whispered to Zell. "All that talk about females being better warriors must have been a little exaggerated, eh?"

"Taking into account that an ancient threat is currently on the loose, I find it plausible most areas would opt to keep best warriors nearby while sending expendable forces only to save face. Keen eye for most obvious of facts, though, Atha. May no one dare hide gender from your wary notice."

He sank down in his seat.

"Well-well-well uh... Shut up, Zell," he grumbled back as she stifled a laugh.

"What manner of wit could form such a response? Give praise that in place of elevated mana you were blessed with a sharp tongue!" Zell snickered, sending Atha slumping further down into his seat as the old man at the front of the group cleared his throat.

"Good morning and welcome to the two hundred and fifteenth Tournament of the Contract Festival! My name is Aeros, and I'm your referee for today's games. Before we begin the preliminaries that will determine who will participate in the actual games, we need to go over a few details. First, these matches are one versus one. Partner entities outside of typical contracts are forbidden. Next up is contract-enhanced items. Basically, if your ability didn't create it, you can't use it."

"My shoes and sword?!" Atha whined to Zell as the announcer glanced up to him.

"Your shoes you can't use," the announcer said. "Your sword is more of a grey area, considering it can be used for or against you, so you may use it."

"Damn, the set of ears on the old bastard, eh?" He chuckled as Zell shook her head.

"No, the participants' collective hearing is linked. Everybody can hear you."

"Does anybody have any more questions for this old bastard in regard to what we've covered so far?" Aeros asked, receiving a slew of laughter from the group. "No? Then let's move on. There will be a ten-second countdown clock to signal the start of every match, but you are permitted to activate your contract and prepare your first attack once it hits the nine second mark. Taunting during a match as well as dirty language are allowed, but until you are in the ring, the crowd will be able to hear you, so keep it to a minimum until crossing plains. Forfeiting is frowned upon, but a participant need only mouth the words I concede defeat freely and without coercion from the opponent's contract. Besides everything mentioned to this point, basically anything goes, so on to finals qualification.

"You will be paired up at random for the first match. The two following matches will pair those who finished first with those who finished last to keep the best from knocking each other out early on. One loss puts you out of the tournament, and the fights continue until the final sixty-four participants are remaining. Captains of the Guard participating in the tournament will fight an extra match to round out the numbers properly.

"Matches will have battlefield selection options granted to the combatant who took the shortest amount of time to get to the current match. Selections are forest, iceberg, beach, desert, or white void. After every match, combatants will be given two minutes inside a healing area to return mana usage and injuries to nil. Now that that's all covered, do we have any questions? No? Then let's start the matches."

The ground behind Aeros rippled and a white matte material covered the ground level as a massive white cube popped out from the center. The participants all stood, and Atha followed suit. Then they began making their way down toward the cube. Atha watched as each fighter placed a hand on the cube and vanished.

"This is it. Come on, give me Deldora," Atha mumbled to himself, before placing a hand on the cube.

The next thing he knew, he was standing in a blank white world. A countdown clock hovered in the air and another young human male stood before him. Red energy glowed across Atha as he met eyes with his opponent, a dull rumble emitting from him as his distant image distorted and bent.

"Some kind of mirage ability? Won't save you for long," Atha said with a laugh. He glanced back up to the counter and noticed that it hadn't lost a second. Several minutes passed before a voice came into Atha's head.

"Apologies everyone, it seems participant Miracle Child was confused and remained in his seat after we started. With all participants now paired up, we will begin."

Atha groaned. I totally forget to keep an eye on him. He's off to a fantastic start.

The timer finally began counting down from ten as red energy pulsed over Atha. He erupted forward as it hit zero. His opponent gasped in disbelief, stumbling back and unleashing a weak blast of rippling air toward him to no effect before receiving a fist to the face. The boy vanished and a second later Atha found himself in a large white room with a handful other combatants. Harika was already there, praying. Others began to arrive. Atha went over to Harika and slapped his shoulder.

"Look who decided to show up! Heard you didn't head down to the big magical teleporter thing once things kicked off." Atha smiled.

"I hadn't paid attention," Harika replied.

"Yeah, sorry. I shoulda thought to check on you before heading down. Still, you got here before me. No problems in match one?" Atha said, checking around the growing numbers for Zell.

"None," he replied.

Someone caught Atha's eye and his attention to Harika slipped. A tall, dark-skinned man dressed in white robes with intricate golden embroidery covering nearly every inch of it sat across the room. Gold rings encircled every finger and a long golden chain hung around his neck. A peculiar pendant hung from the chain just above his waistline.

"God, did anybody tell 50 Cent this was a combat tournament and not a fashion show?" Atha chuckled uneasily, glancing over his own bland black-and-purple robes.

"That is Prince Mikaido," Zell's familiar voice said from behind them. "The favorite to win this year's tournament."

Atha swung around to face her. "Took you long enough. Harika and I won in a few seconds."

"And likely gained nothing," Zell said with a smile. Atha raised an eyebrow.

"Hello, the announcer dude said the first to finish faces the last place person. I'll get an easier opponent next round and select the terrain," he replied. Zell nodded.

"And inevitably robbing yourself of opportunity to face an opponent at their best and the chance to gain experience," she said as Atha rolled his eyes.

"Whatever. So, what's with the Prince? I thought Elise was the only royalty around here."

"He is from a neighboring kingdom," she said. "I suspect he has entered to put his contract on display in a courting effort."

"What the fuck do you mean by that?" Atha nearly yelled.

"To pass contracts through the bloodline, an heir must be conceived. Why would this surprise you?" Zell said as Atha calmed himself.

"I get that, but I'd just never thought about it. So that means the tall pretty boy is trying to hook up with my sister?" Atha, felt his anger already regaining steam.

"In a most animalistic sense, yes. Until this point there has been no whispers of marriage regarding the Queen, which is abnormal for a woman of her age and status in this world." Zell paused as red energy began to glow from Atha.

He growled, "She didn't even mention this to me. I mean, I get that she's not a little girl anymore, but if she didn't talk about it it's probably because she didn't want to. Or maybe because she *won't* go through with it."

"You view this topic through distorted vision. I can see how your conclusion is drawn, but in the aspect of securing the future it is quite the dilemma," Zell replied calmly as Atha continued to stare at the tall man, feeling infuriated at his very presence.

A bell chimed and Zell vanished. Atha, Harika, the Prince, and a handful of other contestants remained, a voice chiming through the air.

"Congratulations! You where one of the first twenty to finish a match. In order to keep Captains from participating in multiple extra matches, you have been designated to sit this round out and are automatically advancing beyond this round. Please take this time to watch your rivals as they finish qualifications." A few dozen screens appeared in a circle around the room that displayed the many participants facing off. "Let's find Zell's!" Atha exclaimed, tugging Harika along behind him to scour the screens. He located her on the second screen he found.

Zell appeared before a young male Shelando dressed in bright red robes. The white world became a dense forest at his selection and she bowed pleasantly to him. He smiled and returned the gesture. The timer reached zero and Zell opened her orange screen, shuffling symbols around as the Shelando stared in surprise. Atha could tell exactly what the young fellow was thinking, having been in the exact same position when he'd dueled her. *What is she doing? Should I hide and try to figure out her contract or attack?*

"Do not take pause on my account. I deemed it fair to conduct my research during the match to give my opponent an opportunity," Zell explained, which only sent him further into confusion.

"Research?" he repeated as Zell began reading information.

"Current match pairs combatant 708 with 294. 294 is registered to Dagult Teser, who wields a combat/transportation contract named Entomologist's Fond Memory. With that information my contract can directly research your own and reveal every strength and weakness. I suggest you make haste."

His mouth dropped. "Nobody can research a contract that fast with a combat/information type! This is some sort of trick!"

"Ah, but this is purely an information type," Zell replied, glancing back to her screen. "Entomologist's Fond Memory allows the wielder to disperse their body into a cluster of butterflies capable of vanishing at a cost of eight mana per—" Zell began as the Shelando erupted into an array of flitting butterflies that shot out into the trees before vanishing. Zell smiled and closed her screen. Blue mana tendrils formed around her back, drawing daggers as she watched her surroundings. Catching a flash of red out of the corner of her eye, she twisted and angled daggers up at the young man, who yelped and lurched back before bursting into butterflies again.

"Vibrant wardrobe betrays stealthy approach. Dress appropriately to remain camouflaged during combat," Zell called cheerfully into the woods, watching the butterflies glide behind her as the Shelando reappeared again. Her daggers had already anticipated this move. "Regain the element of surprise before striking again. The standard attack from behind paired with haste—"

"Why do you keep letting me go? Are you mocking me?!" the Shelando yelled from the thick of the woods.

"Intent was not to insult but to lend guidance that you have clearly been deprived of. You use developed attack patterns but do not appear to have ever learned the key basics. This leads me to the belief you are a self-taught prodigy. I would prefer to see the ember of skill put to tinder rather than crushed. And do not call out to opponent during battle, it reveals the direction of attack," Zell called back, her mana tentacles twisting up toward the canopy as the Shelando stopped again, bursting into butterflies but flitting and reconvening a short distance in front of Zell.

"I get it, I can't win," he sighed, rubbing his eyes.

"Quite the opposite. Though my victory in this match may be inevitable, you have learned something new and taken something with you. I gain nothing but a win. My hopes lie with finding an opponent who can defeat me and to show where improvement is needed." Zell smiled to him as he paused, glancing her over.

"A Denata using an information contract as if it were a combat contract paired with Mana Vectors Wielding Daggers. This is probably gonna sound crazy, but are you Zell Tenzata?" the Shelando asked.

"In the flesh. But please hold tongue until the finals begin," Zell replied with a bow as the Shelando burst with excitement.

"Zell Tenzata! My mom told me stories about you when I was a kid! Oh man, I heard you were a phenomenal teacher but none of the stories do you justice!" he roared. "Well I won't hold you up. As per the tournament rules, I concede—" He paused as Zell raised a hand.

"I have only covered most blatant of mistakes. Please, see them remedied and we may continue," she replied cheerfully before reaching down for a handful of dirt and blotting out the vibrant red of his clothes.

Atha watched in prideful amazement, simply nodding to Zell as she rematerialized as if to say *I expected no less*. He had no time for words regardless; Zell had finished last and already time was winding down until her next match started. She vanished again, and so did Harika and Atha.

Atha found himself back in front of the massive white cube surrounded by the ghostly empty stadium. Aeros was standing beside it.

"Hey, wait my other friend isn't back yet! What the hell, man?" Atha hollered to him.

"Then they must have taken extra time to finish their match," he replied coolly. "Only those with the worst qualifying times are left and must face a captain to be able to move on. Rounding the numbers, remember?"

"Well can I at least watch again?" Atha replied.

"No. Apologies, but we wished only to give a hint at what's to come without giving too much advantage. Be back here at eight p.m. sharp for the finals. If you have any further questions, I can be found in my office just to our left," Aeros replied, motioning toward a room built into the bottom of the stadium. The masses began to disperse and Atha lead Harika off, glancing at his watch.

"We'll wait outside for Zell. Hopefully she'll be out in time for her date with that old Denata," Atha said, glancing off toward the Prince, who walked with a small entourage comprising of a human male and female.

Atha watched him for a few minutes, attempting to get a feel for just who this potential suitor was. The Prince stopped his progress toward the exit, instead chatting with his bodyguards. Atha wasn't close, but definitely within earshot, yet he surprised to find he couldn't catch a single word they exchanged. *Probably some type of contract blocking me from eavesdropping.* His concentration was broken with the sight of Zell dashing past.

"That's what you get for—" Atha started but was cut off as Zell yelled over him.

"Should you need me, make use of my contact function!" Zell yelled over her shoulder to them. "I must make haste to my dinner appointment." She headed into the crowd.

"No sex on the first date!" Atha screamed after her before pulling Harika along behind him.

"Too bad Zell had to buck it. I still don't know how I'm supposed to act around El in public."

"I can teach you. My old city was visited often by royalty."

"Yeah, that would be awesome. What did I do wrong?" Atha asked, finding a less crowded street and heading down it.

"Everything."

"Well thank you, Zell Junior. Just tell me what I should do in that exact scenario next time," Atha grumbled as Harika nodded.

"You remained standing when she entered. If a disaster isn't at hand, you kneel the moment her presence is made known and take directions from the lead guard. If you happen to be sitting, you bow your head to your knees or an inch above the desk or table in front of you. Once the room is permitted to stand, do not approach her and speak only when spoken to. If you are, kneel again and kiss her right ring finger unless you possess a contract activated by touch, in which—"

"Summarize what applies to me, buddy." Atha chuckled.

"When addressing her, initially call her 'your majesty' and every time following as 'ma'am.' Keep firm eye contact and don't activate a contract or reach for a weapon. If you pass her on the street, you only need to kneel unless you are addressed. When addressed in an audience setting, kneel for seven seconds then stand. When addressed

from a distance, move yourself in front of her and kneel. That's all."
Atha scoffed when Harika finished.

"Lots of kneeling. Got it."

A scream sounded from a forming crowd near them. "A fight? Let's check this out." Atha tugged Harika behind him as he pressed forward. He paused in surprise at the sight of Prince Mikaido glaring down at a woman, blood oozing from her nose.

Chapter 19
Wrath Rising

"Put your filthy hands on me again and I will have your head, you wretch!" Mikaido screamed at the woman, who cowered on the ground before him.

"Apologies, sir, I lost my footing!" she sobbed. The Prince's entourage laughed mockingly.

"Liar! You mean to say you fell in a manner that allowed you to completely miss both my guards and into me?" he screamed, raising a fist above her, but Harika shot forward, gently grasping his hand as Atha knelt beside the woman.

"Stop it," Harika instructed plainly as Atha helped the woman to her feet, a cloth appearing in his hand that he used to dab into her nose before handing it to her.

"You should get out of here. I'm 'bout to teach this prick a lesson," he growled as she nodded and vanished into the crowd.

"Take your hands off me!" Mikaido screamed, yanking away with all his might to no effect until Harika released him. The Prince toppled back into the arms of his male guard.

"Did you hit that lady?" Atha asked as calmly as he could muster as a female guard cut in.

"Is that how you address royalty, boy? You should take your own leave before—"

"Shut the fuck up! Ain't nobody talking to you!" Atha screamed, reaching out a hand and snatching the front of the Prince's robes.

"Did you?" he asked again, boiling rage beginning to cripple his thoughts.

The male bodyguard's fist swung for Atha's face, but red energy engulfed his head. With a quick twist of his neck, he slammed his forehead straight into the guard's fist—which, against the Agro-reinforced flesh, released a series of cracks like a snapping glow stick. The guard screamed and stumbled back. Mikaido thrust Atha's hand off and went to his injured ally.

"It's—it's broken, sir," the guard mumbled. The Prince's displeasure twisted into bursting rage as he turned back to Atha.

"You just assaulted the personal bodyguard of a visiting prince. I am at liberty to defend myself," he announced, a blue glow covering his body as a massive winged clock crashed down behind him.

The crowd screamed and dispersed in a frenzy as Atha drew his sword.

"We're in the middle of the capital. You best shut your contract off," Atha instructed as the male guard nodded.

"Please, sir, see reason! This is going too far!"

A small red demon popped out of the top of the clock and announced, "It's time." The number 78 shined over the clock's screen.

"Get back," Atha called to Harika, who nodded and glided back out of the pavilion. "Last warning, asshole. Shut your contract off or—" Suddenly, a dog covered with bandages burst out of a red portal, barking wildly and lunging for Atha. Atha pulsed with Agro energy and shot to the side, pulling his sword back and swinging at the dog. Before he could make contact, the dog erupted into a flurry of bandages, revealing no animal beneath them. The bandages swirled around Atha, wrapping tightly over his arms and the sword. A portion of the bandages loosened and reformed the shape of a dog's head, snapping wildly at Atha. He fell back, frantically pulling at the bandages that remained firmly wrapped around him.

Mikaido erupted forward and slammed a foot down onto Atha's chest, producing a crack in the ground beneath him. Atha desperately swung the sword at him, but the bandages puffed out, releasing their grasp on Atha to shield Mikaido. Atha leapt up, a pistol appearing in his free hand and slowing time as he popped shots off at Mikaido's legs, pinging off the blue glow encasing his body with no effect.

This is bad. At this point its life or death but I can't go all out in the middle of the city, Atha thought.

The dog burst out of a red portal again and leapt at Atha as he swung Shooting Star and rocketed into the sky.

"It's time," the demon resting atop the clock noted again. This time the number 93 appeared across the screen. A black ball fell into Mikaido's hand and he threw it up at Atha, who had manifested a car in between them. The ball jutted past it and smacked him in the chest. Atha's body grew insanely heavy, and he went crashing to the ground, where the dog was waiting. Bandages rolled over top his arm again as the car crashed down only feet away. The dog snapped down on his shoulder and tore at him.

Atha was beginning to lose himself to anger. He manifested a car that sped through the air toward Mikaido. Mikaido flitted out of the way as it slammed into a massive glassy storefront, producing a cascade of glass raining down. Atha swung his sword with a twist, spiraling through the air and flinging the dog off as he roared with frustration. The Prince shot into the air, slamming a fist into Atha's face with enough force to smash straight through the roof of a blue building.

Mikaido turned his eyes down upon Atha who slumped to the floor inside the house, pulling angrily at the black ball stuck to him.

"This is but a taste of what a royal contract is capable of. Bow your head and plead mercy and this need not continue," Mikaido growled.

An AK-47 appeared in Atha's hands and he pelted the preening man with lead.

"It's time," the demon announced, the number 44 appearing across the clock. A red portal opened beside Atha and a massive scaly arm reached through it onto the floor, pulling itself up to reveal a humanoid lizard. A sickening smile was plastered across its face. Its eyes met Atha's, freezing Atha in place he began to panic at the sound of a dog's growl behind him.

Harika shot in and scooped Atha up. Together they flew up and out of the gap in the roof before setting the motionless Atha down on the paved road.

"Coming to save your friend, Shelando? Brave, but costly. Activate force multiplier times two!" Mikaido roared. A second black dog appeared next to the first, along with another lizard. Another black ball fell into Mikaido's hands. He tossed the ball down at Harika, but he didn't budge. Instead, he snatched it from the air and crushed it. Then he yanked the ball off of Atha and crushed it too. The dogs burst toward him, springing into a flurry of bandages that cocooned Harika's left arm. Portions of the bandages reformed the heads of both dogs and their fangs tore fruitlessly at his shoulder and ribs.

"Please stop. I won't hurt you," Harika called softly to the dogs. Healix slithered out of a red portal and onto Harika's arm opposite the snapping dogs. Harika lowered him down toward Atha. "What is wrong with him? He won't move," Harika asked as Healix's eyes focused.

"This is a temporary paralysis spell placed upon him from eye contact from that black lizard. I could reverse it, but it should be just about out of time anyway." Just then, Atha gasped for air.

"Who are you?! To crush a gravity ball in such a way!" Mikaido screamed at them as Harika patted Atha's back, ignoring the Prince. "It makes no difference! You only prove superiority through your aid!" Mikaido continued, pausing as Atha crushed the ground beneath his fist.

"He's right. This is between him and me, Harika. Don't jump in again," Atha replied, getting to his feet and raising his sword as Harika nodded and shot back.

"Between us, you say? You're naïve. Are you truly so clueless that you can't even comprehend the situation?" Mikaido sneered.

"Put another gravity ball on me and we'll continue," Atha sneered back. Mikaido paused before hurling a black ball down at Atha. His weight increased as soon as it made contact.

"I don't need anybody to fight my battles!" Atha declared, focusing all his Agro energy into his left hand and yanking the ball off. He crushed the ball in his hand before turning his sword to Mikaido.

"It's time," the demon announced again, the number 62 shining across the clock this time. A pair of circular blades fell into Mikaido's hands.

"A favorite selection of mine," Mikaido replied, pausing as a figure came to a stop in the air between them. "Get out of my way, guard!" Mikaido screamed as Atha saw Inersha's familiar face. The guard pulled the goggles from over his eyes onto his wavy blond hair.

"Prince, with all due respect, have you lost your mind?" he asked calmly.

"He broke my guard's hand! My cause is justified!" Mikaido retorted.

"So you don't deny that you activated a triple S contract in the middle of the capital for combative purposes? You're just giving a supplementary explanation? Queen's mercy, sir, ever heard the term *international incident*? And you, Atha, a street fight with a prince? Really? What do you think the Queen would have done had you gotten injured or even killed? Hell, maybe you would have even injured him. Do you realize your sister would have been held accountable?"

"He hit a civilian! You don't know the whole story!" Atha complained as Inersha pulled a gem from his pocket and clasped it in his fist. The woman's mug shot appeared above it.

"This woman? Yeah, she's a con artist. Probably trying to get a recording of the Prince's outburst for a profit. What was that you were saying about not knowing the whole story?" he replied.

Mikaido's female guard laughed as Atha's face turned red.

"Bet she didn't count on a recording distorter being present!" she added as Mikaido chuckled and the clock and weapons vanished.

"So what?! That doesn't make it any better!" Atha retorted as Inersha groaned. Mikaido snapped his fingers at his guards before swiveling around and beginning to step away. "Hey, where you going?! This isn't settled!"

Mikaido paid him just as much mind as Harika had paid him. Inersha stepped in front of Atha.

"Stop it! I was sent here to break this up and keep a street fight between a prince and the Queen's adopted brother from escalating. If you keep pushing this, it'll go to the next level!" Inersha whispered, not calming Atha in the least.

"I'll see you in the tournament if you can last long enough!" Atha screamed again, attempting to step around Inersha, who caught him as Mikaido turned around.

"You entered? I hadn't noticed your presence. I look forward to continuing flogging," Mikaido said before turning again and disappearing around a corner.

"Fucking prick. That's the main candidate to marry my sister?" Atha continued, turning his anger on Inersha.

"Calm down. Once again, there's so much more to this," Inersha replied.

"Well then fucking elaborate for me," Atha spat at him.

"It'll take a bit of explaining on my part and a few deep, calming breaths on yours, but just listen, okay?" he replied. Atha's stare continued to burn. "What you just saw was the Prince's royal contract known as 120 Methods of Victory. It's nearly as potent as the Queen's but it is blessed only to the males in his bloodline. If he married Queen Elise, only her contract would pass on to the next generation, which would be a big plus for his family. However, you've seen a bit of the kingdom, right? We're basically on the brink of bankruptcy after all the hardships that have befallen us, and the Prince's family is rich beyond imagination. If we merged lands, our borders would stretch farther than any nation in the history of the planet. All us meager peasants would jump and yell hurray!" Inersha finished sarcastically as Atha's unamused face leaned in closer.

"You think it's a good idea to let that woman-beater anywhere near my sister?" he replied as Inersha's smile vanished.

"Okay, remember, deep breaths. I'm not saying one way or another. I'm just trying very cautiously to tell you why it's practical in terms of the whole bigger picture and that the Queen will be examining it as such."

"It's not practical. That's the only concept you need to drive into your head," Atha growled as Inersha took a step back.

"Not practical! Got it! Well, as much fun as this has been, I need to get back to pulling over drunk flyers. Sorry for breaking up your fight club," he said before slowly becoming airborne. Atha caught his leg.

"Hold on a sec. If I were to beat him in the tournament, would that put a damper on this plan?" he asked.

"Atha, we're talking about a triple S contract. If you could trump that, the talks of marriage would be drowned out by incessant laughter. Has anybody ever explained to you what triple S classification signifies?" he asked, a scheming smile crossing Atha's face as he pulled his meteorite out and began jumbling it between his fingers. "With his contract a toddler would be the favorite to win the tournament. We're talking the blessed few, wielding power the rest of us can't comprehend, power that puts a family permanently above the rest while we all clamor for the chance to fall under their protection."

"How can you say that while flying around fast enough to make a fighter jet blush? Maybe you've just been manipulated by society to think you're not just as blessed as any of them," Atha replied.

"Long ago I had that same thought. Trust me, I've been down that road. I know I appear to be strong, but nothing I could ever do would compare to anybody with power like the Prince's. Take it from somebody who knows, this is a fight you—" His words halted as Roka roared with laughter, yanking Inersha's body off the ground, angling hard into the side of a building, smashing and digging across like a meteor leaving a trail in the ground in its wake.

"Let's toughen you up, then! How did such a whiner ever get my contract?!" Roka roared as Inersha screamed, angling hard toward another building and bouncing off the roof before vanishing behind the skyline. Atha chuckled and glanced back to a praying Harika. He reached an arm over and jostled him for attention.

"Not *a word* about this to Zell. As far as she knows, we were off getting food, okay?" he instructed firmly.

"I hate lying," Harika replied.

"Then plead the fifth."

"I don't know what that is," Harika replied as Atha pulled him along.

"Silence, buddy. Lots and lots of silence. Now come on, we've got a mission."

"Mission?"

"Yeah. Let's go talk to that tournament commissioner and make sure he pairs me up with that royal asshole. Deldora can suck it. Bigger fish to fry."

Heading back to the stadium, they discovered it was still empty, and they had plenty of time before the finals. Not a single soul was around as they approached the commissioner's office.

Atha strode over to the door, Agro energy erupting across his leg, prepared to kick it open. He ended up smashing the door to the ground, causing the commissioner to scream from fright. Atha laughed at his work as he stepped over the door. He hadn't meant to do so much damage, having meant too only kick it open for dramatic effect, but it sure felt satisfying.

"What are you doing?!" the old man gasped, pulling a handkerchief from his pocket and dabbing at the nervous sweat dotting his forehead.

"Sorry, don't know my own strength. It's Aeros, right? Let's have a little chat," Atha replied, pulling the chair out from in front of the desk. He took a seat across from the man as Harika eased through the doorway behind him.

"You kick my door down just to chat? I've heard much about the boy from another world—"

"Don't call me boy!" Atha yelled as the old man flinched.

"Apologies, sir. I've heard much about *you*, but I thought surely the bursting attitude was an exaggeration!" Aeros laughed sheepishly, coming to a stop as Atha didn't join him.

"Look, man, let me just say my piece and then I'll take my attitude somewhere else. You hold some sway over this tournament, right?"

"On certain aspects, yes. What's this all about?" he asked, glancing between the two.

"Match pairings. Put me up against Mikaido from the get-go," Atha replied coldly as the man's face filled with confusion.

"The *Prince*? Why would you want to fight him of all people?"

"That's my business. Can you do it?" Atha watched the man twiddle a finger as a screen displaying the pairing bracket popped up.

"I'm sorry, sir, but it was set the moment prelims finished."

"You've got some pull. Just change it." Atha shrugged, the screen flitting closer to him but shooing it away like a fly.

"Please, sir, I swear I would help you if I could, but a contract created the pairings and it's already set. There's simply just no way that—"

Atha went ballistic, slamming a glowing fist down onto the desk and smashing it in half as the man screamed.

"There's *always* a way! You don't even understand how significant this tournament is!" Atha yelled, standing and kicking the chair back before stepping over the desk's remains toward the cowering man.

"I don't know what you're talking about!" said the commissioner. "You burst in here and start tearing my office up while demanding the impossible from me, but I don't even know why this is so vital!" he cried, easing his chair back away from Atha.

He's just going to keep making excuses with no intention of helping, Atha thought. His snarl faded as his face settled, but Atha was no longer under his own control. He felt himself blacking out. Voices filled his head, voices just as angry if not more so than he was—voices that demanded capital punishment. Their fervent whispers begged for it.

"There you go, son," the commissioner continued. "Are you in some sort of trouble? Is somebody threatening you? I can help."

Atha moved closer and closer, stepping ever so slowly. He didn't entirely disagree with the voices, and he felt compelled to follow their instructions.

He doesn't give a damn about Elise despite all she's sacrificed so worthless shit like him can survive. I should just kill him. Kill him. Kill him. Kill him. Kill him. Kill him. His hand eased up, twitching fingers moving toward the man's wrinkled neck. *It would be easy. Just kill him. Kill him. Kill him. Kill him. Kill him. Kill him.*

"Son? You all right?" the man asked.

Atha could hear his words, but they sounded so distant, blocked by the whispers.

Kill him. Kill him. Kill him. Kill him. Kill him. Kill him.

Atha felt a firm hand fall on his shoulder, and Harika's empty voice sounded, halting the whispers and snapping Atha awake.

"What are you doing?" Harika asked.

Atha glanced around, unsure of himself. *When did I get into over here?* he wondered, noticing his own outstretched hand.

"Um, I was...gonna shake your hand," Atha said slowly, clasping the man's in his own. "Sorry for the damage. I'm still getting used to my strength."

Atha, with Harika behind him, fled out the door.

Atha hurried out of the arena, pausing in front of it and noticing the seats beginning to fill. *What just happened? Did I black out? No, I would have woken up on the ground if that where the case. Was a contract influencing me? Maybe the Prince is messing with me. No, worry about that later. Protecting Elise comes first.*

"We need to come up with a new plan," Atha said and sighed.

"Why?" Harika asked.

"Because I need to beat him! Have you not been paying attention to anything that's happened?" Atha sounded much harsher than he'd intended.

"Yes." Harika nodded. "I just don't see why meeting him in the third round is much of a difference."

"What?! How do you know that?"

"It was on that screen the man showed you. If you both win your matches, you'll meet in the third round."

"Harika! You're a genius!"

"It was right in front of you," Harika replied.

"Details, details. But that's good enough. If I beat him and drop my next match, it'll make it seem like anybody could have done it. Did you see any of the other pairings?"

"I did. Zell and I will meet in the third round."

"Poor Zell. Woulda been sweet if you guys could have been the final match. Oh, speak of the devil," Atha noted, waving his hands at her as she made her way through the crowd.

"How'd it go? Figured you'd be back at the last minute," Atha called as Zell came to a stop.

"He and his family were quite welcoming. And yes, we still have a few preparations to make before appearing before the crowds. You still wear the robes of a monk initiative and I must implore that you see them replaced."

Atha's face fell. "What? But I like them. What else am I supposed to wear?"

"Talks have begun circulating of the human from another world. Why not wear something from Earth?" Zell replied, pausing as Atha closed his eyes and fell silent. "What are you doing?"

"Going over the magazine covers I've looked at to find something suitable for the tournament. Get it?! Suitable!" Atha laughed, reopening his eyes as a magazine fell into his hands. "Mixing functionality with style is a rare thing on Earth, but let's see what options I've got. Oh, here we go, a Secret Service standard-issue suit. Fire resistant, stretchy, sturdy and most importantly, *fashionable*." Atha smiled, flashing the page to Zell.

"Acceptable. Go change."

The suit was a plain black and slim fit, yet was incredibly stretchy. An acrobat would have no problem preforming in it. He pulled a tie around the white dress shirt's popped collar, attempting to properly knot it to no avail. He tossed it into a trash bin.

Atha stepped out of the changing room and went back to Zell and Harika.

"Let's hit it." Atha smiled and straightened his jacket as the three headed to the arena. He eased the door open into the tunnel, pausing at the sound of a crowd gone wild. Their cheers shook the ground beneath his feet. The rest of the combatants stood at the other end, waiting to enter. Atha picked out the Prince with ease as he stood tall above the rest. The Prince noticed Atha as well, pushing through the group and bumping straight into him.

"Better back up, prick!" Atha spat, shoving the Prince back as Zell watched in utter disbelief.

"Why not make me? You did so poorly last time you couldn't possibly do worse," Mikaido taunted, pressing back into Atha's space as Deldora and another captain forced themselves in-between.

"Please, sir, save it for the tournament," Deldora cut in, giving Mikaido a gentle pull back before his arm was thrust off. The Prince gave one last dirty look at Atha before striding off.

"Explain," Zell growled. "Now."

"Oh, jeez, I wish I had answers for you but I'm just as surprised as you are. Maybe he's mental?" Atha laughed. Zell was not amused, turning next to Harika.

"Oh, I haven't forgotten about you. What do you know?" she asked him. Harika glanced up before quickly returning his eyes to the ground. "Oh, marvelous. Having been left alone for half an hour, you taught him *aiding and abetting*." Zell scoffed, throwing her hands in the air.

"Uh, pleading the fifth is neither of those things. Since when has silence been a bad thing?" Atha retorted.

"When it either correlates with withholding information or does not come from you."

Atha began to reply, but the crowd's cheers grew to a roar and the doors at the head of the group pressed open.

"And now, the finalists of this year's Capital Combat Contract Tournament!" the announcer screamed overtop the crowd as the group began shuffling forward. A thankful Atha grabbed Harika's arm and pulled him forward.

"Saved by the bell," he whispered.

"We will find time to discuss this," Zell said as they exited out into the erupting stadium, rows of seats now packed with onlookers reached up into the sky. The same white cube sat at the center, but now screens hovered above it, angling out toward the crowd.

"What are those for? Displaying the fights?" Atha asked Zell.

"In real time. The live feed will also go to viewers."

"Magical TV!" Atha laughed.

"I answer every conundrum that ravages your mind, so please allow me the same courtesy," Zell replied.

"Jeez, fine. The Prince hit a woman, some con artist lady, and we stepped in. Things got heated and we ended up fighting for a few minutes until Captain Inersha showed up." Atha sighed as Zell rubbed her eyes.

"Good intentions that could prove quite costly having been directed upon lofty title," she replied, coming to a stop beside the cube with the rest of the group.

"Whatever. How do I beat him?"

"Beat him? Given your current skill level, I would be surprised if you wounded him," Zell replied. Atha pulled his meteorite from his pocket, juggling it around in between his fingers. His rage from earlier was turning into cool, calculated hatred, and he reviewed the short-lived skirmish in his mind for clues toward future victory.

Zell opened her orange screen, delving into the requested topic. "As most triple S contracts do, his falls under the unique category—even amongst which his is dissimilar. When activated, a countdown clock appears, giving him an additional ability every half minute selected randomly from a pool of 120. Low numerical values signify stronger selections."

"So, I only faced medium- to low-level abilities," Atha said.

"In addition, the contract also gives the user ten rings, each possessing another power that is usable at any time. It is rumored the large gold necklace acts as the contract's ace function, but no further information is listed upon it. Taking all this into account, I would suggest launching an assault before he gains multiple abilities, despite the many unknown factors," Zell finished, whisking her screen away.

"Can you look them up?" Atha asked, but Zell shook her head.

"Royal contracts are considered sensitive information and specific details of actual power would not fall into an information purchase price I could afford."

"Come out swinging it is."

"Studying his matches could prove useful, but it would require us to finish our own early to view them," Zell replied, glancing up as a massive match pairing list appeared above them. A swarm of chatter eclipsed the cheers.

"As I'm sure you all notice, a certain celebrity is listed amongst our finalists. Give it up for Zell Tenzata!" the announcer boomed. A section of tile began to glow beneath her feet before lifting her into the air. Despite the blanket of cheers, a liner of boos threaded about. Betting odds appeared beside the pairings on the screens. "Zell now takes the 3/5 odds from Prince Mikaido, giving him 1/3. With that, betting is now officially open."

Zell waved to the crowd for a few moments before being lowered back toward the ground as the screens continued to display her image.

"*Zell* got better odds than him?" Atha gasped, glancing up for his own name and instantly grimacing at the 1/10,000 odds.

"You fight Miracle in the third round. Think you can beat him?" Atha asked, instantly regretting it as her trademark sly smile displayed her fanged teeth.

"A ten-thousandth would do well to secure concern for itself." She topped her statement off with a wink that sent Atha's eyes into a feverish fit of twitches.

"And now, we will begin the opening rounds with our Queen's blessing," the announcer said. The stadium's onlookers rose up and took a knee as all eyes turned up to a balcony that began to shine green. Elise strode out, a green sword falling from the sky above her and landing perfectly in her hand. She raised it up.

"Let the annual Combat Contract Tournament commence." She smiled, swinging the sword down before heading back into her room.

If I beat my first opponent fast enough, I should have enough of a break to go say hi. Atha sighed, getting back to his feet as he and the rest of the participants shuffled toward the cube and vanished.

Chapter 20
A Flash of Creation

The terrain selection popped up in front of Atha. His opponent was a human male in his mid-thirties with short white hair.

"Hey, where you wanna fight?" Atha asked as the man looked at him.

"Here's fine with me. Thank you for asking," he replied with a nod as Atha whisked the screen away. Atha checked the countdown timer once, then again a few seconds later, equally surprised both times that a single second hadn't left it until a voice called through his mind.

"Apologies, contestants. It appears Miracle Child wasn't paying attention and didn't move to the cube." *Oh my god, I forgot about him again.* "Match timers will now begin official countdown. Please take that time to prepare for combat."

A grenade fell into Atha's hand as the timer neared zero, and he pulled the pin and let the spoon fly as red energy encased his arm, hurling it perfectly on zero. He smirked as the man watched the grenade land before him, the thought of another quick match teasing him.

Metallic threads shot from the ground and encased the grenade. With a loud pop, the threads remained in place, untightening and waving lazily.

"Thing could make some noise. What else you got?" the man called to him.

This guy is way stronger than the preliminary punks. Time to step it up, I guess. Agro energy pulsed through his legs as he whipped Shooting Star out. The black chains encased his arm before a hard thrust ripped him a healthy distance around the threads.

"Control! Anger level six!" Atha commanded, sending a school bus careening toward his opponent. More threads shot up, stopping the bus and sending it flying back toward Atha. He swung the sword hard to the left, blitzing past it and noticing all too late that his opponent had anticipated this and had moved to intercept him. The first set of strings shot out of the ground and toward his foe, entangling around his arm. Atha was fast, but now his speed was challenged. The thread-reinforced fist swung toward his head with incredible speed.

A car shot down between them, but more strings thrust it back into the sky and flung it aside. The man's assault continued. He slammed his fist across Atha's red glowing face, sending him crashing back. The force caused a chain reaction that sent Shooting Star roaring backwards. Slowing leaping back to his feet, Atha was thankful that his opponent hadn't pressed, allowing Atha to take a moment to gauge the situation.

"Control! Return to normal!" Atha pulled the black meteorite from his pocket and danced it around in his fingers. *Safe to say he uses a defensive/offensive ability. He's got speed but not a crazy amount, and it seems like his threads appear without his command since he wouldn't have known to encase a grenade. It did seem like the noise bothered him, though.* Atha returned the geode to his pocket and a flashbang grenade fell into his hand. He hurled it as the man watched it land before him. No strings appeared, and with a roaring flash, a scream erupted from his mouth. Atha zinged forward behind Shooting Star, but as he neared, more strings shot up to catch the sword. Atha sliced through a handful as the remainder began to wave lazily in front of him. He sheathed the sword and ducked around them, Agro energy pulsating from his legs. He ran toward his dazed combatant, but with a twirl of his finger, the strings lashed out, swiping Atha's legs out from under him.

"Already figured out my contract's weaknesses, huh? You're smart, I'll give you that. I'm gonna wrap this up before you give me another scare." Threads swirled over the man's body, encasing him in a metallic exoskeleton as a pistol fell into Atha's hands. He popped off a few shots that simply pinged off him.

His opponent shot forward with speed rivaling Agro energy. Atha dropped the gun and unsheathed Shooting Star, swinging too hard and exposing his side. *Metal safe!* Drawing the image into his mind crippled with anger it manifested in motion, whistling just past him and, just as he'd planned, clipped Shooting Star. The dull blade glowed white, yanking Atha completely off his feet and flinging him far from danger.

Skidding to a halt, the metallic figure pursued. A red glow emitted from Atha's head as time slowed.

I bet I could chop this prick in half. Shooting Star is the only weapon I've used that's done any damage to those strings, but it wasn't much. One good swing should do the trick, but this is gonna hurt.

Drawing the sword behind him, Atha knelt as Agro energy pulsating from his arm and glimmered from his neck to prevent whiplash. He flung the sword forward as a brimming white light shone. The chains tightened down on his arm with incredible force, yanking him forward and slicing cleanly through the armor.

"We have our seventh victor! Atha Lamkos is onto the second round!" The announcer's voice reverberated as Atha reappeared with a soft thud. A guard quickly approached him.

"Apologies, but the large items you left in the ring can't be returned to you at this time. If you require them before your next match, we will need to move the realm door outside of the stadium. This is the only item small enough to be returned promptly." She handed a pistol to Atha.

What? When did I use a pistol? he wondered, grasping it and pulling the clip out and emptying the chamber.

"No, I don't need the other stuff back. Actually, you guys don't need to get anything I conjure back to me in my future matches either. And would you mind pitching this for me?" he replied, extending it back as she nodded. Red energy pulsed from his legs as he leapt into the air and over the barricade into the stands, hurrying up the endless stairs toward Elise's viewing room. A familiar shadowy captain sat in front of the door, rising to her feet as he neared.

"Oh, hey, Shakkoo." Atha smiled as she bowed her head.

"We meet again," she whispered.

"Can I say hi to El real quick?" he asked. She stood and knocked on the door.

"You may. This will be a good test."

"Test?" he repeated, the door swinging open for him. "Thanks. Let me know if you change your mind about my *proposition*." He winked, stepping through the doorway and entering the viewing room. Elise smiled to him as she sat with Dimitri in the corner. Atha stopped, reaching a hand for his sword.

"Who the fuck are you?" he spat as Elise's eyes widened.

"Well, that was absurdly quick. What gave me away?" she replied, getting to her feet as the many panels of glass darkened.

Atha yanked the sword from its sheath.

"Calm down! She's fine I'm just her stand-in until she can show up!" The fake Elise snapped her fingers as both her image and Dimitri's shifted into completely different people. A woman clad in the usual green garb of the guard stood before him as he sighed, replacing the sword into its sheath.

"Sorry, you just took me by surprise," Atha said.

"I didn't wish to trick you, but Shakkoo wanted to see how well a fake would work against someone as perceptive as you. If you don't mind me asking, what gave it away?" she inquired. Atha tapped his neck.

"I gave her a geode and she turned it into a necklace. Hasn't taken it off since. I'd have caught on anyways; your demeanor was off, and she usually has around seven captains with her."

She snapped her fingers back to the Dimitri stand-in.

"Why weren't we notified of the clothing change? Update the manifest for next time." She sighed before turning back to Atha. "I'd heard you were sharp, but you really don't miss a single detail. Please don't tell anyone of this. She's supposed to oversee all combat held within the capital walls, but her schedule has been hectic with everything going on."

"I won't."

"Thank you. Just so you know, the Queen has been moving the very heavens to make time for your next match, so she should be sneaking in and swapping out with me soon." She smiled.

"Kinda disappointed she didn't see the first one, but I'll take what I can get. I'll leave you to it, then." Atha turned and headed back out the door. Pulling it shut, he glanced at Shakkoo. "Can you let me know when the package arrives?" he asked.

"I will see it done," she replied and Atha bounded down the stairs, red energy pulsing from his legs as he hopped over the barrier back into the ring, landing softly beside Zell.

"I don't see Mikaido. Tell me he lost," Atha asked. Zell pointed a finger up toward a screen.

"He mocks me," Zell replied.

Atha glanced up toward the screen displaying his match. Atha could see Mikaido but not his clock.

"He fights while only using a portion of his contract, using similar capabilities to Agro energy. This gives us no insight to what should be expected," Zell said as Atha watched. Another figure zoomed across the screen, swiping and striking fruitlessly at Mikaido.

"His opponent's fast. Not Inersha fast, but he can move," Atha noted, watching Mikaido stretch an arm out and catch his opponent across the neck as the crowd gasped. "That was the mother of all clotheslines." Atha groaned, watching the Prince fall onto his opponent and begin to bash his face with a fist that glowed blue. He broke his opponent's nose

433

and sent streaks of scarlet flying. Seconds later, Mikaido popped up onto the stage.

"Prince Mikaido is moving on!" the announcer boomed, the unconscious opponent falling onto the stage beside him. Green fog lifted him from the ground and carried him toward the healing room. Mikaido reached out a hand and caught his leg, halting the fog's progress and, in an act of pomposity Atha had only read about in books, wiped his bloody fist across the loser's shirt.

"Take your worthless blood back. Why your heart continues to pump it through such a pitiful body perplexes me," Mikaido said, before releasing his grip and allowing the green fog to continue.

"What a fucking scumbag," Atha growled.

"Yet not without skill. The training required to defeat a foe at this level is astounding."

"I'd kick his ass in a fistfight. Wish he'd try that on me," Atha said loud enough for the Prince to hear as he stepped by.

"Did the flogging I gave you earlier cause you to become delusional, or are you just a fool?" The Prince laughed, sending Atha into a rage. He stepped after the Prince, but Zell was quick to catch him.

"Enough! Set mind to purpose free of distraction," she instructed. Atha grumbled but complied. "Your last opponent, where would you rank his contract and what category would you place it in?"

Atha thought for a moment. "Probably primary defensive with sub-offensive capability. And for ranking—I don't know, probably A, maybe even S."

"It was a defensive category and only ranks in the E class," Zell replied, shaking her head. "It was the lowest ranking you have faced so far, but back to the point I made before—he understands and utilizes it prodigiously, causing disillusion. Your next opponent wields an ability ranking in the S category with equal skill, so we should take what time we have to review it." Zell whisked open her orange screen. "Your next opponent is Yug Sekwaf, who wields a combat contract of immense strength. Being the first to wield it, he dubbed it Fire Whisperer. Fire Whisperer not only gives him all the abilities of a pyromancer, but he can also use any manner of fire-based abilities against its user, which includes your guns and explosives."

"What?! Holy shit, that's awesome!" Atha's outburst drew a sideways glance from Zell.

"Put uncouth personality aside for a moment and realize the magnitude of this discovery. Apart from your massive metal constructs, his ability negates your most potent options."

Atha shrugged. "I can wear a fireproof suit then. How hot does his fire burn?"

"The maximum known temperature is 900 degrees Celsius," she answered.

"Hotter than jet fuel but still not up to snuff against Earth's technology." A metallic suit fell in front of Atha, an oxygen tank spilling from the insulated backpack attached to it.

"My next match begins," Zell said, heading toward the cube. "Good luck."

"Hey, I think you're up too, buddy." Atha turned to Harika and gave him a shake as he raised his head from prayer.

"Thank you," he replied, slowly shuffling toward the cube. He halted as Atha caught his arm.

"You good?" Atha asked skeptically.

"I do not enjoy combat."

"I know, but Zell thinks it's necessary we figure out your limits while your mana is suppressed, and I agree. Look, nobody's actually getting hurt by any of this so really you're just taking precautions to make sure people stay safe. Okay?" Atha smiled as Harika nodded.

"Okay," he replied, continuing toward the cube before vanishing.

"Hello, Atha," a silvery voice called from behind. Atha turned and was pleasantly surprised by the familiar face of the winged guard Alkibiades.

"Al! What's up man?" Atha smiled, extending his hand to shake the guard's.

"I was just curious to learn if you knew when our person of interest would be arriving," he replied with a smile as Atha paused.

"You know about that? I thought only the bigwigs did," Atha replied as Alkibiades paused.

"Bigwigs?"

"Sorry, that was an analogy from Earth. They slip out every now and then. I mean to say that I thought that information was on a need-to-know basis."

Al chuckled. "Oh, I see. I may by low ranking, but I am still a member of the guard and aware of key information. I was instructed to ready a detail upon arrival but I'm not sure when that will be."

Atha checked his watch.

"I'm not sure exactly when, but I did ask to be contacted by captain Shakkoo when it does, so just keep an eye on her. They said she should be here for at least part of my next match."

"It is *astounding* how unorganized our guard can be at times, but I thank you for keeping me informed. Good luck against Yug. He is powerful," Alkibiades said before stepping back toward the tunnel as a cheer broke through the crowd.

"Another single hit and Miracle Child is onto the third round!" the announcer yelled as Atha watched Harika step back down from the cube.

"Jeez, you haven't broken a sweat yet, huh?" Atha exclaimed.

"I haven't," Harika replied flatly before folding his hands and muttering quiet prayers. Another cheer mixed with boos filled the stadium as Zell appeared, shaking hands with her opponent before stepping down toward them.

"What the hell?" Atha grumbled. "You've both already won and my match hasn't even started."

"But of course. Seeing as your initial match took the lengthiest time to finish, your recovery segment overlaps into the next round," Zell replied. "Don your suit. The match begins momentarily." Atha picked up the metallic suit, pulled it over his body and turning the air tank on with a dull hiss. For the time being, he left the helmet off.

"Remember, no fire of any manner," Zell advised. "If you get terrain selection, pick the beach setting and hide in the water as a last resort."

Atha took a deep breath and headed for the podium.

Chapter 21
Through Fire and Flames

Atha blinked into the endless void surrounding him. The terrain selection screen appeared before him, and he chose the beach. The white washed away and was replaced by sand and the waves of an ocean. A short distance away, he noticed his opponent waving breezily to him. Tall and slender, the man was completely covered in black, not an inch of bare flesh showing. Most of him was covered in metal plate. What wasn't was wrapped in cloth that appeared to be bandages.

"Went for the gothic look, eh?" Atha joked.

"Not really," the man replied, eyeing himself over. "Just picked something that could cover all the burnt flesh. Didn't want to scar the children for life."

"Burnt flesh? I figured a pyromancer would be immune to fire," Atha replied suspiciously.

"Well, you thought right, but my injury occurred just before I got the contract."

Atha readied himself as the timer neared zero, gasping in disbelief as he realized he'd forgotten the section of suit that covered his head.

"Oh shit, no way!" he exclaimed, the last portion falling into the air in front of him.

"Please, take your time. I'm in no rush," Yug chuckled as the timer hit zero and Atha struggled to attach the hood properly.

"I don't need your charity," he scoffed as Yug shrugged and sat down in the sand.

He smiled. "It's not. I could use a moment to just sit and relax."

"Man, do I ever feel that. I don't know if you know who I am, but I just came to this world a few weeks ago after living a sad little life of imprisonment. What do I do now that a brand-new world is at my fingertips? Sit in a fucking wasteland." Atha laughed, finally ready to go.

"Well, what say we just kick back for a few moments? This beach may be totally synthetic, but I must say, they nailed the texture of sand." Yug leaned straight back into the sand and gazed up at the sky.

"You're not serious, are you?" Atha replied skeptically.

"Nothing says we have to start right when the match begins. Come on, sit down. If I wanted to win with underhanded tactics I could have done that already." Atha remained skeptical but sat down next to him, pulling an arm from the suit and curiously grasping a handful of sand.

"See? Pretty accurate right?" Yug mused as Atha shrugged.

"Dunno. Never actually seen sand before."

"Then take it from me, this is damn close to the real deal. So why did you enter the tournament?" Yug asked lazily, as if he only meant to pass the time. Atha noticed that despite this seemingly aloof display, Yug was keeping a close eye on him. A telltale sign of a seasoned warrior.

"I wanted to see how well I can handle myself in this world. Got a few scores to settle on the side. You?"

"I'm here because I know the Chameleons are planning something," Yug replied and Atha snapped his head up out of the sand.

"R-really?! What do you think they're up to?" Atha replied, noticing Yug's eyes narrow and focus upon him.

"I'm not sure. Actually, I wanted to ask you. You've had contact with them, yes?"

Atha froze at this. This is what he had feared. He could still hear that warning voice croaking in the back of his head, threatening death with the revealing of his experience.

"Not much to say? Don't worry, I assumed as much. Forced you to silence, I'm sure. Fortunately, silence is worth a thousand words." Yug yawned and adjusted some of the bandages around his neck.

"Who are you?" Atha asked, unsure of having found an ally or yet another enemy.

"Calm. Your situation is in good hands. I am no friend to the Chameleons. My purpose for entering this tournament is to get their attention, lure them out. I had a hunch they're keeping an eye on you, so I imagine that's accomplished. Sooner or later now, they will come to me, and the debt of blood I've carried for many years will be repaid." He leaned up out of the sand, groaning as he got to his feet like a child who yet longs to sleep longer.

"So, what say we get to it then? The crowd has waited patiently. Probably." Yug chuckled.

"Well, Mr. Sekwaf, you're a most certifiable badass. I'm ready whenever you are." Atha smiled as Yug snorted.

"I'll be sure to add certifiable badass to my resume. Now let me show you...*IGNIS!*" he roared, thrusting his hands up to the sky.

Fire tore across the clear sky, flits of flame congregating together like a group of fish to form a pair of eyes that stared down upon them. Atha didn't wait. He unsheathed Shooting Star immediately, black chains covering his arm and jolting him forward. Yug sidestepped and released a blast of fire.

"Control anger boost!" Atha yelled. A car appeared between them and careened toward Yug through the fire before exploding and sending Atha hurtling backwards. Shoulda put ear plugs in.

Yug shot flames downward, the sand turning to glass as he flew up over the flaming car and toward Atha. A white canister fell into Atha's hand. He hurled it toward Yug and it exploded in a blast of white fire-suppressing bubbles. Yug's fire didn't stutter, roaring full force across his entire body to turn him into the human version of a jet engine. With speed comparable to Captain Inersha, he shot toward a panicking Atha. With only a few feet between them, Atha drew the image of a massive metal safe into his mind. Yug slammed straight into it with enough force to send it flying into Atha and both he and his makeshift barrier hurtled across the water. Like a rock, Atha skipped across the water a few times before crashing down into its depths.

He hits like a freight train! His abilities go way further than pyromancy, and they must even be self-oxygenating 'cause that ball should have put them out. Oh great, and my suit's ruined,

Atha ripped the top half off and replaced the equipment with scuba gear before descending beneath the waves. The water only went down a few meters, and with his meteorite tumbling around between his fingers he sat at the bottom, contemplating his next move.

Self-oxidizing flames means even the water won't stop them. With air out of the question—oh! No, it's not, I'm just utilizing it on the wrong factor. Still, it'll be hard to pull off. Let's see if I can even manifest the type of metal I need. Atha had never manifested anything he hadn't actually seen before, but with the basic image of a long chain in mind, and imagining it to be made of rare rhenium metal, it came crashing down from the surface to his feet. Tying a knot in it, he laid the knotted end down on the ocean floor, gripping the opposite end and awaiting his prey. It wasn't long until Yug shot down into the water.

Need to keep him away. A cargo container should do. A shipping container hurtled down out of the sky into the space between them. A fiery explosion illuminated the water for a moment as Atha swung Shooting Star forward. He grasped the chain, shooting a safe distance around the burning man. Atha sent random objects of varying sizes down into the water around Yug, who swiveled around, searching for the hiding Atha.

Come on, get above the knot.

Yug's lungs must have been screaming for air and he began to shoot toward the surface, coincidentally coasting just above the knot of chains resting upon the seafloor. Atha pulled Shooting Star from its holster and swung it skyward, a bright flash of light pulsing across the enhanced metal and ripping him up out of the water.

He'd nearly thought his plan a failure until the slack chain in his spare hand tightened as if a fish had been caught. Flinging the sword into the air again, Yug was ripped out of the water, a tangle of chains around his leg. *Now let's get you a bit disoriented before you fry me.* A five-ton weight appeared, flying downward toward Yug who began to jet to the side just as Atha had anticipated. Agro energy absolutely exploded from his body and he thrust Shooting Star toward the blue sky once more, yanking his fish stuck on the far end of the chain straight up and into the weight. Atha winced with empathy for the man he'd just dropped a weight on like the villain in an old cartoon, hardly surprised this hadn't ended the match. Regardless, both Yug's fire and struggle dimmed, and Atha held tight on the chains, once again flinging his sword toward the heavens. He reached high enough into the sky to notice where the white world met the borders of the beach far in the distance.

Well shit, looks like they skimped on the landscape. Let's hope regular oxygen altitude levels are normal. Yanking off the scuba gear and giving another mighty swing, he felt the air thinning and produced a breathing mask to put over his face. Yug was beginning to recover, his flames burning hot once more. He burned as hot as he possibly could, blue fire roaring from his body that Atha smirked at. *Not melting those, homie. You could burn twice as hot and still not touch rhenium's melting temperature.*

As if he'd read Atha's mind, Yug gave up trying to free himself from the chains and sent a blast toward Atha. A large sheet of steel blocked it and Atha was prepared to conjure another, but it was unnecessary as he pulled the gasping Yug higher, feeling his struggle grow less and less until the two appeared back before the crowd that was only mildly satisfied by the lackluster conclusion of victory by suffocation.

"Atha Lamkos is on to round three!" the announcer shouted as Zell slammed into him, bursting with vigor she rarely showed.

"That was amazing, Atha! You strayed from the path of brute strength in favor of a more planned, technical victory!"

"God, he wasn't even as strong as my opening opponent!" Atha laughed, pausing as he realized Yug was gasping for air just a short distance away.

"Now that was just rude. Go apologize. Miracle and myself are due for our match." Zell sighed, releasing Atha and snapping her fingers at the blue Shelando.

"Oh, I forgot! This should be good. Be honest with me, do think you can win?" Atha replied. Zell only shrugged before heading off.

"A fine victory," Yug managed to get out between gasps, extending a hand concealed by bandages. Atha grasped it.

"Thanks. Now call me crazy, but it almost feels like you threw that match the way Zell hyped you up," Atha replied, his spirits sinking at the sight of a glimmer in Yug's eye, a telltale sign that Atha had guessed correctly. "Oh fuck, you did, didn't you? God, I *knew* it was too easy!"

"I'll see you around, Atha," Yug replied as he stepped past him.

"Hey, hold on a second there, pyro, I wanna ask you a question," Atha continued, stepping back in front of the tall figure. "We both have similar agendas. We should work together." Atha had already been feeling the dominant chills of a lone wolf radiating from the icy Yug, and wasn't entirely disappointed even while receiving the response he'd anticipated.

"Sorry, kid. I do my own thing," Yug said, entering the tunnel as Atha watched with dazzled eyes.

"So cool."

"Now it's time for what could have potentially been a final-round matchup!" The announcement made Atha fling his eyes up to the screen. On it, Zell and Harika stood in the forest setting. The stadium shook with the deafening roar from the crowd. "Zell Tenzata, a master strategist, versus Miracle Child, the one-hit wonder, in about as opposite a match-up as I could possibly imagine. Zell has progressed by using information and tactics, while Miracle shatters all who stand before him. It's a meeting of opposite ends of the combative spectrum."

The timer neared zero as Atha watched Zell's mana tendrils pulling together behind her back, forming one long tentacle that eased through the grass toward Harika's back.

What's she up to? It isn't even carrying a knife, Atha wondered. The timer reached zero as Harika's hand flew up and Zell's tendril snapped up out of the grass to pull the hand back into his chest. With a boom, they both reappeared upon the stage as the roaring crowd went ballistic.

"ZELL TENZATA WINS WITH A SINGLE HIT! ZELL TENZATA HAS ONE HIT THE ONE-HIT WONDER!" the announcer screamed over the crowd as Atha stared in disbelief before rushing the stage.

"Oh, Zell, you tricked me," Harika noted as Atha crashed into Zell, laughing with joy.

"That was fucking awesome! How did you do that?!" Atha screamed to Zell over the noise.

"Have you heard the story of the contract possessing unstoppable force pitted against another with perfect defense?" Zell asked as Atha snapped his fingers.

"Oh yeah, Len told me a version of that except with a sword and shield."

"What would you do if pitted against such a foe?" Zell continued.

"Probably just run like the devil had his dick in his hand and was chasing me," he replied as Zell scoffed.

"Shakka's mercy, you shift from brilliance to depths of crude mannerism of increasing undesirability without warning. Assuming fleeing isn't an option and having no defense, the only remaining option would be to turn that force upon itself."

"She told me to give her my best shot or she'd be offended," Harika added.

"Women are sneaky, buddy. Come on, let's go find you a seat," Atha replied, pulling Harika toward the tunnel but lurching with surprise as a shadow rolled across the ground toward him. Shakkoo's covered face popped up out of the shadow.

"It is time," she noted plainly before lowering back down into the shadow and shooting off.

"Magical shadow chick. It was a joke at first, but I kinda dig her." Atha chuckled as Zell pulled his hand off Harika.

"See to your business. I will situate Miracle," she replied as Atha headed off without a word, leaping over the barricade and into the stands once again as a smile crossed his face. He shot to the top, where the door was promptly whisked open by Shakkoo.

"Atha!" Elise burst, standing up amidst the usual swarm of guards. Atha paused, falling to a knee as she stared and smiled. "A proper formal greeting! Please, save that for a more public setting and give me a hug." She laughed and pulled him to his feet before wrapping her arms around him. "I'm so sorry I missed your matches, but I saw replays. Oh, I'm so proud of you."

"You're here now. That's all that matters," Atha replied cheerfully. "But what kept you?"

"I'm sorry, but I'm not at liberty to discuss that. You should get those gears turning on how to bring down the next opponent anyways. And before you say anything, yes, I am quite aware of your dust up with him."

Now would be a good chance to make her second-guess a marriage with him before I even win. "Yeah, sorry about that. I wasn't really too impressed with what he could do, though. Bit of a windbag without much to back it up, so I think I'm already prepared to go in and whoop him," Atha replied snootily as Elise cocked an eyebrow.

"I sense a bit more animosity in those words then what a scuffle should warrant. Is there anything else I should know about?" she asked. Atha twitched, realizing his sly plan had crumbled before the warm smile of Elise. *She deals with people playing multiple angles daily. Can't throw shade on him without it being completely obvious to her.*

"I've got a small grudge against him. We're gonna sort all that out with another go in a bit and that'll bury the hatchet, so don't worry about it. Come on, let's change the subject to something worth talking about. Tell me what you *can* about your day!"

He smiled as Elise sighed and took her seat, motioning for Atha to sit as well.

"My day has been encumbered with meetings, disputes, entitled council members and oh, my personal favorite, publicity matters. That's the normal workload, but now add in that detestable Red Sheep attacking villages as fast as I can dispatch aid and the possible resurgence of the Chameleon syndicate, headed by Erida. To conclude, my day is nothing worth talking about." She hid it very well compared to an average person, but Atha could hear the hints of actual distress and pain strung through her words.

"Hey, buck up!" Atha said "You're sounding more like an overwhelmed princess than a proud queen. You'll get through this. You're doing great and these people are lucky to have you guiding them through these hard times. Either way, I'd rather have a boring conversation with you than an exciting one with anyone else, so just chill out and talk to me."

Elise froze, her eyes glassing over as tears begged to fall. "What—why are you—" Atha started but she waved a hand.

"I'm sorry, that was just very sweet, Atha," she quickly cut in, rubbing at her eyes for a moment as Dimitri stepped to her side and whispered something in her ear causing her head to sag.

"Got something to take care of?" Atha asked. Elise nodded. A captain with a series of screens popping up in front of them came to her side. "Ha, well, I gotta go fight my match, so I'm gonna be busy before you can be this time. Sorry, gotta run!" Atha planted a quick kiss on her head before dashing toward the door. "Love you, princess!" Atha called as he made his escape.

Atha's face twisted with hate the moment he exited, noticing Mikaido watching him from beside the white cube.

That's what you must protect. Now crush this prick into the ground. We can do this, right? Atha thought to himself, glancing down at his open palms that gave no reply. Red energy erupted through his legs, and he burst into the air. With one massive leap, he slammed down onto the white podium just a few feet from the smirking Prince, who gave a quick nod to his nearby female bodyguard, who nodded back.

"And here I thought maybe an inkling of a brain would see you far from my grasp," Mikaido taunted, a faint glimmer shining around his mouth to mask his words.

"Keeping your words hidden from the masses?" Atha sneered back. "If you're gonna speak, you should at least have the balls to let people hear."

"Some of us are held accountable for our actions. We can't all be the Queen's lapdog." Rage flowed through Atha. "I'd like to raise the stakes of this bout. What say the loser becomes the winner's *servant*?" He held a hand toward Atha. Atha grasped it, a tingle of red energy pulsing as he crushed the Prince's hand.

"Not that I trust a bitch like you to keep your word, but it'll be fun to see what excuse you come up with," Atha spat, blue energy pulsing over the Prince as his hand crushed Atha's.

"Looks like Prince Mikaido and Atha are already getting familiar with each other! What a grand display of sportsmanship!" the announcer boomed as the screens displayed their handshake, absent the glowing energies thanks to Mikaido's ally's contract. Atha pulled his hand back, wiping it off on his pant leg before and disappearing into the cube.

The two stood face-to-face in the white void.

"I thought surely you would select the forest for a chance at hiding. This hubris will be your undoing," Mikaido taunted.

Atha raised his fists and took a fighting stance.

"You must be kidding. You really want to go through with a fistfight after seeing my capabilities?" he asked. Atha nodded.

"I try to give weak opponents a fair chance. Go ahead and activate your contract, you're gonna need it."

The Prince's forehead vein popped with anger. He took a stance of his own.

"Have it your way. No contracts, no abilities. Let us see who breaks first," Mikaido replied.

Atha sized up the Prince. *He uses some sort of technique developed to put an opponent down fast. At around his size, he's got a hell of a reach* and *weight advantage on me, which works perfectly with the Judo G taught me. He's got the edge in raw skill from what I've seen, but...*

The timer hit zero as the two sprung forwards. Mikaido launched a fist straight at Atha's face. Atha raised an arm and deflected it, pressing forward to swing a knee toward Mikaido's exposed side. Mikaido lurched back with ease, swinging his left hand toward Atha's face again as he fell forward.

He overreaches because he's never depended on his hands alone to protect his life. Atha nagged the sleeve of his right arm, twisting around and pressing his back into Mikaido's chest and swinging a shin out in front of the Prince's stumbling legs. With a yank on the Prince's sleeve, Atha used Mikaido's own momentum against him, letting it do the heavy lifting, and heaved the massive body up over his shoulder to send him slamming to the ground. Mikaido shot back to his feet, jutting back and away from a fist that angled toward his face.

"How you like them marbles, pussy?" Atha sneered. Mikaido roared with anger, bursting forward but now cautious of his skilled opponent. He threw quick jabs that Atha couldn't catch, and launched a boot toward Atha's chest. With a quick lurch, Atha dodged it, but the Prince let his momentum carry him forward, latching a hand onto the suit jacket and yanking Atha back. His left hand careened for Atha's smirking face again.

Finally. This style doesn't work well when you're being cautious. Atha snapped his forearm up, cleanly redirecting the Prince's fist. He shot forward into Mikaido's chest, sending the Prince stumbling backwards, knowing exactly what his opponent's next move would be. *Come on, give me that leg.* Just as Atha had hoped, Mikaido raised his leg, swinging it toward Atha's side, attempting to keep him at a distance. It was a wise move for a combatant with a reach advantage, but it was exactly what Atha had expected. His hands were already moving to catch the leg the moment Mikaido had raised it. Atha caught it and pinned the leg to his side. *Cobra Kai sweep the leg, sucker!* Mikaido followed his sight to the ensnared leg's twin all too slowly as Atha kicked into it, removing the sole pillar keeping him standing, sending him crashing to the ground hard.

Mikaido hurried to get up again, but Atha followed through with another hard kick, shattering the Prince's nose in an explosion of scarlet. Disoriented, the Prince turned away from Atha, exposing his back—easy prey for Atha, who slid onto the ground behind him. He wrapped legs around Mikaido's stomach and locked his arm around the Prince's neck in a triangle chokehold like an anaconda crushing the life from its food. Blood poured out in torrents from Mikaido's nose. Mikaido pulled desperately at Atha's arm, fighting for air that proved distant as Atha held tight.

"Go to sleep! Go to fucking sleep!" Atha whispered tauntingly into his ear.

Blue energy pulsed out across Mikaido as his arm began to yank Atha off.

"Oh, we're playing that now?" Atha laughed, red energy pulsed out from him to match it, and he dug back into place around the windpipe with another burst of blood. Mikaido vanished from Atha's grip before rematerializing some distance away gasping for air. Atha stood, a white towel falling into his hands and pressing it into his damp clothing to soak up the blood before tossing the rag toward Mikaido. "Take your worthless blood back. Why your heart continues to pump it through such a pitiful body perplexes me." He mocked Mikaido's deep voice as the Prince went ballistic. Blue energy pulsated brilliantly around him as he glided up into the air.

"You fucking peasant!" he screamed. "You don't know who you've made an enemy of or the things I could do to you!"

"Fuck you!"

The massive winged clock crashed down behind the Prince, flapping itself into the air.

"It's time," the red demon announced, the number 108 showing across the clock. Dozens of identical copies of the bloodied Prince appeared in the air. Atha yanked his sword out as a car hurtled toward the back of the original Mikaido, who had vanished. Every copy vanished as well before reappearing at once in random spots around Atha.

Illusions or real? Atha wondered.

A pistol fell into his hands and he popped a few shots off at one of the images to no effect. The bullets passed through it.

Not enough density. What about heat? A set of goggles fell into his hand, and he snapped them over his eyes before flicking a switch. Turning in a full circle, only one heat signature registered. Raising the pistol, he fired again as the heat vanished.

"Cheater! You couldn't possibly have found me so easily without using a contract-enhanced item!" Mikaido screamed.

"No magic necessary, just batteries you sorry ass loser!" Atha laughed, turning to Mikaido once more.

"It's time," the demon announced, the number 112 shining across the clock.

"A pair of bottom selections in a row?! Luck yet smiles on you, you little shit!" A small white demon without eyes and holding a small white cane appeared beside Mikaido.

"At him!" the Prince commanded.

The demon spun its cane as dozens of white sheets of paper shot through red portals, encasing Atha's head and covering his goggles. Atha panicked at the sudden touch from a heatless object he hadn't seen nearing. In pure uncalculated desperation, he yanked and ripped away at the papers that continued to pile over his head. He snapped the goggles off to see the many papers. With no plan coming to mind, Atha flung the sword to pull himself away, but the papers sped up as well, continuing to wrap over his face as he lost his footing and went tumbling down. Mikaido pounced and slammed a foot into Atha's side, sending him crashing off in a different direction.

This is getting bad. Time to step it up, Atha thought to himself. A massive fuel truck hurtled down through the air in between the copies that all glanced toward it.

"What? Did you think I'd step under—" Mikaido began but paused when he saw Atha pull up an RPG and send a canister whistling toward it. A devastating shockwave preceded an enormous ball of fire that spewed out across the white world. Mikaido had been no more than a few meters away from ground zero, yet he showed no signs of damage whatsoever.

"I caught him completely off guard and that still didn't get him?" Atha gasped as the red demon chimed.

"It's time." The number 115 shown across the screen as Mikaido groaned, gliding up into the air amidst the pack of copies. Papers continued to flap across Atha's face, yet he felt another touch across his back. His body went limp and crashed down. A demon the size of an infant laughed crazily upon him, digging its claws into his back despite a pulse of pathetic Agro energy.

Papers began to pile atop one another over his head.

That 115 seems to drain stamina. Let's see how well you can hold on to the roller coaster known as Shooting Star.

Atha manifested a fifty-pound dumbbell in motion, targeting the tip of his sword. With a quick pulse of light, he went rocketing across the ground until the crazed demon lost its grip. Ripping away the papers and snapping the sword up, the demon came at him again. He thrust his sword toward it, but the demon bent like rubber around the blade and was flung away completely unharmed. Atha pulled a pistol up toward the demon, time slowing and taking careful aim before unleashing fire and lead. But again, it was to no avail as the bullets glanced harmlessly off it.

"Struggling like a cornered rat against the most *simplistic* weapons in my arsenal. I did have a mind to draw this battle along even with more formidable selections, yet find myself quite favoring this turn of events." Mikaido laughed.

"That fucking does it!" Atha screamed with rage.

A massive shadow appeared above Mikaido who glanced up, faltering at the sight of metal obscuring the sky from above him. He quickly glanced to the side before vanishing. Atha had manifested a cargo ship, which came crashing down with enough force to shake the entire white world. Mikaido stared in disbelief. A bullet pinged off his shoulder before noticing all too late the missiles that whistled toward him. He flung his hands up as fire ripped across his protective blue shield, leaving a small crack across the portions covering his arms and chest.

That's it! He glances to where he's gonna teleport! I just need to catch him off guard a few more times, judging by that break in the blue covering him.

"It's time," the demon added, the number 102 shining across the clock as a thick blue mist instantly covered the area. It gusted across Atha, solidifying over his body, which went limp with the familiar touch of the laughing demon upon his back. Again, his sight became blocked by papers overlapping across his face.

Atha's sword yanked an arm from the blue encasement, slapping the side of the blade against his chest to free it. Manifesting another fifty-pound dumbbell with a trajectory aimed at his blade, it crashed into it and Shooting Star yanked his body free of the cackling demon on his back before yanking at the papers over his face. The moment he was free, Mikaido's hand snapped around his neck, thrusting him to the ground and pinning his arms.

"What contract do you use?! Tell me!" he screamed. Atha's legs glowed red and slammed up into Mikaido's chest, doing no damage but sending him into the air before he glanced to his right and then vanished. Atha had followed his eyes, twisting his sword in the same direction and smashing it perfectly into the Prince's head, producing another crack in the blue. Atha kicked his feet into the air, soaring above Mikaido as a semitruck slammed straight into him. Mikaido teleported away, coming to a stop amidst his copies as the demon announced, "It's time." The number 117 shone across the clock, sending Mikaido into a fit of rage, tearing his hands across his face in disbelief.

"Why is this happening now of all times?! I might actually end up losing if this run of bad luck continues!" His hands vibrated with energy. He raised them up and pointed at Atha, sending a shockwave ripping toward him. Atha tried to dodge it, but blue fog encased him and hardened, holding him in place as the blast shook his head like somebody had simultaneously clapped his ears while he stared into the sun. The crazed demon neared him as papers once again obscured his sight.

Fearing the worst and panicking, he sent a car crashing into his own back to break the solidified fog before dodging another shockwave.

"Stop him!" Mikaido screamed. Fog gusted around Atha again, but a massive safe meant for storing firearms appeared before him. The door was already open, giving Atha the perfect spot to hide, leaping in and yanking the door shut behind himself. Blue fog hardened over the safe, but Atha kicked the door straight off and thrust Shooting Star toward the many Mikaidos. Tossing a grenade down amongst them, he watched for one to glance away. To his surprise, the group shot up toward him, a shockwave ripping across his head and disorienting him as a fist followed into his face. Blood gushed from his mouth and he crashed down hard onto the ground.

The grenade exploded a short distance from him, pelting him with hot shrapnel as Mikaido slammed a foot down on his head. Atha spun his sword at Mikaido, but blue fog pulsed over him, halting the blade just short of its target, who continued to land blow after heavy blow straight into his face. *I'm gonna lose. NO! I can't lose! I won't!*

"I WON'T!" Atha screamed, filling with rage and glowing a brilliant red. He had no more plans in mind, instead falling back onto his tactless brute strength to carry him to victory. Atha shattered straight through the blue fog and ripped Shooting Star into the Prince's side before erupting into flurry of fists and kicks of his own.

Atha's sword glowed white hot and smashed into Mikaido's legs, sending the Prince spiraling through the air. Atha's heart sank as his red energy dimmed and vanished, its reservoir reaching an untimely end. He sheathed Shooting Star, mostly out of fear that it would break his arm or even kill him without Agro energy reinforcing his flesh. Blue fog snapped over him again, but this time he was free of his protection. Its grip was so firm that Atha could hardly breathe, let alone break free. He felt himself blacking out as the crazed demon latched onto his back and began draining his stamina.

"It's time," the demon announced again, the number 70 shining across the clock. A copy of Atha whisked into existence, standing beside Mikaido, who looked down upon his foe.

"Suddenly and violently the world forces itself back into equilibrium." Mikaido laughed, watching Atha struggle helplessly as he gasped for air. "I had hoped I would acquire this selection. It is an odd draw, not so much along the lines of either offense or defense." He paused as the Atha copy leaned in to whisper something to him. "That's why you hate me so?" Mikaido asked Atha.

"Goodness, you even went as far as to use that woman I struck as an excuse to form a grudge in place of giving clear light to your true thoughts?" Mikaido laughed as Atha paused his struggle. A quiet, perhaps distant whisper began to echo through his mind.

Kill him. Kill him. Kill him. Kill him. Kill him. Kill him.

"That's right, this selection is the portion of your consciousness that hides *secrets*. Nothing held within the confines of that scheming head is safe from me now." He listened to the whispers again, rolling with laughter at the newest gossip. "So that's why you hold such hatred toward the term *boy*. Father used to beat you bloody and fill your ears with the word." He laughed, gliding down in front of Atha, who could barely hear his taunts. The subtle whispers were growing loud and insatiable, perhaps near, demanding one single action be accomplished.

Kill him! Kill him! Kill him! Kill him! Kill him! Kill him!

Mikaido waved a hand, sending the papers converging over Atha's face cascading away. He wanted to look Atha in the eye while he tormented him further.

"You best shut your fucking mouth!" Atha screamed as Mikaido raised a hand and sent a shockwave ripping across him, causing him to nearly pass out from the disorientation.

"You're a recovering drug abuser too? What a filthy wretch you are. I almost regret delving into the depths of your darkest secrets. You have shared much with me, so let me take a turn." Mikaido bent down beside Atha's ear, a smile forming across his face. The whispers dulled as if to let the Prince's words reach his ear, his *mind*. "I hold no love for your sister and find my position of suitor just as regrettable as you. Had only your father moved but a tad swifter in crushing her throat, he'd have saved me much trouble." He ran a hand across Atha's face. Suddenly the evil, suggestive whispers turned to sociopathic demands, screaming bloody murder through his mind and yelling directly into his ear.

KILL HIM! KILL HIM! KILL HIM! KILL HIM! KILL HIM! KILL HIM!

Despite the unquenchable screams and Atha's exploding rage, his expression calmed. The anger and pain in his eyes that Mikaido had worked so hard to nurture vanished, leaving only an empty void. Atha blacked out. The Prince's smile dissipated as he stared into the empty eyes. Scarlet liquid, thick like oil, oozed out of both eyes, down Atha's cheeks like a red river of tears as Mikaido snapped his hand back.

Mikaido watched with disgust, "Is this... *blood?*" Black fog came roaring out of Atha's body, engulfing the entire white world in a supernatural fog.

Mikaido sent a shockwave rocketing for Atha as a mirror popped out of the air, sending the shockwave right back to its sender. The blood continued oozing out of Atha's eyes, soaking the front of his tattered white dress shirt. The torrent of black fog escaping him thickened as his empty eyes studied the hardened fog encasing him. A bottle of liquid fell from the air behind him, shattering atop the demon that had latched onto his back. The demon screamed and vanished before a small gem crashed into the hardened fog encasing Atha, exploding outward and freeing him.

Atha's bleeding eyes turned slowly to Mikaido. The proud Prince who was so sure of victory just moments ago was now on frozen with disbelief. Their eyes met for just a split second before a massive wall of metal came hurtling toward Mikaido, snapping him out of his trance as his instincts kicked in. He glanced to the left, beginning to teleport until another metal wall, over a mile wide, completely blocked that route. A quick glance to his left was stymied by a third wall that was just inches away from him. The gleaming metal began to crush through his blue barrier. The match was over.

Chapter 22
Creation and That Which It Brings

Atha gasped for air as he came to, assuming he had been the one to lose as he glanced around in a disoriented stupor before noticing Mikaido.

"Goddammit! You motherfucker, this isn't over!" Atha screamed, bursting toward the stunned Mikaido and slamming him onto his back and bashing a fist across his face until green fog pulsed over him, lifting him up and away from his prey.

Only then did Atha notice the arena was silent. Mikaido slowly eased back onto his feet, his deep voice cutting through the entire arena. "Unexplainable powers that know no bounds. Fog, darker than that of raging fire. I can't believe I didn't see through you sooner. You're a plague."

This last word, plague, sent a wildfire of whispers up through the stands.

"Plague."

"He's a plague."

"That's right, he is a plague!" a voice yelled overtop the whispers. Alkibiades stepping forward from the tunnel to point a sword up at Atha.

Are they talking about me? Atha paused, glancing up as a pulse of green illuminated overtop him.

"Lower your weapon, guard!" Elise screamed, sending a pulse of green energy down, which he strode through unfazed.

"My Queen, please see reason! He is the plague of Creation; his very existence has brought the Red Sheep from its slumber and into our lands! We must take this opportunity and strike him down!" Alkibiades screamed back, a roar of agreement rolling across the arena.

"We will do no such thing! Lower your weapon now! That's an order!" she yelled back, green light brimming across the sky as thousands of swords of varying sizes appeared. A burst of green energy also pulsed over Alkibiades, but he remained unflinching.

"You would set upon your own to defend a plague?! So be it! I will do what I must to defend my country absent your biased command!" Alkibiades roared back, throwing his sword like a spear, its tip glowing red and picking up speed.

Elise twirled her finger and formed a wall of green fog between the flying sword and Atha. Harika shot up to catch the sword, but it turned translucent and passed straight through both, slamming into Atha's chest in a burst of blood. He screamed in surprise but stopped, realizing it was just an illusion.

"El, wait! He uses—" Atha began but she went white, unable to hear him over the roar across the stadium.

"Nooooo!" she screamed. Green swords descending on Alkibiades, tearing through him. He fell in pieces that vanished. The green fog dimmed and dissipated as she fell to the ground. Her fog evaporated from around Atha, and he fell toward the ground for a few moments before Harika shot out of the stands to catch him, setting him gently upon the ground. Shakkoo caught Elise, who pressed from her grip, hurrying over to the uninjured Atha.

"What—what is this?!" she gasped, feeling over his chest before twirling her finger. "My contract isn't working. Dimitri, my contract isn't working!"

"We must examine the situation. Come, we must relocate to safer settings," he replied quickly, but the arena's attention was drawing to twelve figures standing beside the white cube. They were dressed in black robes and wearing white masks akin to Harika's, except for Alkibiades. His image changed as illusions washed away. Tidy hair morphed to long black dreads that flowed down his back and a bandana worn low. His eyes focused on Elise; a monotone voice emanated from his throat.

"As per a condition placed upon my contract, Thief of all Trades, I stand before you to tell you I have stolen your contract. With that fact now known to you—" He paused, pulling back his robes to reveal dozens upon dozens of black tattoos. A section upon his pale white stomach remained untouched before an image of swords began to darken the empty patch of flesh.

"Your contract is mine." He gave a quick bow as Shakkoo's shadow shot toward him.

"Dibs!" Jun's familiar voice chimed amidst the Chameleons, snatching Shakkoo's face as she popped out of the shadows and promptly smashing it into the ground. The other Chameleons stepped through blue portals that led them high onto the stadium's rim. Jun glanced up at the bloodied Atha, waving a hand to him but flinching as green energy pulsed across Elise.

"Ruler's Right! Queen's last knight!" Elise yelled, green armor forming from the fog and attaching to her as a sword fell into her hands.

"Oh, a contract with a contingency plan for theft? Well, as much as I'd like to test it out, I gotta run." Jun laughed as a blue portal opened beside her. She joined the rest of the Chameleons atop the rim.

"Seize them!" Elise yelled, pointing her sword to the Chameleons but pausing as the screams from the crowd grew. Shadowy hands began snatching up victims.

A voice crept into Atha's head. In singsong vibrato, deep and low, it tolled a dark song.

"I'm bringing home a baby bumblebee; won't my mother be so proud of me?" It began, halting as one of its victims began driving a knife into its fingers. "Ouch, it stung me. I'm squishing"—the voice laughed, bursts of crimson exploding in the open air as the bodies popped like bubbles—"up a baby bumblebee, won't my mommy be so proud of me?"

Torrents of bleeding animals and infected began swarming down the tunnels of the stadium, complete chaos and panic ensuing as all hell broke loose.

"Dimitri! Order target change from the Chameleons to protecting the city! Initiate emergency evacuation protocol type seven!" Elise yelled as holograms began rapidly popping up in front of her. "Attention all citizens! We are under attack!" Her voice echoed through the city as Dimitri began tapping upon holograms of his own. "Mandatory teleportation is now activated and will commence with all children. ETA until elders are relocated is approximately eight minutes so please, take that time to seek safety and shelter of any sort! All forms of transportation are now under royal conscript and are hereby ordered to aid any and all in need of assistance." Beams of light shot down from the sky, encasing children and shooting them off to safety. "Dimitri, Shakkoo, on me! We move to coordinate defense!"

She glanced at Zell. "See Atha from the city. None of you are officially registered with the city roster, so you will not be teleported." Zell nodded, and Elise snapped her eyes to Atha, and despite the chaos and panic, he realized this was the most composed he'd ever seen her. "Be safe, my dearly beloved. We will figure this out. I love you," she said before bursting into the air as Dimitri and Shakkoo followed her out of sight.

"We must make haste!" Zell announced, yanking on Harika's arm, who prayed frantically. Atha's black bike fell before him. A shiver ran down his back and he flipped around to see a massive shadow rising out of the ground. It continued up until it was a few stories taller than the arena, all the while as Atha watched in horror. A figure formed within the darkness with a set of horns protruding from its head, skeletal fingers grasping a huge white scepter in its hands.

"Oh my God," Atha gasped as the shadows continued up past the top of the stadium. Shadowy arms stretched out from the main body across the city in every direction like a squid made of endless tentacles. "That's the Red Sheep?! It's so much bigger than it was last time!" The land within the shadow churned, a massive hole opening as the bloodied beast itself rose out, lifted by the shadows it hid within.

Alkibiades watched from above, glancing to one of the figures surrounding him. "I would be curious to know how the Sheep came to act perfectly in sync with our plan, Blair. He entered on cue with the theft of the Queen's contract, completely lowering the defensive shield surrounding the capital. This might be seen as a coincidence had we not a plague amongst our forces." The Chameleon nodded, a frog popping out from beneath her robes and hovering into the air beside her.

"Yeah, I told him, but only because Erida asked me to," she replied, nodding to another figure amongst them.

"These criminals deserve their fate for stabbing me in the back upon Elise's return," Erida added.

"That's not my concern. If Elise were to perish, I would lose her contract. Blair, convey this message to the Red Sheep. See that Elise is left uninjured in exchange for your information," Al continued as Blair glanced to the frog.

"It will be done," the frog croaked back, turning his sight down to the Red Sheep. "Disease," the croaky voice rang, heard only by Atha and the Red Sheep, who both glanced up to him. "The Chameleons, Plague of Frog included, would ask you to leave the Queen untouched."

"While I do appreciate your tip, Blair, I promised no favor in return, but do owe debt to Creation. Yet take pause, for I have information that will see you equally compensated." The Sheep paused, a sickening smile growing across its face. "Stay out of my way," it said as it moved toward Atha ever so slowly.

"You best stay the fuck away from her or—" Atha began, but shadowy hands shot out from the main mass, slamming into the stadium and sending massive chunks of stone scattering across surrounding buildings.

"Or *what*?! Do you think you have a chance of stopping me?!" The Sheep's voice roared as dust blanketing the entire area. "Imagine having slept for hundreds of years, crazed by hunger, and awakening to a meal of souls ripe with corruption. You took that from me and now stand unprepared to pay the piper for such a slight. I acknowledge you were ignorant to our ways and do hold a fondness for any first plague of Creation, so I will give you an opportunity to bury this."

Atha scoffed in disbelief despite glancing around at the already growing destruction that surrounded him.

"Does it speak?" Zell whispered frantically into his ear.

Atha nodded and spoke up.

"Will you leave the capital and promise to never return? Infected included?" Atha asked.

The Red Sheep nodded.

"Then name your terms," Atha finished, following the beast's gaze to Zell, who stood beside him.

"Kill the Denata," he mused. Atha's face twisted with rage as Zell glanced between them.

"You piece of shit!" he screamed, yanking Shooting Star from its sheath in a fit of rage. A shadowy hand shot out of the ground and flicked the blade, causing a pulse of light to burst from it and sending Atha spinning into the air. Searing pain shot through his arm, the bones of his arm crushing. He was unable to orient himself between the flashes of the ground below and sky above. He landed against something soft, screaming with pain and tucking the sword away as his eyes slowly cleared to the sight of black-and-gold feathers.

"The sky belongs to griffins. Aye, a human would do well to remain upon ground," Shun's familiar voice boomed inside his head.

"Uncle Shun!" Atha conjured a sling and slipped his throbbing arm into it before latching hold of feathers with his left. His arm was thankfully almost completely numb now and rapidly turning a deep shade of purple from where the chains had crushed it. *Either adrenaline or something's beyond broken.*

Zell's orange ball popped up beside his head. "Miracle and I shall remain to render aid! Take this opportunity to have wings carry you far from the plague seeking your demise!"

"Wh-what?! No, Zell, I'm staying!" Atha burst, noting all too late the absent orange ball. "Damn! Shun, we can't leave, we gotta do something!" Atha yelled, the Griffin glancing back at him.

"Please, Shun! We need to—"

"Screeching in the ear of one who gives no argument is quite unnecessary. Aye, we must formulate a plan," Shun replied, gold dust wisping from the air to form a contract before Atha.

"What is this? A partnership contract?" he asked, glancing over the document.

"Temporary partnership. It will connect portions of our minds," Shun replied.

Atha placed a hand across the gold sheet and it vanished. The griffin gazed down, watching the shadows stretching like snakes through buildings all the way across the massive capital.

"His power has grown since our last encounter," Shun observed, but Atha barely heard him. He shared a portion of Shun's sight, grasping aspects of the visual world around him that boggled his mind. "Atha, focus! Time is of the essence, so take it to form a plan!" Shun's voice roared back at him as he gasped, pulling his eyes away from the tiny mouse that hopped through the street stories beneath them. He pulled his rock from his pocket, dancing it around in his hand as his mind cleared.

"Well, we have neither offensive nor defensive superiority, but we do have home-field advantage since you know the layout of the capital. In addition, it's possible to manipulate the Red Sheep. Lastly, our biggest advantage is maneuverability and speed superiority. Adding all these factors together puts us in perfect position to lead the Red Sheep straight out of the capital with minimal damage," Atha explained as Shun listened in disbelief to the harsh shift in demeanor. "Get us close to the Red Sheep and I'll get it to follow us. I need you to figure out which streets are less populated and head for them while keeping us just shy of capture. I'll figure out the rest. Can you do it, Shun?"

Atha felt the Griffin turn sharply to the left.

"Aye, a fine plan. One forcing reminiscence of your mother."

Atha pocketed the rock again. Gold dust began forming additional feathers and gilded the rest of his wings completely gold. Shun's massive wingspan spread out wide, and with a mighty push they shot forward, straight toward the main mass of shadow.

"Do you know why it has grown to such size upon our last encounter?" Shun asked. Atha shook his head.

"Just 'cause I'm one of these fucking plagues doesn't mean I understand a single thing about them. It must have something to do with that skeletal avatar. It was just a skull last time, but it grew with the shadow. Red Sheep also mentioned something about souls, so I'd bet killing people gives it more power," Atha replied, checking around for Elise's image to no avail. Shun stopped in the air a long distance to the side of the Sheep, circling it slowly as Atha watched. A path of shattered buildings lay behind it, its shadowy arms stretching out and continuing the wreckage.

"I must hold this distance or I cannot assure our safety. Can you make do from here?" Shun asked as a megaphone fell into Atha's hands. He clicked it on.

"Hey, Sheep, I forgot to ask before but what was Chernobyl like? I mean, I've seen some nasty shit come out of that place, but goddamn, what in the genetic defect happened here?" Atha yelled, roaring with laughter at his own joke as the Red Sheep slowed to a halt. Even Shun glanced back slowly.

"Chernobyl? Creation, I know not of what you speak," the Red Sheep's deep voice replied through his head.

"I find myself questioning it as well," Shun added slowly.

Fuck me and my references. This must be what a stand-up comedian feels like when nobody gets his jokes, Atha noted to himself before clicking the megaphone back on.

"It's just that I was gonna ask you for a bag of wool, but then I realized I mixed you up with the black sheep! Looks like they accidentally sent the butcher to sheer your fucking mangled ass anyways ri—"

"FILTHY HUMAN! I'LL KILL YOU, BOY!"

Atha flinched, losing his grip and dropping the megaphone as the shadow moved toward him and a bloodcurdling scream erupting through his head. Every single arm shot out from the shadow toward them. Gold gusted over his back, pinning him down onto Shun, who lurched forward, narrowly dodging a closing hand that tore through the building beside them.

"Jesus, Santa, God! I said keep him just shy of catching us Shun, not close enough to whisper sweet nothings in my ear!" Atha screamed as he was thrown around on Shun's back like rickety roller coaster as more hands narrowly missed them.

"Silence! Both his speed and reach have increased, a factor I had not foreseen with elevated mass!" Shun roared back. Atha glanced over his shoulder at the shadow and instantly regretted it. Like a massive spider made of darkness, the arms carried the main shadow across the ground after them, stretching hands that reached for their backs in a frenzied swarm. Shun dipped down between the buildings, swerving and jutting through the tight areas, hoping to slow the assault by hiding their image. The hands pulled together like a wave that crashing through every building before the Red Sheep, forcing Shun back up into the sky as reaching hands licked at his tail feathers.

Shun dipped through reaching hands and chunks of buildings alike, Atha clinging onto his back for dear life with his one good arm.

"How much further?!" he screamed over the wind to Shun, feeling his eyesight connect with Shun's and taking notice of the nearing wall.

"Time is the factor that will dictate distance. The Red Sheep remains active for an hour at a time and will cease attack in favor of rest at that mark," Shun replied as Atha glanced down, noticing a lone warrior dispatching infected with surgical precision.

"What is he doing taking on so many alone?!" he gasped out loud by accident, feeling Shun's eyes follow his own, sensing doubt in them for the first time. "What the hell?! That's Janster!" Atha gasped, feeling panic set in. "He's just a kid. I gotta go help!"

Shun nodded. A tornado of gold swirled around them, the eye of the storm leading to the ground.

"Manifest an outfit like the one you wear. I will give the impression you continue to ride!" Shun replied, a suit falling from the air as gold dust filled it in a shape similar to Atha's body. A tornado of gold dust cascaded into existence around them, entirely hiding the pair from their pursuer's view.

"Jump!"

Atha held his arm, leaping straight down through the gold and landing perfectly behind a building. The shadow ripped across it, unnoticing, and he conjured a sling for his broken arm, grunting at the shooting pain that was spurred by the awkwardness of latching it one-handed. Then he manifested a white mask over his face, dark lines filling it to display an image of anger to hide his identity from the infected. Next came the bike, and he leapt on it and ripped back in the direction they came. It was only a few moments before he had Janster back in his sight, leaping from the bike to send it crashing across infected.

"Janster! What are you still doing here? I thought all the kids had been evacuated!" Atha watched in disbelief as the child tore through the swarms with ease.

"Help me! The swords are controlling my body!" he sobbed as his legs carrying him autonomously down another road. Red energy pulsed through Atha's legs, overtaking the child in one explosive burst and tackling him to the ground. Janster struggled and twisted with incredible strength beneath him, but Atha held firm, grabbing hold of the sword-bearing arm with his own and holding it to the ground.

"Just let it go! Uncurl your fingers!" Atha yelled, twisting his head in a panic as he realized he'dbeen far too loud and receiving a chorus of odious roars across the surrounding area.

"I can't! It won't let me! Tella's all alone!" Janster cried. Atha pressed a knee into his chest before latching his hand onto the hilt's free space above where Janster's hand clasped it.

"This might hurt a bit but bear with me!" Atha replied, glowing red and yanking on the hilt. He gave a few hard tugs, afraid he'd pull Janster's arm clean off. Distorted screams of sick animals grew closer.

Fuck, I can't get a single finger off! Think, think, think! Atha started to panic as the infected began to come around a corner. He manifested a rope and cinched it around Janster before tucking him under his arm and sprinting off.

"Just tell me which direction to go!"

"Take this left!" Janster sobbed back.

"Contact!" Atha announced and Zell's orange ball appearing beside his head. "Zell, I got a kid possessed by a sword, a broken arm, and I'm about to pick up his sister, which is gonna be hard with the way he's struggling! He'll run the second I let him go so I don't have time to tie him up properly and manifest a car with these infected on my heels!"

"Take this side street!" Janster barked before Zell's voice answered back.

"Children yet remain?! My tracker shows you placed deep within the thickest of the swarm so be wary! Backup ETA is a full minute. Can you manage that long?" Zell asked as Atha rounded the corner to pause at the sight of *thousands* of infected. One noticed him, but that was enough. All the rest snapped toward him, a roar flowing across them that shook the windows of nearby buildings.

"Fuck! Hurry, Zell!" Atha screamed, red energy filling his legs as he bounded up onto a rooftop. The infected leaped up after him in swarms. "Control! Anger level seven!" Atha boomed, filling with rage intense enough to send a shipping container to clear off the roof in front of him.

"The house on the right with no door!" Janster announced. Atha hurriedly found an empty patch on the ground before leaping down.

Agro energy's almost gone, he noted as he burst through the door. He hooked a right into the kitchen and Atha's blood went cold and the world stood still. A tiny body mauled beyond recognition lay in a pool of blood filled with bestial and bipedal footprints. A larger, decapitated body lay beside it, bearing an eerie resemblance to the night he shot Dako. Reality faded from his grasp, as did Janster, who he'd forgotten he was holding. The grasp he held on the child released, dropping Janster straight to the floor.

Is this real? Atha wondered and glancing down slowly at his hands. Until this point he'd asked himself the question at least once a day but, until now, he had hoped that is was. Now he felt himself wishing it wasn't and that was supple fuel for the borderline insanity to cross fully into his mind. Retching screams and bodies slammed into the front of the building, cracking the walls that begged to fall. A handful of infected crashed through the windows and bounded through the doorway just two dozen feet behind him, violently dissipating the inner turmoil. His eyes snapped down to Janster, the sword gone as he now lay motionless. Atha could still feel his mind fighting the blur like an out-of-tune TV displaying its worst imitation of a snowstorm. He landed a few heavy slaps across his own face to clear it.

"Break down later, focus!" Atha instructed himself, yanking Janster back up off the floor and sending a car smashing down the wall before him as he dashed behind it. No Agro energy remained and the streets were swarmed. Hundreds of sets of eyes turned to him.

It's over. Completely encircled, he acted on impulse. A heavy metal safe fell open beside him and he threw Janster in with only barely enough time to close the door as the mass descended upon him. Atha screamed and flung his hand up in front of his face. He managed to get his shattered arm one up a few inches, but he didn't notice the pain. He was unable to manifest even one last item with the speed at which they came. Feeling no teeth digging into his flesh, he eased an arm down and peeked an eye, releasing a scream at the sight of bleeding monstrosities just feet away. They surrounded him but moved not an inch closer. He took a step away, easing his back up against the metal safe. All the infected before him taking a step closer as the ones behind took a step away.

"Zell, how far are you?" Atha whispered, expecting the droves to fall upon him at the words. But again, they just watched.

"A half minute out. Be ready. We come by sky." she called back.

"I'm completely surrounded but they aren't attacking," Atha whispered.

"It is rumored a plague cannot attack another without permission from the Antarie. Remain still, appear as no threat," Zell replied.

Atha whimpered, meeting eyes with the Infected who stood nearest him. It was a young woman, probably around his age. Atha guessed she'd probably been out on a date when the Red Sheep broke in, and now this daughter, sister, perhaps young mother, supposed lover, stood leaking blood from her mouth, arms tattered with bite marks from where she probably tried to protect her pretty face. Atha wondered if her family was screaming her name, hoping for a response, maybe at a location of safety or refusing to leave, searching the streets for her.

Atha was smart. Len used to say, *You got the mind of a thinker, kid. Noose be damned, you're quick enough to get out of it while the stupid hang. Problem is, you've got equal empathy, stopping and helping the dumbass dangling beside you.* Len had made it one of his many missions to break Atha of this habit, but Atha had a tendency to stumble when things got dark. A tendency to fall to old ways. A tendency to *relapse*. A baggy of white powder broke his concentration on the bleeding infected, falling from thin air to his feet. A bag of the drug that had been his only comfort in hard times beckoned him to reach down and pick it up. *Come on, you've had a tough run. I'll help you forget everything for just a little bit. Just a little bit and then you'll need some more, and more, and more, and more and—*

"Above you!" Zell's voice barked overhead. A carriage pulled by griffins swooped down as chains lashed out toward him. He swung the safe's iron door open, yanking Janster out as the chains wrapped around his waist to yank him up and into the back of the carriage where Zell sat. Pulling off his mask and tossing it onto the floor, the carriage gusted away.

"Where is the girl?" Zell pried, but Atha could only shake his head. Zell fell silent for a long few moments, glancing over the motionless Janster. "What of the sword?"

"When we—we found Tella, he collapsed and it just vanished," Atha said. Zell whisked her screen open and began shifting symbols about. He didn't watch but buried his face into his hands instead. "How could this happen? I thought kids got teleported out first."

"Assuming they lived outside the capital before relocation to within the walls, they would not yet have been upon the list. Abilities like teleportation typically require some form of authorization from both contract holder and target to activate."

"Where's Shun?" he asked as Zell rearranged her symbols again, displaying an overhead map of the capital and surrounding area.

"After leading the Red Sheep out of the capital, he proceeded to this large clearing," she replied, tapping the screen. "It is surrounded by trees. Shun has begun leading it in circles, attempting to drain time."

A bike fell beside Atha, who proceeded to mount it. "Take pause," she instructed.

Atha slammed his good arm across the handlebar in protest.

"No! Shun's out there fighting all by himself and I'll be damned if I hang him out to dry!" Atha screamed with a cracking voice, struggling to bring the bike to life with harsh reality sending tremors through his arm.

"That is not my aim. We go together. You jump, I jump, as you once forewarned." She smiled at him and he felt a smile creep across his own face. "Master Gabrenuer, please see the child to the Shakka temple," Zell called up to the driver, who gave a nod without taking his eyes away from the sky ahead. "Slide back. I shall pilot this vehicle," she continued as Atha cocked an eyebrow. "I may have practiced a bit with its predecessor while you were occupied with training." Zell winked as Atha scooted back on the bike. She sat down in front of him and Atha wrapped his good arm around Zell. She brought the bike to life and shot out the back of the carriage.

"Uncle, can you hear me?" Atha's voice called to Shun.

"Aye, are you to safety?" Shun responded.

"No, I'm headed back to you. I've got another plan," Atha replied, flinching at a screech that burst through his mind.

"Stay away, you fool! The capital is nearly evacuated, we need not press further!"

"Chill out and listen! Zell checked to make sure and she's certain a plague can't hurt another plague! I can stall him without danger while you take Zell and stay close. She has an ability that can allow her to dig through somebody's head, but she needs to be close by and said she might even pass out. I'm gonna distract him while she tries to figure out some sort of weakness. I'm coming up on your right side so be ready to take Zell and use your dust to put me on the ground!" Atha replied as Shun appeared in the distance.

"There are too many unknown factors! I will not risk you falling on a hopeful gamble!" Shun retorted.

"This isn't your decision! We are literally in the best-case scenario I can think of to try this, so stop arguing with me and get ready to catch Zell!"

Shun screeched with rage, twisting toward them. Atha leapt from the side, gold flakes catching him and lowering him down while Zell leaped straight off the bike on top of Shun. Atha landed softly before the towering shadow which came to a stop in front of him.

"Let's have a chat," Atha growled, a shadowy hand coming over top of him, but he remained unflinching. His second-guessing of the plan only came at the last moment as it pressed over him.

Chapter 23
Enter the Shadow

The hand slipped straight over him, shadows encasing him as every sight and sound fled his senses. He was eased up and through the shaft of the arm, entering the main mass and coming to a stop before the Red Sheep, who stood on the ground, an empty space of air surrounding him within the hollow darkness.

"So you have learned I never posed a direct threat upon you. Yes, let us 'chat' then, Creation," the Sheep's voice called through his head, a sickening smile upon its face as blood oozed from its tattered flesh.

"Fuck you, you murderer," Atha spat back, the Sheep's smile falling.

"Are you incapable of intelligent conversation?" it asked, glancing up to the set of wings whipping by overhead. "You seek to peer inside my mind, I see." It chuckled, Atha stiffening at this as the Sheep glanced back to him. "Does it surprise you that your whimsical tricks are ineffective? Did you really think nobody had schemed against a god before, a god the world in its entirety wishes dead?"

Atha pulled in closer and closer, coming to a halt just outside the empty inner space.

"Holy shit, do you even believe what you're saying? A god? You're just a psycho with a big ego and I'm gonna—" The air left Atha's lungs as shadows forced their way into his mouth.

"Be silent, you preening boy. I have given but a glimpse of the pain and anguish I know as old friends."

Atha drew the image of a car into his mind, attempting to send it flying through the shadow-less space the sheep sat in, but nothing came. "Even when your mouth is absent words, you cast further insult. Neither ability spurred by contract nor plague can pass through my void without my permission. Calling myself a god may have been incorrect after all. It would be more fitting for a god to call themselves the Red Sheep, if only in drunken boast." It laughed, watching Atha grasp as his throat that begged for air.

"I'll let you in on a little secret, boy. My plague may already seem terrifying, but this is *far* from its full power. Many abilities remain dormant until enough souls have been gathered to allow their use. What you have seen so far is Disease at its absolute weakest, and yet even an entire nation could not so much as slow my assault. If even this doesn't dissuade that wrath within you, then we may meet upon field of battle, free of the shackles that restrain us from the other's throat. But be warned, Creation, to challenge me, you must be strong." The beast and its shadows completely vanished and Atha fell to the dirt, gasping for air as Shun slammed down beside him, an unconscious Zell held to his back by gold dust.

"Arrogant fool! Did you learn nothing from my speech of hubris?" Shun's voice roared, leering down upon the gasping Atha.

Air filled his lungs and tears left his eyes, rolling an arm over top to shield them from the gross world.

"I had to try. He killed people, Uncle. He killed *children*." Atha sobbed and Shun closed his own eyes for a moment.

"Aye. We must stay afoot. Danger still lurks," Shun replied, gold dust lofting Atha up onto his back as they took to the night sky.

"Take me to Elise," Atha requested, but Shun shook his head.

"No. You must see Zell to the Shakka village."

"I'll get Miracle to take her. Elise needs me."

"Atha, you are a plague. If you were to place yourself before her after an attack, what do you think the *Queen* would be forced to do?" Shun replied. Atha's fist tightened down on his feathers.

"So that's how it is now? After everything I'm still trapped."

Shun flew for some ways, eventually coming upon a clearing and gusting to the ground.

"I will keep eyes on the Queen. You can find your way?" Shun asked as an SUV popped down next to Atha.

Gold dust lofted Zell onto the back seat as Atha nodded, whispering back, "I've been here before."

Climbing into the driver's seat and twisting the key, a blue path stretched up toward the black sky.

The trip was long and silent. Zell's rhythmic breathing was the only sound within the empty cab.

***

Treetops finally gave way to rooftops and Atha eased the car down, gliding toward the dirt path that ran through the town. Despite the hour, the village was awake, as news of the recent attack had already spread. A few figures illuminated by dull blue light stood out on the dirt path before him. He eased to a halt as a leader stepped forth. They wore the purple robes akin to Zell's, but Atha hadn't noticed, staring in utter disbelief at the weapons of mass destruction they carried in their arms.

All three monks held AK-47s with long banana clips extending down. The leader motioned for Atha to step out, but Atha paused as a dark realization took shape in his mind. *I knew something was wrong when I couldn't remember using that pistol in the tournament. I've been dropping them all over the place since I got here. This is my plague. I gave the world guns.*

The monk continued forward, tapping a finger against the glass as Atha eased the door open, reality beginning to fall from his grasp as he eyed the metal gun. It wasn't one of the exact ones he'd dropped; this one was distinctly different with strange red metal. *They reverse engineered the ones I dropped with a contract. They're manufacturing them already.*

The leader spoke up, a wavering voice stitching together a shoddy quilt of composure. "Elenzer said you would be coming."

Atha's mind couldn't acknowledge his words, taking note only of the monk's finger wrapped firmly around the trigger, a slight shake to his hands begging to cause an accidental discharge. At least the barrel was pointed toward the ground.

"You—you don't put your finger on the trigger. Not until you're looking down sight at a target," Atha muttered, reaching a hand slowly toward the monk's trigger hand, hoping to show him what he spoke of and knowing he wasn't conveying the idea well with a muddled mind. The monk released a dull whimper, snapping away and raising the barrel up to Atha's face. Maybe he hadn't missed everything Atha had said after all.

"Yeah. Like that."

Elenzer shot out from behind them, stepping beside the monk and easing the barrel down out of Atha's face.

"Whoa, *whoa* there. We spoke of this already. Let him pass," Elenzer instructed coolly, his shaking ally abandoning any shroud of his calm appearance.

"He's a plague! Have you so soon forgotten what Disease set upon us that you would welcome Creation with open arms?!" he retorted, Elenzer's firm red hand resting on his shoulder.

"Have you so soon forgotten who kept that rampage to an absolute minimum? Now come, let us see him to the monastery before you incite a panic," Elenzer said as his fellow monk stepped aside. "We must tend to Zell."

Atha rode slowly through town. AK-47's were suddenly commonplace, hanging awkwardly from belts where swords once sat, adequately illustrating the ignorance to the few thousand-year gap in weapons advancements he'd bridged. No, he'd *created.* He rolled to a stop before the quiet stone temple, the massive trees of Shakka waving slowly in the windless night as he heaved Zell into his arms and followed Elenzer in. Atha stopped just after entering, the translucent floor shimmering beneath his feet. A single snap from Elenzer's fingers caused the floor to ripple, and the center portion they stood upon lowered down into a shaft. Lights flickered on farther beneath them. Metallic blue tubes covered the walls and intricately twisted their way down to the ground level, where they all connected into a single helmet resting atop a slab of concrete.

"Put her across the table face up with her head toward the helmet," Elenzer instructed. Atha did as he was told, and Elenzer pulled the strange helmet up over her head as she came to a rest upon it.

"What is all this? Is this for her brain damage?" Atha asked, glancing up the shaft at the glowing metals.

"It is," Elenzer replied. "This is a one of a kind memory reconstruction chamber designed specifically for her. Her contract works in sync with her mind, and when overused, it causes her to become comatose. She should be fully recovered by tomorrow, so get some rest. Your friend Miracle is out just past the Shakka trees. He evaluated the Denata child, Janster, when he arrived." Atha nodded. The flooring pulsed gently around him and lifted him back up.

He walked outside and found Harika sitting amongst the trees. Healix was curled around his arm as white squares formed new organs for a damaged fly.

"Hey, buddy," Atha said and sighed, taking a seat in the grass beside him.

"Hello. How is the capital?" Harika asked.

"*Bad.*"

"I did what I could. Tended to those without bite wounds," Harika replied.

"Zell mentioned it normally took decades for people with your contract to operate capably on humans. I'm so proud of you. How was the kid?"

"He is fine. I never saw the sword Zell spoke of and Healix detected no—what was the word you used?" he asked Healix.

"Anomalies," Healix answered.

"Yes, that. So, we assume it was a temporary enchantment," Harika continued. Atha felt his smile quivering and turned to leave. "Hold on. Your arm," Harika observed.

Atha glanced down to his shattered arm, feeling the dull tingle return with its mention. He'd all but forgotten about it, a pestilential mind placing over his pitiful matter.

Healix eyed Atha's arm, noting the damage.

"Right arm damaged extensively. Shattered humorous, radius, and carpus. Ulna with multiple fractures. Severed radial, musculocutaneous, median, and ulnar nerves," the winged snake said.

Harika got to work. Four cubes of white popped from red portals, gradually shrinking and shifting down into bones. Healix opened his mouth, dancing red light across Atha's arm that pulled the flesh open, yet he didn't bleed. Healix was careful not to break the straps that cradled Atha's arm. With a snap of the snake's tongue, the bones vanished into its mouth, the replacements zooming down into their place. A few more quick zaps over the top portion of Atha's arm and suddenly he could feel it again. With another flash of Healix's eyes, the flesh mended. Atha held the smile across his face, forcing himself to acknowledge Harika's hard work and dedication that he now benefited from.

"That's amazing, buddy." Atha pulled the sling off his arm and dropped it onto the ground. He flexed his fingers and moved his arm around freely.

"It's all right to be sad," Harika replied in his monotone voice.

"What are you talking about?"

"I've been empty for a long time. Empty words don't fool me," he replied as Atha huffed and began to sob. "It's all right to just be sad," Harika repeated. Atha rested his head against Harika's shoulder and started to cry. He cried about how he looked down at two children and promised he'd help them and now one lay dead, the other scarred for life. He cried about the infected woman. He cried about leaving Len and Giuseppe behind. He cried that he came into a new world seeking a fresh start, only to eventually find that old look of disgust when eyes fell upon him.

Atha was all cried out by the time he stopped, feeling practically no better, yet his heart felt full at the fact he'd found allies he could count on. Ones that could share the load when he struggled.

"I need to go get some council. We'll make a plan when Zell wakes up," Atha said as he stood up. He turned and walked away, coming to a stop in front of Cybele, mana streaming off the tree to connect their minds.

"Oh, Atha. Sit down before you fall down little one," Cybele's voice called through his head, helping him slowly down onto her roots.

"I've really messed things up, Granny. I need your advice," Atha replied, staring slowly down at his hands. "I'm the plague of Creation and I've given this world advanced weapons from my own. Do you think I'm gonna end up like the Red Sheep?"

"What happened to that starry-eyed young human who stared in awe at every simplistic construct just weeks ago?" Cybele replied.

Atha couldn't read the tree and couldn't help but let his muddled mind jump to conclusions. "Are you redirecting the conversation because you don't want to answer that?"

"I see optimism has fallen to pessimism as well. I absolutely do not think that, but to make you believe it too, I cannot simply answer your question. See, do you feel any better?" she replied as Atha buried his face. "The times have entered the shadows, darkness is falling upon a land that just barely crept through the last night. Fortunately, that is only half of the duality we know as life. There are promises of bright days in shining equal ahead. Good and evil will always exist but beside that exists the option to fight for the portion you favor, as the Sheep does, prolonging the nighttime until it breaches upon the day. You hold all the power of the universe in your hands, so make a choice of your own."

"But I have been fighting! I've been fighting and everything's still gone to shit! Hell, I made things *worse*! People are walking the streets waving the muzzle of loaded guns in their neighbor's faces!" Atha sobbed back as leaves gently brushed the top of his head.

"Sometimes you can do everything in your power and still watch as it falls to ruin. Sometimes you can do nothing and watch it soar to unfathomable heights. Again, that's just life, and to think that because you fought things should go your way is simply *vanity*. I have never encountered weapons such as those you have released, but that does not mean all is lost," she replied as Atha scoffed.

"Because you haven't seen what they've done, the atrocities committed with those things on a global scale. It's gonna bring on a new age of war where you don't need a fancy contract to rip someone apart."

"Those wishing the worst on another always had that power. Mutual destruction has never been hard to attain at any time in history known to me. Do not think you can goad me into assisting you with your self-hatred." Cybele chuckled.

"That's not what I'm doing. I'm telling you, this is different." He sighed.

"Perhaps it is, but breaking into despair does nothing to change that. All that is left to do is see that destruction is limited, focused," she replied as Atha repeated the words in his head.

"With regulatory laws," he noted as the leaves patted his cheek.

"Precisely. The time to act has passed but the reaction span stretches before you. Don't waste a single second in self-pity. You have the firmest grasp on this force you've unleashed, so who better to implement rules and see them fill the ears of the Queen?" she asked.

"I'll do that then. But what if this is just the start? What if my plague's just getting warmed up?" he asked.

"I've seen unfathomable power like yours only a handful of times before, so that is difficult to answer. It's very likely that you can't control it, or better worded, that it will forcibly ensure the plague continues."

"I think so too. I can't remember dropping any of those guns. It's messing with my head," Atha replied, rapping knuckles against the dome that had done him so well in the past and now mocked him.

"There is little to be done about forcing you under its will, but you can still bend it to your own. How many aspects of this world do you think could be improved with inventions from your own?"

His knuckle halted and eyes widened as he considered the dozens of times he'd seen things that could be improved yet never thought to act. "I can't believe I never thought about that. I mean, this world is different and does a lot of things better, but so does mine. Healthcare, transportation, I don't know, entertainment, even."

"Your power was conceived with evil intent. Abuse it, spur change, and reform for the better of all. Make the powers sorry they ever placed such force in the hands of Atha Honorati. Now do you feel better?"

"Better than I did. Thanks, Granny," Atha replied, heavy eyes glancing toward the cloudy night sky. He fell asleep before he even realized he was exhausted.

A slight bump awoke Atha. Blurry eyes glancing first to his watch, which read seven a.m. It was, the first time he'd slept past 4 in years. When he lifted his eyes from the watch, he saw a shadowy figure standing over him.

"Zell! Should you be up already?" Atha asked, rubbing his eyes and getting to his feet.

"My health has returned to me."

Atha could tell this was a lie before his eyes had even cleared. Deep, raspy breaths noisily sounding from her like a broken whistle struggling to sing and dark purple bags hung under each eye.

"Come, the child has stirred but refuses to move," she continued. "Perhaps your presence will change that."

Heading into the monastery and through to the back room, Atha's heart fell at the sight of the motionless Janster, his eyes staring blankly at the ceiling as a monk offered him a spoonful from a bowl of soup.

"Please, little one, just a few bites and I will take my leave," the monk cooed as she pressed the metal to his lips. Janster's eyes trailed slowly to Atha, a quick flicker of life showing in them.

"Any updates on the swor—" Atha couldn't even finish his sentence as the sword appeared in Janster's hand from thin air. The boy jumped to his feet and twisted the weapon toward the monk's head before Atha could react. Zell, however, sprang into action instantly. Four blue tendrils snapped across each of his limbs to restrain him as her fellow monk screamed and toppled back, the bowl of soup spilling across her.

"Atha, help me! Make it stop!" Janster cried. Atha glancing desperately to Zell for prompts.

"Easy child, you are contained," Zell replied, a wobbly smile forming on her face. "Such a trivial curse properly remedied," she continued, putting him completely at ease.

"You—you can stop it?" he asked.

"But of course," she replied, mumbling, "Memory Bandit," under her breath and pausing for a few moments, only to find that nothing had changed. "Who gave you the sword? Did they use any command words or hint at its origin?"

"It—it's blurry. He said he was the leader of the Chameleons. I can't remember his name. He said it was used a long time ago to make child armies," Janster replied.

Atha drew the winged man to mind. *Alkibiades. That piece of shit.*

"Good, that's very helpful, Janster," Zell replied, her orange screen opening. She rearranged symbols and eventually stopping on a screen displaying a sword identical to Janster's. A few more monks burst in, blue bands popping from the air and strapping over Janster like a straitjacket as Zell dissolved her tendrils and pulled both Atha and Elenzer next door.

"We need an exorcist for the blade. It seems to have been made by Atha's senior Creation plague," Zell whispered, Elenzer's red face panging with blue.

"It attached to his soul?! This situation is far more volatile then you let on," Elenzer replied, flustered. Atha glanced between the two, at a complete loss to what they spoke of.

"Gather Metranta, have her make our need for an exorcist known," Zell replied.

"We must speak upon another plague as well." Elenzer sighed, resting a hand on Atha's shoulder. "He makes the town and our brethren uneasy."

"Wait, what? No, I can't leave the kid behind again!" Atha cut in, feeling his throat tighten.

"No, Elenzer is right. You can do no more to help, but an exorcist will be a difficult resource to precure while a plague is present," Zell replied. Atha had meant to argue this until he was blue in the face but he bit his lip. "Elenzer, move to contact an exorcist. A temporary bandage is required, which we already have. The sword resonates with the host's will to fight. An impossible feat to preform while restrained from emotion," Zell replied. Atha glanced down to his bracelet.

"I don't think that would work. I'd need the target to write information down to get the tethering to work properly."

"She taught you only the most basic techniques of the contract, not their full extent. Just discuss it with her," Zell replied as Atha nodded. The three exited out of the side room with Elenzer heading out toward the front door of the monastery. Atha and Zell went back into Janster's room, a few monks turning to Zell who gave them a reassuring nod.

"Control! Can I talk with you, Dulcina?" Atha asked, the bracelet pulsing for a moment until her blue hologram shone overtop.

"And here I was pleasantly thinking you'd forgotten about me." She smirked.

"Save the jokes for later. That kid over there is possessed by the sword, and I could shut it off by tethering to him. Any way to get around the writing portion?"

Dulcina's hologram turned to face Janster.

"I'm not supposed to give out contract uses that the wielder doesn't know of," she replied, Zell's orange screen springing up.

"Perhaps I could purchase the information. Let me see," she added but Dulcina waved a hand.

"*But* the situation appears dire and you have done right by me in the past, so my superiors should overlook it. Take a blood sample from him and deposit it onto the screen. Write his information down for him, and I'll ask his verbal consent for the tether," she replied. Atha felt a genuine smile cross his face.

"I really appreciate this, Dulcina. Let's get to it," Atha replied, stepping forward. "This might sting a bit, kid, but it's necessary. I need to take control of your emotions until an exorcist can come, but you need to answer some questions, okay?" Janster nodded. Atha manifested a small knife, nicking one of Janster's fingers with it before setting the blade aside on a nearby table. Next, he brought the black portion of his screen up, pressing the bleeding finger against it. With a quick shine of blue, the bracelet made a dull *ping*, and Dulcina nodded.

"Are you under the control of another contract or in any way forced to accept emotion manipulation?" Dulcina began. Janster only shook his head as another dull *ping* came from the bracelet.

"Do you consent to have your emotions monitored and controlled?" she continued.

Another nod, another audible *ping* from the bracelet.

"Tethering complete," Dulcina announced as Atha sighed.

"Control. Set Janster's emotions to null," Atha instructed. The boy's eyes went blank as he sagged like a ragdoll, sword vanishing from existence.

"Very good. Now follow me," Zell replied, slapping Atha on the shoulder as she headed out the door.

"Where to?"

"We gather Miracle. Then, my bug-out location."

"Like a secret hideout?" he replied. Suddenly, a compulsion pressed over him, a sudden want, no, a *need*, to see the shoe seller Hanzel came to mind as he glanced at his fancy boots. "I never properly paid the guy who gave me these like I promised I would. Can I just do this single thing?" he asked, his sad eyes staring down upon the one thing that remained untarnished through this journey in a new world.

"Very well. Be quick. Break words with none but the man himself, stay wary of your surroundings, and for Shakka's love *do not* cause a scene," Zell replied and Atha gave a quick nod. He hurried out the front door, choosing to jog down the dirt path rather than take his SUV, knowing that it stained the peaceful world surrounding it. Or, really, as peaceful as a place swarming with AK-47s could be, but at least air pollution wouldn't be the next calamity he'd enable.

It was a long jog and he slowly manifested coins in his pocket as he gasped for air from the longest run he'd ever taken in his life. He reached the town and found hateful eyes glancing at him. Children hurried inside as he passed. Len had taught him to stay completely aware of his surroundings at all times, saying, *what other people may miss, you will not. You see the whole pictures, no portion of the puzzle missing, while most have only a quarter of the pieces. Where most see a light bump beneath a belt, you see the silhouette of a pistol. Where others see a quick glance, you see the enemy sizing you up, searching for weakness. Nothing will evade your constant vigilance. The whole picture will not evade you.* He did not benefit from this principle now. The principle had been placed to help him notice subtle signs, but they made no attempt to shroud the disdain in their eyes or pause to pull an AK-47 from the loop upon their belts where once sat swords. He kept a wary eye on everything around him, waiting on somebody to make an attempt on his life. Just like back home.

"Just like back home." He chuckled under his breath, the irony not lost on him. Gasping and sweaty, he came to a stop at the shoe shop, the small wooden shop with its sign swinging lazily in the air above him. It appeared closed, the lights dimmed through the massive windows, but he could hear dull bumps inside. He raised a fist to knock lightly on the door.

"Just a moment!" Hanzel's familiar voice called. The short, chubby man quickly twisted the door open and, to Atha's delight, beamed to him with cheery surprise. "Atha! I had heard of your return!" He smiled and extended his hand to shake Atha's before holding the door open. "Come in, son."

"Yeah, bet you heard loads," Atha replied, entering the dainty dark shop.

"Just the whispers of rambling fools, nothing more. Now come, sit. You look like you need to take a load off." Atha smiled at the man, the demeaning words Hanzel cast on his neighbors perking Atha back up more than he knew.

"No, thanks. I just wanted to stop by and pay you the money I owe. I don't know when I'll be able to do that after today," Atha replied as he set the bag of coins he'd slowly manifested over the course of his run on the counter.

"You don't expect me to accept this do you?" he replied, pushing the coins back to Atha who pressed them forward again.

"I do. Trust me, it's no problem."

"I'm not taking your money. After you came through, everybody wanted to see what had the boy from another world so worked up and the shoes caught on," he replied, the word *boy* stinging Atha for a slight moment. He pressed the coins back as Atha finally reaccepted them.

"You're a good person, Hanz," Atha replied, eyes heavy with tears like two storm clouds begging to rain.

"Something you recognize because its true for you, too," Hanzel replied, ruffling Atha's hair. "But there is something I would like to ask you. About these *guns* I believe they're called." A pang struck Atha's heart as he assumed the worst.

"What about them?

"Well, they seem useful for personal defense and after the attack my wife nags that we need to keep better look over my son. Long story short, I bought him a gun. Bought a few actually. Was that a good decision, in your opinion?" he asked. Atha's fears somehow managed to be even worse than his pessimism could imagine.

"Guns aren't meant to be in the hands of kids. I think you should own one, be very familiar with its uses and functions, and pass that knowledge down to him a long time from now. Giving him an AK only puts him in more danger," Atha replied, the shop owner nodding slowly.

"I will do that then. We tested a few out after they came off the assembly line. I've never seen anything like that except from a combat contract. Not the kind of power to put in a kid's hands," Hanzel replied as Atha sighed with relief.

The door erupted open and both tensed. Three large, masked men brandishing AK-47s pointed downrange toward Hanzel.

Chapter 24
Red for Dead

Red energy pulsed into Atha's head, and began to snap into action but instead paused and noticed a fatal flaw in the seemingly murderous assailants; not a single magazine was slotted into any AK amongst them and their slides were cocked back to display empty chambers. Whoever they were, blood was not their intent. Time sped back up as Atha dispersed the Agro energy from his head, watching the three stumble upon one another through the door, moving awkwardly and nearly toppling over as they came to a stop in the room. Atha began to glance back to Hanzel, but the man was swift and already began reaching behind the counter. The only clue Atha had of what was about to happen was a loud click, the flipping of the safety switch from safe to auto. Red for dead.

"WAIT!" Atha screamed but he was cut short as reverberating bangs shook his head and flashes of light briefly engulfed the room, sending the three men down to the ground in a strobe-light effect until they lay bloody and motionless. Atha was stunned, a peculiar thought crossing his mind as he stared in a daze. *So it begins.*

"*Shakka's mercy.* I-I-I just saw red, grab—gun. The monks—get the monks. They must know," Hanzel stuttered, shivering like a man who had never raised a hand in anger would when staring down a smoking barrel upon three dead bodies. Atha was more experienced with death but was chilled himself. He watched as blood oozed slowly across the floor, scarlet covering the dainty brown, hypnotizing. The hypnotic effect dissipated as the bodies slowly shrunk, down and down, clothes and all, into three still little boys.

"Oh my fucking God." Atha meant to think but couldn't control his body at the dark reutilization of recognizing one. Hanzel's son.

"No! Oh, my boy!" Hanzel screamed like a man who had never raised a hand in anger would after having just shot his own blood. Atha fell deeper and deeper from reality as he turned back slowly to Hanzel, unable to comprehend anything, unsure if it was real or illusion, unsure if anything was real at all. Hanzel muttered something, but Atha's head was currently vacant. He watched as Hanzel raised the barrel up slowly, placing it inside his own mouth, the newest head added to the count exploding from the top like a ruptured balloon as blood spattered across Atha's face. Slowly he sank down to the ground, studying every detail of his hands, searching for a pixilation, perhaps a skimped detail, anything to reaffirm the falsehood of this reality.

"Is this real? No, it can't be. You just need to wake up. Wake up. *Wake up*!" He halted his ramblings to the sound of sputtering coughs, blood speckling the boy's cyanotic cheek as he gasped for air. He'd received the least of it, a single gunshot wound to his upper chest bleeding through his clothes. Regardless of whether it was fake, Atha crawled desperately on his hands and knees, the bloody floor turning into a psychotic Slip'N Slide that sent him tumbling down more than once, stopping at the boy's side.

"What do I do, what do I do, what do I do?" he rambled, the young eyes barely awake with skin becoming cyanotic.

"We—we just wanted to try my new contract. Just—just a prank—" His words cut short as he coughed, gasping painfully for air as he went limp. Atha gave himself a hard slap across the face, yanking the boy from the floor and hurrying out the door.

"Medic! I need a medic! Somebody help me!" Atha yelled as panicked screams filled his ears. Onlookers jumped quickly to the easiest conclusion of who was responsible for the bloody mess. "Harika! Harika, where are you?!"

Zell and a handful of monks shot down from the sky, rushing to Atha who screamed and swirled in a dizzied mess.

"Give the child here!" Zell instructed, rushing Atha and pulling the child from his arms and setting the bloodied mess down in the street.

The world swirled around Atha, searching for his Shelando ally who had healed his shattered arm like it was a paper cut. "Harika! Get Harika!"

"I know no one by that name! Atha, you need to *fall silent*," Zell replied. A steak of blue shot through the air. Harika landed a few feet away and hurried toward the child as Healix studied the wounds.

Harika slid to the ground beside him, white cubes already appearing in the air, forming a lung and a rib. Red shot from Healix's eyes, peeling the skin back to reveal the deflated lung. A woman screamed wildly as she rounded the corner to the scene, probably the mother. The lung and rib flashed out for a brief moment as their replacements fell in, followed by a few more quick lasers to reseal the flesh. His color returned, and he began to breathe easier, but still screams broke out.

"He's the bomber!" a man screamed, pointing a finger at Harika as Zell's eyes flashed around, quickly yanking Atha up too his feet.

"We take our leave." Zell grabbed Atha by the arm, pulling him to his feet and pressing him against Harika. "Take him to the location we discussed."And with that, Harika's firm arms reached around Atha and the two shot up into the air.

Harika glided overtop the trees for just a few minutes, angling down past a small waterfall to a nearby cave. He pulled Atha into the darkness, the blue glow of Harika's overflowing mana the only lighting within the large stone cavern.

Atha could hardly slow his sobbing, pausing only long enough to gush out, "I blew your cover, Harika. I'm sorry." He curled up into the fetal position and replaying the scene at Hanzel's shop over in his head with vividness equal to the dreams that would follow for many nights.

"It's fine. I was tired of the name Miracle anyways," Harika replied slowly.

Atha buried his face in Harika's shoulder, both blood and tears staining it this time. A figure stepped through the darkness, coming to a halt before Harika.

"Hello, Lunesella," Harika said, the infected woman nodding to him as she watched Atha.

Bright white light illuminated the entire cave, but Atha's face was busy hiding itself in Harika's shoulder. Harika watched as a woman materialized from the light and he began to speak up but was beat to the punch as she opened her mouth. Like a series of bells, her dainty voice rang through Atha's head with an impetus force, all his sorrow forcibly washing away, every particle of his body focusing on the perfection vocalized gracing his ears.

"Atha Honorati, I have come to deliver an official challenge from the Plague of Disease." His head snapped up, not just to witness beauty that matched the voice, but because *he had heard it before*.

A slender woman clad in magnificent white armor that only left her face exposed hovered a foot above the ground. It took Atha only a moment to deem it the most beautiful face he'd ever witnessed and ever would. Her eyes were slanted at an odd yet mesmerizing angle, irises a deep sapphire blue that matched her long hair that reached down to the backs of her knees like a waterfall. All this paled in comparison to the eight massive wings protruding from her back, stretching like white walls of downy feathers, one half of her body completely symmetrical to the other. Before he could weigh his words, they pulled free from his tongue.

This radiancy defied the bounds of nature, and Atha drew a more supernatural conclusion. "Are you an angel?"

She replied with just a single basic word, a single word that sent tingles through his body, a single word that could be nothing less than the absolute truth. "No."

Of course not. Holiness was not defined by seductiveness. "A devil?"

"No." Again just a single word, but Atha was grateful for it. A sense of nirvana encased his entire being with every twitch of her tongue.

Suddenly it clicked. The woman with blue hair and white clothes that mimicked the armor she now wore—it was the woman who handed him his book in the library all those years ago! He saw her just before he used his plague for the first time. Just before he shot Dako.

"I know you! You returned the book I dropped!" He gasped. The woman nodded one single, firm time to the same effect of her numinous voice. "You're my Antarie, aren't you? You gave me my plague!" Atha continued, already knowing the answer. She gave another single nod in response. Atha fell to his knees before her, bowing his head in gratitude. He knew he couldn't put into words, yet he would still try, if only to hear her release just one more syllable, to force the words of beauty personified.

"I saved my sister because of you. Please, tell me how I can repay this debt," he announced from his knees, somehow knowing she wouldn't, maybe couldn't, ask anything of him. His true intention, while obvious, rang clearly through a mind with only one thought in it—*Please, tell me how I can make you speak just once more.*

"That is not why I have come. My name is Gavreel, the Antarie designated to select Creation plagues and act as their liaison when disagreements with fellow plagues arise. We normally would have reconvened earlier, but you are not accustomed to the typical functionality of a plague and were unaware of how to contact me.

"If you require my presence, you need only speak my name. As to why I appear before you now absent prompt; Disease has voiced his grievance with you to his own Antarie and requests a deathmatch. The location at which the match will begin is warranted to you as the challenged party, should you choose to accept," she replied. Her words still rang through Atha's body, but this was a sobering topic, and even euphoria was overpowered by Atha's all-consuming anger.

He pulled his meteorite from his pocket, rolling it around in his hand as he considered everything he knew to this point. "Just to clarify, if I die, that still puts an end to the Red Sheep, right? He has to go back to sleep?"

"Your demise would mark the moment no living Creation existed. The only factor that could cancel this occurrence would be if Disease possessed a soul of a past Creation plague," she replied.

"Tell it I accept," Atha replied, glancing over to Zell, who had only just entered.

"Do not accept terms of engagement, you fool! Have you not seen what it is capable of?!" she cut in all too late as Gavreel gave a single nod.

"As you will it. Seven a.m. tomorrow the match will begin," she announced. Zell's scarlet face panged with more blue streaks then Atha had ever seen.

"No! Please, take pause!" Zell continued, stepping beside Atha.

"It is too late. Nothing can change his acceptance, let alone his mind," Gavreel replied.

"She's right," Atha replied, Zell snapping firm hands over his face still covered with blood.

"This is not a battle for you to win. This is a glorified death sentence!" Zell replied, Atha's trembling hands resting overtop her own.

"Come on, Zell. Let's not act like my life isn't worth the price of putting that monster to sleep."

Zell stared in utter disbelief for a few moments, finally snapping out of it.

"He is partnered with a griffin! It would be blasphemy to deny them fighting together!" Zell continued, desperately searching for something to tip the currently impossible odds.

"I quote, 'Tell the boy to bring the bird.' So yes, that is acceptable. Do you have a location for the battle?" Gavreel replied.

"The moon. The furthest away. Can you make it oxygenated?"

"I can. I will inform Disease of the location and will return to bring you at the designated time. Lastly, you are permitted to bring your allies so that they may view the match. I will be here to collect you seven minutes early." When Gavreel finished speaking she imploded into white light and vanished into the air. The cave returned to darkness.

Zell eased down to her knees beside Atha in utter disbelief, the woman with a plan was now fully at a loss for what to do.

"Oh, Atha. What have you done?"

Third Life

Colors of the Chameleon

Book Two of the Creation Saga

Preview

The Following work is a preview of book two, and may undergo slight changes before publication.

Chapter 1

Bloodlust Blue

Nestled deep within a forest, the Royal guard constructed emergency relief structures in the form of blue buildings. It had only been a few hours since the Red Sheep's attack. Queen Elise maneuvered her forces quickly and effectively, and before the sun had even set every survivor had food and shelter. A Shelando man, his blue skin barely visible through the dirty black robes he wore walked slowly through the camp like a customer surveying the goods presented by shops. Harmer was this Shelando's name, and he sought neither food nor shelter, only the blood he had not found during the attack.

Al's schemes work too well for my liking. Not even a single full fight for any of the Chameleons, Harmer thought. *I need to satisfy my needs or I'm going to go insane. Plus, it'll be priceless to see the look on his face when he finds out I attacked the royal guard.* A woman crossed his field of view, dressed in all black to even cover her face, Harmer catching the name Shakkoo from the voice of another guard who received instructions from her. A scythe of a smile creased his face, pleased to have so quickly found a worthy opponent. She wasn't aware of his presence yet but in a few moments, he'd be close enough to yank her through one of Leslen's portals and the fight would start.

No sooner did he begin to shift towards the shady woman then did one of those same blue portals, only as wide as a quarter in this case, open beside his ear carrying Leslen's dainty voice. "Hey Harm, Boss requires your presence to go over a few things." Either this was a coincidence or Alkibiades was fully aware of what Harmer was up to. Harmer knew the latter was infinitely more likely, groaning back, "I'm busy. Tell Al that I Don't care about his little schemes, I'll do my part when the time comes." He finished just in time to see a blue portal open beneath his feet, falling helplessly through the blue and appearing within a massive dark building. The windowless walls stretched high around them and disappeared in a black void a few dozen stories up, lit only faintly by dull green lights that hovered around the center of the massive room. Metal boxes of varying size where stacked high throughout and members of the chameleons sat atop them around Harmer who turned his eyes across them with displeasure.

Leslen smirked. "Tell him yourself." She finished while pointing a finger up towards Alkibiades who sat atop a throne the back of which had been carved out to accommodate his black wings, the only place actually intended for sitting in the room. His bandana had been pulled up above his eyes and he made direct eye contact with Harmer who looked up at him with disdain. "Don't make me have Leslen force you here again, Harmer," Alkibiades noted dryly, his monotone voice already annoying Harmer. "I am aware of your lust for combat. You, in turn, are aware of what happens to those who disobey the instructions of the current leader." He finished.

Harmer laughing mockingly back for a few moments, echoing high above him through the high ceiling until he stopped. "Ah, well you know how I love getting under that pale skin of yours. My 'Lust for combat' as you so aptly labeled it is in dire state and may soon be guiding my path." Harmer moaned back, face sinking into a sickening grimace as he sat down upon a box. "Now get on with it." Bloodlust pulsed out of him like icy waves but Alkibiades took no note, only nodding and standing up off his throne.

"Yes, all 13 members of the chameleons are accounted for minus cicada who still has a few weeks before reawakening so let's begin," Alkibiades announced, raising his monotone voice ever so slightly to reach across the group spread out across the boxes. "We will review our previous operation and I will explain how this will correlate into my plan moving forward." *Scheme,* Harmer corrected inside his own head, watching Alkibiades walk slowly closer to the group, angling his wings to allow his black trench coat to slide off his back onto the floor, displaying his many black tattoos that symbolized the contracts he'd stolen over the years that covered his torso.

"Erida, how familiar are you with my Contracts limitations?" He asked, turning his attention to the only figure in the room dressed in a color other than black, a white dress to match her white hair. "That it can steal other contracts and that the victim must remain alive or you lose their ability." Erida replied.

"To further lubricate operations in the future, I will disclose details now that you have proved trustworthy," Alkibiades replied. Erida was the newest member, and at this point the only one without more than a basic comprehension of how it worked. "To steal a contract, the most difficult condition that must be fulfilled is that I must hold a conversation with whomever the target holds closest to heart. The conversation must at some point include a fact that the target's proxy would consider sensitive.

"The only difficult condition after that is I must witness the full power of the targets contract as they attempt to kill me. While these conditions are completed, I must also wield only a single contract I have stolen previously or none." Alkibiades finished. Erida raised an eyebrow, glancing around across the group for a reason behind this information but found none, settling her sight back on Alkibiades and simply stating her question.

"Why would you tell me all that? I could easily stop you from stealing more contracts in the future."

"Because you are now a full-fledged member of the Chameleons. Until given reason, I trust you absolutely and will do anything to ensure our success." He replied, an unexpected blush reddening Erida's face. *The wannabe Queen's taken a liking to old Al, huh?*

"Ok, well what about when I get my time?" She replied quickly, forcing a grimace across her face to mask the reason of her red-toned cheeks.

Alkibiades gave her a quizzical look. "Time?"

"I was told that we are called the Chameleons because every member gets a certain amount of time every year to control the group. What if I use my time to make us hunt Elise down and kill her? You'd lose your fancy Triple S contract." Erida replied with a taunting smirk.

"The group would be under your control and I would have no further say. The only time I can veto a command is when it is likely multiple casualties would befall the Chameleons, but even then, I can only put it up to a vote.

"If the majority or, in the case only an even number of chameleons are capable of voting and a perfect split of votes occurred, we would still move forward with that plan. We have already established that the Luxria Queendom possesses no combatants capable of killing us, so it would never even require a veto." Alkibiades finished, awaiting further questioning from Erida, but none came. Her grimace had left her face and her jaw hung ajar, displaying her surprise at the statement in a literal open fashion. *I know that look. You assumed that Al wouldn't let you kill the Queen because of the long ordeal he went through to steal her contract. The only thing predictable about him is that he is unpredictable.*

Alkibiades spoke up again. "Do you have any further questions, or may I continue?" Harmer watched the little wannabe Queen, hoping she would just continue to lower her jaw until it fell off and remain forever quiet.

To Harmer's disdain, she spoke again. "Just one," Harmer groaned audibly, Jun leaning over and slapping him across the back of the head. "I am only given a pair of days to control the group. In your honest opinion do you think we could kill her in that time-frame?"

Alkibiades took not even a moment replying. "In my honest opinion we could eliminate her in the first minute. Six if she possessed her contract." Alkibiades replied and Erida nodded, folding her hands in her lap to signal that she was done.

"Now back to the topic at hand. We successfully acquired the Rulers Right contract and-" Alkibiades stopped, noticing a small blue portal open beside the massive red skinned Denata Zenta, a piece of blue paper wafting out and falling directly into his open hand. Zenta had to angle it just right to provide the paper with enough light to read the words and his red face panged with streaks of blue as he read and re-read the note in disbelief.

Zenta got to his feet, scurrying the way the weak did, to present the paper to Al. "Zell made her official request, Al." Zell Tenzata, a worthy opponent, and a topic that interested Harmer. He headed to Al's side to read the note, shoving Zenta out of the way as he did.

I, Zell Tenzata, previous third seat of the Chameleons, am officially calling in my one favor given to retired members of the Organization. I request that the member whom wields the Plague of The Frog give guidance to Atha Honorati of how to wield the power of a Plague. It is Imperative that this request is fulfilled within the hour.

"She requests your presence, Blair." Al noted, handing the paper to Blair who sat directly to his left. A green frog hovered just above her shoulder, croaking with surprise and floating beside Alkibiades to read the paper over himself. "Can you provide any speculation upon this request, Kero?" Alkibiades asked the frog who closed his eyes for a moment and pondered the question.

The frog's reverberating croak grinded through the air. "I have a theory, yes. I need not state it now, we'll have a definitive answer within the day if it is what I think. Will you honor the request Al?" The frog croaked back, watching a tattoo flash white upon Alkibiades chest and a moment later the paper burst into a ball of flames.

"Yes. Yusha, how many allies does Zell Tenzata currently have within her vicinity?" Alkibiades asked the giddily smiling red head who ran a hand through his curly locks.

A hologram emitted from the palm of Yusha's hand out into the air before him and within the clear image of a cave he counted Atha, Zell, Harika and an icon designated for Special infected. "There you have it! Huh, look at that. They got a special infected hanging around now too. What's up with that?" Yusha laughed.

Alkibiades slid back into his duster. "We will match their numbers. Reapora, Jun, accompany Blair to their current location. Take Sine with you." The short woman with a scythe larger than her entire body hopping briskly from her box and Jun followed suit, standing and walking across the room to pick up the only Chameleon who sat on the floor. Harmer's blue eyes followed the young blond with hate, watching her stop beside a figure sitting upon the floor. Harmer assumed Sine was insane, the middle-aged man constantly muttering the same words *She's dead, dead again.*

He wasn't sure where the winged schemer had found the mumbling, self-defecating human, nor did he care. Sine was given the 13th seat due to the fact he cannot seem to pull himself out of the fettle position without another's help let alone raise a hand for combative purposes. But, at times, he had his uses. Nobody else in the Chameleons could get more then that same old *She's dead, dead again* line out of Sine, but Alkibiades could get far more than that. Every now and then, he could get *100% accurate* predictions of what would occur within the next hour. A handy tool for any schemer, and probably the only Chameleon Harmer hated more than Jun. He didn't like any of them, ranking them only by how much difficulty he imagines he would have against them in a death-match.

Jun pulled Sine up off the floor and slung his arm over her shoulder, helping him walk to Alkibiades, that same line coming from Sine's mouth time and time again. *She's dead, she's dead again, she's dead again, dead again,*

"Sine, look at me. Focus," Al noted in his monotone voice, slithering his pale fingers underneath Sine's chin and pulling it up. "You are going to accommodate Blair into hostile territory. I need a risk assessment of this operation." Sine's crazed rambling and twitching slowed to a stop, transfixed now fully on Alkibiades who waited patiently for a response.

"Atha- he will- will attack the second- the- the -moment we enter the cave. Out of confusion, not- not deliberate. No other incidents." Sine rattled out, fidgeting and clasping his hands to the opposite arm every few words. Alkibiades nodded, nearing his face in a few inches closer until he was only an inch from Sine's.

Alkibiades pressed for more. "What will he attack with Sine? Focus."

"He will- She is- She's dead! Dead again! She's dead again!" Sine screamed, clasping his arms around himself and wobbling back and forth.

Alkibiades stepped back and Jun pulled Sine's right hand off where it clasped his left shoulder, looping it once more over her shoulder. Al turned to Jun. "Be prepared for an assault directly after teleporting."

Jun, in the way only an entitled little bitch could, groaned and rolled her eyes. "I was standing right here, I heard what he said. Come on, let's go." She spat, finishing in a far more pleasant tone to Blair and Reapora who stood nearby.

Alkibiades next addressed the room. "We will reconvince upon their return. Nobody is to leave." Blair pressed her hand-held button to open a blue portal upon the floor, awaiting Reapora and Jun who assisted Sine. The four jumped into the portal simultaneously. Harmer had reached his tolerance limit for the Schemer, the little blond bitch, and the Chameleons as a whole, pulling his red button from his pocket and clicking it once to open a blue portal of his own. A portal he commanded to lead back to that shadowy captain- *What was her name? Shakkoo?*

"Sit back down, Harmer. We are not finished." Alkibiades called without bothering to turn and verify that it was even he who had opened the next portal. Harmer hated that most about him- how he was always right, how he just *knew* things, how his little schemes always went just as they were supposed to. But more than he hated it, he enjoyed throwing kinks in the plans at every opportunity. Or, at least he thought he was. He'd gone against Alkibiades' commands and entered the royal capital before he met Atha, eventually leading Alkibiades right to the person he needed to speak with before he could steal Elise's contract. Maybe going against Alkibiades' plans was exactly what he was supposed to do. Harmer tried not to think about it.

"Oh, was me leaving not in your calculations? All the more incentive for me to make haste." Harmer teased like a child who just snatched another's favorite toy, all but sticking his tongue out at Alkibiades.

Al's monotone voice, just as emotionless as he was when he was explaining basic concepts of his ability to Erida just minutes ago, defiled

Harmer's ears. "There will be consequences if you do not do as I command."

Harmer could take no more of the schemer. "Oooo, I'm downright terrified." He'd expected to land back in the forestation hiding the survivors of the Red Sheep's attack, but this was not what he found on the other side of that circle of blue.

Endless untouched snow stretched around him in every direction, Harmer first glancing around in surprise, then rage. He pulled the red button from his pocket again, clicking it once to open another portal-none came. He rapidly mashed his finger into it a few more times again to no effect. Pangs of red flushed across his face twisting with anger, selecting a random direction and heading in it. *I yearn for the day you look to the future and see me killing you.*

Chapter 2

Welcoming Unwelcome Guests

Atha sat upon a nondescript blue chair in the brightly lit cave, staring down at his open palms which he repeatedly clasped and unclasped, mumbling words to the supposed being who was the actual cause for his ability to manifest objects. The hour for do or die was still over a dozen away and the odds where bleak, hoping to perhaps secure an ally in the being who bestowed such immeasurable power in him. "If you're in there, just give me a sign. I don't know what your connection to me is but I assume…. I *hope* it would be bad for you if I die." Atha mumbled, receiving no reply and beginning to wonder if it could still hear him.

It sure seemed so when he'd insulted his own power back at the training grounds only to watch a grenade fall from the air and snag its pull-pin on a rock. Regardless, it wasn't feeling too responsive now. Harika prayed silently on the cold stone floor across the room. Atha had caught the premise of said prayers: protection over him in his coming duel. Zell had gone to send a few messages seeking aid. She hadn't mentioned exactly to whom these inquiries would involve. Despite the death-sentence looming, he felt himself counting his blessings that his friends who he had more faith in than himself, where calling in all their favors from gods and mortals alike, looking for an answer to a 5000-year-old riddle named the Red Sheep.

Atha was receiving no response from his plague and decided to give it a rest as he first heard Zell's footsteps. She and Lunesella came walking down the snaking path leading down into the cave. "Any news?" Atha asked, hiding his bursting anticipation at whom he fathomed was his best lifeline.

"There is," Said Zell. "To avoid complication, it is necessary you are brought up to speed on whom will be joining us."

As she paused, a massive blue portal opened about seven feet in the air, four black robbed figures all falling at once to land gracefully on the floor. Zell had intended to give Atha warning that the Chameleons where coming, not having expected they would literally fall from the air just seconds after she sent her message. So much for avoiding complication.

"CHAMELEONS!" Atha roared in tandem with Zell screaming, "NO!" both voices lost entirely in the echoing stone walls and ensuing chaos. Atha drew the image of a car into his mind, rage allowing it to manifest with crippling speed, intending to catch the Chameleons from the blind side and crush every one of them in the straight line they had come down in, but they were ready. Jun was the closest in line to the vehicle, twirling her index finger to send an assault of pink sparkling dust towards the car and as the strange pink collided with the car the metal turned to dust, gusting across the group harmlessly. The vaporized car continued at its original speed, the last particle of its body passing over the Chameleons and the particles returned to their original form, reformed car spinning through the air and smashing into the far wall. All this occurred while Reapora burst forward, pulling the scythe from her back and thrusting the staff end towards Atha's gut. Harika was faster, the blue streak of his body bursting in front of Atha to catch the pole. `

"Enough!" Zell screamed, directing her words to the entire gathering and her commanding presence garnered her intended effect, every set of eyes turning to her. "I contacted them. They are here upon my request to have their plague teach you of how to properly use your abilities." Zell informed him, turning his rage to disbelief in an instant. Harika released his grip on Reapora's syth and she leapt back to stand amongst her ally's, Jun giving Atha a smile and wink as his eyes quickly returned to the threat before them.

Atha's battle ready mind could only speak the one sentence that occurred to it- "Are you out of your fucking mind, Zell?" She stepped across the room and stood facing Atha with the Chameleons at her back, a symbolic gesture representing the truth in her words. "This is no longer about logic. If you are to have a hope of victory, we must spare no effort." She replied, the cool calmness of her expression baffling Atha who stepped to her side to keep his eyes on a portion of the group who had just let a monster into the capital.

"In your craziest dream do you think I'd actually accept let alone want help from THEM?!" Atha finished with a scream that Jun plugged her ears too as it reverberated through the cave, the other two (mostly) sane Chameleons eagerly watching the show. Zell raised a hand and slapped him briskly across the face as a mother might a pouting child, gripping him tightly by both shoulders to keep him from stepping back around. "Have you an inkling of an idea what it feels like for me to call in the syndicate that ruined my life for aid," Zell's voice was low, but every word was packed with rage. "This is me running out of ideas. If we cannot find answers to bridge this immeasurable gap you are going to die. Do you understand that? That is just how much you mean to me, that I would turn to any despite past transgressions." Atha's face softened, replying silently with a nod. His eyes did shift again but only to the blue man who stood just to his left.

"What do you think?" Atha asked Harika, the only member of the Honorati family who had yet to cast a vote. Harika, despite being blindingly fast at times of peril was slow every other and stood quiet for a long few moments.

"Do you know what the basis of my religion is, Atha?" Harika finally replied, Zell releasing her vice grip upon his shoulders as he fully turned to face Harika, realizing he didn't really know anything about it. "It is that no matter how vile or despicable an individual or group may be, that killing them is never the answer because there will always be a time when their life will still have meaning. I think that this is one of those times for the Chameleons." Atha didn't agree with this statement in the least but understood where Harika was coming from, responding with a silent nod again and stepping around past them.

"Alright. Which one of you is the Plague then?" Atha asked. A frog popped out from beneath Blair's black robes and she stepped forward, giving him a smile full of surprisingly white teeth and cocked her head hard to the right side, something Atha would have labeled comical had it come from anyone else.

"At your temporary service, junior!" She cackled obnoxiously loud, reverberating through the cave and continued until Jun gave her a nudge.

"For the love of your mother, shut the hell up." Jun groaned, and Blair recoiled like she'd been branded by hot iron, clasping both hands over her mouth. "Apologies, I lose myself in the moment. Let's move outside." Blair replied, pulling from her pocket a red button and clicking it to open a blue portal. She pulled a long wooden board resembling a snowboard through it and lept on top, Atha watching in surprise (and envy he would never admit too) as it began to hover and glided her up through the winding cave entrance. *Magical hovering surfboards.* Atha thought to himself, stepping briskly up the path after her. Every other member of the cave's occupants followed and Jun, lugging awkwardly along encumbered by Sine who's arm was still slung over her shoulder managed to catch up to Atha.

"Hey, so I gotta ask, what's this all about? Sounds like we were a last resort." She smiled to Atha who didn't even glance to her.

"Don't fucking talk to me." Atha growled back. Jun lived for a good argument and already had over a dozen retorts lined up for this exact response but felt Reapora's eyes hot upon the back of her head and remained silent as they finished the winding walk up to the clearing in the woods just past the cave's exit. Blair sat idly upon her hover board and Atha took a moment to study her blemished appearance. Her skin was pale white but smooth despite the blotches of dirt that riddled it, matching her frizzled rats' nest of hair which was overrun with knots and just as black as her robes. With her dirty appearance adding years to her age it was hard to approximate, but Atha guessed she was probably only a few years older than he. He wasn't sure if being a plague meant he'd follow a similar life-cycle to the one she had, but he knew if he did he'd likely shoot himself in the head. He came to a stop a few feet before her but she paid no mind, instead turning to Reapora and Jun (Who had sat Sine down beneath a tree) who chattered into a blue portal and then began to laugh. He couldn't help but hear what they where talking about and learned that they were, in fact, gossiping about how Leslen (Another Chameleon Atha assumed) had just informed them that she'd sent Harmer out into the middle of some icy continent. Jun was getting the biggest kick out of it, absolutely screaming with laughter, flopping her stomach across the top of Blairs board and banging a fist against it to help release some of her enjoyment. Blair added that the "Squid-headed dolt" probably thought he could walk his way out (he did actually think that, he was still walking in his random direction at that very moment, releasing a loud sneeze as well) but would soon realize he was caught in an endless loop of repeating terrain until "Boss" let him out.

Atha was at first surprised to hear such normal gossip from the group that had just been the cause behind thousands of deaths but quickly switched to intel gathering mode. They could talk in front of him all they wanted, he had already learned that this "Leslen" was the one who wielded the contract that allowed them to teleport at will and that Harmer was currently trapped within one of Alkibiades' contracts. If they gave a shit they sure didn't show it and slowly came down from the high of the topic, Jun and Reapora joining Sine beneath his tree, leaving Atha and Blair alone. Blair's frog hovered out from beneath her robes, stretching its muscular hind legs down and giving him a curtious bow. "Brother." It croaked and Atha scoffed at this label.

"We're not *brothers*," Atha mockingly croaked, glaring back. "Let's just get this over with."

"I agree, but where should we start?" Blair cut in, cocking her head at an awkward angle towards her right shoulder, snapping her fingers and lifting it back up to lean forward off the board to her feet. "Oh, I know! Lets start with introductions! My name is Blair, I'm 19 years old and was born under-"

"Yeah, I don't give a shit. Just teach me about my Plague." Atha cut in and Reapora yelled her agreeance from the side-line.

535

"Stay on topic Blair! Orders are to get back as soon as possible!" Blair went livid at this, screeching with frustration and pulling at her hair.

"Orders, how I hate thee so! If Orders was a living being I'd cut the flesh from its bones and cook its meat!"

Ok, gossip aside these bitches are fucking crazy. Atha noted, Blairs eyes leering up at him from beneath the mess of her hair that now hung in her face.

"When did your Plague first manifest?" Blair growled, continuing to yank at her hair as if she meant to rip it out.

"About a dozen years ago." Atha replied, pretending not to care about her display because he knew in some corner of his mind that this would give her satisfaction. He knew plenty of crazies from prison and 99% of them where just attention seekers.

"In that time have they grown more potent, developed additional abilities or anything along those lines?" She replied.

"They haven't. All I've done is figured out how to use them a bit." Atha replied, sending Blair into an unexpected flurry of cackling laughter. "What's so fucking funny?!" Atha screamed overtop of her and she began mixing words into the maniacal display. "You still black-out when you use your ability! Your power got stronger against your fight with that prince but you don't even remember because you're but a newborn when it comes to its use!" Atha felt the urge to lose his temper but restrained it. So his power had grown but he didn't know how to properly wield it and resulted in a black-out. This was actually turning into useful intel.

"Alright, so how do I stop it from doing that?" Atha replied, failing at his attempt to keep anger out of his voice.

"You can't. You just keep using it until you grow more accustomed to the power flux." Blair replied, abruptly calming.

"Ok well help me expedite the process. How do you do it?" Atha replied but Blair shook her head.

"It is not something that can be *taught*, just as a blind woman cannot be described color. If she was given repetitive glimpses at what they are she can label them herself, but such cannot be put into simple words. The key- for us that is, not the blind man- is that anger activates it." Blair finished and Atha perked up at this.

"Yeah, I get like crazy flashes of anger every now and then. Is that part of being a plague? Does it ever get better?!" He asked but Blair cackled and shook her head.

"No, but it gets worse! Anger grows with the evolution of your power. See, we plagues- us plagues?" Blair paused, unsure of the proper term, tugging at her hair for a moment until she simply shrugged. "Whatever. Plagues start off with a basic portion of our abilities that we can always use. For you, that's your ability to manifest items. As your anger grows, so does that power in some way. During your battle with the prince I saw your eyes bleed and you began manifesting items that could counter his abilities. I'm not much of a theorist but Boss said that your ability had lost one of its governing rules. When that next stage of an ability is hit, we begin to release what I like to call *Plague Particles*." Blair paused, raising her hands as black fog began to lightly drift from them. They swirled above her head and tightened together to form a hat with a large point that sagged at its top third to reach back down towards a wide brim.

"Plague particles are like mana where you consume them to wield your ability. They are accumulated alongside-" She paused, a feverish smile distorting her face and displaying all of her white teeth. "A headcount. Humans, Denata, griffons, trees; only intelligent beings with a soul count. Things like animals or flowers don't count, those ones are just for fun." She finished, once again angling her head hard to the right side and running her chewed off fingernails down her cheeks so hard they left red streaks. Atha was filled with disgust at the display and stepped back as she continued, scratching harder and harder until blood droplets began to eek out of her cheeks. Jun snapped to her feet and in one explosive burst of speed that Atha hadn't expected of her closed the distance, pulling Blairs hands away from her face.

"No, stop. Just a little longer, you can make it." Jun counseled but Blair only dug deeper, hissing at Jun and swatting her hands away. Jun leaned her head in as if she was afraid someone might hear (But still loud enough for Atha to hear) and whispered, "If we finish early we can sneak off and have fun!" She finished, Blairs face brightening and she pulled her hands down, clapping in pleasure as Jun twirled her finger producing a quick spout of her pink-glittering particles. Atha watched in horror as they dissolved Blairs cheeks too the muscle but paused in surprise as the skin layer reformed perfectly intact, leaving no trace of the red streaks or dots of blood. He guessed fun was a synonym for murder to them.

Jun returned to her seat and Blairs eyes returned too Atha, now clearly saner and more focused then they were at any point before. "Where was I?" She asked, glancing too the frog but awaited no response and snapped her fingers. "Oh, right headcount. Do you know what your total is?" She asked.

"I've killed a pair people. Both on earth, if that makes a difference." Atha replied but Blair gave him a puzzled expression.

"That can't be right. When your eyes blead you released tons of plague particles. I'd say at least worth a hundred bodies. Oh, I forgot to mention something. Your headcount is also boosted by those killed by an *effect* of your plague. Any better idea of what it could be now?" Blair asked, and it instantly clicked for Atha. The scene of Hanzel shooting down children and then blowing his own head off. Guns where boosting his count.

His face went white and his legs turned to Jelly but he surprised himself with the fact he could still speak. "What?! But that's not possible! I only started spreading guns a few weeks ago!" He sank down onto his buttocks, suddenly feeling ill but Blair only shrugged and knelt in front of him.

"Maybe its something else then. Whatever the reason, you got a powerful Plague, that much I'm sure of. I've been at this for years and haven't gotten that much. Granted, I go for quality over quantity," She teased like a high-end car manufacturer might too a counter-part of a more common brand. "But stuff like this you could just ask your avatar." She finished, cocking a thumb over her shoulder back towards the frog.

She paused at her own statement, blinking and glancing around Atha and then the surrounding clearing. "Speaking of which, where is your avatar? Is it invisible? Really small?" She asked, snapping her fingers.

"Really small *and* invisible?!" Atha shook his head. "I don't know. The only time I ever had contact with it was when I said something bad about the power. It responded by dropping a bomb at Zell's feet." He replied and Blairs face fell, standing and swiveling back towards the frog.

"You told me an avatar can't wield the plague itself, Kero!" She spat in an accusing tone but Kero nodded at this. "It cannot. Assuming it could, the plague would be far stronger than any I have ever met. Use your Arcana and investigate." He replied, and Blair gave him an accusing leer but formed an X with her index fingers an announced

"Arcana!"

The shadowy hat wisped away from her head and formed a translucent bookshelf, Blair taking a moment to glance through it before selecting a book. Its shadowy form hardened at her touch and became a physical book bound in an archaic cover riddled with symbols and hieroglyphics seemingly placed at random. "Tell me about Atha Honorati's plague." She commanded and the symbols shifted about and started too gleam. She opened the book and sat down beside Atha, holding it open so both of them could read. Blair licked a finger and used it too turn the page, realizing all but the first where blank.

"Hm, doesn't look like anybody knows much at all about your plague. Looks like its official title is "Blood from Water". Oh, and look here, boss was right. It says when your eyes bleed that you can summon items you don't even know exist. All you need is a clear idea of what you want accomplished and the plague will take care of the rest until your particles run out. Also says they will never be the *best* tool for the job but can still accomplish it. That's actually pretty interesting, don't you think?" She asked and Atha leaned over her shoulder too read.

"It doesn't say anything about my avatar?" Atha asked but Blair shook her head. Suddenly Kero snapped down too sit on Blairs shoulder, croaking out "Ask it if his plague is sealed." Blair cackled at this but complied, summoning a wisp of black smoke into her hand as she did. Her eyes widened as the smoke shot down onto the page, emblazing words across it that read

1ST PLAGUE OF THE 10- 1ST SELECTION OF THE 5000. She stared in disbelief, holding the book slowly closer and closer too her face fully expecting that her eyes had failed her and jumped when Atha spoke up.

"What's that mean?" He asked, jumping himself as Blair released a dull screech. "You actually *don't know?!* Of all the things you could possibly be ignorant about you don't know of the plague *selections?!*" She replied in disbelief.

"I'm not ignorant you stupid bitch I'm new. Big difference." Atha spat back, feeling his anger beginning to take hold again. Blair suspected as much and quickly decided to give him the requested information.

"Ok, so there are 10 plagues, right? When plagues die a new one is selected but when that happens they don't get the same ability or avatar as the previous plague. That's because each of the 10 have 5000 different variations of each but unlike how the first plague is the weakest the first *selection* of the 5000 possible abilities is the *strongest.*"

"So I have the strongest variation of the Creation Plague." Atha meant too think but spoke out loud, glancing down at his palms and Blairs eyes followed, expecting him to manifest some monstrosity and kill her with it.

"Exactly. The Avatars that possess power that great are sealed away; too have them exist in this universe even powerless would literally destroy it." She replied, feeling her fear of this discovery melting away as Atha ignored her, stairing down at his hands with a newfound pride that she felt quite distasteful, searching for the right words to wash it away. "Don't get all hard for yourself just yet. Even at the height of your power to this point you wielded only a few hundred plague particles. Snow, or The Red Sheep as you know him, wields *hundreds of thousands.*"

Her screechy, dry voice was hardly background noise at this point to Atha, but his mind skimmed the words nonetheless, picking out the harsh reality in them with uncanny ease. His smile faltered, fanning the flames of Blair's mockery to new heights as she continued.

"At this current point you wouldn't have a hope of defeating me. I, in turn, have no hope of defeating him. That's the reigning heavy-weight champ and if I'm guessing right about what's going through that head of yours right now, I suggest you think hard. Really, realllllyyyy hard." Atha didn't know it yet but being a plague was like being apart of a club. Not the kind that compared trinkets or rare items, no, nothing so carefree, but of how many bodies they stacked. How many villages they burned. But, like any normal club, they communicated to some degree with one another and while Blair didn't have the full picture of just how accurate her words where she *did* know that the tension between Creation and Disease was reaching a breaking point.

"So, teach me." Atha spoke in a clear, anger free voice that caused Blair to faulter for a moment.

"Teach you?" She repeated, Atha nodding, clenching his fists and focusing his attention fully on her.

"How to win. I know I can't; not the way I am now. So, teach me how to wield my Plague effectively. I need your help." Atha was now standing just in front of her and she felt a twinge of comradery shared between them. No, for Blair it was more then that.

She was never quite right in the head, not since the day she was brought into this cruel world. She never knew her parents love, not because she had none but only because they didn't appreciate the fact that they discovered the missing towns pets stabbed to death and buried in their backyard (compliments of their sole heir). She never had friends either, it was difficult to make them when you dreamed more of where you could hide bodies together rather then which boy you imagined yourself wedding. The only ones who got that harsh look behind that bloody curtain in her head and hadn't faltered had been the Chameleons.

But it was made better still. Jun hadn't faltered but even befriended Blair, she who never knew such before, and Blair knew she would love Jun until the moment she died. Not even just friendly love, but what her religious parents would have called Heathen love, love one woman holds towards another beyond simple friendship. She didn't know if Jun shared these feelings, but it was simply enough for her to know somebody on the planet counted on her and would cry should she return to the dust from which she came. And here was another who had seen behind the curtain and counted on her. Perhaps this Creation boy wasn't so rueful after all.

Atha was adept at reading the expressions of another, and while psychopaths where in fact a bit difficult it was still entirely possible to attain what you wished when the right leverage was used. And he knew instantly that is was. Blair's pale skin began to blush beneath the flecks of dirt that spotted her skin and she quickly flipped her eyes too the ground. She wasn't actually diverting her eyes from his but she found her brain cleared and allowed the clearest thought when she tuned everything else out. Which Atha was now worthy of.

"I can't give you the answers you seek; our plagues are simply too different." Blair started in a quiet and calm voice, completely opposite the banshee cry she had voiced till now. "But I know how you can get them. Give me your hands," she instructed but Atha was hesitant, pulling away from her dirty and chewed fingernails that lead the charge of her hands towards his.

"Why?!" He spat, watching her hands retreat too the safety of her birds' nest of hair, pulling at both it and the many burrs that clung too thick too loose free.

"Because while I may not have the answers, I can send you too where your plague sleeps! You can ask it directly!" She screamed, the crazed look once more returning to her eyes like a flash of hot sickness induced by flu. Atha contemplated this for a moment and eased his hands out. Blair snatched them greedily and spat out a chant that Atha's translation magic couldn't translate. Blair's shelves of books burst back into a cloud of black smoke and dashed across her face, black lines edging and contrasting her already dirty features.